Falling
Place

Linda Taylor worked for the Foreign Office in London, Angola and Sri Lanka before teaching in Japan. On her return she read English at Oxford, and taught in language schools in Oxford and London. She now lives in Kent, where she grew up, with her husband and children. When her first novel, *Reading Between the Lines*, was published in 1998 it won the RNA New Writers' Award, was selected for WH Smith Fresh Talent and immediately became a *Sunday Times* top ten bestseller. Her subsequent novels, *Going Against the Grain, Beating About the Bush* and *Rising to the Occasion* were published to great acclaim. *Shooting at the Stars*, was short-listed for the Parker Romantic Novel of the Year Award.

Praise for Linda Taylor

'Linda Taylor writes so well and so wisely. Her characters are compelling and she knows how to tell a story with honesty and compassion. When you find yourself sneakily reading when you really shouldn't be, you know it's a good book!' – Jill Mansell

'Funny, original and thought provoking' – Katie Fforde

'You'll be flipping pages so fast, the breeze will keep you cool on the beach' – *New Woman*

'Take the phone off the hook and pull up your favourite chair . . . Unputdownable' – Christina Jones

Also by Linda Taylor

Reading Between the Lines
Going Against the Grain
Beating About the Bush
Rising to the Occasion
Shooting at the Stars

Linda Taylor

Falling *into* Place

arrow books

Published in the United Kingdom by Arrow Books in 2006

1 3 5 7 9 10 8 6 4 2

Copyright © Linda Taylor, 2005

First published in the United Kingdom in 2005 by William Heinemann

Arrow Books
The Random House Group Limited
20 Vauxhall Bridge Road, London SW1V 2SA

Random House Australia (Pty) Limited
20 Alfred Street, Milsons Point, Sydney,
New South Wales 2061, Australia

Random House New Zealand Limited
18 Poland Road, Glenfield
Auckland 10, New Zealand

Random House (Pty) Limited
Isle of Houghton, Corner of Boundary Road & Carse O'Gowrie
Houghton 2198, South Africa

The Random House Group Limited Reg. No. 954009

www.randomhouse.co.uk

A CIP catalogue record for this book is available
from the British Library

Papers used by Random House
are natural, recyclable products made from wood grown in
sustainable forests. The manufacturing processes conform to
the environmental regulations of the country of origin

ISBN 9780099427056 (from January 2007)
ISBN 0 09 942705 2

Typeset by SX Composing DTP, Rayleigh, Essex
Printed and bound in Great Britain by
Cox & Wyman Ltd, Reading, Berkshire

For Gedas and Thomas

'We did not change as we grew older, we just became more clearly ourselves.'

Lynn Hall

Chapter One

❧

At Heathrow airport, two mothers were disguising broken hearts. Their two daughters were, trainers twitching, aching to leave them behind.

'*Tempus fugit*,' Rebecca, who was Emma's mother, said.

'What was that?' Marie glanced up.

'Time flies.' Ginny gave Marie, her daughter, a tight smile. 'Got your passport?'

'I left it on the cat's head.'

'Malaria pills?'

'No, Mum, the dog ate them.'

'We don't have a dog.'

'Then who was it who ate my malaria pills? Not a boyfriend at long last, surely, Mother?'

Hearing the familiar sarcastic quips, Ginny wanted to grab her daughter and hold her so tight that she couldn't leave. She'd miss her demands, her expenses and, most of all, her sarcasm. Did she get that from Ginny? All those years, eighteen years to be precise, of bringing up her daughter and any theories of child-rearing she'd eaten up and digested over the years had resulted in this, an Olympic medal in sarcasm. Better, perhaps, than no Olympic medal at all.

At least it was likely the two girls wouldn't fall out, Ginny was reassured. She couldn't imagine Emma storming off and leaving Marie high and dry with a 'And you can find your own way out of the jungle, bitch!' Or Marie sneaking off and leaving Emma in the clutches of a snake-hipped drug dealer as he slipped a suspicious packet into her handbag. But what if . . . ?

Ginny pulled on the brake. Sprawled over the seats in Starbucks, backpacks propped up by their sides, cheeks and eyes glowing, Marie's trainer tapping the table leg impatiently as they waited for their flight, the two girls tried to hide their jitters for the sake of their mothers. They couldn't wait to get away. They were well brought up enough to be polite to the two creased-looking parents with furrowed brows watching over their offspring as if it was the last time they would ever see them alive. But it was clear they wanted to get through the gate and on their way as soon as decency would allow.

'Not long to go now.' Rebecca glanced at her watch and only Ginny noticed the lump as she swallowed.

'Yep. Best be on our way. C'mon our kid.' Emma stood up, gazing out over their heads towards the departure gates.

'Now you're not going to go sloppy at the last minute, are you?' Marie wrinkled her nose at Ginny. 'Are you? You are.'

'No.' Ginny managed a whisper, gripped Marie's arm and propelled her towards departures. 'Bugger off. Go and explore. Find yourself. See how different the rest of the world is. It's your duty. I'd have done it if I could. I would do it if I were you. You have my absolute blessing and everything we've ever said.'

'And everything squared.'

'You know how happy I am for you. Go forth.'

'And say hello to Auntie Charlotte, you forgot to say.'

It was a family joke. When anyone went abroad, somebody would always tell them to say hello to Charlotte. It was because Ginny's sister, Charlotte, had been abroad for many years, usually on the move. Wherever the holiday was, from Crete to Cairo, banging into Charlotte was something of a possibility. Although in recent years Charlotte seemed to have settled for Mumbai, the wandering-star joke still stood.

'Say hello to Charlotte.'

'Mission accepted. And we'll email every five minutes so there really isn't any need to cry.' Marie sounded anxious. 'Is there?'

'Absolutely not,' Ginny almost bellowed in her attempt to keep the tears from crawling up her throat. 'Now come on or you'll miss your flight.'

'Why are you shouting?'

'Because it's fun. You should try it some time.'

And then they really were off, looking impossibly young, Marie's fine brown hair shining, soft like baby hair, on her combat jacket, Emma blonde and chubby like a young cherub. A final wave, a wide, toothy smile. After they had disappeared beyond passport control and couldn't be seen, Ginny and Rebecca stood in total silence. They must have stood there for about ten minutes, not saying a word.

'Oh God.' Rebecca heaved a long sigh.

'Yes.'

'It's what I dreaded most.'

'Me too. I wanted it for her, but I wanted to stop it as well.'

'I travelled when I was young. I went to Europe. It

3

was fantastic,' Rebecca said. 'I'll never forget it. I got trains everywhere, studied art and architecture, slept on floors, ate what I could, when I could. I couldn't deny Emma the same thing. Except these days it's India, Thailand, Malaysia, the Philippines, they go so much further and the dangers are different. And yet they treat it as if they're just popping up to London for the day. All they need's a ticket, a few quid and a good novel. I'm not sure it's such a good thing that travel's so easy now. It's too easy. They don't respect it like we used to. I wish I'd never read *The Beach*.'

'I'd have gone,' Ginny said, 'if things had been different. I'd have leapt at the chance.'

'You didn't explore when you were Marie's age?'

Ginny thought about it for a moment, then laughed. 'In a way.'

'But your sister went off travelling, didn't she? Charlotte?'

'Yes. And she never came back.'

'I thought she came back occasionally?'

'For a few weeks here and there. Not really. This isn't her home anymore.'

They gazed helplessly at the queue threading its way through passport control. Their daughters were well out of sight.

'I just can't believe she's old enough. She can do whatever she wants now. I can't stop her.'

'I remember when Marie was a kick in my stomach.' Ginny stopped abruptly. Did she really want to think that far back? All week it had been clawing at her.

'You must have had her very young.' Rebecca appraised Ginny.

'Yes.'

4

'You've always looked the youngest of the mothers. I've always envied you. Such a stupid thing to be jealous of, youth, when you can't do anything about it.'

'I'm not even forty yet,' Ginny mused.

'Blimey. Lucky you.'

'Yes. Lucky me. I was eighteen when I became pregnant with Marie. The same age she is now.'

On the way back from the airport Ginny stopped off at Rebecca's house for a cup of coffee, at Rebecca's request. It suited Ginny. She wasn't rushing to get home to an empty house.

The two women had known each other for eight years – since Marie and Emma had found themselves in the same class at senior school and become friends. They were always warm when they met, often shared a joke, occasionally stayed as long as a cup of tea, but there were no attempts to force anything more demanding upon each other.

'Why don't you ask Rebecca and Gareth round to dinner?' Jane, Ginny's mother, had quizzed once when Ginny had been feeling isolated.

'Interesting threesome that would be. No, Mum. I don't want happily married parents giving me sympathetic looks over the carbonara.'

'I'm sure they wouldn't pity you. You're way beyond that anyway, what do you care what other people think? You need to meet more people of your own age.'

'I've got old friends I see sometimes.'

'Yes, but you hardly see them. I mean new people.'

'You mean men of my own age.'

Well . . . You're still youthful and fun and pretty. In

fact, I've often said I think you're prettier now than when you were younger. You've got more striking with age and you've got a lovely figure. You should be able to meet men. It's normal, dear.'

'If I invited Rebecca and Gareth round, the man of my own age would be Gareth. I don't think that would be very diplomatic.'

'He's probably got friends.'

'Er – have you met him?'

'You've always got a quip, just like Marie,' Jane sighed. 'Everyone's getting divorced at your age. It's the perfect time to start meeting men again. And they'll have children too so they'll understand.'

'There's no perfect time.'

'There is. When you're in your twenties everybody's matching up. If you don't meet the right man then you have to wait a good few years before they start coming up on the market again, when those marriages fail.'

'God that's cynical, Mum.'

'It's a fact. You're in your late thirties now. There are hundreds of them about. Keep your eyes peeled.'

Gareth had looked a lot more charming when he was younger, Ginny concluded as her eyes were drawn to the wedding photo on the wall. Rebecca, with bouffant blond hair like candy floss, swept up with flowers and ribbons, looked good enough to eat. A Lady Diana dress, full skirted with balloon sleeves and frills and lace everywhere. A tiara perched with geometric accuracy probably held into place by gallons of gel and spray. Rebecca's hair had probably been like uncooked spaghetti when Gareth had tried to push his fingers through it later that night. Next to her Gareth was wearing an unfortunate pair of glasses that looked as if they came off with the nose attached, but there was a twinkle in his eyes and a kind of grin hovering around his mouth. He looked nerdy but approachable. He'd probably had a stutter when he was a child and spent his sixth-form years playing Dungeons and Dragons and feeling sick every time a girl spoke to him. Charming, really. From what Ginny had seen of him in recent years, he had lost his approachability but was still nerdy. Not quite so charming.

Ginny never missed not having a wedding. You can't regret not doing something you've never aspired to do. She enjoyed weddings and romantic photos, like this one, as much as anyone, but a wedding was something that happened to other people. Like baldness. Or spiritual enlightenment.

'Milk and one, isn't it.' Rebecca put the mug on the coffee table and Ginny made herself comfortable on the sofa. It was olive green, like the carpet, and had walnut features built into the arms. It was formal but surprisingly comfortable, like the rest of the house. Rebecca sank into the matching armchair. Her blond hair was short now, cut into wisps that suited her, and the white and blond hair mingled subtly in an attractive way. Unlike Ginny with her brown hair that showed each stray grey the moment it popped up – before she spotted it and yanked it out with the tweezers. Not that she'd had many. It seemed Ginny had always been a late developer and was destined to be one for the rest of her life. She knew women five years younger who slapped on the hair dye, whereas she only occasionally had to pluck a hair out. Rebecca had the same colouring as her daughter, blue eyes and chubby cheeks. Emma was lucky she hadn't inherited her dad's nose, Ginny always thought privately and Marie always said out loud.

'I never know where you put everything,' Ginny marvelled. 'My house has so much clobber. Where are all your books?'

'Oh well, Gareth doesn't keep books. We value them as much as anybody else, but he doesn't like hanging on to old things for the sake of it, and you can see his point. He's very practical. Typical scientist, I know.'

Yes, it was a fact. Nothing in the house had any sentiment clinging to it, apart from the wedding photo and a couple of pictures of Emma and her older brother as children on the mantelpiece. It was a pleasant house but the personalities of the occupants seemed to dodge between the furniture and flit away, like ghosts. It was as if somebody there was embarrassed by emotional things, by emotional displays. Ginny could guess who.

'Books do collect dust, it's true.' Ginny thought of the walls full of wonky shelves crammed with anything from Jilly Cooper to Plato that formed the environment that she'd brought Marie up in. Ginny had the opposite problem to Gareth, it seemed. She couldn't throw books away. Every so often she and Marie would just hammer another shelf up so that the small house had reached a point now of full insulation by bookshelves. Even the bathroom hadn't escaped. Ginny was a scientist too – or at least that was the way her career had been going before Marie. But Gareth was a pure chemist; he worked at a well-known research firm. He was a very unemotional man. He was probably the one who volunteered to give the guinea pigs their eyedrops. But that was unkind. Although Ginny was

8

allowing herself a moment of self-satisfaction knowing that Marie had been able to pull anything off the shelves and read it from the age of about five upwards and had thus acquired an impressive general knowledge, for her age or for any age, the fact was that she and Emma had both done equally well in their A-levels and secured deferred places at the universities of their choices, so she wasn't sure what it all proved. They'd both spent a lot of time in the school library, studying there rather than at home. Perhaps Gareth's book purges had had something to do with that on Emma's part. She wasn't sure what Marie's reasoning was. Other than to avoid Ginny, of course, but that thought was hurtful even if avoiding your mother was standard in a teenage daughter.

'Emma has a bookcase in her room, of course. And I've got a shelf in the bedroom where I keep what I'm reading at the time.' There was a pause. 'But I rather like your house, I have to say, although Gareth—' Rebecca stopped herself abruptly, clearly about to reveal Gareth's negative opinion of Ginny's den. Ginny hid a smile. 'I like your house. But a marriage is such a compromise, isn't it?'

'I guess so.' Ginny sipped her coffee.

'Oh, I'm sorry. I don't mean . . . '

'Don't be silly. I've got opinions on marriage even though I've never been married. Every relationship's about compromise, isn't it? With your mum, with your children. I'm sure it's even more so with a husband.' Though Ginny wondered whether Rebecca ever had much opportunity to compromise. For such a mousy presence, Gareth loomed large in both Emma's and Rebecca's lifestyle.

'They're in the air now. They'll be somewhere over the Alps.' Both women looked at their watches and fell silent again. Rebecca had opened a window and the sound of an English garden seeped into the polished room. A warbling thrush, the flutter of dry leaves falling from branches as birds wrestled for position in the cherry, a strimmer in the distance, the waft of damp lawn on an uncharacteristically mild October afternoon, a spatter of lukewarm rain on the mulch. So calm other than the twitter of a blue tit distracted from his berry-pecking as he spotted a neighbourhood cat taking his afternoon stroll. Thailand would be so different. So . . . fantastic. Ginny felt the tug of excitement and fear again. Yes, she would have gone herself, like a shot, if things had been different. Sending Marie was the next best thing. She should be happy. She *was* happy about it.

'The thing is,' Rebecca said, bringing them both out of their reveries as her voice cracked, 'that Gareth's been having an affair for a year and now that Emma's gone I think he's going to ask for a divorce.'

Missing Marie became a physical ache as the day went on. It became so physical that as she brushed her teeth that night Ginny took two Ibuprofen tablets. When she lay in bed, hot tears running down the side of her face, Ginny remembered Marie when she was just a kick inside. And she allowed herself to be drawn back seductively, like silk in the wind, to a time before the kick. The thing about Barney had been that she had been so mad-damned-head-over-heels in love with him.

To start with, he didn't even have a name. He was

Blue Scarf. She saw him in the faculty library. The first time she saw him her breath caught in her throat, her heart pounded and she forgot to swallow. He had dark-brown hair, a little long and twisted with hair gel at the edges to smooth down the curls that wanted to fly away, magnificent tawny green-brown eyes and the most supple, sensuous, fantastic pair of lips she had ever seen in her life. Eighteen years old and sexually inexperienced, Ginny had been plunged into the world of erotic fantasy. To be kissed by those lips, to taste his tongue, to be gripped by his strong hands. Oh my God. That would be beyond heaven. So as much as she tried her absolute best to keep her mind on anatomy and her next tutorial the library became a place of hot sweats and secret aches, thanks to Blue Scarf.

She saw him speak at the Oxford Union in a debate on world famine. As he was introduced and stood up to speak she found out his name was Barnaby Middleton, and was deeply disappointed that it wasn't a more romantic name, but the cries of support were for 'Barney', which she and her fantasies could live with. The cheers were mostly from girls. Pretty ones. Ginny had observed them from her bench at the back with narrowed eyes. It was a lesson learnt. If you think someone's drop-dead gorgeous the chances are someone else does too. And in the case of Ginny – who at eighteen was awkward and tall for her age, with fly-away hair and unimpressive breasts – that somebody was probably prettier and curvier than she was. He was an intense speaker, those lips that curled and threatened to turn into a teasing smile every so often remaining straight and serious. She was moved by his

11

words. He wasn't just posturing for popularity or so that he could put 'debating' down on his CV, or so that it would further his political skills, or so that he would become a familiar face in time for the elections for President of the Oxford Union. She could see that he was debating because he firmly believed what he said. He spoke of the lack of funding, of aid, of healthcare and education, of medical supplies. He compared the contributions of the European countries and criticised the USA. He seemed to be a big fan of Médecins Sans Frontières. In the five minutes that he spoke Ginny learnt something. He was intelligent. He had integrity. He was studying medicine too. He was handsome. He was sexy.

He was perfect. It was complete and utter agony.

We can't get married, Virginia. We hardly know each other.
My name's Ginny.

Ginny snapped her bedside light on and sat up, her T-shirt sticking to her chest. She pulled it off and flung it against the wall, then got up and fetched herself a glass of water. Mr Mistoffelees, their ginger tom, frowned, got up and settled down again. Ginny looked at herself in the bathroom mirror. How could it be that she looked exactly the same as she had that night, nearly twenty years ago, when in a college bathroom she had waited with a heart pounding like a piston to see if a ring appeared in the bottom of the *predictor* test tube? She smoothed a finger over her eyes and pulled at the skin. Some laughter lines yes, the rings under her eyes were probably darker. But they were the same brown eyes. Her hair was tamed now into a sleek shoulder cut that swung around her neck; it suited her, but it was the same brown hair that flew away given half an excuse. And her soft, pale-pink lips, they were the same lips that Barney had kissed all those years ago.

She blasted cold water into the basin and splashed her face. Then she went back to bed. It wasn't a good idea to allow the past back in. It was better to stay in the present. Nineteen years ago she and Barney had gone separate ways. Eighteen years ago her life had changed utterly as her beautiful daughter had burst into the world. She was the perfect child created by her parents' imperfections. Twenty-odd years ago Rebecca had covered herself in hairspray and got married to Gareth with the big nose and funny grin.

And in the present, she wondered as she turned off her light and rolled over on top of Mr Mistoffelees, had Gareth come home and asked Rebecca for a divorce?

Chapter Two

❦

It was Charlotte's fault that her parents' house was full of animals. Four cats and a fish tank with six fat goldfish. The fish had died, one by one, and Jane hadn't replaced them. The cats were still hanging on in there. Every time Charlotte went abroad she deposited an animal back at home, and they added up. In theory, it was a temporary arrangement, just until she got back and got settled in a place of her own. In reality, whenever Charlotte came back to England she became bored and dissatisfied and it was never long before she took another job abroad. When Mr Mistoffelees arrived Jane had put her foot down and insisted that he'd have to go to the Cats Protection League. That's what they were there for. Jane was starting to feel like an animal rescue shelter and she had to get them past Harry, who always shrugged in the end and got used to it but had a damned good moan to her when they were alone. Charlotte had found Mr Mistoffelees in a London squat, she'd said when she arrived with him in a cardboard box. She was on one of her temporary stays in England and it was never clear how long her temporary stays were going to last. She was sleeping on the floor of a friend's studio flat in Pimlico and teaching English as a Foreign Language in Vauxhall.

'I can't dump him on the Cats Protection League,' Charlotte had protested. 'D'you know how over-stretched they are? Nobody will ever want him and they'll have to keep him for ever, maybe caged. He's six months old, and the kids only want cute new-born kittens.'

At that point, Marie had intervened with floods of tears at the thought of the ginger bundle of fur being put in a cage.

'Oh Jesus.' Ginny gave Charlotte an arch look as she took eleven-year-old Marie in her arms. 'Why can't you keep him? He likes you best. You rescued him.'

'He'd like anyone who fed him.'

'He won't fit in with the others.' Jane had felt her protests becoming more and more futile as Mr Mistoffelees snuggled up on one of the sofa cushions, closed his eyes and began to purr like a machine gun.

'You can never have too many cats, Mum. It's not true what they say about them being loners. They need their communities. Once you've got two you could have six and it wouldn't make any difference.'

'It makes a difference to the number of tins of cat food I have to buy.'

'Oh come on. You can't put Mr Mistoffelees in a cage for the sake of a few rotten pence. And they are excellent mousers. You don't get any rodents in the garden or the shed, or the garage, do you?'

Jane thought doubtfully of the four other cats who at that moment were snoring upstairs in various bedrooms. Then Harry peered in from the garden, probably hearing Marie's howling, spotted the ginger kitten and mouthed, 'No bloody way,' to Jane. That, for him, was quite a strong stand.

15

'I'm sorry, dear, but we've got four cats already. It will really put them out. We had to keep Blossom in a sort of granny flat in the dining room for nearly a year before the others got used to her. There were lots of fights before they settled. Especially with Blackie, he doesn't like intruders at all. It's not as easy as you say.'

'We can have Mr Messilees in our house,' Marie told Ginny with wet eyes.

'You've got animals here, darling.' Ginny kissed her. 'You're here so often, you've got all Granny's animals to play with. If we took Mr Mistoffelees you wouldn't be able to give him as much attention as you wanted to. He'd be neglected. It wouldn't be fair.'

'Then I'll spend more time at home.'

'You can't, sweetie. Who will look after you when you get home from school? I have to work.'

'Granny can come round to our house and look after me instead of me coming here.'

'Granny's got Granddad to look after.'

'And four bloody cats and a tub full of fish,' Jane added, standing up and breathing heavily through her nose as she did when she'd been pushed too far. Both her daughters were humbled by it. 'The answer's no, Charlotte. I'm sorry.'

Left alone while Marie followed Jane out to the kitchen, Charlotte and Ginny eyed each other warily.

'No,' Ginny said firmly.

'Please, Ginny. I don't ask you for much. I don't ask you for anything, in fact. That's not a bad track record for a little sister.'

'You've got to take responsibility for your own actions.'

16

Charlotte was genuinely surprised. 'I do. I've never asked you for anything. Especially not money. I've never asked to stay with you, I know you don't have much room. I do my jobs, live my life. I do take responsibility.'

'You keep rescuing animals.'

'So, I rescue animals when I see they're neglected or being abused. All of these cats were in dire straits when I found them. I really don't think that makes me a monster.'

'Then keep them yourself.'

'But I can't. I've got to be in Cairo in three weeks for my new job. You know that. And before you say take them with you, I can't do that either. A, I don't work in countries where the people are particularly nice to animals. They're not always particularly well fed and watered themselves so you can see how animals get pushed down the chain. And B, I'd never be able to bring them home again because of our loony quarantine laws. That poor cat's better off in England. And he is a bag of bones, look at him. How could I leave him where he was?'

'You've got to stop dumping animals on Mum. She's got a houseful. It's not fair.'

'Well,' Charlotte said slowly, 'at least I don't dump children on her.'

It had taken a moment for Ginny to realise what Charlotte was insinuating and then the penny had dropped and she'd been furious. They'd rowed and Ginny had left with Marie. A couple of hours later, worn down by Marie's wailing, Ginny had rung home, knowing Charlotte was still there.

'Bring him round on your way back to London,'

she'd snapped. And that was how Mr Mistoffelees had come to live with Ginny and Marie.

As Charlotte was touching down at Heathrow, unbeknown to her mother or her big sister, Ginny was agreeing on the phone with Jane that she would pop in later that evening. Since Marie had left, Ginny had been in a kind of spiral. This was her first Saturday on her own since Marie had been born. Not literally the first, but the first Saturday that she'd spent with her new status of being 'on her own'. It had started with hyperactivity. She'd got up at seven and hoovered the house. Then she'd cleaned the bathroom and set about the kitchen. While in the kitchen she'd noticed through the window that the back garden needed doing properly and added that to her list of things to achieve that day.

'It is amazing,' she told her mother on the phone as she picked a string of brambles out of her hair, 'that when you do all the things that you can literally do in a day you shock yourself. If Marie was around it'd take us months to do all these little jobs. And I've cleaned the oven as well. I can't believe how quickly I did it. I'm almost disappointed.'

'I know how you feel. When Charlotte went off I learnt Spanish,' Jane said.

'But that was logical. That's because she was going to do languages at university, and you'd always wanted to learn Spanish. That was more of a thwarted ambition. I don't think cleaning the oven was an ambition.'

'No, I don't mean when she went to university. She'd only been gone half a term when you came back, don't you remember? There wasn't time for me to do anything before you were here, needing me again. I mean when she went off travelling to South America. That's when I started learning Spanish.'

'It's not really the same,' Ginny said after a pause.

Maybe it was the same. That wasn't the point to Ginny in her ravaged emotional state. At the same time, Jane was wishing that Ginny wasn't so dismissive of things that she said. Sometimes Jane sifted through two or three possible comments to make before she said anything at all, just to avoid Ginny's breezy, cutting replies. But it was too late, it had happened again, and now Jane felt stupid. But she covered it up, just as Ginny covered up her irritation, and the conversation continued a little more stiffly.

'So this letter. . .' Ginny continued.

'I haven't opened it.'

'Do you recognise the writing?'

'I haven't opened it, dear,' Jane protested again. Was she protesting too much? 'It's obviously from someone who knew you when you lived here. Or someone you gave our address to because you weren't sure where else you'd be, but that would be years ago, when you were at university. It's someone who doesn't know where you are now. I think it's a man's writing, though. You can usually tell.'

'How can you tell?'

'I don't know. But I'd put money on it.'

'Look, I'll see you later and pick it up then. I need to go and have a bath. My skin's itching all over.'

Ginny felt guilty after she'd put the phone down. She always did when she'd snapped at her mum. And Jane was on her own now, after her father had packed

19

his things and left. She seemed to be adjusting to it well, without high drama and histrionics. It had been three months since he'd gone. Then Ginny realised she hadn't even asked her mum how she was in the space of their phone call and felt even worse. She flicked bubbles impatiently around the bath, unable to relax, feeling that something ought to be done. But there was no Marie to pander to or organise any more. Perhaps her mother felt the same, with no Harry to cater for. But then Jane had four cats whereas Ginny only had Mr Mistoffelees. She lay in the bath hoping vainly that the scented water would somehow permeate her skin and soothe her heavy heart. Then she shook herself and tried to think about her mother instead. She became so preoccupied with imagining what Jane's day had been like for her without Harry around that she completely forgot about the mysterious letter that had fascinated her mother so much.

Chapter Three

That Saturday evening in a blustery, mild October, Charlotte came home. Her skin was peppered with freckles, her fringe now pale blonde and wild over a brown face. She was in jeans, a T-shirt and a denim jacket, trainers on her feet and a rucksack slung over her shoulders resting with casual comfort. She sauntered with the arrogant ease of the wanderer returning to familiar turf. She was home. It was Saturday, Mum and Dad would be in. They were going to be so pleased.

Patrick Road seemed to exhale a self-satisfied sigh. The evenly spaced detached houses, geometric gardens, neat little windows and doors all painted and polished, glass cleaned to diamond sharpness reflecting the pinky-orange of the autumn setting sun. No noise, no sprawl, no shouted exchanges from the doorways, no children running to greet a new arrival, no smell of woodsmoke or coconut milk, nobody conducting their business on the doorstep, sweeping sand from the path. This was England. Everything was barracaded inside, everybody buttoned up, each house creating a barrier to the outside world, like a puffed-up chest daring anybody to approach it. Four hours back in England. Could she be missing Asia already?

When she'd left India she'd been so relieved to be

coming home and leaving her troubles behind. When the plane was late taking off she'd found herself pulling the corners from her in-flight magazine with agitation. She wanted to come home, she was ready to do this now. There was a time to be away and a time to be home, and this was most definitely a time to be home. The swell of sadness she'd felt on leaving was now replaced by a breath of hope. It was just that each time she came home she felt as if she was seeing the road she'd grown up in for the first time. It was so organised and so affluent that it annoyed her. It was like a spoilt child that you were torn between hugging and slapping.

The mature front gardens of Patrick Road were decorated with sprawling mossy foliage, the waxy leaves of evergreens and glossy cars. An electric saw droned, a dog started to bark but couldn't be bothered to continue. The road, like its occupants, was sleepy with overfeeding. A couple of children's bikes were spreadeagled on the pavement. And there was number 12. Charlotte stopped and lit a cigarette while she gazed at her home.

It was plain enough, a four-bedroomed detached house, with chocolate-brown tiles that started halfway up and spread to the peaked roof. Two front windows gazed out to the front like wide-open, dazed eyes. The red front door was placed with accuracy to the bottom right – except that it had been repainted in navy blue. It had looked better red. A neat row of shrubs bordering the path led to the doorstep. They'd been a lot smaller last time she'd seen them. It was a Lego house, she and Ginny used to joke. You can't miss it, it's the one that looks like a child drew it.

It was three years since she'd last seen it. Charlotte took a long drag on her cigarette, visualised her mum, dad and a heap of gorgeous cats inside, everybody pottering about, doing Saturday-evening-late-in-October kind of things, and thought about how thrilled they would be that she'd come home. She dropped her cigarette and walked up the path. She hadn't meant to start smoking again anyway. It was a ludicrous time to regain a bad habit. Hopefully now she was home her nerves would settle. It was time to sort things out.

When Charlotte rang the bell she wasn't going to find her dad, Harry, at home. He was in Portugal that weekend, as it happened. He didn't speak Portuguese but Denise did. Denise owned a villa on the coast – owned it outright, not one of these time-shares that Harry had read about. Denise was a dentist, divorced, two sons, one at university studying to be a dentist, one in Australia being a dentist. Harry had met Denise when he'd gone in for a check-up. That had led to a filling, which had led to polishing, which had led to the possibility of capping, and further discussion had ensued about a bridge until Harry, running out of ideas and fearing he was going to lose perspective completely and ask for his jaw to be wired or all his teeth to be extracted, admitted that he would like to ask Denise out to dinner and that was the only reason he kept making appointments to have spurious work done. Flattered, lonely and curious, Denise had agreed to meet him for dinner. They met in a restaurant, and she reminded him of a holiday in Greece. She was tanned, weathered, with copper eyes and perfect teeth,

wearing a crisp white linen dress that made him want
to touch or smell it. She made him giddy. He lied about
being married and pretended that he was a widower.
Then he pretended it was years ago and he'd rather not
talk about it just yet. Jane was so used to him going out
on his own, either to golf or to play snooker with Roger
and Peter or just spending hours in the garage finding
things to tidy up or reorganise, that she didn't wonder
where he'd been that evening after he'd mumbled
something unintelligible about an evening with his
friends. Their relationship had finally reached the
point of no possessiveness whatsoever. As he'd got
ready for bed in the bathroom, brushing his teeth
(avoiding carefully the new fillings), his eyes had filled
with hot tears. Jane had already turned the light off
and he could hear light snoring. The cats hadn't
missed him; Blossom only yawned as he stepped over
her on the landing, but other than that he could have
been invisible.

A nagging voice, like a child's chant, sang in his ear
that this was the meaning of trust. Jane didn't ask
where he'd been, the cat didn't squint at him
suspiciously. They just assumed that what he'd been
doing that evening was in keeping with a retired
senior marketing manager with a lovely wife and two
lovely grown-up daughters. In fact, he knew that he
was starting an affair and the realisation sent a cold
wave of excitement over him.

Three months before Charlotte rang the doorbell,
Harry had moved out.

As Charlotte walked home from the station, Ginny
was sitting at the kitchen table at 12 Patrick Road,

turning over the letter her mother had given her while Jane fiddled with mugs and teaspoons in the sink and pretended not to watch. Finally Jane couldn't stand the suspense any longer.

'So I thought it was probably a man's writing, you can usually tell. They tend to have small, spidery writing.'

Ginny nodded. A frisson was spreading over her skin.

'No doubt you'll want to open it at home. In case it's personal. It probably is personal, especially written in ink like that. I'd have said it was an older person because of that. It's so unusual to see nowadays. People just don't bother, do they?'

Ginny was contemplating the quality paper of the large envelope, the weight of the letter and most of all the handwriting, spidery as Jane said, and in real ink. She had only ever known one person who liked to write in ink. But that would just be stupid. It wouldn't be.

'You've lived in your house for years, so it's somebody who's lost touch with you and doesn't know where you are. So I thought of all your friends. I was wondering who on earth would want to contact you after all this time. I can only think of one person who might do that.'

'Yes,' Ginny breathed in agreement. Her strongest feeling was disbelief. Jane pulled up a chair, her eyes eagerly searching her daughter's face.

'Yes? Do you think it's from him?'

'Yes.' Ginny put the letter down again. She blinked at her mother. 'Good God, what does he want?'

*

The first time Ginny had spoken to Barney had been in the bar of the Oxford Union, after he had been debating. She'd felt like a groupie, sitting against the wall with her friends waiting for the moment he headed for the bar. Then she'd seized her opportunity and appeared at his elbow. Her pulse was racing, making her feel sick and giddy.

'Hello,' she said.

He gave her a cursory glance and she withered and died inside. Just then a gorgeous redhead tapped him on the shoulder on her way past and demanded a rum and black. Ginny swallowed, self-consciously twiddled with the edge of her shirt and gave a false laugh, which she instantly hated herself for. 'I saw you debating. You were very impressive.'

'Thanks.' Another glance, no interest there and no attempt to promote conversation.

'So that's all I wanted to say. That and I really agree with everything you said. I thought it was bloody cool.'

'Cool?' He pulled an elaborately surprised face. He obviously wasn't impressed by her vocabulary. She would just have to wind back time and remove her ridiculous comment. Her face was becoming redder and redder, her eyes stinging they were so bright with nerves.

'I'm really into Médecins Sans Frontières as well.' Could she have put that any better? Could she have put it any worse? His quizzical expression remained. 'In fact, I used to have a badge. . .'

He laughed out loud. Her pulse was so strong she could hear it in her ears, and now her mouth had dried out completely. The only benefit of that was that she could no longer speak. She used to have a badge? What on earth did that prove? Only that she was a kid who used words like 'cool' and wore political badges in a pathetic attempt to look deep. Her shame was complete. What made it worse was that he'd done nothing to provoke her idiotic behaviour, it had come entirely voluntarily from her. There really was nothing more to be said. She slunk away.

As she was pushing through the small crowd at the bar, tears of embarrassment now stinging in her eyes, she heard him say, 'Are you a first-year medic? I've seen you in the library.' She couldn't look back. In any case, now a tear had escaped and had dribbled right down her face leaving a white streak in her foundation. She reminded herself that you never, ever approach somebody who's so far better looking, funnier, cleverer and more popular than you are yourself. It only ends in tears.

'Oh, who's that?' Jane tutted, leaving a bemused Ginny fingering her unopened letter at the table while she went to answer the front door.

The next thing Ginny heard were whoops of delight, squeals and cries coming from the hall. She went to investigate and felt a bolt of shock to see her sister, Charlotte, enveloped in her mother's arms.

'Good God!' she said, for the second time in an hour, and added, 'Bloody hell,' for good measure.

'Nice to see you too.' Charlotte grinned over her mother's shoulder. She looked great, was Ginny's first thought. She had always had an ability to abuse herself with alcohol and cigarettes, late nights and unsettled living, while still looking healthy and pretty. Ginny was somewhat jealous of that. At the same time she felt a wave of relief that her younger sister was home and well. It surged up through her and she had to knock it back as her eyes started to smart with tears. But Charlotte looked different from when they'd last seen each other, too – she looked older. It was there in her pretty tawny eyes, streaky lines under and in the corners.

Then Charlotte stepped forward to greet Ginny and Ginny let out a gasp of shock. She instinctively glanced at her mother. Jane was pulling a funny face, somewhere between humour and total astonishment.

'You're pregnant!' Ginny said a little unnecessarily. In fact, Charlotte looked as if she had a bus stuffed up her T-shirt.

'Thirty-two weeks,' Charlotte said, hovering somewhere a few feet away from Ginny, her embrace less certain now.

'Oh my God.'

'It's great, isn't it?' Charlotte grinned again. 'I'm really happy.'

'You're not still smoking are you? I can smell it.' Ginny wrinkled her nose.

'Is that all you can say?'

'No, of course not. There's lots of things I can say. Why didn't you tell us? Blimey, Charlotte, how can you get yourself this pregnant without telling anybody at home?'

'I was happy just getting on with it. I haven't had any complications, I was quite content living where I was. I was going to have the baby first then bring it home.'

'But . . . why?' Ginny had reached total incomprehension fairly early on for one of their conversations.

'Because if I'd told you all I was pregnant and living in an animal sanctuary in the middle of Mumbai with my Indian boyfriend you'd have all freaked.'

There was a brief, baffled silence. Then Jane said, 'Boyfriend?' at the same time as Ginny said, 'Freaked?' It seemed neither of them was surprised about the animal sanctuary.

'Don't worry about it,' Charlotte soothed them, tossing her rucksack on to the hall carpet. 'It's all over now, anyway. Both boyfriend and Mumbai were interesting experiences but that's all behind me. I'm home for good now. My wandering days are over.' She glanced around. 'Where's Dad?'

Jane and Ginny exchanged glances. Jane spoke, touching her younger daughter's arm. 'You've been out of touch for a long time, darling.'

'He's not dead?' Charlotte looked pale for the first time.

'Not dead exactly,' Ginny began.

'He's in Portugal with a dentist named Denise,' Jane stated factually, wiping her hands to demonstrate her feelings. 'And good riddance.'

'What – on one of his golfing holidays, you mean?' It was Charlotte's turn to struggle to understand.

'He's not golfing,' Jane said.

'What's he doing then?'

'I should imagine he and Denise are spending most of their time having it off,' Jane snapped.

'Mum!' Ginny frowned and took her arm. 'Come on, let's all go through to the other room. I think we've had enough revelations in the hall.'

'I just can't believe Dad would do this,' Charlotte said as she curled up on the sofa after dinner. Ginny was stacking the dishwasher in the kitchen. 'Don't mind if I put my legs up, do you? They get very achy and puffed up in the evening. I mean, what on earth was his motivation? What can he get from some other woman that he can't get here at home?'

'Do you really want me to paint you a picture?' Jane said sharply, sitting down with a gin and tonic for herself.

'But – sex? Not Dad. He's not that kind of bloke. Okay, I guess he thinks about it from time to time, but he's a family man. He wouldn't just walk away from all that for a roll in the hay.'

'I suppose we don't really know our parents at all,' Jane mused. 'I don't expect I knew either of mine. I think we're all amazed at what's within ourselves. We're all capable of doing pretty shocking things, it just usually takes a catalyst to make them happen.'

'What catalyst?'

'In this case, a check-up.'

'Well she's a bitch,' Charlotte stated. 'Any woman who'd break up a happy family for her own ends is just a selfish cow. I hope I meet her, I'll tell her what I think of her. How dare she do this to us?'

'Us?' Jane queried lightly.

'Sorry, Mum.' Charlotte flushed. 'I mean you, of course. I know I've hardly been here in recent years. I'm so shocked. How can he walk out and leave you with a houseful of cats to look after? It's like I hardly know him at all. When he gets back from holiday I'm going to call him, then we'll see what he's got to say.

He'll want to know he's going to be a grandfather, so I'll have to call him anyway. At least he'll be thrilled about that.'

'He's already a grandfather, dear,' Jane said flatly.

'Well, yes. Apart from Marie, though. . .' Charlotte sighed, laying her head back on the cushions. 'But it's bloody weird timing. Who'd have thought that I'd be coming back to live at home just at a time when you'd been left here all on your own. You'd have thought I'd planned it like this, except of course I didn't know anything about Dad's sleazy little fling. But don't worry, Mum, you're not on your own now. I'm here – and him, of course,' she finished, touching her swollen stomach affectionately.

Chapter Four

It was much later that night when Ginny walked home, gazing up at a misty sky, white with hidden moonlight. The letter was in her handbag, forgotten since Charlotte's dramatic homecoming. Although not forgotten by Jane, who'd whispered, 'Do tell me what he wants, won't you?' in Ginny's ear as she'd kissed her goodbye on the doorstep.

The air felt clear and fresh after a shower of rain and Ginny could smell wet leaves and earth. She walked out of Patrick Road, down the opposite crescent, down a narrow lane lined with terraced houses, cut through an alleyway and was on her own lane, a cul-de-sac of small cottage-like terraces – hers on the end. Her parents had helped her to put down a deposit when Marie was three years old. Up until then she'd lived at home. At first she'd worried that Jane would feel burdened by her sudden return from university and the arrival of a screaming baby (and Marie screamed a lot) but as the months passed, and Marie became a gorgeous, giggling, squirming bundle of fun, Jane seemed to have gained a new role – as Marie's second mother.

Ginny went out and found work and before long the three adults in the house were politely stepping round each other. There was no one terrible row that told

Ginny it was time to go. There were little moments, adding up to an obvious conclusion. She'd been out with friends from work one night and Jane complained about the smell of wine on her breath when she got back. Harry started to mutter about having to live his life in the shed as Marie's toys expanded and took over the house. Jane would make comments about aching legs and back, as Marie grew heavy. Fighting for space in the bathroom became difficult as Marie seemed to absorb water like a sponge. Feeling guilty about burdening Jane, Ginny hardly ever went out, but as Marie got older she ached for some adult company in the evenings. There was a spell when she went out on Friday nights, just for an hour or two, and Jane seemed content. Then Ginny went out twice in one week and although Jane agreed to sit for Marie she sulked over it, and the word 'obligation' cropped up. Then one evening, when she came home from a particularly hard day at work, she heard Marie say to Jane, 'Thank you, Mummy.' Bursting into tears and proclaiming her identity, Ginny decided then that there had to be another way.

She would always be grateful to her parents for what they did for Marie in those first three years, but when they discovered that a neat little two-bedroomed end of terrace was for sale just three roads away they all decided it was time to galvanise themselves. Her parents gave her a loan for a deposit, which she'd never been allowed to repay (in the end Jane had just told Ginny, 'You can't take it with you, and you'll get it in the end anyway. Let's just call it an early inheritance.'), and the mortgage was in her own name. By then her job – working in the pathology laboratory of the local hospital – was regular and safe, and as the house was small and a bit run down their low offer was accepted. It had worked out very well.

Her house had provided a cosy, safe home for her and Marie. She swung open the garden gate and took the four steps up the short path to the front door, stopping to pick a dry twig from the overgrown lilac bush by the door and push the dangling threads of the vine growing round the door and twisting along the telephone cable out of her eyes. Marie had always said how much she loved walking through the vine to get into the house. It was romantic, she claimed. The lilac brought back memories of many springs, coming home together. Marie would always stop to smell the blossoms and make loud snorting noises to make Ginny laugh. Ginny felt a satisfied swell that she was home. But, of course, Marie was away and that brought a dull, empty thud that she tried to clear with a deep breath.

In the hall she hung her coat and went through to the narrow kitchen to fill the kettle ready for a cup of tea before bed. Then, as she pulled out her unopened letter and considered it again, she flicked the kettle switch off and helped herself to a glass of wine from a bottle in the fridge. The kitchen was too small for a table – a galley kitchen was the euphemistic selling term for narrow and useless for anything other than cooking – but they had a breakfast bar in there and a couple of stools. Still, it was pretty, re-tiled only four years ago with colours of Marie's choosing and fitted with spot-lamps that seemed like a great idea at the time but kept popping bulbs that were incredibly expensive to replace. But the result was cosy and they considered it a success. Marie had good taste, and they'd done the work together. Ginny stopped to sigh as she left the kitchen. Would they work together on projects again? Surely from now on Marie would want to embark on such adventures with friends, or even boyfriends. From now on, Ginny would only be in the way. The thought made her feel miserable.

The living room had one wall of red brick framing an open fireplace. The other walls were lined with bookshelves. In the wall to the right of the fireplace was a French door with square panes that led out to a small patio and a long garden. Ginny pulled the heavy curtains over it and the hooped wooden curtain rings rattled. There was a red velvet two-seater sofa and an upright armchair – which Marie always complained didn't match anything and called Granddad's chair. It was Ginny's favourite chair for reading, letter-writing and general contemplation. Next to it was a small high-legged coffee table of dark mahogany, which they'd found in a second-hand shop when they were in Brighton one weekend. Ginny had always had a sneaking feeling it was an antique of some value but she loved it so had no intention of selling it. Two tall dining chairs that were seldom used stood against the wall. She carried her wine and letter across the tufty green rug and sat down in her favourite armchair, took a swig of wine for sustenance, then ripped open the envelope.

She read the letter, which was short. Enclosed with it was another envelope that was more bulky. The letter read,

35

Dear Ginny,

I've sent this letter to your parents in the hope that it will find you now.

I have drafted this letter so many times and none of my words have been right. Instead I'll just keep it short. I've enclosed a card for Marie's eighteenth birthday and a letter. Would you give it to her, please? As she is now eighteen I hope you will give her the choice of whether to accept it or not.

I'm sorry things turned out as they did, but I hope you think you made the right decision. I have many regrets and have felt great sadness, but all I wish you is goodwill.

Yours respectfully,
Barney

Ginny squinted at the envelope for Marie then pressed it with her fingers. The bulk seemed to be on the card – perhaps one of those comedy cards with things stuck to them. Then a metallic tune peeped out from the envelope in response to her prodding – the tune to Happy Birthday.

Ginny read the letter again and took another of mouthful of wine. Then she started to laugh. After a few moments she was all but clutching her sides. Wiping her eyes she stood up and went over to the phone – noticing as she picked up the receiver that she had an answerphone message. She could deal with that in a minute. First of all, she had to share this news.

'Mum? It's me. Yes, it is from him. You'll never guess what he says.' Ginny laughed again. Perhaps it was the warmth of the wine releasing the tensions since Marie's departure, perhaps just because Barney's words were so goddamned funny. She read the letter out to Jane.

'Oh my goodness!' Jane exclaimed. 'What is he thinking of?'

'Such polite regret after all this time. It's just so strange. And the card,' Ginny finished, hiccupping a giggle back down her throat, 'sings Happy Birthday!'

'No!'

'Yes.' She played it down the phone. 'It's probably got a badge on it saying "Birthday Girl". He probably thinks she'll wear it at her party while she plays pass the parcel dressed as a fairy.'

Jane laughed then lowered her voice. 'I'd better be quiet. Charlotte's dropped off on the sofa and I don't want to wake her up, she looks so tired. Well, darling, what are you going to do?'

Ginny decided to ignore the reference to Charlotte for now. Charlotte's behaviour was all too familiar. Ginny was riled by her sudden arrival, bursting in and demanding to stay while she'd been away for years without giving any of them a second thought. Yes, Ginny was going to speak to Charlotte about it all later, but for now she concentrated on Jane's question.

'What do you mean, what am I going to do? There isn't anything to do.' Jane said nothing. Ginny scratched her chin. 'You mean about giving the card to Marie? Of course I'll give it to her. I'm not going to stand in his way. I wouldn't deprive her of a singing birthday card. No doubt it'll have a profound effect on her.'

37

'Yes, it probably will,' Jane said seriously and Ginny could feel her frowning. She straightened her face. 'Mum, I've always been perfectly fair. She knows all about her dad – as much as I last knew, anyway. I've never said a bad word about him. How could I? I don't even know him. And all those photographs and letters I sent him, all those requests for him to visit Marie that went unanswered – she hasn't got a clue about any of that. You know that. I've been an angel. I'll give her the card when she comes back from travelling, that's what I'm going to do.'

'Darling, I mean what are you going to do about Barney? For eighteen years you've wanted him to get in touch with you and now he finally has. What are you going to do about it?'

'Mum!'

'What did I say?'

'I have not by any stretch of the imagination been waiting for bloody Barney to get in touch. How could you think that?' Ginny screwed up her nose and glared at a finger mark on the white gloss of the door. 'What's got into you? You know I don't give a damn about him or where he is. All that faded many, many years ago.'

'But I assumed, love, that you still felt a need to see him.'

'Oh God, will you stop this. No I do not need to see him. What on earth for?'

'For closure, dear.'

Ginny felt angry by the time she came off the phone, which was not the idea of the call. The idea was to have a good laugh with her mum, vent her feelings and go to sleep with an easy mind. Instead, she'd been irritated at the image of Charlotte all spread out over her mother's sofa, waving her pregnant stomach around as if it were a great personal achievement, landing in her mother's lap like a stone.

And, yes, she knew she'd done a similar thing when she'd been younger but it had not, in any sense, been the same. She had only been a teenager when it happened to her. She was bewildered, jobless, penniless, then, after Barney's final word, boyfriend-less (and she'd had no choice whatsoever about that one). She'd really had nowhere else to go. Charlotte on the other hand – from what she could piece together from the evening's conversation at least – had decided to leave her boyfriend, the father of her child, on a whim, just as she did everything on a whim. She'd just changed her mind about the way of life she'd bought into that year (or that month, perhaps, her lifestyle changed so quickly, with the wind). So the animal sanctuary, the selfless job teaching English to kids in Mumbai, the life at one with nature, or whatever crazy New Age philosophy she'd been embracing, was out, and a detached surburban house in the home counties was in. But how long for? And how were Jane's emotions going to be pulled about when Charlotte changed her mind and headed off abroad again? She'd done it so many times before – made grand claims about staying, made Jane happy, then flipped a coin and disappeared again, leaving Jane confused and anxious about her.

But Ginny was also annoyed at the suggestion that she could have been nurturing ideas about Barney all these years. Since it had become clear – abundantly, painfully clear – that he wanted nothing to do with his daughter and was heading off to fulfil himself, Ginny's feelings had mutated from hurt and disappointment briefly to anger, and then finally to indifference. This had happened very quickly, perhaps in the space of a few years. Then she'd stopped wishing that he could see Marie each time she passed a milestone, or said something adorable, or something clever, or, as she got older, something witty that made everybody laugh. It just didn't matter any more what he might think. Ginny had spent months at a time, maybe years, not even passing his name through her head. Marie was so much her daughter, so loved by her mother's side of the family, that Barney had become vestigial, like an appendix. He was something nobody needed anymore.

So why had her mother annoyingly suddenly piped up with the idea that she should write back to him? Apart from anything else, if she wrote back to him he'd think she was still interested in him in some way, and that would be abhorrent. After the way he had sauntered away holding all the cards, not a care in the world, off to live his full life with his full set of advantages, his parents patting him on the back, his bloody parents. . .

Ginny downed the remainder of her glass of wine and stabbed at the answerphone button.

It was Rebecca. Her voice sounded strained. At first Ginny's adrenaline raced, thinking that she'd heard something from Emma and Marie that was worrying, but it wasn't about the girls at all.

'Er, hello, Ginny, this is Rebecca. Um, I was just wondering, really I was only wondering if you'd like a cup of coffee some time. That's all. I'm fine really. Okay. Bye.'

'Shit,' Ginny said aloud. So Gareth had left her after all.

Chapter Five

When Charlotte woke up she instinctively reached for Raj, but he wasn't there. She opened her eyes. She could smell soap powder and could hear a lawn mower. A soft, apricot light filtered through the pastel flowers on the bedroom curtains. The cotton of the duvet was crisp and clean. When she slid herself into a sitting position and touched the carpet with her feet it felt smooth and silky against her rough skin. She eyed her toes critically. The skin was calloused from living barefoot as often as possible, the sparkly pink nail varnish, popular in Mumbai, was chipped. She put her hands over her stomach and rubbed.

'Hello, mystery baby.' Her lips widened into a smile. 'Hello, little darling. Nothing to worry about. We're home now. Yes, do you like that? I felt that kick. Yes, you're glad to be home aren't you?'

After a few minutes of this one-sided conversation, Jane put her head round the door.

'I heard your voice. Are you awake? Are you all right?'

'Of course. Just chatting to the baby.'

'Oh, that's nice.'

Jane wasn't wearing make-up and was still in her dressing gown, her hair ruffled. Charlotte glanced at her watch. It was very out of character. Jane was always up and about before any of them, cleaning up, making toast, organising their day.

'You're up late, aren't you, Mum? Not like you.'

'Harry was an early riser. I just take my time now. It's nice to lie in. I'll put the kettle on now.'

Jane disappeared leaving Charlotte feeling puzzled. It sounded almost as if Jane enjoyed mornings more now that her father wasn't at home. That couldn't be right. It had to be bravado. That was typical of Jane, to try to make the best of things. It took Charlotte a minute or two to push herself up off the bed – her bump was becoming heavier daily – then she padded downstairs yawning and joined her mother in the kitchen.

'Did you have any thoughts about what you wanted to do today, dear?' Jane quizzed as she made tea.

'Not really.' Charlotte rubbed her eyes lazily as she slumped into a chair at the kitchen table. 'Can't see the doctor until tomorrow, being Sunday and stuff. I'll ring some old friends I think, see if anyone's still around. I expect I'll sleep a lot. Afternoons are worst. I go out for two hours at a time, sometimes.' She took her tea and stirred it. 'When's Dad back from Portugal?'

'Don't know,' Jane replied crisply, wrestling with the plastic wrapping of a loaf and whipping out two slices of wholemeal.

'Don't you care?'

Jane watched her daughter with steady grey eyes. 'Not as much as you think I do.'

'Why not? I don't understand it.'

'I know you don't, darling, but it's been a long time since things went wrong.'

43

'Three months. You said he'd been living with that dental – tart – for three months.'

Jane's lips twitched. 'She's not a tart, actually. It would have been nice to think she was, but she's actually rather nice.'

Charlotte gaped. 'You've actually met her?'

'Of course. She was our dentist, remember? Just before I knew that your father was liaising with her I'd been in for a clean and polish. I'd thought at the time that her hands were very shaky, for her that is, she was usually so steady. She must have been wondering what I knew, poor woman. The torture she must have been through. And just because your father left three months ago doesn't mean that's when things went wrong.'

Charlotte shook her head. 'I don't get it, any of it. If she is nice and professional and all that, what the hell does she see in him?'

Jane let out a shout of laughter, which had Charlotte staring in surprise again. 'Now you sound more like Marie.' Jane took her mug of tea and sat down. 'I suppose your father is a thoughtful man, and he can be kind. She's a mature woman, divorced, possibly lonely. Your dad's always been presentable, quite the gentleman. He used to be very good looking, you know. And he's able to be very charming when he wants to be.'

'But how can you tell if he's charming or not when he's totally bloody silent?' Confusion made Charlotte harsh. It was easier in this bewildering situation to blame her dad for everything. It had to be someone's fault.

'Perhaps he'd become silent around us. Perhaps

he'd just run out of things to say. Perhaps there were things he wanted to say, only not to me.'

'But aren't you even going to sort it out with him? Are you talking? In negotiations, or whatever it's called?'

'We're not getting divorced, Charlotte, if that's what's worrying you. There's hardly any need. It's not as if Harry's about to start a new family.'

'That's a point. Does this dental tart—'

'Her name's Denise.'

'All right, *Denise*. Has she got her own family?'

'Two grown-up sons.'

'How grown up?'

'One's in Melbourne being a dentist, one's studying to be one in London.'

'Jesus. Then it's simple. Just send Dad a video of *Marathon Man*. He'll be on the next plane home.'

'Has it occurred to you,' Jane said, clearing the table, 'that I may not want him on the next plane home?'

'Not want?' Charlotte echoed feebly, her hand resting on her bulging stomach.

The doorbell rang.

'Ah. That'll be the handyman. It's about time we got that gate fixed.' Jane put the tea towel down and wandered off.

Ginny met Rebecca for Sunday lunch in the Anchor, a crooked country pub on a lane sheltered by beech hedges that was well known locally for a good roast. They ordered lunch and a drink each at the bar then took their drinks over to a table in the corner where things were quiet. It was a crisp, bright autumn day and it took Ginny's eyes a while to adjust to the gloom created by the small windows, dark wood and yellow ochre walls of the interior.

First they discussed their daughters at length. They were in Bangkok. Ginny had received an email every day, and two phone calls. So far she was tensely content that everything was going well. It was fair to say that she was torn between moments of panic and moments of complete jealousy.

'He's gone,' Rebecca said with sudden brittleness, like a dry biscuit snapping. Ginny widened her eyes sympathetically and waited for her to continue. Rebecca put down her gin and tonic, her hand trembling. 'I don't want to burden you with this, believe me, Ginny. There's nothing worse than a depressed friend. I'm not even a friend – it's really the kids that brought us together.'

'Oh, I think of you as a friend, no question about it,' Ginny said warmly.

That was a trigger. Rebecca's pale-blue eyes brimmed with tears and they slopped messily on to the over-polished surface of the table.

'God, I'm so sorry,' she snorted, wiping the back of her hand over her running nose and gulping. 'It's just, you see, I thought I could talk to you.'

'Of course you can.'

'I'll regret burdening you tomorrow. I'm so sorry.'

'Please, Rebecca,' Ginny patted her wet hand, 'stop apologising, and please don't keep thinking it's a burden. I'm not exactly the expert on husbands, errant or otherwise, but you can talk to me about anything.'

'I – just – you strike me as someone who would never betray a confidence. You've got that air about you, someone trustworthy. And you've known us all these years. I mean, am I so stupid? I knew something was brewing but I didn't realise it would be so destructive. Now I feel like such a – an idiot. He's made a fool out of me, he's made our marriage a sham. I feel betrayed in every possible way. I hate him for making me feel like this. I *hate* him.'

Ginny opened her mouth and shut it again. She was about to agree that Gareth was a prize bastard for walking out on Rebecca just as she found herself alone, her son grown up and at university, her daughter on the other side of the world. His timing was bloody awful. It would be easy to say 'Yes, I hate him too,' but it would hardly be helpful. She just thanked the Lord that she'd never been married and had all these fears to deal with. If you didn't have a husband he couldn't walk out on you.

'He says he'll explain it all to the kids when Emma gets back. At least he hasn't done it in front of their eyes.'

'No, men never do.'

'But that is good of him, isn't it? Shouldn't I be grateful for that, at least?'

'Yes, I suppose you're right,' Ginny lied. What a coward, sneaking away to avoid the harsh judgement of the two people in his life who would challenge his decision the most strongly. Rebecca may be hating him at the moment but that would come from hurt and regret. It was nothing compared to what his children's reaction was likely to be. There was nobody more judgemental than a teenager. Gareth must have been quietly quaking. 'Do you want to tell me what happened?'

Rebecca's chest heaved. 'It's a woman from work.

My God, what a cliché that is. Younger than him, of course. They've already set up a home together. How could that have happened without me seeing it? He was already making another life for himself, when he had a life at home, with us. It's greedy, isn't it?'

Ginny wanted to make Rebecca feel better but had no idea what to say. She felt her parents' situation might be worth running past her. 'You know, my father ran off with somebody else recently.'

Rebecca was shocked. 'What? When?'

'About three months ago.'

There was a moment's stunned silence and Rebecca sniffed and rubbed a tissue under her nose. 'Oh my God, I had no idea.'

'No, nobody really knows about it. We haven't talked about it unless we have to. But it's unfathomable, when it happens. I'm not saying there are any parallels at all, but I do think sometimes men go a bit mad.'

'And what about the women they run off with? Are they mad too?'

'Maybe. Or maybe just grateful for the attention.'

'You'd think there weren't enough men to go round, the way some women behave. I wasn't brought up like this. In my family, marriage was permanent. My parents were strict Catholics. But your poor mother. And in her retirement as well, it's just cruel.'

'Odd,' Ginny mused, 'she doesn't seem too bothered. She's got a part-time job she enjoys now and sometimes I do actually think she's all right.' She didn't mean to sound flippant but it was hard to put it any other way. 'I guess I was stunned. Perhaps I still am. My mother doesn't seem to be surprised at all and whenever I mention it she plays it right down and changes the subject. But that's another story really, it's you I'm interested in.'

Rebecca let go a large sigh, her flow of tears ebbing. 'And you've managed all these years on your own. You must think I'm pathetic.'

'Not at all, 'Ginny said severely. 'It hasn't been easy. There have been times, sometimes months, sometimes a week, sometimes just at night, when I've been desperately lonely, when I've wished hard for a magician to make it all better, to make the right man walk into my life. But there's never been one right man who I've been prepared to risk Marie's stability for.'

Rebecca gazed at Ginny with red-rimmed eyes, her expression close to awe. 'You're so strong. I wish I could be strong like you.'

'It's not strength, Rebecca, just necessity. Barney wasn't interested, so there it was. Me and Marie, end of story.'

'Barney?' Rebecca quizzed gently. 'That was – he was, was he, the, er. . .'

Ginny realised how easily Barney's name had slipped out. It was funny because she never referred to him by name, hadn't done for years. Until the letter had arrived, Barney had been shut in a drawer in the back of a dusty attic in her mind, a drawer labelled 'Do not open'.

'Yes, he was responsible, as my father might have put it.'

'He was a – Emma said – I mean, you know how girls talk – but I gather he was a student, is that right? I don't want to ask if it's painful.'

49

Ginny laughed, a carefree laugh. 'It's not in the least painful. He wasn't even a boyfriend. He was my first lover. I was a gauche, innocent, swotty medical student. He was gorgeous, I was flattered. To be honest, I was madly in love with him. I think I was so grateful to have his attention, even just for one fumbling night, that I was prepared to give him anything. And that's how Marie came about.'

'Oh, you unlucky thing. Just one night.'

Ginny sighed. 'And the odd thing is that since then I've known so many stories about people taking months maybe even years to have a baby. Sometimes it's as if they're collecting pregnancy points over the months. But at the end of the day it's very crude biology. One happening, one baby. But no, I'm not unlucky. I've often realised that I'm one of the luckiest women in the world. Marie's been everything to me, I shudder to think what my life would have been without her.'

'But now she's gone,' Rebecca ventured, her hand more steady as she lifted her gin and sipped from it, 'what on earth will you do?'

'So you'll come with me to the doctor's tomorrow, won't you?' Charlotte looked up from the Georgette Heyer she'd found in her mother's bookcase. 'I could do with the support. It's ages since I've been to a doctor in England. They're always so moralistic, it'd be good if you could wait with me till I come out.'

'Tomorrow? Oh, no I can't, dear. I'll be at work.' Jane perched on the edge of the sofa and rubbed Charlotte's leg affectionately. 'You'll be all right on your own, though, won't you?'

Charlotte blinked at her mother. 'Work? What do you mean, at work?'

'I've got a job.'

'What? Why?'

'Because I wanted one. Everybody's got a job. It's completely normal, Charlotte. You're reacting as if I'd said I was going to Soho tomorrow to buy some sex.'

Charlotte was puzzled. 'Soho?'

Jane tutted. 'It was a little joke. I'm not working in Soho, I've got a job in the hospice shop on the High Street.'

'Oh you are joking! In a charity shop?'

Jane looked genuinely hurt. She sat back, literally putting distance between herself and her daughter. 'I would have thought,' she said slowly, 'that with your experience, your travelling and your perspective, that you would be the one person who would appreciate working as a volunteer for a charity. You know more about unfortunate people in the world than anyone else I know. I'd have thought you'd be pleased.'

'Of course I am! Oh God, Mum, that's not what I meant.'

'Then what on earth did you mean?'

'It's just a job that old people do. And you're not old.'

Jane took Charlotte's hand, and Charlotte raised her mother's hand to her lips and kissed it warmly. She noticed as they pulled away from their embrace that the skin there was drier, more speckled, more frail than she remembered. Was her mother old enough to work in a charity shop already? Just what had been happening while she'd been away?

51

Chapter Six

Jane had disappeared and was doing something in the garden. Their conversations were leading nowhere; Charlotte couldn't make head or tail of Jane's strange mood, and she felt she'd rather be on her own for a while. A bit of pampering would do her good. After they'd had lunch she wallowed in a long bath. As the afternoon lazed on, Charlotte took the opportunity to make herself a mug of tea, steal the phone and take it upstairs to the bedroom. She pulled the battered remains of her brown leather filofax – bought fifteen years ago and now, like her, well travelled and somewhat the worse for it – out of her rucksack and sank back against the luxurious pillows, wiggling her toes in the calm coolness of the room. A few phone calls then she'd have another nap. This baby was like a succubus, stealing all of her energy for itself. She snapped herself awake and flicked through the pages of her address book.

Four disappointing phone calls later, she flapped through the pages again despondently. Nobody lived where they used to live. Two answerphones with unknown voices on them, two complete strangers with no knowledge of the friends she was looking for. It couldn't have been that long since she'd been in touch with these friends, could it?

Her best friend whenever she came back to England had always been Helen. They'd worked together once in a language school in London Bridge and Charlotte had taken over her sofa, or her floor, more than once on previous visits. At least she knew where Helen was for sure, but unfortunately that was in Washington D.C. with her new lawyer husband, who she'd met quite out of the blue in a pub in Putney while watching the Oxford and Cambridge boat race. Here in sleepy Kent Charlotte was starting to feel friendless and isolated.

She took a gulp of tea, wishing she could drink something stronger, as she was getting agitated, and flicked through the filofax again. She'd already checked out the people she liked the most and was starting to look dangerously closely at names of people who she'd never really liked in the first place. If only she had Internet access here in the house she could probably track at least half of these people down from searches, maybe even from old email addresses. She'd used an Internet café in Mumbai sometimes and perhaps she could check her own account for new messages. Not that she expected any. Yes, it probably was her fault that she'd lost touch with everybody. This made her feel even more bad tempered. The thought came again – had she done the right thing in coming home? She shook it away.

The obvious thing was to go to Ginny's house and use Ginny's computer to access the web. Marie had been online for ages, and Ginny had been communicating with her by email since she'd gone travelling so she knew everything was up and running there. But to do that she'd have to face Ginny's frosty, moralising face again and she wasn't ready to do that yet. It wasn't as if Ginny had anything to be moral about. She'd done exactly the same thing herself eighteen or so years ago – tipped up pregnant and in need of support. Somehow when Ginny did it everybody had rallied round, yet Charlotte felt distinctly as if they were disguising their annoyance with her predicament. And while both her sister and her mother had eventually reacted very warmly to the idea of the baby last night, they'd both seemed pretty cool when it came to being interested in Charlotte herself. So far nobody had asked a proper question about Raj yet. Not one that she could answer. But then there was so much that nobody here would understand about her circumstances that perhaps it was just as well that nobody asked a sensible question. It saved her having to dig into her soul and heave up strong emotions that were better left sinking down, like an anchor, into the depths, out of sight.

If only she could nip outside and have a quick cigarette. She could just imagine Jane's reaction on seeing her pregnant daughter trying to sneak a fag. The image was pretty grotesque, it was true, but Charlotte had had moments of not caring in recent days. If everything had fallen apart, what did a stray cigarette matter? Who cared if she damaged her health if her heart and soul were already ripped to pieces? Maybe she could just have a puff through the open window?

She crept to the window and opened it. Beyond the pink and cream concrete apron of the patio the garden stretched like a green bathmat, rectangular, soft, even and a rich green. The bushes seemed stunted by comparison with the eucalyptuses she and Raj had loved so much on their long walks when they'd gone up country. For a moment, gazing over the tame little English garden, she was transported back to the forest they'd visited often, one she'd grown to love, remembering the wild colours of the birds in the sunny branches and the massing of the fruit bats at dusk. Her eyes filled with tears and they spilt out uncontrollably, her throat contracting as she let out a sob and put a hand to her face.

'Raj,' she whispered. 'I'm so sorry.'

How hurt would he have been when he realised that she had gone? A little? A lot? She hadn't left any note, no word of where she was going. She'd deserted him utterly and completely, and brought his child to her own country. As the tears fell, she fumbled for a cigarette, then heard her mother's voice rounding the corner of the house and heading into the garden. A man's voice was droning in response. Panicking, Charlotte lost her grip on her cigarette packet and it flapped on to the patio. She ducked out of sight.

'Yes, of course I appreciate your thoroughness,' Jane was saying in what Charlotte recognised as a politely friendly tone. 'When Maude talked to me about the job you'd done on her rusty railings out the back I said to her, give me his number and I'll get in touch. That gate's been sticking every damp spell for the last five years. It's such a relief to have it seen to.'

'In the unlikely event of the need for a full and total overhaul,' the handyman replied, 'I would, of course, warn you about any extraneous or excessive charging that might be necessitated by the completion of my duties as they would have been laid out to you in the – er – first instance.'

'Yes, Mr Wells, I understand.'

'Call me Malcolm, please. Everybody does.'

'Malcolm then.'

'You see nobody appreciates thoroughness in this day and age. The young men, they just seem to be more interested in the rapidity of certain tasks and thus the efficacy is mislaid along the byline.'

There was a slight pause, then Jane agreed. 'I'm with you wholeheartedly, Malcolm. Perhaps you can shave a bit off the gate so that it fits?'

'Now there's a fine example one can exhume for the benefit of explaining what I'm saying. Your gate there must needs require a removal from the post and a repositioning in order for the overall imaging and solidity to be maintained.'

'Oh yes, I see. Well, perhaps if you could make a start?'

'I would, of course, have to consult.'

'Oh yes, of course, it's the weekend. Please call your wife – you can use our phone.'

'I'm a widower, Mrs—'

'Call me Jane, please.' A small laugh. 'Everybody does.'

'Well, Jane, I'm a widower now. I have been afflicted with this circumstance for two years so this employment you see is beneficial to me not only in a pecuniary capacity but also on account of the inevitable social intercourse that arises from it.'

'Oh, I say,' Jane said, then cleared her throat. 'Oh, I see what you mean. I'm sorry, Well, maybe you could consult – who is it you need to consult?'

56

'Only my diary. It is placed conveniently on the front seat of my van. Perhaps you'd like to accompany me in retracing our steps.'

'Yes, why not.' Jane laughed again, a girlish sound. 'Do you think you could come next week then?'

'My movements, Jane, are not exactly concrete.'

Charlotte winced as the voices began to trail out of her hearing again. Did anybody really want to know about Malcolm's movements? Had she been mistaken or had her mother been flirting?

She peered through the window at the retreating figures. Her mother looked tall and even regal next to the squat man wearing an inappropriately thick jumper, his bald head reddened by the surprising strength of the autumn sun. In a brown sack he'd have looked just like a little fat monk, pottering about his monastery garden. Pouting down at her lost cigarettes, she decided to go back to the phone again, and, in a burst of hormonal defiance, tried another number. This time she heard a voice she recognised.

'Stuart? It's Charlotte.'

'Charlotte?' There was a pause then disbelief. 'Charlotte Simpson?' Then utter delight. 'Oh my God, what are you doing? Where are you? How *are* you?'

She smiled. That was the warmest welcome she'd received since she'd come back to England. Perhaps it had actually been a good idea to ring her ex-boyfriend. After all, he was obviously over the moon to hear from her. He might have had a girlfriend or two in the interim, but clearly he was single now. And she had dumped him, and he had been broken hearted. What harm could it do if they saw each other again? Her spirits needed a boost and she was hugely pregnant, after all. It was laughable to think that anything would happen but maybe she could salvage a friendship. She desperately needed one.

'I'm back in England. It's a long story, but I was wondering what *you* were doing?'

Ginny read Barney's letter again when she got home. Then she put it away again. Peace settled over her. Poor Rebecca, her life in turmoil, her expectations dragged away from her and dumped in a skip. Thank God, thank *so* God that she'd never married. She'd often observed from a safe distance the power that married couples wielded over each other. It was perverse, head games of the worst order. She was angry with Gareth on Rebecca's behalf, mostly on account of his cowardice, but she secretly thought that she'd be far better off without him. It would just take Rebecca time to realise that. She didn't entertain the possibility of him coming back, although she suspected Rebecca would probably have him back. She was like a wounded animal, barking and in need of pain relief in whichever form it arrived. Gareth returning with a packed suitcase would do the trick nicely.

She went to bed and considered, as she stroked Mr Mistoffelees's head, what she had told Rebecca about Barney. Did it matter? No, not at all. It hadn't touched her emotions to talk about it. The knowledge was liberating and she smiled to herself.

The fact was, that night in his college room had been incredibly exciting for her, even though it had ended in drama of the highest order. Parents screaming, everyone in tears. Yes, it had turned ugly, but, just for a fleeting night, it had been beautiful.

After the Oxford Union debacle it had been a week before Ginny had even set foot in the faculty library again. She'd wrapped herself up in a scarf and woolly hat, her collar up, and sidled in like a burglar. She'd worked, her pulse thudding painfully in her throat as she sneaked glances around, hoping he wouldn't see her and remember what an idiot she'd made of herself, all but making a pass at him at the Union bar. When she had finally spotted him among the book-shelves her heart had shot into her mouth. She'd darted her eyes back to her work and stared unseeingly at her notes, probably for an hour, before, eyes bright, she'd sneaked out of the library again, unnoticed. After that milestone, trips to the library had gradually become easier. She saw him at times and always shot out of his way, finding an excuse to dive out of sight or bury her head in her work. Once they were in the same queue at the check-out desk and he murmured something to her with a smile, but she turned rigidly to face the librarian, checked out her books and steamed out like a train on a one-way track.

After a few weeks her life returned to relative normality, aside from her occasional sightings of Barney, which always left her red faced and nervous. In any case, he wasn't the only source of entertainment that she had at the university. She had other friends and she'd joined a few clubs at the freshers' fair, signing up to all kinds of things at the time that she'd dropped out of later. However, she still went to the chess club. That was how she'd been chosen to play on her college team for Cuppers, the inter-college contest. The St Anne's team were good, and she knew she'd been lucky to be picked for it. Unsurprisingly she played board four of four, and she wasn't in the least offended. It gave her a chance to pick up the occasional victory, and the way things were going she had a success rate of about sixty per cent.

And then they went to play St John's.

They rendezvoused with the other team in the bar.

'Sorry about this,' a tall, blond graduate who she always remembered was called Daniel told them. 'One of our lot's late. Just changing from rugby. Can we get you a beer now you're here?'

Well, ruminated the St Anne's team, we don't normally drink before a match, but then again it's very tempting. . . Before long the teams were fraternising with unusual relaxed humour at the bar and they'd all had two pints.

'Do we really care who wins?' Daniel had grinned. 'Perhaps we should just toss for it. From what I can tell from the table, we're pretty much evenly matched. Our record of wins and losses is the same.'

St Anne's team captain, Theresa, annoyingly attractive and clever in equal measure, had agreed. But she fancied Daniel, that much was clear, and the atmosphere was becoming increasingly frivolous.

'In any case, we're a board short,' said Daniel. 'Some bastard's nicked it. I'm really sorry but we were hoping you wouldn't mind taking it in turns on one of the boards.'

'No need for that,' a voice came from behind. 'Look, I've made one.'

Everybody laughed as the fourth member of the St John's team joined them brandishing a board drawn in felt-tip pen on two blank pieces of A4 paper stuck together with Sellotape. 'Sorry I'm late, sodded my knee up in the scrum. That's the trouble with being so tall. Second row, no arguments.'

But Ginny wasn't laughing. Blue Scarf, otherwise known as Barney, was the fourth player.

'So who's your board four?' he asked, eyes roaming over the team and stopping at Ginny with a quizzical frown of recognition, then a light in his eyes.

'I am,' she said, almost shouted, with a confidence she didn't feel fuelled by two pints of overly fizzy lager.

He held out his hand. 'May the best man win.'

'You're not board four,' she stated, too startled to acknowledge the handshake.

''Fraid so.'

Ginny turned to Daniel, fired up with adrenaline. 'Are you doing reverse order?'

'As if we'd reveal our tactics to you,' Daniel replied with a good-humoured wink. 'Okay, let's grab one more beer and take it with us. There's a free room up the corridor we can use. We'll have to flip for the naff paper board, but at least we've got four sets of pieces. Couldn't imagine Barney knocking up a spare set of those in his free time, talented bugger though he is.'

Ginny wandered down the corridor with the group, her cheeks flushed, her eyes smarting.

'Virginia the virgin, you may have me here.'

'That is just childish.'

'No, it's a fair recognition of mate in three moves.'

61

'I meant what you called me.'

'Virginia?' Deep set eyes roved her face. 'Isn't that your name?'

'Oh,' Ginny stood up, pushed herself away from the table, 'have the game. You're just tedious.'

'You're resigning from a winning position?'

'Fuck off.'

It had all the members of both teams glancing up in surprise. She walked away and didn't look back. So what if she forfeited the game. So what if the team lost. She would not sit there and be the butt of Barney's jokes. It had been painful from beginning to end, especially with the teasing glances he was giving her, peering up from under his eyebrows, trying to put her off with the confidence of a young man who knew he could distract women if he felt like it.

So he thought himself so attractive, so popular, so funny, she huffed as she strode vigorously through the quad. So cool, the man who could be anything to anyone and be loved for it. In one transformation he could pore for hours over his textbooks, the next he could debate articulately the state of medicine in the third world, the next he could have them all laughing at the bar, later he could make crude comments to a female student he hardly knew. Correction, didn't know at all. Cocky sod, arrogant bastard, thank God they'd never got to know each other, she'd hate him. It was better not to go through all the motions. Life was too short; she would just stick to the company of people she liked and who liked her. How difficult was that?

She laughed into the night air, her warm breath sending cobwebs of white smoke into the cold. In that one dig at her name he had made himself unattractive to her. He who had looked down his nose at her because she hadn't put her praise for his speech into particularly good words, he who, fresh from the rugby club, was still talking in macho soundbites. What a total, utter posturing arse.

'Arse!' she yelled into the air, apologising to the night porter as she went through the lodge.

'Did I offend you?' The breathless voice caught up with her and, having just reached the main road, she turned round in astonishment. It was him, bright eyed under the streetlights, looking seriously concerned.

'Oh don't make things worse. Just go back to your bar, drink some more and fall over.'

'I did offend you,' he confirmed.

'You can't offend me, you don't know me. You're just clearly very juvenile and I've got better things to do with my time, like an essay that's due in on Thursday.'

'Just stop for a sec.' He held her arm as she turned to walk away. 'I'm sorry. I've been making silly jokes down with the rugby blokes all afternoon. I guess I didn't really think about what I was saying. Really, I am sorry.'

'Accepted. Now get lost.'

He blinked at her again. Surprised by her spirit? Good. 'You were winning from about six moves in. You play a mean game of chess.'

'And?' She turned back in irritation.

'I'm board one normally. We switched tonight thinking we'd have a couple of boards in the bag, including mine.'

She stuck a hand on her hip. 'And?'

'You beat me. And I'm board one.'

She gritted her teeth. 'And?'

'I should have thrashed you, but I didn't, because you're too good.'

'Hoorah. Can I go now?'

He let go of her arm. 'Yes.'

'Thank you.'

She stalked home, her chest heaving, and stayed awake all night replaying the conversation in her head.

Chapter Seven

'We went through the motions, you know, blood tests and the like. I weed into a pot and they had a good prod around. I heard the heartbeat – that was lovely. They said everything was fine, but this is England, of course, and they started going on about excess water something. Said I was big for my dates. So they're going to scan me on Thursday,' Charlotte told Jane as she ate her way through a packet of biscuits and Jane busied herself making a salad for supper. 'And I told them it wasn't necessary. I did have a scan at twenty weeks.'

'You did?' Jane stopped chopping tomatoes and turned round. 'You didn't tell me.'

'There's a lot I haven't told you. We haven't really talked properly about it at all, have we?' Charlotte couldn't help sounding sulky as she wiped a biscuit crumb from her lip.

'We haven't really had a chance yet, dear. I'm sorry I had to go to work but we all have our routines, don't we?' She might have added that she wasn't prepared to drop everything just because the prodigal daughter had returned, Charlotte guessed moodily, but she didn't.

'It would have been nice if you'd come with me today. I don't know what it is about going to see a doctor in England, or a midwife even. They always make you feel you've done something wrong.'

'I don't think that's true. Ginny had wonderful support when she had Marie. Not everything in England is as negative as you make it out to be,' Jane said with half a sigh. 'We all like it here. It can't be so bad.'

'It's just so strange, so different from what I'm used to now. They make such a fuss. If they could see how people manage who don't get all this medical attention.'

'Yes, and babies and mothers get ill in other countries because they don't get this medical attention. You know that. Especially older ones. There can be complications.'

'That's another thing that's pissing me off. I'm only thirty-six. Anybody would think I was fifty-six. They talked about screening and how do I feel about not being offered amniocentesis. Honestly, Mum, there's risk of miscarriage after amnio. As if I'd risk doing anything that might hurt this baby, especially after all I've been through to—'

There was a pause, Jane raised her eyebrows in anticipation but Charlotte didn't elaborate.

'Well,' Jane said soothingly, 'that's your mother's instinct coming out already.'

The soothing tone made Charlotte feel more sorry for herself. She really had felt quite intimidated seeing a doctor, midwife and nurse all in one afternoon. They'd bustled around her, frowning their disapproval at her history so far (or so it seemed), and she'd felt utterly wretched. She saw that they'd ticked on her notes 'unsupported pregnancy'. She did want some sympathy from her mother but since her arrival it had been very thin on the ground. Perhaps Harry leaving had hardened Jane. Something had changed. Or was her memory faulty? Had Jane always had a business-like side to her, that could sweep sentiment aside and see things clearly and logically? Had she lost her ability to recognise that all her daughter needed was a big hug?

'It's a pretty momentous event for me, after all. I know you and Ginny have been here before so it all seems pretty mundane.'

'Oh darling!' Jane's eyes filled with tears and she swept across the room to the table. 'A baby is *never* a mundane event.' After a hug Charlotte felt mollified, although she was put out when Jane went back to preparing the salad. Hadn't the hugs lasted longer when she was younger?

'It's just all been – quite difficult.'

Chop, chop, chop. A silence fell on the kitchen, then Jane said, 'You know I'm ready to hear it when you want to tell me, I just don't want to pry.'

'Well it's hardly prying to find out about the history behind your grandson.'

'Grandson?' Jane took a chair and put her elbows on the table, her chin in her hands, all attention. 'I didn't like to ask. Did you find out when you were scanned before?'

Charlotte nodded and bit her lip, suddenly emotional again. 'You'd have thought that would have made it all all right, wouldn't you?'

Jane nodded, her face showing total bafflement, then Charlotte sighed and began.

'The baby's father is an Indian man, Mum. His

name's Raj. I met him at work at the school in Mumbai, he was one of the managers there. Oh, I had a lot of friends there of all kinds of nationalities; that was fine for a couple of years, we had a lot of fun. But after a while I sort of opted out of the whole expats abroad thing, it was annoying me too much. Too much money, not enough sense, not enough perspective, everything's better back in England, every foreigner is stupid, you know how it is.'

'Not really, dear, but I can imagine. That's not you at all.'

'Oh they're not all like that. But I just became more and more involved in Indian culture. It made more sense to me. And Raj became my one good friend.' She swallowed noisily. 'Then he became my boyfriend.' At last Jane put out a hand, and Charlotte curled her fingers around her mother's and went on. 'We kept it secret for a while.'

'But why? You're both adults aren't you?'

'Huh, yes. But his family are quite well-to-do. They wanted him to marry a nice respectable Indian girl, probably a lawyer or a doctor. They'd never have approved of me.'

'But you were a teacher?'

'A white English girl. And an English-language teacher, not a proper schoolteacher, even. A big, resounding no all round.'

'And?'

'We decided to live together. Then we started rescuing animals. So his family ostracised him.'

'Goodness.'

'And then, when there was a baby, well, you can imagine. They didn't want to know. He'd ruined his

68

life, I was a typical loose white woman who'd wrecked his life and his chances of a respectable marriage. I'd ruined everything for him, it was all my fault. He had the choice, leave me and go back to his family and they'd cover it up. Or stay with me and they'd disown him.'

'Gracious.'

'So I made the decision for him. I couldn't bear to see him in so much pain over it. So I left.'

Charlotte let the tears fall. All the tiredness, the emotion, the hormones racking her body overcame her. She could still see his sister's hard face telling her to get out of her brother's life.

'Oh my brave girl.' Jane squeezed her hand. 'Well, you're home now.'

'And he'll be glad. I know his family will be, and he'll do the right thing. I can't be held responsible for ruining someone's life. It's too big. It's not fair on me, or our son.'

Jane hugged Charlotte again, this time a long, slow, warm hug.

'There, there,' she tutted, sighing again. 'Who would have thought that history could repeat itself in this way. My poor girls. Whatever did you do to deserve the men you ended up with.'

'Girls?'

'Ginny too.'

'What's Ginny got to do with it?' Charlotte was irritated.

'Well. . .'

'No, don't talk to me about Ginny at the moment.' Charlotte sniffed. 'She's being so uptight and moral. And please, I must ask you, please don't tell her a word of what I've just told you. It's far too private, far too. . . special for her to walk all over. I trust you, Mum, not a word.'

'Of course, I'll be as silent as the grave if you insist. Although Ginny is the one person who would understand just how you feel.'

'How come?'

'Have you forgotten? Well, I suppose you were preoccupied with school and exams and you didn't really get involved in all the drama, thank heavens. But Barnaby's family were absolutely awful about the baby. They even tried to buy her off with money, can you imagine? They insisted that she have an abortion, and when she refused they booked her into a private clinic and tried to force her to go.'

Charlotte blanched. Now that she was pregnant the story had a far greater impact on her than she could have imagined. She certainly didn't remember any of this. It had all gone on around her in a blur. All she remembered afterwards was that Barney's name was practically taboo, and apart from a few acid comments here and there, that was it. 'Oh my God, poor Ginny.'

'Yes, poor girl. Still, she was saved from the in-laws from hell and that has to be a blessing.'

'But what about Barney? Didn't he have any say in it?'

'From what we could all make out he wanted to run away from it all. I think he must have been a very weak and vain boy. All he cared about was his career. I'm sure he was glad to have a battleaxe for a mother doing his dirty work for him, coming here, thumping the table, waving her cheque book around, scaring us all to death.'

70

'She came here?'

Jane raised her eyebrows. 'But this was a long time ago. Perhaps it's better that you don't bring this up with Ginny. It was all very unhealthy at the time and I'm amazed she survived the pregnancy and birth as well as she did. She got through it because we cocooned her with love and support. And we'll do the same for you, darling.'

'But Dad's not even here.'

'Never mind.' She kissed the top of Charlotte's head and rubbed her sun-bleached hair. 'I'll look after you.'

'So, Barney never kept in touch after that?'

'Never showed any interest at all. Harry and I were determined to protect Ginny from that terrible family, so we made sure she didn't suffer any further humiliation. And, as you know, Marie has turned out to be a wonderful girl.'

'I don't know about Marie.' Charlotte felt a spear of regret. 'I hardly know her. I haven't been here.'

'But it's never too late to catch up,' Jane reassured.

'I wonder, though.' Charlotte wiped her face with a tissue and settled with a deep breath. 'How can a father go all those years knowing he's a father and not do anything about it? Whatever he does, where he goes, he's still Marie's father.' Just as Raj would be their baby's father.

'Well, Barney was clearly very young and immature. Perhaps your Raj will be different.'

'Oh, he can't be involved.' Charlotte shook her head resolutely. 'It's just too complicated.'

'Well then, dear, it's not what we would have wished for you or for Ginny, but we'll make the best of it. That's what parents do. As you'll find out.' Another kiss, this time on her cheek. 'I'll come with you to your scan on Thursday if you'd like me to. Now stop eating biscuits, all that sugar's bad for the baby. And you won't find the packet of cigarettes you dropped on the patio, I've thrown them away. No more smoking. The salad's ready now.'

Chapter Eight

'I never took a gap year,' John, one of the pathologists in the lab, said as he shifted his swivel chair, adjusted the slide in the clips and peered into the microscope. 'Couldn't afford it. Thought it was just the spoilt kids who did that. You know, driving Land Rovers through Africa, going camping in South America, all that fake Indiana Jones stuff. Little kids pretending to be explorers armed with Daddy's credit card. Can't see how that teaches them anything. Sticks in my throat really.'

'Not that you're jealous,' Ginny replied with good humour, collecting a tray of test tubes and heading for the centrifuge. She had, of course, considered all of that before she'd agreed to Marie going. She wasn't going to let her go just because everybody else did it. She'd had to be reassured that Marie was going to learn something, that it would enrich her life in some way. Her daughter's attitude had been so mature that it had surprised her, and Ginny thought she knew her better than anyone. She'd always encouraged her eclectic interests, it should hardly have come as a surprise that she wanted to get out there and see things for herself. 'Marie had set her heart on it so much.'

'But that's the thing. Your Marie's not spoilt. And no

offence, Ginny, but none of us earns much in the NHS. How has she managed it?'

'Well, everything's a lot cheaper than it used to be. They seem to manage on a shoestring now. Marie's never been extravagant and she's saved so hard. She's worked all her holidays down at Next and she did extra work packing videos at Christmas up on the industrial estate, and she didn't spend a pound of it on herself. In the end I said I'd try to match her savings to give her a good start. And my parents chipped in a bit.'

John looked impressed and nodded his frizzled greying head, glasses glinting in the flickering light (they'd asked repeatedly for the strip light to be replaced). 'Fair enough, I s'pose. You must miss her, then.'

Like her right arm had been hacked off, but Ginny said, 'She's in touch with me so much I'm actually wondering how she's finding time to do anything else.' She felt a surge of pride. Marie hadn't let her down. At least, not yet. She'd been in contact through some means every day.

'I don't suppose you went travelling, did you?' John glanced back from his microscope as Ginny finished stacking trays. 'Course, sorry, I guess you didn't go to university. You'd be sitting where I am otherwise. Not that it's much more fun.'

It had been years since Ginny had felt any edge about people's assumptions about her. She hesitated. She'd never wanted to sound too big for her boots and alienate people, either. It had been convenient to train on the job as a laboratory technician when Marie was small. She'd used her interest in science, in medicine, and applied it practically. Over the years she'd been

74

promoted, and now her work involved anything from maintaining the lab to developing cultures. Sometimes it was dull and routine, sometimes she felt that her brain had been badly underused, but the people were nice and she liked being behind the scenes. The work they did in the labs was important, it just didn't carry any of the status of the higher profile medical professions. It was a steady job with benefits and she made the best of it. 'Actually, John, I did go to university. You wouldn't believe it now, but I'd started to study medicine.'

'Really?' John took this news affably, even though there was a definite 'them and us' issue between the skilled laboratory staff and the doctors. The 'them' usually came in the form of the word, 'wankers'.

'Yes. I was going to be a doctor, if they'd have me. But Marie came along after only a few months, and that was my life mapped out.'

'Hmm. So now Marie's gone off, will you go back?'

Ginny stopped as she was heading for the steriliser. 'Go back where?'

'To university.' And as she must have looked baffled he added, 'People do, you know, especially when they're still young.'

'Don't be silly, John' She laughed at him. 'It's far too late for that.'

'Okay, only asking.' He went back to his slide and, as he often did, involved her in his work. 'Bingo. Take a look at this, Sherlock, and tell me what you think.'

She went and sat on a grassy bank next to the nurses' home to eat her sandwiches. It was a glorious afternoon, the late-autumn sun warming the dry grass. The air smelt sweet and rich, like earth. It lifted the heaviness in her heart. It was amazing, she had to concede, that one small person could have affected her life so profoundly. Since Marie's arrival there hadn't been a minute of a day that she hadn't been thinking about her in some way. It was an obsession, really. Perhaps it was an obsession that Charlotte would come to understand once her baby was born. She seemed so casual about it at the moment. It was most definitely the calm before the storm for her. But that was a good thing. She needed to grow up.

As she munched on a ham roll Ginny decided harshly that having a baby was probably the *only* thing that was ever going to make Charlotte grow up. She'd been flinging herself around the world in a pair of trainers like some eternal student for long enough. At least she was company for Jane at the moment. Ginny had to admit that since Harry had left she'd felt uneasy about Jane being alone in that big house. All it would take would be a burglar or some kind of crisis when she was all alone there and her confidence would be badly shaken. And what about the future? Ginny had pretty well resigned herself to being the only child in England, the only one who had looked out for their parents and would continue to do so into their old age. Charlotte would be off again before long, that could hardly be in doubt, but how would she do it this time? Would she go and leave the baby, just as she'd left a string of stray animals in the past? Although it was an ungenerous thought, Ginny believed it was perfectly possible. With Charlotte, anything was possible.

She sighed and bit the end off a spring onion, having

a silent argument with Charlotte in her head that involved the word 'selfish' in every sentence. Then she closed her eyes, let the sun warm her face and tried to calm down.

Unbidden, Barney's scrawled handwriting flashed across her inner eye: *I have many regrets and have felt great sadness, but all I wish you is goodwill.*

She opened her eyes, blinked and stared at the rows of square windows of the nurses' home studded across the grim red brick with military precision. Bloody Barney. She just couldn't shake him out of her thoughts these days.

The knot in her stomach had been growing. The longer she stayed in the library revising, the more work there was to do. Her list, instead of getting shorter, was growing longer as she uncovered areas that she hadn't studied in sufficient depth. The exams were creeping up; now there were only two weeks to go. It was sudden death. If she failed she'd have one opportunity to retake, then bang, out.

Ginny wasn't eating properly and she knew it. That morning she'd seen herself in the mirror in her underwear and been horrified. She looked like a lollipop. She was pale and her eyes were edged with grey smudges. Thank God her parents couldn't see her like this. They'd be sending her hampers and jumpers, more vitamin pills and God knew what. It was a good job they didn't know about the caffeine pills, or the fact that she had an occasional cigarette to stay awake.

She picked up her biro again and underlined the word 'endocrinology'. It became blurred and fuzzy, a squiggle of blue. She blinked at it and it seemed to recede and zoom towards her.

Break often, her tutor had advised her. Don't run at it like a bull. Save some stamina for the exams. It was easier said than done. She stood up unsteadily and headed in a wavy line for the library exit. Outside, she sank on to a low wall and put her head in her hands. She felt sick, shaky and tired, and what was worse she had a sudden urge to burst into tears and cry her eyes out, there outside the library in front of everyone. She could hear snatches of conversation over her head, the tick-tick of bicycle wheels, bursts of laughter, drones of cars in the distance.

'When did you last eat?' A hand rested gently on her shoulder. She looked up blearily into clear, attractive eyes. Oh God, not him. She was too tired to stalk away.

'Ages ago. I'm sorry, I can't stop to talk, I'm revising.'

'You look like death.'

'Thank you.'

'Come on, stand up.'

'I'm all right, Barnaby, leave me alone.'

'You remember my name. Well that's something, but call me Barney.' He examined her expression. 'Or bastard if you'd rather. Barnaby's such a mouthful. At least all the girls say so,' he added in a quip, then straightened his face. He helped Ginny to her feet and supported her arm. 'You look as if you're about to fall over. You need a good meal.'

'Yeah.'

'I'm taking you to the St Giles. Egg, beans and chips.'

'Oh please leave me alone, I've got a place at the

table and half a ton of books out and I'm working to a timetable.'

'That doesn't involve food? I'll go and get your bag, the librarians can put the books back, make a change for them to do something they're bloody paid for. You wait here.'

She was going to walk off indignantly but found that her legs weren't strong enough to carry her, so she waited docilely for him on the wall, and allowed him to lead her away when he returned with her bag packed up with her notes.

'I won't know where anything is, now,' she complained, taking her bag from him, not stopping to wonder how he knew where she'd been sitting.

In the snug St Giles café he ordered for them both, and she drank a mug of strong, sweet tea, alarmed to see that her hands were trembling. 'Oh God!' she exclaimed, looking at her white fingers. 'What's happening to me?'

'I hate to tell you this, but you're not unique. It's standard Mods burn out. Been there, seen it, survived it. Luckily, I've caught you in time. There is a cure but you're not going to like it. Food, alcohol and a day off.' He gave her a teasing mock-serious look. She didn't smile back. 'You really don't like me, do you?'

'What did you order?' She dodged the question.

She ploughed her way through a heap of chips, eggs, sausages, bacon, beans and mushrooms and ate all the toast as well. At the end she still felt light headed but the shakiness had gone. After eating she felt peaceful. She was too bloated to complain when, after half an hour, the owner insisted they move on to make room for others.

'Hey, where are you going?' Barney caught her arm in the road.

'Back to the library.'

'You are joking.'

'Not at all.'

'It closes in just over an hour anyway. You won't get much done.'

'Nonsense. I'll get loads done. Thanks very much for making me eat, I do appreciate it actually and I feel miles better.'

'You should know better,' he tutted, 'med student as well. You always finish a course of treatment.'

'What do you mean?'

'I told you, food, alcohol and a day off. It's decently late. I'm taking you for a beer.'

'Oh no way at all.' Ginny shook her head adamantly but inside felt a wiggle of curiosity.

'No arguments. Kings Arms. Now, Virginia.'

She stopped and looked at him, frowning. She'd assumed, especially after his crass joke about virginity over the chess match, that he had realised that she didn't appreciate his joke. She didn't like his teasing about her name. She'd just been another woman for him to wind around his little finger.

'My name's Ginny,' she told him flatly.

'Hey, that's what I said.' He widened his eyes. 'And I'm taking you for a beer, however pedantic you're going to be about labels.' He winked and she felt herself responding. Resistance was one thing, being in love was another. She stood uncertainly for a moment longer and then decided to go to the pub with him.

Chapter Nine

In fact, Stuart was a lot better looking than Charlotte had remembered. She met him in Gordon's wine bar next to the Embankment, slightly regretting her choice as she awkwardly picked her way down the narrow steps into the gloom. The cigarette smoke didn't bother her anymore, she'd got over her sickness months ago, and somehow now that Jane had given her a big hug her urge to have an occasional rebellious cigarette had died away. Jane had also given her a long lecture about smoking and pregnancy, but little realised that it was the hug that had done the trick. It was dark in the vaults and, her hands protectively around her bump, Charlotte pushed her way through the drinkers to the cellar, where Stuart was already installed at a candlelit table, a bottle of red and glasses at the ready.

'Wow, you do look great.' He stood up the moment he saw her and stepped forward to help her out of her loose jacket.

'You too.' She beamed at him, allowing a flutter of the eyelashes. Yes, he'd improved with age. He was squarer jawed, more rugged. 'You must have a good job now. That looks like a tailored suit.'

'Oh, yes. I have got a— Oh my word, you are full of surprises, aren't you?' Well it could only have been a matter of time before he noticed that she was seven months pregnant, and large for it. He chuckled as they both sat down. 'Charlotte, Charlotte, there's always something with you. Congratulations. Why didn't you tell me on the phone?'

'I just wanted to surprise you. What do you think? Does motherhood suit me? Am I blooming?'

'Hard to tell in this light,' he teased, 'but you've got a damned fine suntan. It was India, wasn't it? The last place?'

'Yes, yes, but tell me all about you first.' Of course, she'd have to share all her news, but she'd provide an edited version. She wasn't about to give him the story she'd given her mother.

'Oh, well, I guess I've got some surprises too, but look at you. You can't sit there massively pregnant and not tell me what's going on. Are you married now? What've you been up to?'

'You know me,' Charlotte teased, accepting a small glass of wine. 'Never been one to settle. Of course I'm not married, dummy. Can you see it, really?'

'I must admit it's hard to picture you in flowing white. Maybe just at the moment.' He winked and she felt warm inside. How nice that he hadn't backed off just because she obviously wasn't going to be a sexual conquest. A little bit of flirting would do her spirits the power of good.

'I am extremely happy with my life, Stuart, and that's all you need to know about the circumstances of my, shall we say, delicate state.' They both laughed. He'd always loved the rebel in her. He'd always been more square. That's why he'd fallen in love with her and she'd left him.

'So did you dump some poor bloke halfway round the world and run away? Did his parents want you to stay at home, barefoot and pregnant? Or did the poor sod make the mistake I did and propose to you?' Stuart sipped his wine, chuckling. He scarcely noticed Charlotte turn pale in the dimness of the candlelight, sit back in her chair and take a long, slow breath. She took a sip of wine to compose herself.

'Spot on. You always could read me like a book.' She swallowed it. Nice, mellow wine and she remembered that, of course, Stuart rather prided himself on being a connoisseur of such things. And he'd been a good cook, too, that came back to her now.

'Oh, no no. That's the thing about you, Charlotte, you are completely impossible to read at all times. That's what made you interesting. Perplexing, definitely, but interesting.'

She wetted her lips with her tongue. 'Made? You're talking in the past tense. That's a shame. I'd like to think I'm still interesting, even though I am the size of a small country.'

'Oh you are most certainly more interesting in this manifestation. Definitely not something I expected. So you're staying in London at the moment?'

'No.' She felt slight irritation that he'd forgotten what she'd told him on the phone. Or perhaps he was playing hard to get? 'I'm down with my mum. Just for a bit while I sort myself out. Oh and my God, you'll never believe it, my dad's left home.'

'No!' Stuart was suitably shocked – just for a second, then he stood up, his eyes roving the back of the room. 'Aha, here she is. Early, but that's her all over.' He waved his hand. 'Lisa! Over here.'

Charlotte twisted round, puzzled. Walking towards them, or rather sauntering, was a coolly blonde, undeniably pretty woman with a full figure, a smile of pure delight on her lips as she approached Stuart. No, it wasn't delight. It was love. She was clearly utterly smitten with him; she even closed her eyes when he kissed her cheek. Then she turned to greet Charlotte and the smile remained on her lips.

'You must be Charlotte. I'm so pleased to meet you. Stuart's always talked about you and I was dying of curiosity. I hope you don't mind my joining your get-together. I did say that I thought you'd want to catch up on old news, but he insisted I come. You're the only one of his old friends I haven't met yet.'

Charlotte held out a hand limply. She hadn't got the energy to heave her bump into the air and stand up in response to this woman's enthusiasm.

'Charlotte, this is Lisa, my wife,' Stuart said. 'I'll grab another chair and a glass. You take my chair, baby, I'll find another one.'

'Can I have your wine, too?'

'Of course, love.'

Charlotte stared at Stuart's hands in dismay. Had she been so dense, so preoccupied that she hadn't noticed. . .? And there it was. A plain gold band slap bang on his ring finger.

'May I ask about it?' Lisa leant across the table, nodding at Charlotte's bulging jumper. Her blue eyes shone with wonderment in the flickering light and Charlotte realised with descending spirits that she was going to have to sit and make polite conversation with this charming person because there was no excuse not to.

84

She moved the conversation away from her baby. 'So how long have you been married?'

'Two years, almost. It's just great. I love being married, the best thing that ever happened to me. I can't understand people who say it doesn't change anything. It's changed everything for me. I love more than anything being Mrs Putnam. Mrs Stuart Putnam. It's so primitive, all about ownership and possession. It makes me feel like something worth having, something he's proud of. God, I'm wittering on already, I do talk too much. Let me just grab a mouthful of wine, I had a pig of a journey over here on the tube. Did you come by tube?'

Charlotte shook her head. 'Straight up to Charing Cross.'

'Don't touch the tubes with a bargepole tonight. Someone's thrown themselves in front of a train at Knightsbridge.' After talking to you? Charlotte wanted to snap. 'It doesn't help us working on opposite sides of London, but it was inspired of you to choose somewhere slap bang in the middle. We used to meet in Covent Garden, way back, when we were first seeing each other. That was before Stu proposed. God, a moment I'll never forget. It was absolutely tipping down with rain—'

'Has he found a chair, I wonder?' Charlotte peered vaguely over Lisa's shoulder.

'No, I don't think so. Still struggling to find one. But anyway,' she took another sip of her husband's wine, proving her earlier point about ownership, Charlotte thought. 'I know he proposed to you once, but I think we're the only two. I thought I would say that just to clear the air, and it's obviously all ancient history. I did wonder about you, though. You know what they say about ex-girlfriends lurking unhealthily in the background.'

'What do they say? I think you're supposed to try to make friends with them.' Charlotte tried to smile in pleasant way. She didn't want to be a bitch. Lisa was far too keen, far too nice to deserve any sniping. In any case, it would only make her look jealous. Which she was, but fairly pointlessly.

'But anyway,' Lisa nodded at Charlotte's bump again, 'your life's obviously moved on incredibly dramatically. Congratulations. I always think there's nothing more exciting than a new baby. I'm so happy for you. When you arranged to meet, neither you nor Stu knew the other one was already married, did you? Fancy that.'

'I'm not married,' Charlotte stated. Then, for reasons that she could hardly understand, added bluntly, 'And neither's my sister, and her daughter's eighteen now. And, as my parents have just split up, neither's my mother.'

Lisa blinked prettily, momentarily stunned into silence. Stuart returned with a chair.

'Here we are. So are you two getting to know each other?'

'We're three unmarried mothers, according to Charlotte,' Jane laughingly told Ginny on the phone later in the week. 'Makes it seem like a disease that's catching. Or maybe genetically inherited.'

'You'd better add Rebecca to that list then. Remember Emma's mum?'

'Of course I do. You told me her husband was a charmless geek.'

'Yes, he is. Well, at least I thought so, but Rebecca's really devastated that he's gone and he must be having an affair with someone who thinks he's nice. He's not having an affair with himself.'

'A bit like Robin Cook,' Jane mused. 'And Stephen Hawking. And that Blunkett man, too. It always amazes me.'

'And Dad,' Ginny ventured, curious for the response.

'Oh yes, and your father.' Jane's voice was even, calm; sometimes Ginny wondered if it seemed to her mother as if it had all happened to someone else. 'Charlotte's going to see him, did she tell you?'

'I haven't spoken to Charlotte for days. She's not going to do the outraged daughter demanding that he comes back to the nest, is she?'

'I don't know what she's going to do, but that's between her and her father.'

'What have you said to her?'

'I've just told her the truth about the circumstances, dear. She seems more confused than anything else.'

Ginny felt that she was getting over her confusion now. It wasn't that anything in particular had resolved it, just that the longer his absence went on and the more her mother accepted it quite affably, the more normal it seemed. Charlotte had some catching up to do, just in the matter of time she had spent around the situation. 'Actually, I'm surprised I haven't heard from Charlotte. I'm getting all my news about her from you. It's like she never came home.'

'Well I keep her in touch with your daily news, too. I'm like a post office, really. I'm quite used to it. Mothers always are.'

'I'd have thought she'd have been round here by now to use Marie's computer.' In fact, Ginny was a bit put out that Charlotte hadn't been round to see her, just to talk about pregnancy or new-born babies, or even to ask about how she'd brought up Marie. Or even just to talk about Marie. 'She obviously doesn't need me,' she added huffily.

'She has her scan tomorrow. Go gently with her, won't you, Ginny. She's not as robust as she looks.'

Ginny ruminated but didn't answer. It was always everybody else's job to understand Charlotte. Where had she, Ginny, gone wrong? She'd brought up her daughter nicely, she had a decent job, she had enough money and a small but nice house. There were no histrionics, no dramas, no tantrums, no grand entrances and exits. That meant she was expected to do all the understanding, she was never the one needing to be understood. Well not, at least, for a very long time.

'Ginny?' Jane went on gently. 'She will need you, she just doesn't realise it yet. Be there for her when she comes to you, won't you?'

Chapter Ten

Charlotte was growing paler as they sat in the waiting room in the women's centre at the hospital waiting to be called for her scan. She could feel her energy sapping away. The baby kicked her several times, vigorously. She winced, but couldn't bring herself to talk to Jane, who was peacefully flicking through *Woman's Own* next to her, casting her occasional concerned glances. She didn't want a fuss. It was all such a fuss. It was only a baby, a natural happening in a woman's life. Nothing was going to be wrong. By the time her name was called her palms were clammy and she was nervous.

'All right?' Jane queried as they stood up and followed the sonographer down the corridor to a side room. She shut the door after them. Charlotte nodded tensely.

After she'd given the sonographer her notes she lay on the trolley and raised her T-shirt up to her chest, as she was instructed. Jane quietly took a seat at the back of the dim room. A cold, clear gel was squirted on to her skin and the sonographer began to probe. All the time she talked soothingly to Charlotte, turning the monitor towards her so that she would be able to see her baby.

'I'm not ill,' Charlotte muttered. 'It's not necessary really.'

'Did the midwife explain properly the reasons for your referral?' she asked pleasantly.

'I'm big. I think that's it.'

'In your notes there's a query about the dates of your pregnancy. They've also queried hydramnios, which is excess fluid retention. How many weeks are you?'

'I think thirty-two, or thirty-three now. I did know, but I've got a bit confused since I saw the midwife.'

'I wonder why they're so late in querying your dates. Didn't it come up at the twelve-week and twenty-week scans?'

Charlotte's mouth was dry. 'I didn't have any scans. I've been abroad.'

'No scans so far?'

There was a silence, then Charlotte shook her head and annoyingly felt her eyes fill with tears. This dark room, the kind voice, her mother's benevolent presence, hovering like a guardian angel in case she was needed. It knocked all her rebellious spirit clean away. 'No,' she whispered, but her words were clear. 'I haven't had any scans at all.'

'Oh but darling, you mean in England,' Jane inserted for her. 'My daughter did have a scan in India, where she's been living. At twenty weeks. They told her she was expecting a little boy.' Jane looked at Charlotte, approaching and touching her hand. 'That's right isn't it, dear?'

'No, Mum. I'm sorry, that wasn't true. I just didn't want you to worry.' Charlotte closed her eyes, not even able to look at the screen. She hadn't seen her baby, she wasn't sure she could bear to see it. And suddenly the fears for her baby's health approached, grew like a swelling wave, and overwhelmed her. She burst into tears. 'I'm sorry, Mum. I didn't mean to lie. I just didn't want you to say it was all primitive where I was living, when it wasn't at all. It was my fault I wasn't scanned. I didn't consult anyone. I just stayed away from everyone.'

'Oh my dear girl.'

'I just didn't want to make things worse.' Or to see the baby, or to think of it as real, or to have to deal with what happened next. Being pregnant was a bit like being in limbo, a state between states. Or like being on an aeroplane, flying off to a new country. You could read a travel guide but nothing could prepare you for the experience of actually living there.

The sonographer gave Charlotte a tissue and she wiped her eyes and blew her nose.

'Would you like to see your baby now, Charlotte?'

'I don't know. Yes, of course. Mum, I'm scared.'

Jane squeezed her hand tightly, then Charlotte heard her exclaim aloud. 'Oh my Lord. A baby, Charlotte, look at your beautiful baby!'

Charlotte turned her head, and her mouth opened in awe and remained open as she gazed at the tiny features of the baby in her stomach. He was moving around, the sonographer deftly catching up with him with the probe.

'I think we'd better measure and count everything and do a full check-up. I don't see any sign of excess fluid, but this is a big baby and we'd better be sure of your dates. Do you want to know the sex of your baby, Charlotte?'

'I always thought it was a boy,' she breathed. 'Please tell me.'

'Yes, you're right, it is a boy. Good guess.' Charlotte

91

nodded, hot tears flooding her cheeks, which Jane mopped up quickly with a hanky of her own. 'Let's get to work then.'

'My little boy,' Charlotte whispered to the screen as Jane gripped her fingers hard. 'My little boy.'

'He's so perfect,' Charlotte said later as she lay on the sofa fingering the photograph they'd been given to take away with them. Jane bustled around, making mugs of tea and delivering them, as Charlotte seemed to be more prepared to talk to her than before.

'Absolutely perfect. Nothing wrong with him at all.'

'Nothing they can see,' Charlotte amended cautiously. She couldn't drag her eyes away from him. 'So wonderful. I can't believe it.'

Jane settled beside her. Ever since the scan she'd seemed unable to stop smiling. It made Charlotte's heart bound with joy. At last, her mother was happy, truly happy about the baby.

'Now, dear, are you all right with everything she said?'

'Hmm? Yes, of course. I just can't believe all that's inside me. I mean, of course it became more real once he started moving. Little butterfly tickles at first, then stronger kicks, and now sometimes he seems to roll over completely. I get the weirdest shapes sticking out of my stomach.'

'About your dates, Charlotte.' Jane nodded at her encouragingly.

'Yes. I'm an idiot, aren't I?' But she felt hazy, like she was in a mist. A protective mist that made her feel happy and shielded her from anything that wasn't to do with the baby. 'I'm a month out. I should have guessed. But I've never been pregnant before. My periods are always unpredictable anyway, it was really hard to remember.'

'Darling, it means you have to think about getting ready.'

'Hmm?'

'For him coming.'

'Oh, yes. I realise. I'll just have to think about it. Look at his toes, isn't that incredible that they're all there and little. I think his feet are the most amazing thing.'

'If she's right, Charlotte,' Jane tenaciously held her daughter's eye, 'if you are thirty-six or -seven weeks, he could come at any time. As she said, he's a first baby so it's more likely he'll hang on, but we need to be prepared now. You and Ginny were both early.'

'That's so exciting.' Her cheeks burnt with pleasure. 'To think he could just turn up. Fantastic.'

'I'm sorry you felt you had to lie to me about the scan. I think I understand why you did, but, for the baby's sake, let's not do that any more, hmm? Shall we be completely honest now?'

Charlotte glanced up guiltily. 'I am being honest. I just didn't want you to fuss.'

'All right' Jane shifted up the sofa awkwardly and touched her daughter's arm. 'And there's something else I want to say to you, darling.'

'Yes?' Charlotte's eyes were fixed on her baby's photograph. Her stomach was fluttering with excitement. Maybe just another week or two, then she'd meet him, this brand new person that she'd made, for the first time.

'About your friend.'

'Which friend?'

'About your Indian friend?'

Charlotte's head snapped up and her eyes darkened. 'What about him?'

Jane gathered herself then spoke firmly. 'I want you to think very, very hard about contacting him to tell him that the baby's nearly due. I think you should . . .consider carefully telling him where you are and giving him the choice—'

'No.'

'Darling, I think—'

'No.'

Jane sighed. 'I just don't want you to do anything you'll regret later. The birth of a baby is an incredibly emotional time. You don't know it yet, but you'll need a lot of support and you may find that you wish with all your heart that his father was there beside you, to help you and to share it with you.'

Charlotte pursed her lips, fighting back difficult emotions. Then she said, 'Mum, you said you'd come with me to the hospital. In the car you said you'd be my birthing partner. Have you changed your mind?'

'Of course not, darling. If there's no boyfriend here for you, of course I'll be there. I promise with all my heart.'

Charlotte relaxed. 'That's all right then. I don't think I can do this on my own.'

'But this is it, you see, Charlotte. There will be other moments, many of them, from his birth onwards, where you'll say to yourself, "I don't think I can do this on my own." It's a very tough thing, to have a baby and no father to support you.'

'Ginny did it.' Charlotte stuck out her chin, more out of defensiveness than confidence. 'Didn't she? Somehow Ginny managed on her own and brought Marie up to get a string of A-levels and a university place. She's doing all right, isn't she?'

'Darling,' Jane said softly, 'Ginny is a very brave woman who has had a very difficult life.'

Charlotte propped herself up on her elbows, baffled. 'In what way?'

'I mean that it's been hard for Ginny, and she's made enormous sacrifices.'

'What sacrifices? Money, I suppose, but of course I know babies are expensive. I think that's common knowledge.'

Jane stroked Charlotte's forehead affectionately. 'Sometimes I think you have the arrogance of youth, then I remember that you're not the teenager you once were, full of confidence, daunted by nothing.'

'What do you mean?'

'You sound very young, my love.'

'Immature, you mean.' Charlotte pulled away, hurt.

'Ginny's given up everything to be a good mother to Marie. She gave up her career and she gave up any opportunity to have a husband and family. She didn't take any risks that might make things harder for Marie. She's put herself second in every decision she's ever made about that girl. I also happen to know, because I'm her mother, that she's been very, very lonely.'

Charlotte saw Jane's eyes were bright with pride for her eldest daughter. She was jealous and she was daunted by it. After a while, she answered, 'Okay, it's fair enough. I haven't been here often enough to see what she's done. I probably don't even know her very well.'

'I think, don't you, that now might be a good time to get to know her?'

Chapter Eleven

Ginny had met her father in a pub to talk, shortly after he'd left home. It had been an immense shock for her. She was all the more shocked that her mother hadn't said anything about the problems they were having until one evening in the week, when Ginny had popped into the house and after an hour or so asked, 'Where's Dad?' and received the simple answer, 'Oh, he's left.' Her mother had seemed catatonic. Ginny had even wondered if she was on tranquillisers and had grilled her about it, but it appeared this was a frame of mind unattributable to drugs of any kind.

For that reason, she *did* understand Charlotte's utter bafflement. She wasn't prepared to admit that she had shared the feeling, though, or acknowledge that she still didn't really have a full understanding of what had happened to her parents. After all, she'd been here, the dutiful daughter, on her mother's doorstep providing company, fellowship, help when required, and a granddaughter; all things that enriched her parents' lives. She should have seen it coming; she, with insights into her mother's life, should have sensed that it was happening. But she hadn't. She might as well have been halfway across the world, trekking barefoot round temples, sunning herself and drinking beer from the bottle, or whatever it is Charlotte did that was so compelling.

She'd slapped her handbag down on the table and slammed herself into the chair opposite her father. He'd glanced at her nervously and edged the glass of wine he'd bought her towards her.

'Forget drinks, Dad. I want an explanation,' she'd fumed. Then without waiting for him to speak had continued. 'I mean, how *dare* you do this? Who do you think you are? After everything Mum's done for you for all these years. All the support and love she's given you. She needs you, Dad, and you've just walked away from it all.'

'Actually, love, she doesn't need me.'

'Of course she does!'

'No, she doesn't,' he said slowly, taking a sip of his pint of bitter and wiping the froth from his lip. 'Oh don't look at me like that, Ginny, you may not need a drink but I do. You're not an easy woman to talk to when you're angry.'

'I'm listening,' Ginny snapped. 'Go on.'

'She needed me,' he began carefully, 'all the time you were around with Marie. She needed to support you, and I needed to support her so that she could be strong for you. It was like a chain, and the links all needed to be strong. Without me being there I think it would have been very difficult for her. But Marie's grown up now, she's going off travelling then she'll go to university. You don't need the help from us that you did before. Things are different now.'

Ginny blanched, amazed by what she was hearing. 'Oh just hang on one minute. I see what you're doing here. You're going to bring me into it to make me feel

98

guilty. I'm not having it, Dad. You'd better come up with something else.'

'I'm not blaming you, my love.' He tried to reach out for a hand but she tucked them firmly in her lap. 'I love you and I love Marie with all my heart; you are precious to me.'

'I should bloody hope so. Marie is your only grand-daughter. Your only grandchild, in fact, and quite possibly the only one you'll ever have.'

'A granddaughter, yes, but in a funny way I've always thought of her more as a daughter – an unexpected one and all the more of a gift for that. Think about it, Ginny. We've all stepped in and given her what she needs. In fact, it was like one of those card houses. You supported Marie, your mother supported you, and I supported your mum. And I'm proud of that. But our marriage became lost along the way. It would have happened anyway, I think we just stayed together longer because we were so busy.'

'But you're stable, you're good together, and by God, Dad, you've stuck it out all these years. Of all the times in the world to split up, why would you do it now? You've been married forty-two years. I mean, for God's sake, doesn't that mean anything to you?'

'Yes, it does.' Harry's eyes misted over and he covered them with his fingers, rubbing them so that Ginny wasn't sure if he was upset or had something in his eye. 'It does mean a lot, but it's not a reason to stay married.'

'Why not? Please explain,' Ginny had choked, partly on fury partly on tears. 'I don't understand any of it.'

'I'm sixty-six, Ginny. Does that mean I'm already dead?'

'What do you mean?'

'I mean that I'm alive, I'm still here, a person with a brain, a heart, an imagination, and, God help me for saying this to my own daughter, but I still have a body, a man's body that wants to behave like a man's body.'

Ginny swiped at her wine and drank a large gulp before shooting at him, 'As far as I can see your man's body's doing what all men's bodies do – running away.'

'But I'm not, love. I'm not running anywhere.' He held his beer glass in both hands, considering it carefully. 'Have you talked to your mother about it?'

'Of course. Well, I've tried.' Ginny sighed heavily and slipped off her jacket, hanging it on the back of her chair. This obviously wasn't going to be a short conversation. 'I can't really get any sense out of her. I think she's still in shock.'

'Oh no, it's not shock, Ginny, it's indifference.'

'No.'

'Yes, love.'

'No, Dad. That's just you blaming her.'

'I'm not.' He put his hands up to protest his innocence. 'I am not blaming your mother, please be clear.'

'Do you still love her?'

'Of course I do, I'll always love her.'

'Then how can you run off with someone else? Doesn't it make you feel sick every time you touch her and think about Mum? Don't you feel guilty?'

'I feel shame, yes, Ginny. You'll be very glad to hear that I'm totally ashamed of myself. I'm sorry for all the gossip your mother's had to put up with, well-meaning phone calls, enquiries from nosy neighbours, fake sympathy, all that. . .*balderdash*!'

Ginny jumped. Her father was so mild, he might have well have sworn his head off; the effect was the same. 'Steady on, Dad.'

'Well it's hypocritical cant, I tell you, I hate it. She has had far more fallout to deal with than I have, and that isn't fair. And for inflicting all that on Jane, I am sorry and I'm thoroughly responsible.'

'But then, why—'

'One of us had to go, Ginny, and it made sense for it to be me. I was the one who'd found someone else.'

Ginny felt hollow inside, as if she was hungry but as if eating wouldn't solve the problem. She wasn't hearing anything that she wanted to hear. She wanted him to be remorseful, to beg forgiveness, to ask her if Jane would have him back. That wasn't happening.

'Dad, are you coming back?'

He reached for her hand again and this time she let him take it although she couldn't respond to the affectionate pressure he put on her fingers. 'I don't think so, dear. I think I'm happy now.'

'And Mum?' she asked weakly.

'I think your mum's happy now too.'

'What the heck is going on?' Ginny found Charlotte in the kitchen laughing like a hyena, watching a frenzied scene taking place in the back garden.

'Oh, Ginny, come and see this. Malcolm's found a wasps' nest in the back of the shed. So Mum asked if he could deal with it, so he said yes and asked if she'd got any squash racquets, and she said she'd got a couple of old badminton racquets. Remember our old ones?' Ginny did. More recently she'd played on the lawn

101

with Marie. They'd used the washing line as a net. 'So he's put some kind of chemical in the nest, and now he's swatting the stray wasps with the racquet. Oh look!'

Ginny watched, amazed, as the short, red-faced handyman swiped at the air with her old badminton racquet. From a distance, Jane shouted encouragement, hopping from one foot to the other.

'There's another one, behind you!' Jane called.

'Got it.' Malcolm swivelled round and swiped.

'Oh my God, everyone's finally gone mad.' Ginny shook her head, wanting to laugh but not really wanting to share Charlotte's joke. 'She'll get stung.'

'He's already been stung.' Charlotte shouted with laughter as he aimed at one way above his head, jumping as if he were Pete Sampras trying to smash a tennis ball. 'He's such a potted shrimp. You don't really think she fancies him, do you?'

'What, Mum?' Ginny peered out at the scene critically. 'I wouldn't have thought he was her type at all.'

'She flirts with him.'

Ginny was intrigued by that, but she didn't like the new arrival informing her about her mother's behaviour, so after a moment she said, 'I know, but there's nothing in it.'

'Have you met him before then?'

'Not really, but she's talked to me about him. She tells me most things.'

'Yes.'

They turned side by side, not looking at each other, both fixed on the spectacle taking place on their lawn.

'I suppose Mum's told you the latest news about the baby then, has she?'

'About your dates? Yes.'

'And that it's a boy. I'd always thought it, but it wasn't confirmed until now.'

'You are a twit, Charlotte. You'd better get your act together now.'

'I am.' Charlotte turned defensively and gave Ginny a hostile look. 'I know what I'm doing.'

'So what have you decided, a crib or Moses basket? Have you looked around at pushchairs yet? Don't get one covered in knobs and gadgets, it'll irritate the hell out of you when you've got a screaming baby inside. Or have you gone for one of those three-wheeler buggies?'

There was a pause during which Ginny felt, rather than saw, Charlotte staring at her. 'You're not really asking me, are you?' Charlotte said, and Ginny realised with annoyance that she was tearful. 'You're just saying all that to make me realise how little I know. I'll see you later.'

Ginny was left alone in the kitchen as Charlotte went upstairs on her own. After a moment her bedroom door banged and Ginny sighed loudly.

Several moments later, after a hurried conversation with the still-swatting Malcolm, Jane arrived in the kitchen, rubbing at her hair.

'Oh, hello, Ginny. That's the thing about insects. The more you see, the more you think are covering you. I'm convinced I've got one in my hair, can you see it?'

'No.' Ginny checked. 'Nothing that I can see.'

'Where's Charlotte?'

'Upstairs.' She might have added, sulking, but

103

didn't want to explain the conversation they'd just had. Perhaps she had been mean. But somebody had to make Charlotte face reality. Perhaps she could have done it in a nicer way. It was just that every time she saw Charlotte her stomach tightened and she wanted to have a row with her. Now that Charlotte seemed to be nearer her due date than anyone had imagined, it was impossible to start an argument. That really wouldn't be fair. And yet she felt it wasn't going to be possible for them to move on until they cleared the air. She turned her attention back to Malcolm, outside on the lawn.

'Is he actually doing anything out there?'

'Oh yes,' Jane said breathlessly. 'He's swatting them.'

'But the racquet's got holes in it. They'll just go through the holes.'

'No, no, they're not. They're on the floor.'

'Doing what?'

'Rolling around.'

'Are they laughing?'

Jane frowned at Ginny. 'No, dear, they're dying.'

'Jane!' Malcolm's red, sweaty face appeared at the window, making them both jump. 'If you might be so kind as to assist me,' he bellowed through the glass of the closed windows. 'Do you think you could come outside and stamp on a few?'

'Oh, of course, Malcolm, I'll be right out.' She bustled to the back door. 'Put the kettle on, will you, dear? Make us both a cup of tea for afterwards. And if Charlotte's upstairs, this might be a good moment to talk to her. Between you and I, I think she needs some advice.'

104

'But she needs to ask me, Mum, and she hasn't asked me anything.'

'Well. . .' Jane hesitated, a concerned frown over her eyes, 'maybe you need to make the first move.'

'I'm not the one who wants help. She is. I think she might at least swallow some pride and make an approach to me.'

'Is it that important to you, Ginny? Does she have to come crawling to you?'

Ginny was irritated, not just by her mother's defence of her younger sister, but by the language she was using. It sounded bolshy, as if it was straight out of Charlotte's mouth. 'Of course not, she doesn't have to crawl anywhere. She just needs to ask me, nicely, if I can help, and then I'll give her all the help I can.'

'It's not as if she's a stranger, darling, she's your sister. And she's your little sister, and in this situation you're the one with the experience. You might think about acting a bit protectively towards her. She's more confused than she's letting on, that's all I'll say.'

'About. . .' Ginny fished. 'Is this about the mystery man back in India?'

'I don't know anything about that,' Jane rattled on. 'I just think that in families we need to drop the niceties sometimes and just move in when we know we're needed.'

'Of course I'd be the one to help her if she needs me. It's completely logical. But she doesn't need me, Mum, and as far as I can see she's going out of her way to show me how little she values my advice. She hasn't even rung me since she's been home.'

'I still think you could volunteer some help even if it hasn't been asked for. At least you could have told her you've still got things like Marie's cot up in the loft.'

Ginny pursed her lips. Yes, she'd never been able to bring herself to throw those things away. Perhaps she was being sentimental. Perhaps somewhere in the back of her mind she'd always thought she might meet somebody really special (and he would have had to have been extraordinary), and maybe in those circumstances she might have had another child. For whatever reasons, she did have some things that needed dusting down and perhaps re-evaluating, but they would do in an emergency. Ever since Charlotte had come home, Ginny had been ready with the offer to give her everything she had in the attic, as soon as the request came. But the request hadn't come. 'I'll tell her when she asks me.' She stood her ground, feeling ever more ungenerous as Jane increasingly seemed to be standing alongside Charlotte.

'I do think time's running out,' Jane said a little more firmly. 'One of you is going to have to back down and act reasonably.'

'We haven't even had a proper conversation since she came home,' Ginny defended hotly. 'In fact, I can't remember the last time I had a decent conversation with my own sister. She hasn't even remembered little things, like Marie's birthday. Frankly, Mum, she's such a poor example of an aunt I fear for the kind of mother she's going to be.'

Jane stopped at the back door, her hand on the handle, and gave Ginny a piercing stare. 'That, Ginny, is just downright cruel and you must not to repeat anything of that kind to Charlotte.'

'But you must know what I mean.'

106

'Yes, I do. And when you came home pregnant, young lady, I feared for the kind of mother you were going to be. Never forget that. Never let hindsight make you smug. Motherhood is like learning to swim while you're already at sea. You learnt that, and Charlotte will learn it. You have no right to judge her just because you did it first.'

'Mum!'

'That's all I'm going to say. Now I'm going to stamp on some wasps. I'll just pretend they're my two obstinate daughters and I'm sure we'll get the job done in no time.' With that, she let herself out of the back door and pranced back across the lawn, muttering something under her breath out of Ginny's hearing.

Chapter Twelve

❧

The thing that grated on Ginny's nerves more than anything was the quietly confident way in which Charlotte seemed to *know* everything. She hadn't asked her any questions at all. Ever since her return Ginny had found herself hovering around the phone when she was at home, playing answerphone messages in the expectation of hearing Charlotte's voice asking if she could come round to talk to an expert. But no phone call came, and no message. The only messages were from Jane, as usual, or Rebecca, who was now clearly in dire need of a confidante. Ginny had called her back twice since they'd met for a drink and they'd talked for a good hour or two. But these things, as Ginny knew without being the expert on that particular area of life, would not be resolved by a couple of hours of conversation, or even many hours. Rebecca needed to talk to her husband – he was the only one who could provide any answers. Ginny's opinion on matters was, at the end of the day, completely irrelevant.

It was a strange thing, Ginny thought as she ran herself a bath that night and sank into it, smiling wearily at Mr Mistoffelees in compensation for being too tired to talk to him as he curled up on the bathroom carpet next to the radiator, that she had more in common with Rebecca than she did with her own sister. Even given the fact that Charlotte seemed hell-bent on history repeating itself by coming home alone and pregnant. Ultimately, marriage or no marriage, it was the relentless reality of parenthood that had bonded her with Rebecca over time, whether they liked it or not. An understanding of the plight of being the mother of an eighteen-year-old girl, and of every year that their daughters had experienced in their development leading up to now. For Ginny, Marie had simply been it. Everything that she might have wanted herself had come second: work, money, clothes even, and most definitely relationships. But perhaps, she mused, squinting at her clean toes through the bubbles, perhaps things had been the same for Rebecca. Perhaps she had put her relationship second, too. Perhaps there were times when you didn't have any choice.

'What a sad bunch of harpies we are, Mr. Meths,' she mused.

She would have thought, at least, that Charlotte would want to talk about the birth. What did she think was about to happen to her? Did she think it would be a bit like a headache and she'd just take an aspirin when the time came? It was typical of Charlotte to float into it in a hippyish bubble of independence and self-assurance. No doubt she'd be telling the midwives what to do.

That was a point, though, that Ginny didn't quite understand. If Charlotte was so set on natural ways to do things, why hadn't she insisted on a home birth? Jane hadn't even mentioned it. Or perhaps they'd had a row about it and Jane didn't want to go over it again.

She couldn't imagine her mother wanting to get the hoover out after that little escapade. It was one thing clearing up all the endless cat hair that Charlotte's feline donations had left over the years, but to mop up after a birth would be asking a bit much. (And what would the cats make of a birth in the middle of their living room, she wondered?) But, nonetheless, the subject hadn't come up, and the more she thought about it the more Ginny felt that it was out of character. Could Charlotte be more insecure about the birth than she was letting on?

It was so strange being a woman, Ginny decided, rubbing soapy hands over her thin form and her flat stomach, which had once been so distended with Marie inside. And before that, of course, it had been flat, slim, girlish. When Barney was the one running his fingers over her flesh, trailing a hand down her stomach to her thighs. Her body, all things to all people, a sexual stimulant, a temple of protection. So strange.

Would it be an emotional strain, she wondered, closing her eyes lazily, if she allowed herself to remember exactly what had happened with Barney that night? She sighed and let her body loll in the water, wiggling her fingers luxuriously in the warmth. But all that would come back were patches, like looking at an edited selection of holiday snaps with all the links missing. Like a cruise around the world with all the glamorous moments remembered and all the trundling along on a diesel-soaked ship forgotten. Like prising the pyramids out of the clutter of Cairo and placing them on a calm ocean of sand. As long as she lay, her hands rubbing her flesh, her eyes closed, steam condensing on the mirrors, windows and taps around her, she couldn't bring back a sequence of events. She had a vision of the back of his head with soft brown curls tapering into his neck. But that may have come from later, when he'd been walking away.

Admit it, Virginia, we hardly know each other.
My name's Ginny.

She sat up sharply and opened her eyes wide. 'I never wanted to marry you, Barney.'

She got out of the bath, towelled herself down roughly and threw on a bathrobe, padding out across the landing into her bedroom, where Barney's letter was lying on the table next to her bed. She threw it in the wastepaper bin in the corner of the room, then after pacing for a few moments decided that Marie probably needed to read it when she came home. So she got it out again, smoothed it out and decided to take it into Marie's bedroom. Out of sight was out of mind. In fact, she'd put it under Marie's bed, so that she couldn't see it, waving at her, each time she pushed the hoover round. She got down on her knees and stuffed it out of sight, her fingers brushing against something soft and woolly as she did. Laying her head flat on the carpet she could see the rough outline of an oversized, misshapen soft toy.

'Oh! It's George! What are you doing down there?'

Retrieving George, the old woolly toy dog, from the dust and cobwebs that never got to see the Hoover (especially when Ginny was in a bad mood, Hoovering being her least favourite job) Ginny felt a wobble of her bottom lip. He had stuffed, lopsided ears, huge brown

111

eyes and an enormous lump of a black nose, like a piece of coal, stuck on the wiry wool of his muzzle. His body was baggy as he had been intended as a pyjama case, which is what Ginny had used him as when she was a little girl. When he was passed on to Marie, however, she fell in love with him instantly and insisted that he was too important for pyjamas. When Ginny complained that he looked thin and scraggy without any stuffing, Marie stated that it was the shape he was meant to be, and wouldn't have anything put inside him other than her secret possessions.

George had seen Ginny through her childhood. She'd even, in the kitsch way that students did in those days, taken him to university and planted him on her bed as a mascot. And he'd been held and kissed by Marie as she'd grown from baby into young woman. Fashions had changed. Now Marie's identity was more determined by an aeroplane ticket and a computer keyboard than by a cute stuffed toy.

Ginny sat alone, holding the motheaten dog to her chest. She allowed herself tears of nostalgic regret. It was all too fast, all over too quickly. She'd been cheated. She wanted some time back. She didn't want to do anything differently, even the awful moments, but she did want to do it all again. Marie was supposed to be her project, her purpose, the reason she hadn't fulfilled herself in other ways. Marie was the greatest achievement of her life. With Marie gone, what on earth did she have to show for herself?

Sadly, she took George back into her bedroom with her, tenderly brushed away the last of the cobwebs and laid him on the pillow next to her head.

Chapter Thirteen

Charlotte realised now that coming up to London to spend an evening with Stuart and Lisa had been a really stupid thing to do. She lay between the freshly laundered sheets of their spare bed, inhaling the overwhelming perfume of fabric conditioner. She'd been allocated their beautifully newly decorated spare bedroom with its rocky seashore theme of shells, oversized pebbles, ropes and wicker chairs, inside their pristinely painted white Georgian-fronted house on the outskirts of Notting Hill. She willed the time to pass so that day would break and she could get up and leave. She had only accepted Lisa's enthusiastic invitation because she'd felt so incredibly lonely.

For a start, she should have realised that Lisa, being the life and soul of the party and self-proclaimed princess of the house ('He's my Prince Charming,' she'd said of Stuart, 'so that must make me Princess Charming'), would have hosted a dinner party. Of course she would. As if it would have been a cosy threesome. Even the most generous-minded of wives would not want to spend an evening locked in conversation with her husband and her husband's ex. So she had invited two other couples to join them, both successful married people with no children.

Handpicked, one could ungenerously conclude, to make Charlotte look as odd as possible. As the evening had worn on and Charlotte had felt tiredness melting her body from the inside out, she had begun to feel that perhaps Lisa's invitation had not been born out of munificence after all. Charlotte felt, with every question, every polite 'Oh I see', that she was a freak. She'd tried to fob off the questions about her life of travelling, her misfit situation of impending single motherhood, by making jokes. The more jokes she made, the more the women shifted uncomfortably, the more the men guffawed, the more pointed the questions became, the more she felt like somebody on display, somebody who made other people feel normal. By the time the brandy came out and she pleaded exhaustion and excused herself to flee to the safety of the salt-fumed spare room, she felt Lisa had probably achieved her goal. She had made Charlotte, the potentially threatening ex-girlfriend, look like a dangerously irresponsible flake that nobody in their right mind would touch with a bargepole. Certainly she'd seen Stuart's hand fly to Lisa's and squeeze it several times during the dinner, 'Darling,' he seemed to say with every look and every gesture, 'I'm so glad I found somebody stable, somebody who fits in with my ideals, my world, my friends. I'm so glad I married you, not her.'

And then, to finally make her feel sick and wretched, one of the married men had made a pass at her, upstairs on the landing, as she'd been making her way out of the bathroom and towards the bedroom. Soaked with wine and brandy, he'd started waltzing with her, and, as conversation from downstairs was now

114

coming in loud laughs and shouts, he had gone unheard.

'Well, now, Charlotte,' he'd breathed at her, 'I always think a woman is at her most beautiful when she's pregnant. You are all woman.'

'All woman and one baby,' she'd fobbed him off.

'You are a bit of a challenge, aren't you? I can see what Stuart saw in you. I bet you were dynamite in the sack.'

Surprised as he lunged towards her for a kiss, Charlotte had pushed him away. 'I'm sorry, I don't think you understand. I'm going to bed. Alone.'

'Of course you are.' He'd winked, taking his cue and backing away. 'But I've just slipped my business card into your pocket and you make sure you call me when you're out the other side of this messy business. It can get very lonely being a single mum, and there'll be times when you may want some company.'

Charlotte had, indeed, found his card in the pocket of the guest bathrobe, which she'd borrowed. She'd stared at it blankly. 'Why have you given me this?'

'Just call me when you want a real man, and some uncomplicated fun. You know, uncomplicated.' And, with a wave of his eyebrows and another wink, he'd headed back down the stairs, whistling loudly.

She'd stood on the landing on her own, swallowing back annoyance and humiliation. What did he think she was? A cheap bit of skirt? Is that the impression she gave? That because she was doing this alone she was up for it with just anyone? A wave of nausea and sadness had slid up her stomach, and she'd dropped the card on the landing carpet, as if it was a hot poker.

'Bastard,' she whispered. 'Seedy, nasty little bastard.'

She'd taken herself to the bedroom and stood there, dazed. Then as she'd heard footsteps coming up the stairs to the bathroom she'd jumped to the door to try to lock it. There was no key. So with great effort she'd put all of her weight behind the chest of drawers, which, thankfully was almost empty, and shifted it so that it was in front of her bedroom door. She'd hoped that she wasn't going to have any more interruptions, but at least any drunken attempts to invade her bedroom would now be thwarted. Then she'd lain down in the bed feeling miserable, vulnerable and, above all, very, very lonely.

Suddenly she felt a tightening of her stomach muscles and she opened her eyes wide in shock. Was that a contraction? She hadn't had one before. It was like a spasm. A tight pain that made her jump. She lay perfectly still, her hands over her stomach, and waited for it to happen again. Perhaps half an hour passed, then another spasm came. Oh for God's sake, why had she moved the chest of drawers? Why hadn't she just gone downstairs in her nightclothes through Stuart and Lisa's beautifully lit arched doorway and into the dining room to ask if everybody could control their husbands as she needed some sleep?

Most of the night, she fretted. She found herself sweating, waiting for further contractions, wondering what the hell she was going to do if they became stronger. She thought about Raj, and cried. Then, probably in the early hours of the morning as the voices began to die away downstairs, she managed to fall asleep.

In the morning she was woken up by banging and scraping at her bedroom door. She opened her eyes, then shot up in fright, for a moment not recognising where she was or what she was doing there. Then it all came back to her in a heavy, depressing blanket of memory and her first thought was that her contractions had gone away again. Her second thought was for the baby's safety, and she pushed at her stomach, thankfully feeling the baby shift. All that happened in an instant, then she had to concentrate on the fact that somebody was trying to get into her room.

'Who is it?' she called, pulling her bathrobe around her body tightly.

'It's me, Lisa,' came a terse reply. 'What the hell have you done with the furniture?'

Not so polite this morning, Charlotte noted, but then again, now that she'd managed to embarrass her rival so publicly, perhaps Lisa felt there was no need to maintain any pretence at liking.

'I – I moved the chest of drawers. I'm sorry.' Charlotte got up and struggled to pull the item of furniture back to where it had been.

'Be careful!' Lisa yelled from the other side of the door, and Charlotte's momentary relief that somebody cared for her well-being was shown to be misguided as she added, 'That's an antique and one of the legs is wobbly. You really shouldn't have moved it without asking one of us first, Charlotte, you might have broken it. What were you trying to do?'

Red faced and puffing, Charlotte opened the door wide to an unsmiling Lisa, holding a mug of tea for her. 'I'm sorry, I just – it's just—'

'I brought you a cup of tea,' Lisa snapped, handing it over. 'I'll just come in and check that nothing's broken, if you don't mind. Oh look, it's left marks on the floorboards. Stuart took hours over those, he painted and varnished them himself. Did you think somebody was going to attack you? I don't really understand why you did this.'

'I was attacked once,' Charlotte lied, willing the floorboards to give way and drop Lisa down right on top of the Liberty dining table below. 'In India. By – it was a complete stranger, a madman just came into my room once. I'm sorry about your furniture but I'm afraid it's a habit I've got into. There was no key, you see.'

'Well, there's no madmen in this house,' Lisa stated, then swept away muttering, only just loud enough for Charlotte to hear, 'only a mad woman, apparently,' as she went back down the stairs.

Charlotte only made a cursory attempt at goodbye. Stuart was at the dining table when she went downstairs, fork of scrambled egg in hand. It seemed Lisa excelled herself at producing king-sized breakfasts as well.

'I won't stay to breakfast, if you don't mind,' she said as Stuart gave her a fairly alarmed look and a faint smile. 'I'm feeling rather tired and would you believe it, I think I had my first contractions last night.'

'You'd definitely better be on your way then.' Lisa bustled in, now appearing to be the picture of concern. 'You need to get home and rest as soon as possible. You shouldn't really be travelling on your own this close to your due date anyway, surely?' Charlotte marvelled at how she made it sound like a criticism, seeing as it was Lisa who had insisted that she come.

'Oh well, perhaps I should walk with—' Stuart's offer to accompany Charlotte to the station was interrupted quickly by Lisa.

'Sit down, Stuart, your eggs are getting cold. If Charlotte knows the world like the back of her hand, like she told us, I'm sure she's independent enough to find Notting Hill Gate station. I'd think she'd be rather insulted at the idea that she can't make it up the road on her own, wouldn't you, Charlotte?' She winked at Charlotte in apparent conspiracy. 'Men just don't understand women who can go it alone, do they? Would you like me to make you up a sandwich to take with you for the journey?'

'No, thank you, Lisa.' Charlotte hooked her rucksack over her shoulder. 'Thank you very much for a lovely evening.'

'And let's stay in touch,' Stuart said uncertainly.

'Definitely,' Lisa nodded.

'Of course.' Charlotte played along. 'I'll let you know as soon as there's any news with the little one.'

'Just not on the train on the way home, I hope,' Stuart joked.

But it didn't feel like such a joke on the way home from Charing Cross when Charlotte again felt the sharp bands of pain shooting across her stomach. To try to distract herself as her heart rate shot up and her anxiety increased, she ferreted through her bag and found the leaflets that were scrunched up in the bottom. Information that she'd been given at the doctor's surgery by the midwife, and that she'd plunged into her bag without interest, thinking it didn't apply to her, in her unusual circumstances, knowing that she wouldn't look at it again.

There was a flyer about an ante-natal group that she could join and one giving the details of a class she could go to for relaxation and breathing exercises. They were free of charge and the leaflets claimed she could meet other women locally who were in the same situation. Suddenly the words were warm and welcoming. She just hoped that she hadn't left it too late.

Chapter Fourteen

❧

'You'd better get yourself round here, and make it fast,' Jane said.

Ginny was dazed, rubbing her eyes, playing with the cords on her bathrobe. What time was it? What day was it? She'd been woken up by the phone ringing and she'd stumbled across the bedroom, yanked up the receiver and been met with Jane's tone of forboding, and something strangely urgent and sharp in her voice, like an intake of breath.

'What's happened?'

'Nothing's happened. Nothing that can't be dealt with sensibly, anyway.'

'Oh God, it's Charlotte, isn't it? Is it contractions?'

'No.'

'Have you rung the hospital? Ring them first, they'll tell you what to do. I'll be right round.'

'Charlotte's in London, visiting friends,' Jane said after a pause.

'What the hell's she doing in London? She's just about to have a baby! What will she do if her waters break on the train?'

'I know. I think you should have talked to her about that, but we can discuss Charlotte later. This has nothing to do with Charlotte.'

'Then what? You've been burgled.'

'No, no, I'm fine.'

'Are you sure? I'll just throw a tracksuit on. I'll be there in five minutes. I don't like the sound of your voice.'

'It's not an emergency, trust me. Just come home, as soon as you decently can, Ginny.' And she added in a low voice, 'And you might want to run a comb through your hair first.'

'Why are you being so bloody cryptic, Mum? Just give me a clue. It's not like you to be a drama queen.'

'I'm not—' she dropped her voice to a hoarse whisper. 'He's come back. And I'm blowed if I know what to say to him.'

'Oh, I see.' Ginny was grim.

'I'm not sure you do see, Ginny.'

'Oh it's all right, Mum, I understand. I'll have a shower, then I'll be right round.'

It was Saturday morning, she remembered. And when she put the phone down she realised she was still clutching George.

She threw herself into the shower. So her father had finally walked back through the door and poor Jane, caught on the hop, no doubt faced with a suntan like a wet teabag and a set of pearly teeth that had outshone their potential in every sense, was flummoxed.

On the other hand, Ginny reasoned, running her hands through her fine hair as she blow-dried it in the bedroom, she wasn't sure she wanted to get involved in the nitty-gritty. She'd told Jane that she had met Harry, but Jane hadn't been particularly interested in what Harry had had to say about the state of their marriage. Or if she had been interested she hadn't wanted to discuss it with her eldest daughter. So why drag her into the middle of the marital crisis now?

In any case, Ginny decided, throwing on a pair of jeans and a cotton shirt and shoving her feet into trainers, she'd been summoned and that was all there was to it.

She made her way to her mother's house and, as usual, went round to the back door and let herself in with a call inside to warn Jane she was there.

'Mum, it's me.'

'In the living room, darling.'

Odd. There was a tremor in Jane's voice, something nervous and unfamiliar to Ginny. And in the living room? It was all rather polite.

But as Ginny stood in the doorway and gazed at the scene in the living room it all came into focus with a thud of shock. First shock, then confusion, then shock again. But one thing was certain. It was nearly nineteen years since she'd seen this man and she knew him again instantly.

Barney stood up first. Jane stood up too, but Ginny wasn't looking at her mother. She was inspecting with keen curiosity the face of the man who'd changed her life. He was scruffier. He had stubble, as if he was halfway towards growing a beard. His hair was lighter, a tawny brown. It was still thick, though, and not touched by grey as far as she could see. He was thinner than she remembered. He'd lost some of that party-balloon muscle that had made him such a big thing in the rugby camp. His eyes were the same. But, now that he took a step forward, they were different. He'd always had attractive eyes, of a greeny-brown colour that was so striking when he was younger. Now they looked hazier, less clear, more thoughtful. He

123

was, without any question, the same man but older. Much, much older. In fact, standing in the same room as him, knowing without doubt that they were the same age, Ginny felt young, sprightly and, quite frankly, next to his physical roughness, very pretty.

'Ginny,' he said. He took another step forward and stopped.

'I got your letter,' she said, as she couldn't think of anything else to say. Her heart was thundering, but that was with the surprise of it all. She was nervous and her mouth felt dry, but she wasn't reacting to him in any of the ways she might have imagined. She wasn't in awe of him at all, and, in fact, she found it hard to see the heartthrob she'd had such a huge crush on. He didn't look like anyone's heartthrob. He looked, sort of, damaged. In fact, he reminded her in that first meeting of George the pyjama case. Battered and thin, with wide, appealing eyes giving an aura of fragility. An odd thing in such a tall man with such broad shoulders. He was just out of proportion, like poor old George. And at that thought she had to bury a smile.

He seemed heartened by it. 'Well, I'm glad you're not throwing anything at me.'

'Like what?'

'Oh, I don't know.' His voice was the same. That was a funny thing. Nineteen years of not hearing a voice, only to recognise it instantly, as unique as a fingerprint. Although it did sound as if he needed a cup of tea.

'Mum,' Ginny turned to Jane, as she seemed frozen to the spot, her eyes like saucers as she watched this exchange, 'do you think you could put the kettle on for us? It'd be so kind.

124

'Oh! Of course, dear, I'll make more tea. I'll go out to the kitchen. I'm sorry, off I go.'

She bustled away and pointedly closed the door behind her.

'I thought you were my father,' Ginny explained, almost laughing again. Barney watched her; he seemed intrigued by the humour in her face and voice. His eyes were devouring every detail of her face and figure, as if he was trying to memorise her. Or maybe, like her, he was trying to adapt the memory he had to the reality standing in front of him.

'Your father?'

'The way mum was whispering down the phone when she rang me, making it sound like a huge drama. I thought my dad had come back. He's been away, you see, but it doesn't matter now. I'd just got the wrong end of the stick, that's all.'

'Oh, I see. Well, I – the thing is, I've been away myself and as I'd come back I thought – I wasn't sure, but I had this address for your parents and as I—'

'Look, sit down, you look as if you're about to fall down.' Ginny indicated the sofa as Barney had indeed turned very pale. 'Let's have a cup of Mum's tea before you say anything else.' She spotted an empty cup and saucer on the coffee table. Of course, Jane had already been the perfect hostess. 'Another cup, then. You look awful, if you don't mind me saying so. I'm sorry, that's probably not the reception you'd imagined, but you look as if you need a square meal.'

'I am – I've been working. Actually I was going to just drop in and ask about you, maybe try to get a phone number.' He sank on to the sofa and draped one long denimed leg over the other. 'I didn't expect you to be down the road. I didn't think for one minute I'd see you today. I'd have shaved.'

Ginny nodded, listening earnestly to him, wondering where he'd been to get himself into this state of tiredness and depletion, then suddenly stopped and thought about the incongruity of his not shaving before they met again for the first time in nineteen years. In fact, for the first time since Marie was born. Barney had never seen her. She couldn't help herself, but this time she laughed aloud.

'Oh, I'm sorry, it's just the idea that you shaving would make any difference to anything. It's really funny when you think about it.'

He gave a half-smile. 'I just meant out of politeness, really.'

'I think it's usually people's mothers who are impressed by clean-shaven chins, and I have a feeling that it's a little late in the day to try to impress,' she let out a spurt of laughter, 'my mother with your shaving habits. Oh, I'm sorry. You have to admit, it is funny, you being here, worrying about not shaving. Just you being here is funny. Look, I'll go and get the tea.'

When she came back, feeling oddly light headed, with two mugs of tea and the bowl of sugar, he was pacing slowly around the room, surveying the family photographs. Ginny stood silently, puzzled, watching him stop in front of the mantelpiece where her parents kept a collection of photographs of Marie. He picked each one up, examined it closely, then placed it with painstaking precision back where it had come from. He looked like an archaeologist examining a new priceless find with awe and disbelief.

'You'll have seen those,' Ginny ventured, making

him jump. 'Those are standard mugshots we've sent out to the family, and you always got one of those. I've got albums full of ones you won't have seen.' And she suddenly felt generous about it. He was harmless. Helpless, almost. She felt sorry for him. She added more softly, 'I can show you the albums if you like.'

He turned round and Ginny saw that his face was white, his eyes darkened. If anything he looked worse than he had a few moments ago. He seemed very distressed.

'What do you mean? What should I have seen?'

Ginny put his mug down on the coffee table for him and sipped her tea, trying to understand his question. 'The usual photographs, posed at school, for photographers, those kinds of shots that most people frame and put on the mantelpiece. Hey presto, like my parents. They're not the ones I have up at home, mind, I don't think any of these do her justice at all.' She squinted at Barney and said slowly, 'You were sent all of these. To your parents' address. You must have seen them.'

He sounded as if he was choking. He cleared his throat loudly. 'I'm sorry, I don't understand. You're telling me you sent me things.'

'Of course. Right up until her eighteenth birthday. Now I feel it's up to her what she does.'

'I don't understand,' he repeated. He looked bewildered.

'Barney? Sit down again, you really don't look well. Have you been up all night? When did you last sleep? Did you drive a long way?'

'Ginny, I've come blundering in here straight from the airport, and I think I've done it all wrong. I've got it all wrong. I don't understand anything. My parents said you never kept in touch.'

There was a long silence. Ginny felt her body grow cold. She curled her fingers into her palms. It was a long, long time since any mention of Barney's parents could make her angry.

'Oh dear,' she said pointedly. 'I think they are going to have to give you an explanation.'

'I don't get it.' His eyes were misted with tears. He struggled with himself, then said, 'Your mother, Jane. She told me that Marie's away. Travelling. I thought, how ironic, when I've just got back to England.'

'You too?' Ginny raised her eyebrows.

'What? Oh, your dad, you mean?'

'Oh, my sister, that's all, but it doesn't matter. Where have you been?'

'Oh. Everywhere. I—' He stopped abruptly and squeezed his thumb and forefinger over the bridge of his nose, bowing his head and closing his eyes as if lie had a migraine that was sucking all of the energy from him. Ginny watched with some concern, but then he stood straight again and opened his eyes, and he seemed stronger.

'Ginny, I owe you an apology. I'm going to leave now, sort myself out, get a bed, shower and a proper meal. But please can I ask you, may I contact you again when I've got somewhere to stay. Perhaps tomorrow?'

'Um, yes.' She didn't think to say no. There seemed no reason not to see him now. He obviously had questions and she obviously was the one to answer them. That only seemed fair. There was something rather confusing about the situation that needed to be cleared up. And something was gnawing at her now, about his dismay and his confusion. A knot of anger was working its way into her, but there'd be time to talk about it properly when he was in a better state.

'It's Sunday tomorrow, you won't be working?'

'No, I work weekdays.'

'All right, may I phone you? Perhaps in the afternoon or evening?'

'You can come round to my house if you like. You might want to see some more photographs.'

He swallowed again, looked dangerously shaky for a second then asked croakily, 'If you could write down your address?'

She did, and she described where it was. 'Easy to find, from the station or by car. I don't know which way you'll be coming'

'Neither do I yet. So,' he put his hands together, 'I'll see you tomorrow.'

'Yes.'

She showed him out, then closed the door, not wanting to watch him walk away. In the kitchen Jane was flicking the kettle switch on and off as if she had a nervous twitch.

'Oh my God, Ginny, I didn't know what to do with him all this time. You were ages coming round. I showed him the photos of our holiday in Crete from five years ago. I just didn't know what else to do.'

But Ginny was too dazed to think straight, and she ran the conversation through her head again. 'Something's not right about this, Mum, but I'm not sure what it is yet.'

Chapter Fifteen

❧❦❧

By the time she got home, Charlotte was near to tears. Jane jumped up as she walked through the back door.

'Oh, Charlotte, there you are! We've had such a morning, you just won't believe what's been—' Then she stopped, absorbed Charlotte's pale face and bleary eyes and grabbed hold of her. 'Oh, my poor girl. What is going on with you?'

'I'm fine, I'm just so tired, Mum, and I've had such an awful time. I wish I'd never gone.'

'Have you got contractions? Is something happening? Why are you holding yourself like that?'

'No, no, I'm fine now.'

'Why in bloody hell's name didn't you ring me and tell me which train you were on? I'd have picked you up from the station. I told you to ring me. I thought that's what we'd arranged.'

'It's only five minutes' walk.' Charlotte was amazed by the vehemence of her mother's tone.

'Five minutes when you're heavily pregnant, my girl, is not the same as five minutes at any other time. You mustn't take any more risks. That's it now, no more trips to London. I don't want you on a train again.'

'Please don't make a fuss. I didn't get much sleep

last night and I really want to go to bed. Is that all right? Can I just go up now?'

'Of course.'

Jane took Charlotte upstairs and tucked her up in her own bed, in her own bedroom, and Charlotte, instead of feeling rebellious about being at home in the safety of suburban England, was suddenly grateful for the familiarity of home and her mother's touch, and she burst into tears.

'I had contractions. Last night and this morning. I didn't know what to do.'

Jane stiffened and began to fire succinct questions at her daughter while she stroked her forehead. Charlotte answered, grateful for the attention. She didn't want to be ignored anymore, she wanted to be noticed. She wanted somebody to see her fear without her having to spell it out. And Jane could see it, in the staccato replies she received and the whiteness of her daughter's face and the blackness of her eyes.

'And you say you haven't had a pain for an hour? Are you quite sure?'

'Yes, it was about an hour ago, but they've gone away again now.'

'Well,' Jane sighed, 'at least we've got you home safely and we can take it from here. I knew I should have stopped you from gallivanting about in London. I told you not to go, but you are one for knowing best, Charlotte.'

'It's not you, Mum, it's me. You couldn't have told me. I didn't know I was going to feel like this. And I haven't had any pain before. It took me by surprise.'

'I'm going to ring the hospital and tell them what

131

you've told me and get their advice. They may want you to go in, just in case.'

'No, it's fine, Mum. The baby's not coming. I'd know if it was coming. That's what everybody says. And the contractions didn't hurt much, they were just new and weird and I wished I could have talked to somebody about it.'

'What about your friends – who was it you were staying with?'

'It doesn't matter. They're not friends really. Just people I knew.'

'I don't think you can count them as friends if they ignored the fact you were in trouble and didn't offer to help.'

'It's not their fault either, Mum. It's me, don't you see? It's me.'

'My baby,' Jane soothed, kissing Charlotte on the cheek. 'I'll make a call and I'll be right back.'

'Okay.' Charlotte closed her eyes and snuggled into the sheets, wincing as the baby decided to try to change position. She felt like a small spin-drier loaded with an oversized duvet that was fighting to make space for itself.

By the time Jane returned, Charlotte was feeling a little soothed, although the alarm she had felt when she'd been on her own and frightened was still hovering close by. She shifted herself up on to her elbows to drink the cup of tea her mother had brought her.

'What did they say?'

'I'm to keep an eye on you and we're to time the contractions. I've given them every detail you've given me and they said they're probably just Braxton Hicks.'

'What the hell are they?'

'Just your body limbering up – practising, if you like. They don't normally lead to anything. Ginny had them for about four months before she had Marie. It made it quite difficult for her to know when Marie was coming.' Jane gazed at her daughter, and if she tried to disguise her concern she failed. 'You haven't heard or read about Braxton Hicks? Even now? Didn't the midwives talk to you about it?'

'No,' Charlotte said in exasperation. 'Or maybe yes. If they did I don't remember exactly what they said. Look, I don't know anything. I'm stupid. How can I make it clearer? I really don't know what's going on or what's going to happen next. I don't know anybody who's pregnant. I don't know anybody who's been pregnant. I have nobody to guide me, Mum, so please don't look at me as if I was a total idiot. Just tell me what's going on, please.'

'Oh, my silly girl.' Jane held her hand. 'Of course you know people who have been pregnant. There's Ginny and there's me, for a start. Your sister and your mother. We're here to help you.'

'I've just had so much on my mind it's all seemed like a million years away. I know that sounds stupid when I'm so big and so pregnant, but sometimes it still seems as if it's never going to happen, and all my other thoughts crash in and take over.' She heaved a sigh. 'I'm glad you're here, Mum, so glad.' She ignored the reference to Ginny for now. 'Thank God I came home. I've never needed you so much in my whole life.'

'Your big sister said that to me once,' Jane ventured. 'I know she seems to know it all now, but I can remember when she was nothing more than a frightened girl, asking me to explain it all to her. I'll give her a call in a minute. I'll ask her to come round.'

'No, don't.' Charlotte lay back on the pillows and covered her eyes.

'What is going on with you two girls?' Jane shuffled closer to Charlotte and peered into her face. Charlotte kept her eyes firmly shut. 'There's an atmosphere and it's got to be cleared. I'll call her.'

'No.' Charlotte opened one eye in appeal. 'She'll only make me feel more guilty than I already do. For coming back here, for landing in your lap, for being a burden. And I *am* sorry, Mum. That's the thing. There's nothing that Ginny can say to me that I don't already know. She thinks I've been miles away, living it up, not thinking about everything back at home. But she's wrong. I thought about you all, every day. I'm just not so good at expressing things as she is. And I wanted a life for myself. That's all I ever wanted. To see what was out there, not to take a moment of my life for granted but to live it to the full in as many places in the world as I could think of to visit. I wanted a different life. A life that wasn't ordinary. Is that so wrong?'

Jane squeezed her daughter's fingers. She didn't answer straight away. 'I think we've all wanted lives for ourselves that aren't ordinary.'

'Oh, I know. I didn't mean to say that your life is ordinary.'

'Well, perhaps it has been ordinary. If you think putting your family stability above and beyond everything else is important, yes, my life has been ordinary.'

'Oh, Mum, that's not what I meant.'

'And Ginny's life hasn't been ordinary either,

134

although you'd be forgiven for thinking so, just because she chose to live her life near her family home and she hasn't been anywhere exotic or done anything that might be considered daring.'

'I don't think that either,' Charlotte complained weakly. 'At least, that's not quite what I meant. I wouldn't ever offend Ginny by telling her she's ordinary.'

'But maybe she thinks that is exactly what your opinion of her is. Maybe she thinks you feel you've been the exciting one, exploring and discovering. . . Maybe when she's around you she feels like the boring one, left at home with her responsibilities. Except that she's been discovering things too. She's just been an adventurer in a human sense. Finding out about being a mother. That was daring of her, at the young age she was. It was her choice, and, whatever you think about it, it was a brave one.'

'Well I'm going to do that too, aren't I?' Charlotte appealed. 'Isn't that clear to Ginny now? I'm going to understand some of her experience. Maybe at last we'll have something in common.'

'Yes. And maybe Ginny feels that you've had a bite of both sides of the cherry cake, or whatever the metaphor is.'

'Had my cake and eaten it?'

'Maybe.' Jane nodded gently. 'Maybe that's it.'

Charlotte closed her eyes again. Jane sat with her in silent companionship for several minutes. Then she ventured quietly, 'How do you feel now?'

'Fine. Just very, very tired.'

'Any pains?'

'No pains at all.'

'Baby moving?'

'Yes, baby moving occasionally but just as he usually does. Please don't worry, Mum. I wish I hadn't said anything now. It's probably four weeks to go, anyway. I should have known it was just a silly false alarm.'

'Nothing's silly when it comes to a baby.'

'You said Ginny and I were both early?'

'Ginny by a few days; you were a week early, but then second babies often do come early.'

'You see, I didn't even know that. I don't know anything. I'm a complete ignoramus.'

'Stop beating yourself up,' Jane chided, and as Charlotte allowed a brief smile to flit over her lips she added, 'I want to ask you about your friend again. Your Indian friend. You said his name was – Raj? Is that right?'

This time Charlotte didn't have a ready answer. She covered her eyes with her arm and took a deep breath. 'What about him?'

'I'd like to know something, Charlotte, but it's personal.'

'Go on.'

'Do you still love him?' Jane held her breath and Charlotte sensed her tense expectation.

Did she still love Raj? There was never any question about it. She loved him as if her heart would break. That was why talk of being brave gave her pause for thought. She had walked away from the only man she had ever loved, and if anything took courage that did. Nobody was ever going to understand that, and it was pointless trying to explain it. Charlotte had been many things over the years that she didn't like, but she didn't

136

consider herself a wimp. At least, she hadn't thought she was afraid of anything, until these last days when the birth was growing more imminent and a horrendous fear was creeping up on her. Fear for her baby's safety, fear of the unknown. But to sneak away in the night like a thief from the man who was the guardian of her heart. That had taken a strength that she had never known she possessed. Compared to that she had felt that the physical pain of birth would be nothing. In some abstract way, she expected it to be painful. In some perverse way, she wanted it to be painful. She wanted it to take her over, possess her, blot her mind of any other images. She needed to be overcome by something bigger than her love for Raj; maybe this would be it.

'Yes, Mum,' she answered in a small voice. 'I love him.'

'And, may I ask something else?' Jane tiptoed.

'Yes.'

'Does he know where you are? Does he have any way of knowing?'

Charlotte clenched her jaw and bit back the emotion that swelled up. 'I didn't want him to know. I didn't tell him where I was going.'

'Do you not think, darling,' Jane ventured very, very gently, 'that he would want to be with you at the birth of his son?' Charlotte became so still and so silent that after several minutes had passed Jane began to worry about her. 'Charlotte?'

'If you love me at all, Mum,' Charlotte managed in a trembling voice, 'you won't ask me that question again.'

*

137

Of course, Jane did ring Ginny, once Charlotte was asleep and she was sure that she wouldn't overhear any of the conversation. And Ginny, knowing nothing of Charlotte's false alarm, leapt straight in with her reactions to the sudden arrival of Barney.

'My God, Mum, I still can't believe that Barney turned up on your doorstep. I'm so sorry I was so long coming round. It's no wonder you were shaken up. What did you think when you opened the door?'

Jane, suffused with worry about Charlotte, now flipped her thoughts back to the other great event of the day. Not that she could have put it to the back of her mind. It was a mother's job, after all, to be a bridge, and she did it well. For Ginny, as for them all as a family, the return of Barney into their lives was the biggest thing – apart from Charlotte's pregnancy – that had happened for eighteen years.

'To begin with I didn't recognise him,' Jane said. 'He doesn't look a bit like he did when he was a teenager.'

'Oh, he does,' Ginny corrected. 'He really does look the same. Just older and more weather-beaten.'

'I couldn't see it.'

'Well. . .' Ginny let that go. Her mother hadn't been in love with him. She hadn't once studied every detail of his face and body as if it were a precious work of art. She hadn't seen the spirit inside of him, the character that she had known. Her mother didn't sometimes look at Marie and see her father in her eyes, or in her gestures. Maybe that was what had kept Barney with her for all these years that he'd been absent, whether he'd known it or not. 'The essence of him is the same.'

'I just felt very glad, very glad indeed that Marie was abroad.'

'Oh yes!' Ginny agreed, settling in her favourite armchair. 'Thank God for that. I can't imagine what I'd have said to Marie if she'd been here. I'll have to handle that very carefully. At least I've got plenty of time to think about it before she comes home.'

'And, to be honest, whatever we might have said over the years, I felt rather sorry for him. He seems a bit of a mess.'

'What on earth did he say, when you answered the door?'

'It was all very ordinary. He asked if I was your mother, and then he recognised me and apologised for not recognising me immediately, then apologised for intruding, then apologised again and asked if it might be possible for me to give him an address or phone number where he could contact you directly. And when I told him you lived just up the road so I could call you and ask you to pop round he seemed a bit shaken up. But he agreed, so there we were. Then as you were about to arrive I thought I'd better leave everything else up to you. So I got out the holiday albums. He was very polite about them.'

'I felt sorry for him, too. He seemed very wobbly.'

'He'd just flown in that morning, as he told you. He'd been in Africa, he said.'

'Really. Where?'

'I'm not sure.'

'Doing what?'

'You must ask him yourself, I didn't really get to grips with it.'

'Maybe he'll tell me, if it's relevant at all. I'm not sure I really care where he's been all these years. It's strange, though. When I got his letter I was amused by it, annoyed by him, too. But he's not how I thought he'd be. I'm going to see him again, tomorrow evening. I'll be interested to see how things go. I'll just play it by ear.'

'And do keep an open mind, won't you, Ginny.'

'Of course,' Ginny said instinctively, then added, 'About what?'

'About him.'

'Yes, of course. Why?'

'I just have a feeling that things might not have been as we thought they were.'

'Well, I do too, but it doesn't change anything, does it?'

'Probably not. But you never know.'

Chapter Sixteen

❦

What a difference a day makes, thought Ginny, as she opened the door to Barney on Sunday evening.

He'd obviously had a good night's sleep. He'd shaved, showered and changed his clothes. He still looked thin, but he looked very different from the shadowy figure she'd seen the day before. He was in a faded denim shirt and jeans and DMs. It was possible he'd even had a haircut – at least he'd combed it or dampened it down so that the brown curls were more in place. He looked just as craggy but much more solid than yesterday, as if he could stand for more than ten minutes without caving in. His eyes had a certain light, a certain life, as though he'd plugged himself into the mains and come away recharged.

On Ginny's part, she'd had a chance to think about how she'd like Barney to see her again, after all these years. Not, now the reality was here, how she might have imagined it. When she was much younger, in those first two or three years that he'd maintained his stony silence, she'd fantasised about hurt drifting back and her pointing a finger at the door, Gloria Gaynor style. Or draping herself kitten-like on a sofa and flashing her eyelashes at him and puffing up her cleavage so that he could see the sexy woman she had grown into. Perhaps, that fantasy assured her, one day she would be the one to reject him. But those fantasy images had expired long ago. The bigger Marie got, the bigger the demands of her role as mother had become, the smaller her fantasy had become until it had shrunk away, and, through lack of nourishment, died.

So, instead of any of those things, when she got ready for Barney to come round to her house on Sunday evening she dressed as she normally did. She wanted to look good, of course, but she didn't want to be particularly alluring or to make any statement to him. She was herself, Ginny, mother of Marie, and he was here about Marie, not about Ginny. That being said, she did take some care with her make-up and she did put some mousse on her hair before she blow-dried it. She wanted him to see how well she'd done her job and emerged the other side, still young-looking, still slim, still with energy, and still pretty. If Jane's encouraging remarks were true, she was prettier than she'd been when she was younger. But now she was only concerned for her feminine pride. She was passionate that he should not find her lacking, as a mother or as a person.

She took a step back to allow him in to her hallway. Again, strangely, she felt towards him a combination of sympathy and warmth. Maybe even companionship. In truth, she was looking forward to talking about Marie to somebody who appeared to be genuinely interested. Just how interested he was she would gauge as they went along. She wasn't about to overwhelm him with detail, neither would she hold back. She'd just give him what he wanted. There seemed no reason not to. She caught a whiff of aftershave, or maybe it was just his deodorant or shampoo, as he stood in the hall, his shirt crisp and clean about his lean body. It was a smell that only a man would exude, strange in a house so full, normally, of feminine scents. She quite liked it.

'I made some food. I wasn't sure if you'd have eaten or not but it's there if you want some. I've already eaten but you're welcome to whatever you want. Just let me know if you're hungry,' Ginny said practically as she led him into her cosy living room. He glanced around him with interest then back at her.

'It's a nice house.'

'Yes, it is. Small but nice. Marie and I designed it together.'

He nodded. He seemed sombre again, as he'd been the day before.

'Would you like a drink?'

'Thank you. Just whatever's easy.'

'I've got a bottle of white wine in the fridge. Or there's whisky, gin, over there in the sideboard. I don't normally drink spirits but you're welcome. Or a cup of tea or coffee.'

'A beer?'

'Actually, that's the one thing I don't have.'

'Just a glass of wine then, that would be very nice, thank you.'

She nodded and took herself into the narrow kitchen to pour it. Out of sight of him, as she gathered two glasses down from the cupboard, she found herself marvelling again at the turn of events. It was so very, very odd that Barney, father of her daughter, cause of the seismic shift in her life, was now hovering awkwardly in her living room and waiting for her to pour him a drink. On the other hand, they had so much in common in the form of Marie that it seemed entirely natural for him to be here. She did feel a flutter of nerves, it would be a lie to pretend that she didn't. But quite why, she wasn't sure. And as she poured the wine she decided that there were two reasons. One was that she wasn't used to entertaining men on her own in her house. The other was that she was extremely protective of Marie, especially in her absence, and she was just hoping that she wasn't going to have any reason to be defensive about the way she'd brought her up or about any of the decisions that she'd made.

'Here you are.' She handed him his glass of wine and held hers up. 'I suppose we should say "cheers" or something. It has been a long time after all.'

Barney held up his glass. 'Cheers, Ginny. Thank you very much indeed for having me round to your house.'

'That's okay.'

'It's more than that. It's very generous of you. I think under the circumstances it says a lot about you. May I sit down?'

'Of course, please do.'

She had forgotten, it was true, and it was coming back to her with each minute she spent in his company, how well brought up he was, for want of a better phrase given the horrors that his parents had turned out to be. They had sent him to an expensive public school, and perhaps the fees had eventually paid off in some way. She had known that much about him after they'd fallen into bed together. There was something his mother had said about not investing in her son for all those years for him to throw his life away on a mistake. . . But that had been a long time ago, and she pushed the memory of his mother's shrill voice away. What was evident now, as was evident when she first met him, was the fact that he knew how to be polite, how to push buttons. Or perhaps, by now, as he must have been nearing forty, it wasn't about pushing buttons. Perhaps now he was genuinely respectful of other people. He seemed respectful of her, at least.

'Yes,' he continued, almost to himself as his eyes roved her room, the stacked bookshelves, the layers of life squashed into the small space. 'It says a lot about you.'

As he seemed to be about to veer off into a world of his own, she indicated a number of photo albums that she'd uncovered earlier in the day and piled up on the table for him to see. 'I put those there, for you to look at. It's up to you, you can just flick through them on your own if you like, or I can explain anything to you. I don't want to bore you with acres and acres of family snaps.'

'Bore me?' His head flew up and his eyes were pained. 'How could it bore me?'

'Well, I just...' She took a large mouthful of her wine and sat in her favourite chair so as not to impose on him on the sofa. Besides, he took up most of the sofa himself with his long arms and long legs. 'I'm sorry, that wasn't meant to sound negative. I just don't know how you feel.'

Barney shifted forward on the sofa and put his fingers to his temples, closing his eyes to concentrate. She'd seen him do this yesterday, as if he had a headache. Now she wondered if in fact it was something he did habitually when he was trying to concentrate. She couldn't remember him doing it before, but then, of course, she hadn't known him very well before. And they'd largely been young, formed physically but not entirely formed in other ways. He'd probably developed many of his characteristics later in life, just as she had, in response to what had happened to him. Whatever that was. Eventually, however, he sat up straight again and disconcerted her with a straight, clear-eyed look.

'Before we go any further, I need to get some things straight, Ginny. Some very important things. I need to ask you some questions.'

It all sounded very formal and Ginny found herself shifting forward on her chair and sitting up straight, all attention. Other than the background ticking of a clock in the room, there was no noise while they both thought. It lent an appropriate gravitas to the atmosphere, one that matched Barney's expression.

'It's been a long time, Barney. I don't mind you asking me questions, but of course you'll understand if I'm a bit defensive.'

'That's the last thing I want. When I say I want to ask you questions, I think it might be better if you hear me out.'

'Go on.'

'The first thing I want to say is that I'm daunted by actually being here, in the house where you've brought Marie up. It's very difficult for me. I can feel her, everywhere. It's like a kind of electricity. I'm overpowered by it.'

'That might be the cat hair.' Ginny regretted her quip the moment it was out. She was so used to verbal sparring with Marie that this sudden solemnity took some adjusting to, but she wriggled uncomfortably

146

and looked suitably apologetic. 'Sorry. I'm being silly.'

'It's all right. I know it must be hard for you to know how to react to me. After all these years I just turn up. You must feel very odd.'

'A little.'

He sipped his wine thoughtfully. 'Yesterday, you said something about photographs. That you'd sent them.'

'Yes. Every few months when Marie was little. More recently it was when she changed or had a school photo taken.'

'I feel you have to know that I never saw any of those.'

Ginny frowned. Then she sat forward and stared at him intently. 'What do you mean? I assure you I'm not lying.'

'No, please don't think I meant that. I know you're telling the truth. Instinct tells me, apart from anything, and I trust my instincts. I think that you have done the decent thing – or at least, you've tried to – and I think others have blocked your efforts.'

'And by others you mean – who?'

'That will be for me to find out. I'm pretty sure I know what's being going on, but I've been so busy, so preoccupied, so—' He stopped, laughed under his breath and pushed a hand through his hair, which was becoming more unruly the drier it became. 'Listen to me. As if you care about what's been going on with me for the last God knows how many years. Ignore what I've said. Let's just say I think you've been let down. I think I've been badly let down too. I'll deal with it in my own way, it's just going to be very painful.'

'Are you saying that you never got a single photograph or letter I sent you?'

'Not one.'

'Jesus.' Ginny sat back in her chair and considered this development. In fact, she realised that she was shocked. She'd just assumed that the parcels she'd bundled off in good faith to Barney, care of his parents' address, would have been passed on to him. It wasn't as if she'd ever asked him for anything. Not after those first couple of letters when Marie was a baby and where Ginny was eager to know whether Barney wanted to see her. She was such a beautiful baby, she couldn't imagine anybody not wanting to see her. She couldn't imagine how he could resist his adorable daughter. But the response had been silence. 'I'm stunned, Barney. I don't know what else to say. I'm so very, very sorry.'

'I'm touched that you tried to stay in touch with me.' He looked moved. Again his clear eyes had misted over. It struck Ginny that the insensitive boy had turned into a very sensitive man. Or perhaps he was just sensitive where his own feelings were concerned. It was impossible to tell.

'I didn't try to stay in touch with you,' she corrected, feeling it was an important point. 'I tried to tell you about your daughter. It's quite different.'

'Yes, yes, of course. Sorry, that's what I meant.'

'But,' Ginny pondered further, 'the letters I sent you when Marie was first born, telling you about her, you must have got those at least.'

He paled and tightened his grip on the arm of her sofa. 'No. I've had nothing from you.'

'Nothing at all?'

'Not a word since the last time I saw you. Of course, I know after that our parents met and everything was pretty much decided by them, but—'

'Hang on. My parents didn't decide anything for me. I chose my own path. When your parents came down to our house there was a huge scene. I'm afraid I have to say your mother got quite hysterical and it all got really out of hand. In fact, it was terrible.'

'I didn't know the details but I can imagine,' he said grimly. 'And no doubt your parents told you about it.'

'I was there. I met your mother and father.'

'They never told me that. They said they'd had a meeting with your mother and father, there was no mention of you being there at all. My God, has anyone been telling me the truth?' he shook his head, bewildered.

'I can tell you what happened. Your dad didn't say much. Your mother was rather strange; she kept insisting on talking over my head, as if I wasn't there. I think that's what I remember more than anything else. She addressed all her comments to my father. I don't think she even thought my mum was worth consulting. The essence of her argument was that you were an investment and she wasn't having her plans for you ruined. She said you didn't want anything more to do with me or us, that I'd been a silly mistake, somebody you weren't even interested in. She kept telling my father that a marriage was out of the question. Even when I told her I didn't want to marry you, she just kept on and on. *There will be no marriage.* You know, I'm not surprised she didn't tell you I was there, because she didn't notice me at all. She didn't see me and she didn't hear me. To her, I was completely, utterly invisible.' Ginny took a deep breath to let the anger subside. This wasn't supposed to happen. She wasn't supposed to be reliving all the unpleasantness from years ago. She wanted the meeting with Barney to be positive. She poured herself another drink before offering him one. Her hand was shaking very slightly, but annoyingly she saw that he noticed.

'Ginny, I'm sorry. The last thing I want is to come here and make you go through this again.'

'I'm not going through it. I'm just telling you what happened. I never did want to marry you, Barney, I think you'd better be clear on it now if you weren't clear all those years ago. If somebody's been telling you lies, let me set the record straight. If I had had the luxury of choosing a husband for myself, it wouldn't under any circumstances have been you. Have no doubt about it. You are the last man I would have considered marrying.'

There was a silence. Ginny stared down at her fingers twisting in her lap. It needed saying but, God, she wished it hadn't just leapt out like that. For nineteen years she'd wanted to tell him to his face that he was the last man she would ever have married, and now she'd done it. She couldn't bring herself to apologise, but she couldn't make herself say anything else either. In the quiet of the room, the clock ticking rhythmically, she could hear his soft breathing. After a while, he stood up.

'Ginny, I've imposed on you and I think it's time for me to go. I am truly sorry for what my parents did back then. As you may gather, I didn't have much control over what went on and I don't seem to have had any control since. Believe me when I say that the very last thing I wanted was to upset you.'

'I'm not upset.' Ginny stuck out her chin and stood up too, so that she could look him straight in the eye.

'Perhaps you needed to tell me that. You must have built up a lot of resentment over the years, especially if you thought I was ignoring you.'

'I will only ever tell you the truth, Barney. If you knew any thing about me at all, which you don't, you would know that. And, no, I haven't resented you at all, not at any time. At first I was confused because I didn't understand why you wanted to shut Marie out when she was so wonderful. Since then I've only felt very sorry for you because you've missed out on the life of a beautiful, clever and funny girl and you can never have that time back.'

She'd wanted to hurt him and she saw his face crumple. It was a bull's-eye. Nobly, under the circumstances, he sniffed, kept his head high and walked from the room. She followed him into the hall, starting to feel naggings of guilt.

He turned to her at the front door. 'Thank you for having me and for the wine.'

Ginny examined his face. Part of her wanted to slap him. But another part of her wanted to comfort him, 'Wait here. I'll get the albums. You can take them away with you and bring them back when you've finished. In fact, you'd probably want to look at them on your own anyway, without me breathing down your neck. I should have thought of that.'

'Thank you.' He nodded. 'I will take them. When can I bring them back?'

Ginny's lips twitched, despite herself. 'I don't think we need to make a formal arrangement about custody of the photo albums. Just call me, I gave you my number. Or pop them back, I'm usually here when I'm not at Mum's.'

Suddenly he took her hand. He was probably going to shake it, but in the end he just held it. It took Ginny by surprise, so much so that she didn't pull away. His skin was warm and a flashing image shot through her head of a passionate man, which she shook away again as quickly as possible.

'Thank you,' he said, and brushed his lips on her cheek. 'I really mean that. You are majestic.'

Slightly dazed, Ginny watched him walk away with the albums tucked under his arm, into the darkness and out of sight.

Chapter Seventeen

❧

It was the last thing Charlotte would have imagined herself doing, but on a dull, grey midweek afternoon she found herself at the cottage hospital two miles from home, walking into a relaxation class for pregnant mothers.

Jane had given her a lift as she wasn't working that day, and Charlotte had hesitated as she'd been about to get out of the car.

'I'm still not sure if this is a good idea.'

'It is,' Jane said firmly.

'I won't have anything in common with any of them. They'll all be twenty-two and married to the boy from next door.'

'And what, exactly, is wrong with that?' Jane arched a critical eyebrow at her daughter. Sometimes Charlotte felt she'd said completely the wrong thing.

'Nothing, that's not what I meant.'

'Even if they are all local women who've lived here all their lives, you've got no place to be judgemental. But it's much more likely they won't be. This town is full of commuters now. It's such a quick train journey into London, you'll probably meet a lot of stressed businesswomen panicking about having time off from their careers. In any case, women are having babies much later in life. You don't need me to tell you that. You'll probably be the youngest.'

'Daft, Mum, but thanks for the encouragement.'

'And what makes you think you're the only person round here who's ever had the courage to get on an aeroplane?'

'Yes, all right, point taken. So you'll pick me up in an hour?'

'I thought it was an hour and a half.'

'It is, but the first hour's exercises and breathing, the extra half-hour's just for a cup of tea and a chat, if anybody wants to stay. I don't want to stay for that.'

'Why not? I'd have thought it's just what you need.'

'They'll just want to know too much. I don't want to face another barrage of personal questions and another sea of critical faces,' Charlotte said tensely. 'I just want to get in there, relax, and get the hell out again.'

Jane's lips twitched but she nodded and drove away, promising to return in an hour.

As Charlotte walked down the corridor, following the directions she'd been given at reception, she saw ahead of her another pregnant woman. It took her by surprise because she realised that since her pregnancy had been confirmed she hadn't actually been around anybody else in the same situation. They reached a pair of heavy swing doors together. The other woman turned to Charlotte, looked her up and down and her face broke into a smile.

'You haven't got long to go, have you?' she said.

'Oh. A few weeks.'

'How many weeks are you?'

'Thirty-seven-ish.' Charlotte tried to look pleasant

without venturing into any overtures of friendship. 'And you?'

'Thirty-eight. I've just taken maternity leave.'

The funny thing was that although she didn't know this woman at all, when Charlotte looked at her stomach and compared her own shape, she felt as if they had something in common. It was an unexpected feeling of conspiracy. Even warmth. 'Well, me too. In a way. I've been abroad.'

'Really? Where?'

'India, most recently.'

'Fascinating. I met my husband working in Belgium, we've just come back in the last few months. Bit of a shock coming home to roost, isn't it? Makes you feel like one of those salmon, or is it trout.'

'I feel more like a whale, myself,' Charlotte admitted. The other woman laughed, and Charlotte could see in a flash that she was happy. She took a deep breath and tried to be happy herself. 'Yes, it feels strange being home but it has some advantages, I guess.'

'Is it your first baby?'

'Yes. And you?'

'Yes. Bit surreal, isn't it. Have you been to this before?'

'No, first time.' And if she was honest, she was nervous, but Charlotte wasn't going to be honest.

'Me too. I don't really know what to expect. Do we have to blow into bags or try synchronised groaning, or something?'

'I've got no idea.'

'My name's Polly, by the way.'

'I'm Charlotte.'

'Nice to meet you.'

In fact, they didn't have to blow into anything. The session was taken by a midwife, looking very sporty in a tracksuit and bare feet, with a soft voice and smiling eyes. She didn't ask Charlotte or Polly anything at all about themselves, only how far pregnant they were. She also advised them only to follow the exercises they felt capable of doing and to stop the instant they felt uncomfortable. Charlotte spent an hour bending and flexing on a rubber mat, hoping with all her heart that the baby wouldn't take this as a cue to arrive. But, to her astonishment, some of the women there were already due, and one, to her shock, was a week over-due. She kept watching her to see if she showed signs of going into labour. Despite herself, Charlotte felt her nerves settle, especially at the end of the session when they ail lay on their mats with their eyes closed and listened to the midwife read a relaxation mantra.

'Imagine yourself holding your baby. Visualise your baby's features,' she finished, seducing them into motherhood. 'Visualise its tiny fingers and tiny toes. . . That's the end of the reading. Lie still and quiet with your eyes closed for as long as you want, until you're ready to sit up.'

Practically in tears as the mental and emotional tension ebbed from her body, Charlotte eventually sat up to find that tea, coffee and squash was already laid out on a table at the far end of the room. One by one the women stood up and wandered over, sat down and began to talk about their pregnancies.

'Oh, I'll just. . .' she began to mutter her excuses, patting down her hair and wondering if Jane was already outside waiting.

'Charlotte!' Polly waved her over. 'Are you drinking tea or coffee?'

'I'll have to, er. . .' she glanced at her watch. Polly was smiling; the other women were already talking.

Then she heard somebody say, 'Have you had any Braxton Hicks' yet?'

This was something she wanted to stay to hear.

'I'll have a cup of tea, please, Polly.' She made her way over to the table.

Ginny had thought it might be a nice distraction for her and Rebecca to go to the local fireworks' display on Guy Fawkes night, but, as Rebecca jumped with every whistle and bang, Ginny realised that it hadn't been such a bright idea to inflict pyrotechnics on somebody with such jangling nerves. She'd been concerned about not hearing from Rebecca for a couple of weeks and when she picked her up from her house, as they'd agreed, felt instantly that she was in the presence of somebody struggling with depression. Ginny wasn't stupid enough to think that fireworks would cure Rebecca, but she hadn't expected the shock almost to kill her. Several times Rebecca had grabbed the arm of Ginny's jacket and exclaimed 'Oh my God', as a firework had gone off. Eventually, thankfully, it was over and only the bonfire raged at them from beyond a rope barrier.

'I think that's it then,' Rebecca said. 'They must have spent a lot of money on it.'

'Oh look, there's a fair.' Ginny pointed to the other side of the grassy hill. 'Shall we wander over?'

'Yes, all right.'

With no enthusiasm at all Rebecca traipsed around

the stalls with Ginny. She really didn't want to do anything and Ginny couldn't blame her. At one point Ginny took her arm and squeezed it.

'Are you okay?'

'Hmm? Yes and no. Normally we would have come to this event as a family. In the past, you know. Emma's going to be very angry. She's really going to be livid when she finds out the age of this woman.'

'Really?'

'She's thirty. Only thirty. That's only ten years older than Emma.'

Give or take a year, Rebecca was right, and Ginny could only feel deep sympathy for the awful rejection that she must have been enduring.

'Have you talked to Gareth properly now?'

'You can't call it talking really. He shouts and I cry.' Rebecca gave a brittle laugh. 'I don't know why he's the one that's shouting. It should be me.'

'Guilt, probably.' Ginny pursed her lips. She'd always disliked Gareth, but she liked him less with every snippet of information. 'Perhaps you should try shouting at him. It might get a lot of your feelings off your chest.'

'I know, but I can't. I've never been a shouter. I never wanted the children to be raised in a family with lots of conflict.'

'Were you, then?'

Ginny heard Rebecca's sharp intake of breath. 'Sometimes you're very perceptive, Ginny. Yes, my father was a violent man. Only with words, but the result was probably as bad. I was terrified of him.'

'Is he still alive?'

158

'No, thank God. Oh, isn't that awful, I can't say that. He was my father after all.'

'Yes, but people do sometimes let us down, don't they?' Ginny thought of Barney's mother suddenly, a strange, unbidden memory of her open, red mouth screeching at her parents. Poor Barney. He can't have had an easy time at home either. It had been so convenient to think of him as the boy with all the advantages, but they'd lied to him and deceived him over his own daughter, something of great importance. It made Ginny realise how lucky she was to have Jane and Harry as parents. Even Harry, in his absence, was a benevolent figure, a kind man who would do anything for his family whether he lived at home or not. For a fleeting moment she had an understanding of the amicable arrangement her parents had come to, then the waters muddied again and it was gone.

'Cross my palm with silver!' An old woman in a headscarf, with weathered, tanned skin suddenly leapt from nowhere into their path. Rebecca half jumped into the air.

'I didn't think people really said that,' Ginny addressed her, trying to be humorous. The last thing she wanted was to be shadowed around the fair by a gypsy fortune-teller.

'Lucky white heather?' She whipped a sprig of heather from her pocket and waved it at them.

'How much?' Ginny asked.

'Two pounds.'

'I'll give you a pound.'

'Two pounds. Otherwise it won't work.'

'And no extended warranty, I bet.' Wrily, Ginny fished out her purse and paid, taking the heather. As she did so, the gypsy grabbed her hand fiercely and stared at her palm.

'A man from your past,' she croaked. 'He will change your life for ever.'

Ginny tugged her hand away. She certainly didn't want her fortune told. 'A bit late for that warning, but thank you for the heather.'

'And you, darlin'? A bunch for you?' She turned to Rebecca, who was nervously shaking her head.

'No, thank you.' Ginny frogmarched them both along the muddy walkway and they stopped next to a round stall where children were trying to throw rings over impossibly large goldfish bowls. 'Here you are.' She handed Rebecca the heather. 'For luck. I think you need it more than I do at the moment.'

'Thank you.' Rebecca took it without complaint. 'That is kind of you, Ginny. I'll keep it.'

Chapter Eighteen

It was a week before Barney appeared again. Ginny was replying to Marie's latest email using the computer that they shared but had put on a desk in Marie's bedroom, as she used it the most. Mr Mistoffelees was curled up on Marie's bed, snoring. It was a bitterly cold mid-November night, and every so often the sash windows rattled in response to a blast of wind. Ginny was wrapped up warm in a thick jumper and tracksuit bottoms, one of Marie's fleeces thrown over her shoulders. She was also wearing Marie's old hockey socks from school. They were too big for her and beautifully warm. As she typed to her daughter, giving her Charlotte's latest news, she curled her toes into the carpet, transported to a hot, clammy world where Marie and Emma's latest adventure had been visiting a Buddhist temple. She could only imagine the sights and smells, how different the atmosphere was from the cosy little bedroom Marie had inhabited as she packed her rucksack to leave.

Then the doorbell rang and Ginny glanced at her watch. It was only seven-thirty but it felt much later. She'd been looking forward to a glass of wine with the news, then bed. And her first thought, of course, was that it could be Barney. She had after all in a fit of generosity, in a last bid to make him feel welcome, told him that it wasn't necessary to call before visiting. Now, as she went down the stairs, pushing her hands through her lank hair, she really wished she'd insisted that he call her first. Most of her make-up from her day at work had rubbed itself off and she gave herself a quick appraisal in the hall mirror. It was too late to put any lipstick on now. It would look as if she'd put it on especially to answer the door. She'd have to do as she was.

Barney looked very cold, but he hovered on the doorstep and handed over the stack of photo albums she'd lent him.

'I've brought these back. Thanks very much for lending them to me.'

'Oh, that's no trouble. Come in.'

'No, I won't intrude on you again, I just wanted to return them promptly in case you thought I'd kidnapped them. It was very moving for me, looking through them. Perhaps we can talk about me getting some copies. I wondered if you have any negatives for them.

'Yes, of course, so come in.'

'No, not now, Ginny. You're not expecting me, but I was passing and I thought now would be a good time . . . I didn't want to ring you because I didn't want you to stand on ceremony or think you had to entertain me.'

'Barney, it's sub-zero out there. I'm cold if you're not. Please come in.'

He stepped tentatively into her hallway and she shut the door behind·him. He was strapped up in a thick jacket. It had a strong leather smell, like a worn saddle. He was in jeans again and his DMs.

'I'm not used to this temperature, I have to admit.' He followed her through to the sitting room.

'Really? My mum said something about you being in Africa.'

'Yes. I've been working there for some years.'

Ginny was intrigued but let it pass for now. 'Glass of wine? I'm just having one.'

'No thanks, I really won't stay.'

'All right.'

They looked at each other for a while. Ginny felt it again, this strange feeling of familiarity with the man she hardly knew. He was giving her a curious look too. Could it be that he felt the same?

'Where have you been, then?'

'I'm sorry?'

'Your job. In Africa.'

'Oh. I've been in East Africa, mostly.'

'With the bank?'

He looked confused. 'What bank?'

'I'm sorry, I should have explained. Some years after – after I last saw you,' Ginny said carefully, 'I spoke to someone who'd been at college with you. A friend of a friend. He'd said that you'd joined an international bank after Oxford. So I did know that, but that's all I knew.'

'Oh God, *that* bank.' he laughed, a shout of laughter, like somebody remembering something they had done at a party when they were fifteen and had hoped everybody else had forgotten. 'I did join a bank, yes. Briefly. It was about a year after university. I was tired at the time, the dog's life of an intern, you know.'

163

'No don't know.' Ginny tried not to sound sharp; she smiled to cover her tone.

'Sorry, that was a stupid thing of me to say. I realise—'

'You don't have to tread on eggshells, Barney, I'm interested in what you did. Tell me.'

'It was just, I was a junior doctor in a busy London hospital, not coping well with long hours and sleepless nights. Suddenly the world of international finance seemed easy, well paid and alluring. It was a kind of misadventure. It didn't work out for me, or for them.'

'Oh, I see.'

'So I went back into medicine. Sort of ran back into it, really.'

'Oh.'

'And I've been there ever since.' He nodded to show he'd finished his tale. 'I took work overseas and I've been in Asia then Africa.'

'Whereabouts?'

'Ethiopia. Then most recently the Sudan.' Then he looked stricken again, much as he'd looked when Ginny had first seen him in her mother's living room. Ginny sensed that this was not the time to ask him to talk about his work. She could almost see images dancing across his eyes as he gazed at her. But she was curious to know one thing.

'So you did work for Médecins Sans Frontières?'

'Yes, I did. Then I moved to work for Save the Children. I've been with them a while.'

Ginny raised her eyebrows at him approvingly. 'Well, in that case you did what you set out to do and you must feel very fulfilled. Good on you.'

'I – I wanted to work with children,' he said, then

164

pursed his lips. Ginny felt the emotion emanating from him although he tried to conceal it. He went on, 'It's not—' he stood awkwardly for a moment. 'It's hardly comforting for you to know I've been off fulfilling myself, if that's what you want to call it, when you were. . .when your life changed so that. . .I mean. . .'

'I'm fulfilled, Barney. I'm a mother.'

'And your work? Did you – I mean. . .?'

'Look, if we're going to talk about all this, why don't you sit down and I'll put the kettle on or open this damned bottle of wine? It's hard to have this entire conversation standing up either side of the coffee table. My legs are starting to ache.'

'Actually, I did want to ask you something. Perhaps it might be a way for us to talk without me always being inside your house, invading your territory.'

'I don't feel like that,' Ginny said reasonably, although in truth she did feel somewhat invaded by this tall, curly-haired, leather-smelling man who was, gaunt or not, still very much all man. 'But what did you want to ask me?'

'I wondered perhaps if we could have dinner. Meet somewhere, if you like. It could be local so that you don't have to travel far. I think I'd be more comfortable talking about myself, and you, and Marie in that environment.'

'Well. . .' Ginny considered. For some reason the thought of having dinner with Barney sent a butterfly dancing over her stomach. 'I suppose we could, if you think it's really necessary to go out somewhere.'

'I do, to be honest. Here I feel as if I'm encroaching on Marie. Spying on her, almost, when she's not here. Being in her house, where she lives, without her approval makes me feel a bit uncomfortable. I feel bad enough, really, about looking at all the photos without her knowledge. I'd just like to take a delicate step away from her, to give her a bit more space. I don't know if that makes sense.'

Ginny thought about it and nodded. It was actually something she hadn't thought of; she'd only been relieved that Marie was away from home so that she couldn't complicate matters. Not yet, anyway. It showed, again to her surprise, how sensitive Barney had become, and she found herself liking him for it.

'Yes, Barney, let's have dinner locally somewhere. What about you, where are you staying?'

'I've got a room in a friend's house in London. I can easily get the train or borrow the car and meet you.'

'A friend's house?' She couldn't help probing. Wasn't he married either? She hadn't thought to ask him. He wasn't wearing a wedding ring, now she looked for it, but then men often didn't. He was wearing a plain silver ring on his right hand, but that could have been a present from anyone, or something he fancied himself in (although she thought that seemed less likely; he wasn't the sort of man who would wear jewellery). If Barney did know what her question was angling for, he refused to provide it. Either that or it sailed innocently over his head.

'Yes, an old friend,' he said. 'I can stay there as long as I want so there's no pressure. When are you free to have dinner?'

'Erm. . .' Ginny pretended to think hard. In fact, in terms of evenings and weekends, she was free until the lab's Christmas party dinner way off in the middle of December, but she really didn't want to admit to that.

'How about this Saturday?' he suggested, and a gleam of eagerness was in his eyes. Of course, she realised, he'd be desperate now to ask lots of questions about Marie. Of course he'd want it to be soon.

'Well, in fact, a friend has just cancelled on me for this weekend,' she lied. 'We could make it Saturday.'

'Where would you like to go?'

'Intimate and candle-lit suit you?' She arched an eyebrow at him, then realised she was almost flirting with him. His eyes widened in response and she pulled a straight face immediately. 'I'm joking, Barney. But somewhere quiet would probably be good so that we can talk.'

She told him about a small pizza and pasta restaurant on a side-street not far from the station and they agreed to meet there at eight o'clock on Saturday.

'Do you want to keep the photos until then? You could make a note of which ones you'd like copies of and I'll see what I can do, that's if we've still got the negatives.'

'It's all right, I've already put a note to you inside the album. I'll be off now, Ginny.'

'Are you getting the train home? At least let me give you a lift to the station. It's getting colder by the minute out there.'

'Oh no, it's fine. I borrowed my friend's car this evening.'

'You did? That's good of him.'

'She doesn't use it much. People in London either tube or bus it or walk everywhere, don't they?'

'Hmm? Yes,' Ginny answered casually, having clocked the *she* that she'd been fishing for and finding herself, as she let him out and he sprang off with a set of car keys in his hand, wondering who this old friend was and whether Barney was romantically involved with her.

Before she went to bed, she sat with her glass of wine and read the note Barney had written her.

Dear Ginny,

Once again I can't thank you enough for welcoming me so warmly into your home and allowing me to see these photographs. It is far and above what I expected.

I have listed separately the photographs that I would like, if at all possible, to have copies of. I can arrange the processing. If this isn't possible I'll understand.

I found seeing Marie's life through film a profound experience. She is much as I had imagined her in some ways, and in other ways so completely different. She is, as you told me, a very beautiful girl and I can only imagine how talented. Her vivacity shines through. She is lucky to have inherited so many traits from her mother.

With kind regards,
Barney

Ginny read the note through again several times before she let it fall gently on to her lap. She drank her wine slowly.

'You damned charmer,' she uttered to herself.

Chapter Nineteen

❦

'It's so good to see you, Charlotte,' Harry said, flashing his daughter a broad grin. 'And congratulations on your news. You really do look well. Motherhood suits you, but I always thought it would.'

'Well, thanks, Dad,' Charlotte said a little stiffly. She couldn't help seeing the signs of expensive dental work when he grinned at her and she couldn't respond to the warmth of his welcome. Not yet. 'I do feel like I'm having an affair with my own father, having to arrange a meeting in a restaurant.'

'Denise would like to meet you but I guessed now wouldn't be the best time.'

'No, I don't think now would have been the right time,' Charlotte agreed with some edge. 'I haven't seen you myself for a couple of years and it's probably a good idea if we get to know each other again first before I meet your new girlfriend.'

They were meeting in Pizza Express, on a weekday lunchtime. As a youthful waiter was hovering, determined to take their drinks order, Harry ordered a lager and Charlotte a lime and soda before he loped away.

'I suppose we'd better decide what to have. He'll be back in a minute.'

Charlotte peered at her dad from behind her menu. He was tanned, she noted, and he looked well. She was surprised by the crisp mint-green shirt he was wearing, and the fashionable chinos. They were new. He looked younger, that much was true. His hair was brushed differently, more straight than across, as he used to have it. Then Harry leant back in his chair and assessed Charlotte's expression carefully.

'Am I going to get a rerun of my meeting with Ginny?'

'I have no idea, Dad. I don't know what she said to you.'

'That I'm a selfish bastard who's abandoned your mother, basically.'

Charlotte was surprised. Every impression she'd had from Ginny had been that this was a situation she was at ease with, as if Ginny knew some secret or had some underlying insight into the reasons for Harry's departure, something that made it all make sense. She'd had no idea that Ginny had railed at him for leaving. She had been about to do exactly that, but it made her rethink.

'Well, aren't you?' she quizzed him, trying not to sound too judgemental. If Ginny had been the accusatory one, perhaps she could be the understanding one. It might give her a role.

'What do you think, Charlotte? I want your opinion. You, of all people, should have a view on this.'

'Why me?' She was flattered. Did he really think her opinion mattered?

'Because you've been out there, you've done something different with your life. You took the road less travelled by.'

'It's true that I've done that. But you never approved of me.'

170

'Yes, I did, actually.'

'You never said so.'

'There was no need. You were going to do it anyway. You were always strong willed. When you were a child you always went off to do your own thing. I remember you climbing over the garden gate and racing off down the road. We kept bringing you back and you kept climbing over that gate. You must have been about two years old. You had wanderlust and you had it really bad.'

'I know. I've never been able to control it. But I had no idea you understood any of that. I thought you thought I was a dangerous maverick who'd gone off the rails and had to be patiently tolerated until I somehow got better and came home.'

Harry quirked his bushy eyebrows. There was humour in his brown eyes. 'I didn't think you were ill. But you see, we do have a lot in common. I always thought we did.'

'How?' Charlotte flushed. The drinks arrived and she sipped her lime and soda through a straw. Did her dad really think they had a bond? Perhaps they had, and she'd just never realised it.

'I think everyone's waiting for me to get better and go home. But I don't think I am going to go home, Charlotte, you may as well know that straight away. Even saying that, I remind myself of you when we used to take you to feed the swans on the river. You hated to be told it was over. You used to say "I'm not coming home and that's that."'

'Why all the reminiscing, Dad?' Charlotte frowned. Then Harry put his hands over his eyes and she could see that he was silently crying.

171

'Oh dear God, I'm so sorry.' He heaved.

'Hush.' She took one of his hands and held it firmly. 'Shh, Dad, people are looking.' In fact, there were more waiters than customers in the restaurant at that moment and Charlotte was annoyed with herself for sounding so starchy. What did it matter if somebody else saw her father cry? What mattered was that she didn't want to see him cry.

'I don't care who sees me.' There was a sob in his voice. 'Ever since you rang I've been dreading this, knowing you're going to launch an attack on me like Ginny did. It was like being nuked. She thought I had all the answers, but I just came away feeling like a beaten-up dog. And all I can think about are my two beautiful little girls, my daughters, when they were children. Oh, it breaks me up.' He clutched a hand to his chest. 'I can't get these images out of my head. It's like an endless loop of cine film with you two running towards me, hands waving, arms outstretched, calling "Daddy, Daddy, come and see what we're doing!" But then I wake up from it and you're not there. Neither of you. Instead there are two self-sufficient women who don't need me any more. One of them never even needed to visit me. Not even to send me postcards or ring me up once in a blue moon.'

'That's me, of course.' Charlotte felt very uncomfortable.

'I am sorry.' Harry cleared his throat loudly and wiped his napkin over his face. He took a large sip from his cold beer, his fingers slipping on the wet glass. 'I'm all right now. Sometimes I just find it all overwhelming. People think that the person who leaves runs off into the night laughing and dancing.

They have no idea that sometimes it's harder to leave than be the one who's left. If you leave you will never, ever get any sympathy for it. Everybody will accuse you. Everybody will support the person who's been left. If they want they can just shrug their shoulders and claim they don't know why you went, so you have to give all the answers. It's not fair, when the decision is mutual. It isn't fair for people to think you have answers when you don't.'

Charlotte put her menu down and stared at her father. She knew how hard it was to leave. But she'd never heard him so eloquent. 'I had no idea you felt like this, Dad.'

'It's been hard, Charlotte. I'm not asking for your sympathy but just believe me when I tell you that leaving somebody you love is the hardest thing in the world to do.'

'Oh yes,' Charlotte whispered, almost to herself. 'I know that much.'

'Denise had nothing to do with it. She was just a catalyst. Your mother and I haven't been good together for many years, you know. Perhaps if it hadn't been for Denise we'd have even staggered on a few more years until we fell into our graves, neatly laid out side by side, fifty or sixty years of marriage carved out on our gravestones. It would have looked better that way. We'd have been remembered as a devoted couple. But we weren't devoted, we haven't been for a long time.'

'But I hadn't noticed anything. I feel so stupid.'

'You haven't been at home, Charlotte. You haven't even been in the country.'

'I thought you weren't angry with me for that.'

173

'I'm not. I'm just stating a fact to you. You can't expect to have seen any signs of our marriage being unhappy.'

'No, I know, and I'm sorry about that.'

'God, what difference does it make?' Harry seemed exasperated with himself. 'Even if you had been here, you may not have noticed anything. Ginny didn't. She was too preoccupied with her own life, with Marie.'

Charlotte glanced up again, curious. So Ginny was as surprised as she was, was she? Why couldn't she have said so? Why did she have to pretend to be the one who knew everything, to make Charlotte feel like the outsider who'd walked in at the end of the play, someone it wasn't worth explaining the plot to, because it was nearly over anyway. In fact, Ginny hadn't understood the plot herself. Couldn't she just have been honest about it?

'Well I'm listening, Dad.'

'You've got enough on your plate now, Charlotte. Look at you. You're about ready to pop. We should talk about you instead.' He took a shaky sip of his drink. 'Are you happy?'

Charlotte laughed, the question was shot at her so suddenly. 'It's a bit more complicated than that.'

'Is it? Is it really?'

'Are *you* happy, Dad? Can you give me a simple yes or no?'

He shook his head. 'When I'm with Denise, I'm happy. When we were in Portugal I was happy. When I'm not talking to you or Ginny, or thinking about the past and filled to the brim with regrets, I'm happy.'

'Well I guess it's a bit similar for me. When I think about the baby, I feel incredibly happy. I feel scared, too.' She was amazed at how easily that confession came out to her father. Even in his tearful state she had the instinct of the daughter who knew she would be protected by him.

'Well I'm sure birth is pretty scary. I'm glad it's something I've never had to go through. But women do make it and then they do it again, so it can't be that bad.'

'Either that or you just forget how bad it was. That's what Polly was saying – she's one of the women I know from an ante-natal relaxation class. We were talking about pain the other day. It's great in theory, you always think you can withstand anything. But it's like a big wall between me and the baby. I can't see the other side of the birth at the moment.'

Harry nodded wisely, although Charlotte wasn't convinced he was really following her thread. 'Yes. Ginny had a difficult birth, but she came through it.'

'Was it difficult? You know, I can't remember anything about it. I think I only got a sketchy account.'

'You weren't interested in babies then.' Harry smiled indulgently. 'And we did try to protect you from too many gory details. I remember you coming home from university in your holidays and holding Marie. You couldn't wait to give her back to Ginny.'

'Oh don't say that.' Charlotte swallowed a mouthful of lime and soda and it tasted acidic. 'I'm trying to persuade myself I'll be a good mother.'

'Of course you will, now. You were very young then and your mind was miles away. You said to Ginny "Rather you than me." I think it upset her at the time that you didn't show any interest, but it takes all sorts, and she wasn't your baby. That makes all the difference.'

'I hope so.'

As the waiter returned they gave their food orders. Charlotte ordered the biggest pizza on the menu, with garlic bread. She was just so hungry, all the time, that she then decided to order a starter as well.

'Eating for two?' the waiter quipped in an awkward attempt at flippancy.

'No, just trapped wind.' Charlotte indicated her stomach and he laughed lightly and thankfully left them again.

'So, about the father,' Harry leapt in after the waiter was out of earshot.

'Oh, don't ask me, Dad. Please don't.' Charlotte rubbed her eyes tiredly. 'It's not easy to explain.'

'I've got all day. I'm retired, as you know, a man of leisure now, and I want to talk to you. As you said, we need to get to know each other again.'

Or, perhaps, Charlotte could have added, they never really had known each other. She gazed at her father's curious face, his kind eyes. Would now be a good time to try to bridge that gap, to make a start on a relationship that actually meant something to both of them? She sighed.

'It's a long story, Dad.'

'Have you told your mum, or Ginny?'

'I've told Mum bits and pieces. Ginny and I aren't – let's say we're not communicating very well at the moment.' To her relief he didn't pursue that, but let it lie with a nod. 'So, no, I haven't really told anybody the whole story. I haven't told anybody the truth.'

Harry lifted his beer to her lime and soda; they clinked glasses. 'Here's to being completely honest with your old dad.'

Chapter Twenty

It was Saturday and Ginny wondered why she was taking so much time to get ready. At six o'clock she'd run the bath. An hour later she was carefully putting make-up on and had several combinations of clothes laid out on the bed so that she could think about them as she flitted from the bathroom to the bedroom and decide what to wear. Then Jane phoned, and she was annoyed to be interrupted, especially as Jane wanted to have a good talk about Charlotte, who it seemed had gone off to meet up with some women from the ante-natal group she'd joined.

'Well it's great that she's joined a group, at last. Good of her to admit that she actually needs someone else.'

'Yes,' Jane replied rather fiercely. 'It is good, so there's no need to turn it into an excuse to have a dig at her, Ginny.'

'I'm not!'

'Anyway, I want to talk to you properly. Is now a good time?'

'Actually,' Ginny said awkwardly, trying not to get the foundation from her fingers all over the handset of the phone, 'I'm just going out.'

'Oh.' Jane was surprised. 'That's nice.' There was a long pause. 'Meeting Rebecca, are you?'

'No.'

'Oh.'

It was Ginny's turn to feel exasperated. 'No, Mum, I'm actually meeting Barney.'

'Oh!' Now Ginny could imagine Jane sitting bolt upright, all attention. She still hadn't forgotten Jane's advice to her to, well, in essence, do exactly what she was doing. And nobody liked to feel that they had been following somebody's advice to the letter when in fact they were acting independently. Especially when that advice came from their mum. 'Oh, that's interesting. So he contacted you again after he came round.'

'Yes, he did.'

'That's good.' There was another long pause. 'You don't want to talk to me about it, then?'

'Not at the moment, Mum.' Ginny felt mean. She knew it was a sea-change in her feelings towards discussing things with her mother, and she guessed Jane would feel a bit rebuffed. But somehow she'd gone beyond wanting to have a giggle about Barney on the phone with her mum. She wanted to pursue things privately for a while. Perhaps she'd talk about it later, when she had a better idea herself of how she felt. 'There really isn't anything to say. I'm meeting him for dinner—'

'Dinner?'

'At a restaurant in town, then he's going home. We're going to talk about Marie.'

'In a restaurant? A nice one?'

Jane was impressed when Ginny told her where they were meeting. 'It sounds very intimate. I think it's quite dark in there. It always looks dark from the outside.'

179

Ginny tutted. 'As long as we can see the menus I'm sure it'll be light enough.'

'You know, in retrospect, I had forgotten how good looking he was,' Jane mused, as if she was talking to herself.

'Well, I hadn't, Mum.'

'Yes, very manly. A bit on the thin side, but that's just temporary, I think. I'd say he's been overworked and hasn't been eating properly. But the essence of a man is always there, like an aura. He has got nice hair, I have to say. I always did like men with curly hair. And he doesn't seem to be greying much.'

'Any more observations?'

'He's sort of Harrison Ford-ish. Don't you think?'

'He's nothing like Harrison Ford.' Ginny rolled her eyes at the ceiling. 'Anything else?'

'Yes, he seemed a lot nicer than he used to be. I know it sounds strange to say this, but he struck me as a kind man. I didn't get that feeling about him before.'

'Well you hardly saw him before. Only that time you came up to college to talk to us both, right at the start when I was panicking, and he only stayed five minutes.'

'Exactly. He was obsessed with himself then. I remember thinking, what a selfish young man. But I don't think he's selfish any more. Whatever he's been doing with his life, it's obviously been good for him.'

'He's been working for charities, as a doctor. He told you that, surely?'

'Oh, yes.' Jane sounded as if she was feigning vagueness. 'Yes, that's right. I think it was Save the Children. No doubt that will have changed him quite profoundly. Yes, I've been thinking a lot about it in the last few days. I think he's a much nicer man than he ever was.'

Ginny jammed her teeth together to stop herself from agreeing. The last thing she wanted just before she went out and met Barney again was to feel too warm about him. It was inappropriate. He had his own life, she had hers. Perhaps they would cross somewhere in the middle now, like two great ovals in a Venn diagram with a little area that overlapped, hatched and labelled 'Marie'.

'It does seem a shame about his wife.'

Ginny blinked, and tried to stop her lashes, laden with a new mascara she'd bought that afternoon, from sticking. 'What wife?'

'Just something he said, but I can't really remember the details now. Well, he'll tell you all about it, no doubt.'

'Hang on, Mum.' Ginny gripped the phone. 'You can't just casually throw these lines into the conversation and expect me not to bite.'

'Oh, it's not my story, dear, you'll have to ask him yourself.'

'I am hardly going to walk into the restaurant and start grilling him about his marital status.'

'So he hasn't told you then?'

'And when exactly did he share all the intimate details of his life with you?'

'When he was here, that morning, of course. I was here with him for nearly an hour. What do you think we talked about?'

'Crete!'

'Yes, I did show him the holiday album, but there's only so much you can say about Knossos. And he

181

asked me if you were married, of course. That's only natural. He must have been wondering if some great big bloke was going to walk in and punch him in the face on your behalf.'

'So of course you told him I'd never married and had very few boyfriends.' Ginny sank on to the corner of her bed, depressed.

'No, of course not! Oh, maybe if he'd been a different kind of man. . . I don't know. . .but I made it clear to him that you'd had lots of offers, you were just very choosy. He seemed very surprised that you'd never married, and so he should be. Lovely girl like you.'

'Oh my God, I don't think I want to hear any more. You had no right, Mum. It's all so embarrassing. I can't believe you talked about me to him.'

'I just made him think a bit about what he'd given up. That's all. I didn't do anything wrong. I think you'd have been proud of me.'

'Mum, let's get something completely clear. This is not a date. I am only meeting Barney to talk about our daughter.'

'But he's not married,' Jane peeped like an insistent little bird tugging at a worm. 'And neither are you.'

'So what are you saying?' Ginny gaped in shock, then nearly shouted her disbelief. 'That I should marry him?'

'Well. . .'

'Mother! What planet are you on? Go and have a cold shower or a large gin or whatever it takes and think about what you're saying to me. You are completely crackers if you think I'm going to take up with Barney again.'

'But when you came into the room that morning, I

182

thought there was something there. A little, I don't know what, a chemistry.'

Ginny stared, aghast, at her reflection in her bedroom mirror. If she'd looked a bit pink when she'd put her blusher on, she looked like a strawberry now. 'There is no chemistry between us!' she asserted. 'It's all about Marie!'

'But all the same, he is a bit special. I mean, if you forget the past, and I don't think that's entirely been his fault either, he's quite a hunk. Don't you think so?'

'I can't talk to you. I've got to get dressed and go. Just – just clear your mind of all this lunacy and I'll call you tomorrow.'

But thanks to her mother, when Ginny walked into the restaurant at eight o'clock that evening to find Barney waiting at the bar for her, there were three words that leapt into her mind. The first was 'hunk'. When she'd rejected that one, forcing a smile as she joined him at the bar, the second two words to crash in on her thoughts were 'Harrison' and 'Ford'. She pushed those away, too, forcing a grin so wide he must have been wondering if she'd taken a pill before she'd left the house. (In fact, she'd had a glass of wine, deciding therefore to take a taxi in as she'd probably drink with the meal too, but that didn't justify the false jollity plastered over her face.)

He looked nice, she noticed, as she slid on to a bar stool next to him. He was casual in fawn denims and a lightly clinging black polo shirt. Perhaps he'd been shopping – although the trousers looked fairly worn-in.

'It's a nice restaurant. It's busy tonight.' He nodded

over his shoulder. 'Our table's currently occupied, but it'll be ready in ten minutes, they said. Would you like something to drink here?'

'Thanks. Just a white wine, please.'

He ordered it for her from an efficient waitress then turned back to appraise her with an unreadable expression. 'You look nice, Ginny.'

'Thank you.'

'Do you mind me saying that?'

She pretended to be preoccupied with the clasp of her handbag and then with hooking it over her shoulder. 'No, not at all. It's always busy in here on Saturdays, but once you're at the table it does seem very private. They're all well spaced from each other.'

'Yes, as I see.'

So his casual compliment managed to be swallowed between ordinary observations, like a sandwich filling, and yet Ginny found it gave her a boost. She had taken care with her appearance. She'd fluffed up her fine hair and sprayed it into place. She'd put a bit more make-up on than usual (after all, as Jane had pointed out, it was quite dark in the restaurant, most of the tables being candle-lit or illuminated with soft wall lamps), and she was wearing a soft crossover top that showed her curves and a loose skirt that swung sensually around her calves. She was wearing heels, too, something she didn't do too often these days.

Her wine arrived on a tray and Barney took it and handed it to her just as she was about to reach out and take it for herself. She accepted the glass with a gracious smile.

'Thank you, Barney. Always the perfect gentleman.'

He half laughed to himself. 'Do you know, over all

these years the one thing I remembered about you was your ability to cut me down to size.'

'What do you mean?'

'Just with a look or a sharp remark. It was always as if you could see right through me. You can still do it.'

Ginny opened her eyes wide at him. Her cheeks felt warm and probably her pupils were dilated, as much through the ever-present flutter of nerves as anything, but whatever happened in that moment they ended up staring at each other, deep into each other's eyes. It was just a fleeting moment, then the waitress jumped up again.

'Your table's ready, sir, if you'd like to follow me.'

They settled themselves at a table right in the back corner of the restaurant. They took menus and sipped at their drinks. The waitress lit the candle at the table, and the cutlery gleamed in the glow. Ginny gazed at her menu for some time without reading anything on it. She was still disconcerted by the look they'd given each other at the bar. Was it just her, or had there been a sexual frisson between them? If it wasn't just her, what should she do about it? It had to be squashed, and quickly. After all, if her mother was right and if they were both unattached at that moment, just being in the presence of each other was enough to spark curiosity, intimacy, perhaps even the comfort of a link with the past, something that in a perverse way could suggest a familiarity that bypassed the proper norms of meeting somebody new in these circumstances. It could suggest a reunion, especially in the absence of Marie. It could suggest a sexual reunion. They were adults, after all. They were only human. And Marie, the one person who brought them together but at the same time held them apart, was on the other side of the world.

It had to be squashed. Ginny heard Barney clear his throat self-consciously as he flicked through the pages of the menu. He had felt it too. She suddenly knew it, and she knew that he felt as tantalisingly challenged by her presence as she felt by his. She knew that in that moment at the bar they had unwittingly aroused each other's sexual curiosity. It was fleeting, it was inappropriate beyond words, Marie would die, she would die, it could never, ever happen. Once was a misfortune, twice would be more than carelessness, it would be suicide, for her self-esteem and for her role as a good mother to her daughter. She could not, must not, sleep with Barney ever again, and yet she knew with a growing sense of alarm that they had both felt something in the air, something that could, given a good meal and a bottle of wine, lead in that direction.

She had to do something, and quickly, to save them from themselves.

'So.' She picked up her glass and held it out to him. 'Cheers again, Barney. Let's hope your girlfriend's as understanding as my boyfriend is about this.'

And he just nodded, agreeing with ease to her casual statement. 'I guess we're both lucky to have partners who understand we're in quite an unusual situation.'

'Yes,' she said faintly. 'It's what I've been thinking all along.'

'Good.' He smiled an easier smile, just as her stomach knotted. 'So, what are you going to have?'

186

Chapter Twenty-one

They talked about Marie and it seemed to Ginny that a couple of hours passed in a flash. She had to admit that Barney was good company. He listened to what she said, he asked a lot of questions and gave suitably fascinated replies. Although he was affable throughout she often saw a flicker of discomfort cross his face, of pain or regret perhaps. Eventually he asked the question she'd been anticipating.

'Do you think Marie would like to meet me?'

Ginny turned her glass around, playing with the stem. Their plates had been cleared away and coffee was coming. Now she felt a surge of protectiveness for her daughter. 'I really don't know. It's possible. I think you'll have to ask her yourself. As I've told you, she's very mature and very capable of voicing her feelings.'

He played with a leftover dessert fork, concentrating on the prongs glowing in the candlelight. 'Would you mind if I asked you what she knows about me?'

'She knows the truth. I've never embellished it and I've never put an angle on it, positive or negative.'

He glanced up at her, disconcerting her again with that straight, clear-eyed gaze. 'What do you think the truth is?'

Ginny took a deep breath, allowing herself half a

smile. 'We were young, it was impulsive, you weren't ready for fatherhood.'

'You weren't ready for motherhood but it didn't stop you.'

'That's true.'

'So she must conclude that I was pretty selfish to abandon you.'

Ginny hesitated. It probably was Marie's conclusion, but she had lived her life without any knowledge of her father, so her feelings were weak towards him, to say the least. 'You have to remember that as far as she's aware there's never been any interest from your side. That means she's never expected to meet you. It may sound strange, but I don't think she's given you much thought, especially as she's grown older.'

'No, it doesn't sound strange,' he replied quietly, his lips straight and humourless. 'Does she know you attempted to contact me? That you sent photographs?'

'No. I didn't raise her expectations. It wouldn't have been fair.'

The coffee arrived and Ginny sipped her latte. Barney flicked through the drinks menu, which was still lying on the tablecloth. 'I'd like a shot of something, will you join me?'

Ginny considered. She wasn't driving, she felt relaxed, it would help them over a tricky part of the conversation. Or, perhaps, after the niceties were over with, it would all be tricky from now on. 'Go on then. I'll have a brandy.'

He ordered then scrutinised Ginny again. 'I've been going through my mother's things. Not a pleasant job.'

Ginny frowned at him. 'Why? Where is she?'

'She died this year.'

'Oh, I'm sorry,' Ginny said out of good manners. In fact, she couldn't be sorry. She'd thought his mother was a complete nightmare.

'We didn't have much of a relationship, especially in later years. She was a difficult woman, as you know.'

'Yes, I have to say my meeting with her at my parents' house was pretty dire. But it was under unusual circumstances.'

'Fair of you to say so. I was always closer to my dad, that's when I could get close to him. My mother had an ability to stymie things. I'm not even sure she knew she was doing it, but that included relationships and, well,' he shook his head, 'all kinds of things have her fingerprints on them. Anyway, he's on his own now and this is the first time I've been back since the funeral to sort things out.'

'You're not staying with him?'

'No, we're both too old for that, but I'm just up the road, in terms of London. I'd rather be staying with my – girlfriend – anyway, at this time.'

Ginny nodded her eager agreement. So he really did have a girlfriend. Of course he would have one.

'Anyway,' he went on, frowning, 'I found your letters and your photographs in a box tucked right at the back of one of her old wardrobes in the spare room. After we last spoke I went hunting for them, I have to say; practically turned the house upside down. But I think I can say, if I try to find one kind thing to say about my mother's actions, that she did keep them and that tells me that she must have had at least some doubt in her mind about what she was doing. Perhaps she thought that one day she'd show them to me. Perhaps she'd even have done it soon. I'd like to try to give her the benefit of the doubt. It's hard, but I'm trying. She can't defend herself now.'

'No, of course.' Ginny tried to look understanding. The subject of the missing letters and photographs made her blood boil and she took a deep breath to let the anger subside again. Who had this woman thought she was? And she couldn't help saying, 'But she had no right, Barney.'

'I know,' he said softly. 'And it makes me very sad.'

'What about your father? Couldn't he have told you I'd stayed in touch?'

'He knew nothing about your attempts to get in touch. All the information he had was from my mother. I'm afraid she might have even been delusional, the things he told me, things she told us both that it seems now were completely invented. She'd managed to convince him that it was your family who'd forbidden me to ever go near you again, that there'd even been threats.'

'What?' Ginny was aghast.

'All nonsense. He was as shocked as I was to go through the box with your letters in. Especially the early letters and photographs, when Marie was just . . .' He cleared his throat and rubbed his eyes. 'I'm sorry. My dad and I were both very moved, that's all I can say without dancing on my mum's grave here. I don't think either of us had thought she would have been capable of deception on such a grand scale. I had no idea what she'd been doing. Dad told me he has always wanted to know what happened to Marie. Became quite obsessed by it, he says, but all that was bottled up inside him. My mother stamped on any questions from him, so he'd assumed he'd never meet his granddaughter. Anyway, you're a sensitive woman. I think you can imagine how we both felt to find all the things you'd painstakingly sent us over the years. It was – what can I say? A huge thing for both of us.'

The brandy arrived and Ginny noted that they both grabbed their glasses and took a large swig. Emotions were definitely running higher now. Barney was clearly agitated, scratching at his ear and shifting in his chair, picking up the fork again to fidget with it. He must have been astounded to find out that his mother had lied to him all his adult life, and she felt a niggle of sympathy for him.

'Your mother must have adored you,' she told him, trying to see it through a parent's eyes. 'She was trying to protect you.'

'Don't make excuses for her.' He snapped the fork back on to the table suddenly. 'As I said, I hope she was about to put things right but that she just ran out of time. She had cancer, steadily progressing, but it suddenly overtook her. Maybe she was planning a confession. But it was so quick, in the end. By the time I got back to England she was unconscious.'

'I'm so sorry, Barney. It sounds awful'

'Oh, this was six months ago. After the funeral I had to go abroad again, back to work, to tie up loose ends before I could really get away and come and sort it all out with Dad. But I'm back now and maybe at last it's all falling into place. There were so many things that didn't make sense before.'

There was a pause as they sipped their drinks and were lost in their own thoughts. Then he seemed suddenly to answer the question that had been on her mind for days now. 'And I haven't explained the most important thing to you properly – you must be asking yourself, why now? You must have been wondering why I needed to go through my mother to get in touch with you, especially as I managed to find your family address. Why couldn't I have done that before? Well, my mother told me you'd married and moved away. To another country, she said, to start afresh somewhere else. That doesn't excuse everything, but it did mean I felt you'd built a new life. I knew I'd have to go through your parents to try to contact you and I'd been told it was the last thing you wanted. I didn't want to force my attention on you, on Marie.'

'I see. It makes a kind of sense.' Ginny accepted his explanation although inwardly she shuddered, especially at the blatant lie his mother had told about her marrying. She found herself pitying her; she must have been very insecure about her son to shroud herself in so much fiction.

'Then when I knew Marie was eighteen I felt I had more of a right to do something. At least then she was an adult and I could try to contact her directly. I felt she'd be capable of telling me to sod off if she wanted to, but I hoped she'd also be mature enough to give my approach some reasonable thought.'

'Oh yes, either of those things is possible.' Ginny couldn't help a smile as the ache of missing Marie rose in her stomach again. 'How did you know when her birthday was?'

'My mother had told me, way back, that your parents had given her formal details of the birth. She must have got it all from your first letters. Just after Marie was born she gave me a date of birth and a name. That's all I knew. Any other questions I asked my mother were deflected. She made it sound as if she was in touch with your parents, as if they'd all reached an understanding of a sort, which was, in essence, that I was to stay clear of you and let you build a life without my interference. I was too young and stupid to argue with it, at first. Then as the years went on, as I became more and more concerned about not having done the right thing, I felt paralysed with indecision. What if you'd told Marie that your new husband was her real father? What if I turned up and wrecked her secure life? Was it selfish of me to want to get to know her, when as a kid I'd accepted my mother's explanations, let her be a buffer? I let it go on and on, and it turned me inside out. But, well, as you can see, here I am, trying to do something now.'

'And what is it you really want to *do*?' Ginny asked him, hoping her question sounded friendly and open. 'Have you thought that far ahead?'

'I don't know.' He shook his head, confused. 'I really don't know. I guess to take my lead from Marie.'

Ginny watched him bite his lip, his cheeks sucked in with the effort not to show the emotion he was feeling. Was it possible for a father to be so convinced that his attention was unwanted that he could stay away from his own daughter for eighteen years? Even in a time when communication was easier than it had ever been? Perhaps, she decided. If somebody worked on you, fed your fears, gave rise to insecurities and nourished them, told you lies and backed them up. If that source of misinformation was somebody you cared about, somebody whose word you trusted, it could be possible. She ruminated further, finishing her coffee.

193

'Did you never marry, Barney?' She found herself wondering if a wife would have wanted to know about an illegitimate child floating around out there somewhere. Or if he would have come clean. 'If you don't mind me asking.'

'I did marry, yes, Ginny.' He looked at his empty glass as if at this moment in time he had need of another one. Then he eyed her squarely. 'It wasn't a happy marriage. It didn't work. My wife left. I don't think there's any need for you to express polite regret about that.' He gave a sardonic smile. 'No need to say anything at all. It was over more than four years ago.'

'Were there . . .' she probed tentatively, then stopped.

'There weren't any children,' he answered firmly. Then he elaborated. 'In some ways I've been living with the ghost of Marie for all these years, of the child I never knew. Of that child's mother. Unresolved events, unfinished business.'

'Unstarted business.' Ginny raised her eyebrows.

'Yes, that's true. I've imagined Marie so many times, had so many dreams, nightmares, visions of her. Of you now, married again as I thought, with other children, in a family where I was blotted out. I've had a recurrent dream for eighteen years, can you believe it, of the last time I saw you, walking away. For eighteen years it wouldn't go away.' He swallowed painfully, and she could see tears in his eyes. 'I know it must have been so hard for you so please don't even think I'm comparing our experiences, but I do want you to know that I've almost gone crazy over the years. I can't tell you how good it is to see you.'

Ginny's hand had been resting on the table. She was

taken aback when he reached out and put his hand over hers. She snatched her fingers away quickly.

'Don't, Barney.'

'I didn't mean to startle you. God, Ginny, I'm such an idiot' He dashed tears away from his eyes with the back of his hand. 'I just can't tell you how good it is to see this ghost as a real, live, warm person. As someone who can talk to me, who can see me, who even smiles at me. Who will share Marie with me. The little girl who was hidden from me.'

Ginny felt tears rising in her throat, too. Whatever she had imagined his life to be like away from all the duty and responsibility of raising a daughter, she hadn't pictured anything like this relentless self-questioning, the intense pain of separation that he had endured over the years. And his intensity towards her, the looks, the sudden grabbing of the hand; this was all about Marie, about trying to reach out to a link with his daughter. It made sense. She shouldn't have snapped at him.

'You'll have to contact Marie, when she comes home,' she told him, holding his gaze as warmly as she could without being intimate.

'I will. I'll do everything properly and it'll be up to her.' He seemed resolved, sitting up straighter now, a curl falling over one eyebrow and reminding her of his attractiveness. 'In the meantime, you've given me the greatest gift anyone could possibly have given me. For the first time in my adult life I can feel hope.'

'It is only hope,' she said cautiously. 'Marie is a law unto herself. I don't want you to be devastated if she decides not to see you.'

He nodded, lost in thought again. Then he said, 'But

195

you saw me, Ginny, and I never thought you would. It does give me reason to believe.'

They parted company outside the restaurant. Ginny's taxi had arrived and was parked a little further down the street. The wind ruffled Barney's hair as he huddled into his jacket and put out a hand to say goodbye.

'Thanks so much for tonight, Ginny. It's been great. I can't tell you how much it's meant to me.'

She could see, had been able to see all evening, just how much it meant. It had taken her by surprise. She'd been forced to review a lot of her preconceptions – most of them in fact. 'It's been a pleasure. I enjoyed myself, actually.'

'You sound surprised.' He raised an eyebrow.

She laughed. 'Yes, I am surprised.'

'Brutally honest, but fair.'

'And you know your way home?' she teased, sounding like a mother.

'Home.' He pondered the word. 'Yes, I know my way.'

'You know,' she considered carefully, 'it's going to be a while before Marie comes back. Maybe even months. You are ready for that, aren't you?'

'Of course. And I think you're right, it is just as well I haven't jumped right in and startled both of you at the same time. It'll give me a chance to think of a way of approaching this delicately.'

'It'll give you time to think about the possible outcomes, too,' Ginny advised cautiously. Strangely, having seen so much of this man's soul over the evening, she didn't want him to be hurt. She found herself hoping that Marie would want to meet him.

'I was going to ask you a favour,' he began hesitantly.

'Shoot.'

'It's just – it's been so many years, such a desert, without any information. I was wondering maybe if I could see you again. To talk like this.'

'Well. . .' Ginny shifted in a stiff blast of wind. She was only too aware of how handsome Barney was. Her mother, annoyingly, had been right. He wasn't better looking than he used to be, he'd always been a gorgeous man, but he was much nicer, and when you combined his personality with his sex appeal, it all made for a fairly potent package. Even just one more evening in his company had made her aware of him in a personal sense, as a woman reacts to a man whom she can't help being attracted to. It was fairly dangerous terrain and she'd have to be very careful indeed not to trip up. But was it fair for her to shy away from meeting up with him just because she didn't want to acknowledge that she was attracted to him? His eyes were searching her face eagerly. 'Yes, we could meet,' she hedged.

'It brings me closer to her. Makes her seem real. I need to know more about her, it's like a hunger. I wish you could understand.'

'Well, if you'd arrived at any other time in my life it might have been harder. But she's gone away from me, for the first time ever, and I miss her like hell. It's like a disease that I won't recover from until she's home. I have some sympathy with that ache of missing someone so badly. I know it's not the same, but it gives me a bit of insight into how you feel. Of course we can meet. It's not a problem at all.'

Barney's tone was instantly brighter. 'But I don't want to cause any problems for you.'

'Oh, it won't really.'

'With your boyfriend, I mean.'

'Oh, don't worry about him.' Ginny faked a laugh. 'He's very easygoing. He'll understand. And it's not as if there's anything between us, is it, Barney? That really would be absurd.'

'Yes, wouldn't it,' he said in a lowered voice, and took a step towards her. In a second, so quick that she thought she'd imagined it, he touched her cold cheek with his fingertip. Then he took her hand again and raised it to his lips, kissing the skin gently.

A shiver ran along her skin, up her arm and into her body. Her stomach tightened. Her breath came out as a whisper. 'Barney. . .'

He took her face in his hands and kissed her lips softly. It was so quick, she might have imagined it.

Her mouth was still burning, her spirits thrown up in the air and down again, and he'd already moved away, dropped her hand and turned up his collar ready to leave. 'I'll miss my train if I don't hurry. Let's talk next week.'

She stared after him as he walked away, then quickly recovered herself and dived into her taxi. The driver chatted to her on the way home but she couldn't concentrate on a word he was saying. She was touching her lips, feeling the skin that Barney's lips had brushed, shocked by the frisson that was running up and down her body.

She really couldn't deny it any longer. Whatever

logic she tried to impose on the situation, her body was speaking for itself. She was still overwhelmingly attracted to Barney. She could only be incredibly grateful that he didn't feel the same way about her.

Chapter Twenty-two

'What on earth did you say to your father when you met him?'

Charlotte was confronted by Jane when she drifted downstairs in a T-shirt and dressing gown at breakfast time on Sunday morning. The baby had woken her up with a session of frenetic kicking, and she was starving. But Jane's demeanour put her on her guard, and she found her pulse stuttering defensively. Of course, she'd told Jane she was meeting Harry, but she hadn't told her how the meeting had gone, and Jane hadn't asked.

'Nothing, why?' she asked nervously as she put the kettle on, grabbed a loaf and put two slices in the toaster.

Jane seemed very uneasy. She was turning a coffee cup round and round and she looked preoccupied. 'He wants to meet me. To talk.'

Charlotte raised her eyebrows and couldn't help a sneaky smile as she buttered her toast. 'He does? That's great.'

'Why do you think that's a good thing? We've done all the talking we need to do. I don't want to go over it again and again. I want us both to move on!'

'But, Mum,' Charlotte took her plate and sat opposite Jane at the kitchen table, 'there's so much still to talk about.'

Charlotte watched warily as her mother's jaw tightened. She looked angry. Charlotte had been amazed at how many times since she'd got home she'd seen flashes of annoyance in her mother's expression. It wasn't the way she'd used to be.

'You're making a lot of assumptions, Charlotte.'

'How am I? Explain it to me. Please, Mum, I don't understand why you want this all done and dusted so fast. There are so many years behind you. Surely you and Dad've got to think about it more carefully before you throw it all away.'

'You see, this is where you show just how young you are,' Jane asserted, then added, to soften her tone a little, 'Darling, when you've been married to somebody as long as your dad and I have been married, there's a deep understanding of how things are, deeper even than either of us can put into words, even to each other. You end up almost psychic when you're in the presence of that person. You know their every thought, can anticipate every response. Talking doesn't come into it.'

Charlotte chewed on her toast unhappily. 'But maybe that's the mistake you're both making. Maybe you should be talking. What if you're wrong about what Dad thinks, what he feels. What if you thought you were psychic but you weren't.'

'You haven't been married for forty-odd years, Charlotte, so you really wouldn't understand.'

'I know he still loves you,' Charlotte entered triumphantly, feeling she couldn't keep that card up her sleeve any longer.

'Of course he does,' Jane explained, flattening Charlotte's spirits. 'And I love him, too, dearly, as you would a very old friend who's been a part of your life, of your family history, for so many years. I just don't want to live with him anymore. And he obviously feels the same way.'

'Why, Mum. Can you tell me why?'

Jane sighed and put her elbows on the table, staring intently at a knot of pine. I don't want to put it into words. Not to you or Ginny.'

'But you've got to give us something, just toss us a bone to chew on.'

Jane hesitated, looking worried. 'I was lonely, Charlotte.'

'I know, Mum,' Charlotte leapt in. 'That's why I'm so glad I came back when I did, but if Dad was back here. . .'

'No, dear. I was lonely when he was here. And I think he was, too.'

'But. . .' Charlotte flailed around for ideas. 'But you can't have been less lonely after he left.'

'Sounds silly, doesn't it? But, yes, I could have my own thoughts, not have to worry about a silent man living in my house, living a separate life, unhappily drifting past me every so often.'

'But if he was so silent, and yes I know Dad's never been a great talker at the best of times, couldn't you just have had your own thoughts and not told him?'

'Yes, I did that for many years. And you've probably put your finger on it without meaning to. Oh, I know, married couples often live separate lives as the years go on, but mentally they often draw closer together. That didn't happen to us.'

'I just don't get it.' Charlotte dropped her toast back on to the plate miserably.

'I know.' Jane stood up briskly and started to wash up, clattering the crockery in the sink. 'So it's better not to ask me to explain it, because I really can't. I don't expect your father can, either.'

'He said he was lonely, too,' Charlotte said quietly, poking at her toast with one buttery finger.

'Well, there you are.' Jane crashed a plate on to the draining board.

'But you will meet him though, won't you? Maybe if you met in a different environment, somewhere away from the house, somewhere where you can see each other in a new light. . .' Charlotte pondered. Then she added, clumsily as she realised afterwards, 'I mean, it's not as if this Denise woman really matters. Loads of people have affairs and stay married. It's all just symptomatic of a problem in the relationship. It doesn't mean they actually want to be with someone else, so I will say I'm glad you're not having hysterics over the other woman thing. We're all grown-ups after all.'

Jane heaved a loud, impatient sigh. 'Really, Charlotte, is this all about you and your baby?'

Charlotte sat up, startled by Jane's sudden sharpness. 'What?'

'Do you want your father to come home so that we can be parents to your baby? Because I think you have to reconsider your motives. Don't forget we've already been parents to you and Ginny, then just as you girls both grew up and left we were parents to Marie. Marie's a young woman now, and neither of us was expecting to become parents again.'

Charlotte gaped, open mouthed, guilt tugging at her. Well, yes, perhaps she did think her mum and dad

203

had enjoyed having a role to play in Marie's life. Perhaps she had thought they'd missed it, and would throw themselves with enthusiasm into a similar role with her baby. She hadn't exactly visualised it, but somewhere in her imagination it was something they did. 'I don't – I'm not – Mum, how can you say that?'

'How are you going to support your child, Charlotte, have you thought about it much?'

'Well,' Charlotte plucked at the fluff on her dressing gown, trying to cover her swollen stomach, 'of course I've thought about it. I'll have to go out to work.'

'And how are you going to do that?'

Charlotte hadn't really thought it through. 'Easy. I'll get a job at a language school in London. With my background and experience they'll snap me up. Don't worry, Mum, I'm employable. I will be able to pay for all the nappies and all that stuff.'

'All right.' Jane wiped her soapy hands efficiently on a tea towel. 'And who's going to look after your baby while you're at work?'

'Well, I . . .' Charlotte went red. 'I thought – well, you will, Mum, won't you?'

'There you have it.' Jane flapped down the tea towel with vehemence. It was as if she'd slammed a door. 'As I thought.'

Charlotte floundered, her heart thudding at the rare confrontational stance that her mother was taking. 'I – look, Mum, you don't have to look after him all the time. I know you've got a part-time job. Maybe I can get a nanny or something when you're at the charity shop.'

'Exactly as I thought,' Jane said grimly.

'Mum, don't look at me like that.' Charlotte

squirmed and then winced as her stomach muscles contracted. She took a deep breath and continued. 'It'll just take a bit of organisation, but it'll be all right. Please don't worry about it.'

'You know, Charlotte, you really have become an incredibly selfish young woman. All these years of travel and exploration, of getting to know the big wide world, of leaving behind a little Britain that you've despised, it's all been about nurturing your own interests. It makes me sad to see that it's just made you very good at putting yourself first. And I know you've worked in countries where teaching was important, where you were paid little and put in a lot of effort. You've been where people needed your skills, I know that. But the irony is that when it comes to your own family you can't see beyond your own needs. And you're walking all over the needs of other people, people who you know love you, people you can take advantage of. And by that, if I'm being too cryptic, I mean me and your dad.'

'Mum!' Charlotte was shocked. She pushed her plate away, all appetite completely gone. Tears of injustice stung her eyes. 'It's not fair! I'm not selfish.'

'Then if it's not true, you must concentrate on organising yourself instead of organising me,' Jane's breath whistled through her nostrils and she clamped her jaw shut again, her eyes flashing.

'But, I—' Charlotte swallowed back the urge to cry. 'I can't organise myself. I don't know what to do.'

'You should start by contacting your boyfriend and discussing it with him. That would be more appropriate than giving me a lecture about the importance of communication with my own husband.'

205

Charlotte was abashed, her face now hot with humiliation. Her mother had never spoken to her in this way since she'd been an adult. She found herself putting her fingers under her dressing gown and holding the baby protectively. 'But you're my family, Mum,' she protested weakly. 'It's where you go when you need help. A family's supposed to be there for you, through thick and thin.'

'Your boyfriend is your family,' Jane retorted with a steely calmness that took Charlotte's breath away. 'He's your baby's father. You, your boyfriend and your baby are a family. You're hiding from that fact, but it's still a fact. And you told me you still love him. I can't think of any better reason to contact him and tell him where you are.'

'Mum, hang on.' Charlotte put a hand out, emotion rising and threatening to overwhelm her. 'I have told you that's a taboo subject.'

'You don't decide on the taboos where your child is concerned,' Jane issued, pulling out a chair again and slamming herself into it. She held her daughter's eye fiercely. 'Listen to me, Charlotte. We helped to bring up Marie because the circumstances were desperate. We helped Ginny because she had absolutely nobody else to support her.'

'Yes, like me!' Charlotte defended.

'No!' Jane banged the table with the flat of her hand, making Charlotte jump. 'Nothing like you at all. She tried very, very hard to involve Barney in the upbringing of Marie. She did everything she reasonably could, short of going to court, which she never wanted to do. And she was practically only a child herself, one who made a very costly mistake. You are making a choice as

206

a mature woman. You don't have any right to expect everybody to flock to your aid. I'm sorry if I sound harsh, but somebody's got to talk to you straight.'

'Mum, I'm pregnant,' Charlotte said weakly. 'Can we not have a row, please?'

'We're not rowing. You're just hearing some things you don't want to hear.'

'Just, not now, please.'

'Charlotte,' Jane put out a hand to her daughter and Charlotte cagily took it, 'I'm only trying to help you to think ahead. Ginny has had a very difficult life on her own. I've seen it all first hand and I don't think you should put yourself in the same position if you've got any choice. I think you should contact your boyfriend.'

'Mum,' Charlotte took an unsteady breath, 'I'm having contractions again, only they're stronger. Does that mean the baby's coming now?'

'Oh dear God,' Jane said.

Chapter Twenty-three

Late on Sunday morning, while Jane was driving Charlotte to the labour ward of the local hospital, Ginny was still in bed, and she was still thinking about Barney. Cosseted in her duvet she rolled backwards and forwards, trying to shake the images that surged into her mind. But they would not go away. And now she could remember, in every detail it seemed, the night she had spent with him at university.

She could visualise Oxford again. Hear the traffic in St Giles, the bells chiming, the clatter of bicycles around the Bodleian Library. It had been late when they'd left the pub, their college scarves wrapped tightly around their chins to ward off a biting wind. She could remember the blast of cold air that had hit her face as they'd fallen out of the pub door. It was strange how that sensation suddenly returned. She'd been sparring with Barney all night, so it had been an odd evening, strangely stimulating. She'd been so young, she hadn't realised what she'd been experiencing was merely a preamble. That what they'd been doing all evening, bouncing off each other's remarks, generating friction so strong it was practically visible, playing with the sexual attraction between them, was adult foreplay. That it was leading her somewhere, and that was not going to be the number fifty-two bus down the Cowley Road, where she lived in a shared house, but rather to Barney's room in college.

He'd offered to lend her a book. That was right. She lay back on her pillows and remembered. It wasn't that he'd told her he'd got a bottle of vodka in the fridge – that had come later, once she was in his room. Then they'd drunk vodka shots, giggling like schoolchildren, making fun of their lecturers.

Then, as she'd made herself comfortable on his floor, her back propped up against his bed, he'd come and sat next to her and, quite suddenly, put his hands to her face, held her still and kissed her very firmly on the lips. It had taken her breath away, and she'd closed her eyes, enraptured, waiting for more. He'd kissed her again. And again. And again. Then they'd abandoned themselves completely to physicality, wrestling with each other, their clothes sliding off. They'd made love there, on the carpet, and it had been brutal and exciting. Afterwards, Barney had dragged Ginny into the painfully narrow single bed with him and somehow, amid more giggling and fondling, they'd fallen asleep.

In the morning Ginny had woken up with a jump as Barney's bedroom door had crashed open. One of the scouts – an odd name, Ginny had always thought, for the army of middle-aged women who cleaned the students' college bedrooms – had walked straight in. She'd apologised and walked out again, but not before Ginny had discovered she had a headache, a dry mouth and a body that ached all over. Barney had rolled over, moaning and pulling a pillow over his head, and fallen asleep again. Ginny had slipped out of bed, dressed herself and escaped to save them both from the embarrassment of analysing what they'd done.

What had they done? Ginny wasn't sure, but she knew it wasn't something either of them had intended to happen. That was confirmed to her the next time she saw Barney in the library, deep in conversation with a stunning brunette who was clearly flirting with him. She'd stopped dead in her tracks, shocked by how hurt she felt, how jealous, how rejected. He'd seen Ginny over the other girl's shoulder. After a flush of embarrassment, he'd winked at her, but carried on his conversation without breaking it off That was it, then. She'd become what she'd been determined not to become. Another notch on his bedpost.

Furious with herself, she'd thrown herself into revision for her exams. Several times after that he'd come up to her with weak attempts to start a conversation, but Ginny had brushed him off. Perhaps she was rude. Perhaps she was sharp with him. Maybe so. But she couldn't forget the pain in the pit of her stomach at the way he'd handled things. There hadn't really been any need to flaunt his next conquest so openly, to display his indifference so blatantly. He might have just said, 'Ginny, I don't think we should have slept together. I hope you don't mind, but I don't want a relationship.' She would have at least respected his politeness. And she would have agreed with him, at least verbally, so that he wouldn't have been able to see how deeply she had fallen in love with him.

In the present, in her bed in the house she shared with Barney's daughter, Ginny sat up abruptly and rubbed in agitation at her hair. How on earth had it got to this? That she, a mature woman with a grown-up daughter, was tossing and turning in bed, worked up into a sweat with feelings she'd really rather not be having, over the man who had got her into this predicament in the first place? And the more she thought about the previous night in the restaurant, his casual charm, the touching of her cheek, the kissing of her hand, the careless kiss on the lips that had sent her into a turmoil of confusion, the more she felt he had been flirting with her. And what a result. Her body hadn't felt this warm, this sensitive, this alive, for many years.

'Oh my God.'

This could not happen. She had to put a stop to it, for everybody's sake. She had to make an excuse to see Barney and attempt to control the situation. She had some photographs for him. That would do nicely. She got up, stamped across the bedroom floor and found her handbag. In a pocket was the piece of paper where she'd scribbled down the mobile number he'd given her. She stabbed out the number and sat on the edge of the bed, closing her eyes for concentration.

'Barney? It's Ginny. I'd like to see you.'

'Ginny!' He paused. 'Is everything all right?'

'Yes, everything's fine.'

'Is it Marie? Has something happened?'

'No, it's not Marie. I just need to talk to you. And – er – I've had the photos you chose developed. They're ready for you. When can you make it?'

She heard him shuffling about, perhaps looking at a diary or maybe just absorbing her strident tone. 'I can do Friday evening. Are you free?'

'I can be free then.'

'I'll come down to you.'

'No, I'll come to London. We can meet somewhere.'

'Well, come to my house then. It saves hanging about in the cold.' She heard him breathing, could practically feel him frowning. 'Are you sure everything's all right?'

'Yes,' she said edgily. 'Where do you live?'

'Ginny, have you changed your mind about all this? About me getting to know Marie? If so, please warn me, because if all this is going to disappear again. . .'

'No, it's not that.' She took a deep breath and softened her tone, sympathy for him creeping up again. 'It's all right Barney, I just thought you'd like to have some photos of Marie after all this time without any. And we probably should talk again.'

'Yes,' he said after another pause. 'Yes, I think you're right. Well, I live in Wimbledon.' He gave her his address and directions from the tube. 'That's if you're sure you want to come to London.'

'It'll be fine. I can be there by seven.'

'I'll see you at my house at seven then.'

After she'd rung off, Ginny found that her hands were trembling. She stared at them, troubled, then ran herself a hot bath, piling bath foam into the water. She immersed herself in water and allowed the perfume to invade her nostrils. The water lapped over her body and relaxed her muscles. At least she was no longer trembling. Now she needed to think about what she was going to say to him, and that was going to prove the hardest thing.

*

'You're lucky. We've got a quiet day in here so far,' one of the midwives on duty at the labour ward greeted Charlotte and Jane with a broad smile. 'We'll get you into a room and check you out. How are you feeling?'

Charlotte could feel her eyes growing as round as saucers as they followed the midwife down a narrow, polished corridor and into a small room, one of several off to one side. She could smell disinfectant, and the posters on the walls were of mothers and babies, encouraging breast feeding, early skin contact, vaccinations. The babies in the posters looked tiny, red faced, damp haired. Would her baby look like any of these? Would he be dark, like Raj, or fair, like her? Suddenly her son seemed much more real. In the calm, medical setting, all the equipment set up and ready, like a party waiting for the guests to arrive, the birth itself seemed imminent. It boggled Charlotte's mind as she padded obediently into the room and stood next to a raised bed. There was an array of tubes and monitors and, it seemed, a spaghetti of wires everywhere. Then her eye was caught by a small plastic container in the corner of the room, like a storage box but longer.

'Oh God,' she said to the midwife in an explosion of nerves. 'Is that where the baby goes?'

'Once he or she's out, yes usually. But not until you've had a good chance to hold him and perhaps feed him, too. Let's get you up on here and fix you up to some monitors.'

Charlotte lay on the bed. Jane, it seemed, melted effortlessly into the background, always there and yet not interfering. Charlotte had to acknowledge her

213

mother was handling the situation just as she'd have wanted. Later she'd hug her for it.

'I'm not even sure if I'm wasting your time,' Charlotte half apologised, annoyed to hear that her voice was still shaky. She lay back and allowed to midwife to probe her stomach with soft fingers. 'I don't think the contractions are as strong as they were an hour ago. He's still wriggling a lot, though.'

'Yes, I think it's wise to check any sustained increased activity. Ooh, yes, there he goes again, I can see a little leg moving around there. I'm more interested in his restlessness than your contractions at the moment. You said on the phone you've been having Braxton Hicks' quite regularly.'

'Yes.' Charlotte swallowed.

'Normally we wouldn't call you in until the contractions were very regular and very strong, so strong perhaps that you'd need some pain relief. First babies are famous for taking their time to arrive. But we'll have a look at him and see why he's wriggling so much.'

'Why? What could it mean?' Fear for the baby's well-being struck at Charlotte's heart. All she cared about at that moment was that he was well.

'He could just be a bit impatient, or sometimes babies do get themselves into distress for all kinds of reasons.' She took Charlotte's notes from Jane and flicked through them with an expert eye. 'You're not really due for another two weeks but we'll just make sure everything's OK. It's nothing for you to worry about. You're in good hands.'

'Thank you.'

The midwife attached an elastic strap around Charlotte's stomach with a sensor pressed against the skin. Next to Charlotte a monitor whirred and thin paper began to feed through it.

'This will show your contractions and the baby's vital signs. You see?' A flick of a button, and they all heard a strong heartbeat.

'Oh my word!' Jane breathed from the chair she was perched in next to the wall. 'It's your baby's heart!'

'Nice and strong. Sounds like a boy,' the midwife cajoled. 'Now just relax. This will take some time. I'll leave you strapped up and come and check on you every few minutes. Can I get you a glass of water?'

'Yes, please.'

They were left alone and Jane inched her chair towards the bed and gently took Charlotte's hand.

'Are you all right, dear?'

'I'm scared, Mum. I've never been so scared in my life. But not for me, for him.'

Jane squeezed her hand. 'He's fine. Listen to that lovely strong heart. And he's a big boy, we can see that. He'll cope.'

Charlotte felt another contraction coming and closed her eyes. But this was less strong and it faded more quickly than others she'd had.

'I don't think he's going to come today,' she said to Jane.

'That would be a relief.'

Charlotte turned her head on the stiff cotton pillow and gazed at her mother. 'I thought that's what I'd feel, but I don't. I'd love him to come now. I don't care about the birth anymore, I don't care if it's really painful, I just want to meet him. I want to start to get to know my little boy. The waiting's just making me really anxious.'

215

'It will all happen in good time,' Jane soothed. 'Babies have a way of knowing when that right time is. It's one of the miracles of life.'

They settled together in peaceful silence, broken by the whirring of the machine, the occasional bleep of Charlotte's blood pressure monitor, listening to the baby's heartbeat echoing around them like a little tin drum.

'I love him so much,' Charlotte said, emotion swelling inside her.

'I know, love. It's natural. You're a mother now.'

'I mean Raj. I wish things were different. I wish he could be a part of this.'

Jane mopped the trickle of tears that ran down Charlotte's nose with a tissue from her handbag. 'I know, darling.'

'But I did a terrible thing to him.'

'You left him, that's all. Maybe it was a mistake. Sometimes you don't realise you've made a mistake until afterwards. That doesn't mean it's too late to put it right.'

'No, I mean I did something terrible.'

'Hush, Charlotte. You need to be calm.'

'But I've got to tell you. I told him it wasn't his baby.'

Jane fell silent, her face crumpled with concern. 'Oh dear,' she said quietly.

'I didn't want to ruin his life, his family's plans for him, his future. His family were going to ostracise him if he married me. They would have disowned him, he would have lost them for ever. I had to get him off the scent, so I told him a terrible lie. Then I left, in the middle of the night, so that we couldn't argue about it anymore.'

216

Jane absorbed all of the new information, her eyes troubled. 'You poor girl,' she said eventually. 'I'm sorry now that I called you selfish. You did a very selfless thing.'

'But I hurt him so badly. You should have seen his face. I broke his heart.'

'You know,' Jane rubbed Charlotte's fingers, 'he probably didn't believe you anyway.'

'Oh, he did. I did such a good job of lying. I made up a really convincing story, and he went so pale I thought he was having some kind of seizure. He couldn't speak, he was so devastated. Oh, he believed me, there's no doubt about it.'

'Don't worry about it now.' Jane kissed her daughter's hand. 'Listen to your little baby, thriving in there. You've done a good job, bringing him this far. Now you need to relax and let him be happy inside you until he's really ready to come out.'

Yes.' Charlotte put her head back on the pillows unhappily and stared up at the white speckled tiles on the hospital ceiling, lost in a miserable world. 'And that's why I can't go back.'

Chapter Twenty-four

'And you're sure you're all right now?' Ginny asked Charlotte with concern. They were back at home on Sunday night and Ginny had come round in response to Jane's call.

'Yes, I'm fine. I just panicked a bit earlier. It's all so new, you know. Feel a bit silly now. He's stopped thrashing around and the contractions have died away again. It just gave me a shock.'

Ginny went and sat on the armchair, seeing as Charlotte was draped over the sofa, a blanket over her legs. Somehow she didn't want to squash up next to her on the narrow cushions; it would be too intimate. But she could hardly just nod and go back to the kitchen to talk to her mother, leaving Charlotte worried. Compassion niggled at her, but she still needed Charlotte to ask her for help. If only she'd swallow her pride and do it. But Jane had given Ginny a good telling-off on the phone. What if, after all, that had been the baby's time to come? Wasn't Ginny ever going to offer Charlotte some of the baby goods she had stacked away in the attic, doing absolutely nothing? Wasn't she going to offer a bit of advice? Or, Jane had snapped, some support at least?

'I've got a cot you can have,' she told Charlotte bluntly.

Charlotte twisted round, wincing as the baby kicked again. 'You have?'

'It looks a bit knackered but it's strong and safe. You can have it. It's in the attic somewhere.'

'I was just thinking of buying a cheap Moses basket or something. That's what the other women have been talking about doing. But—'

'Well if you're sorted, that's fine. I'm just offering.'

'No, I'm not sorted.' Charlotte propped herself up on her elbows to examine Ginny's face. 'I'm just saying the other women all seem to be getting baskets so that's what I was thinking of. I was just picturing something small that would do for now.'

'It's fine, Charlotte. The thing about pregnancy is that it's best to listen to everyone and then decide what to do for yourself. You can put the baby in what you like.'

'No, I'd like to put him in a cot. That's what I meant. I was just saying—'

'Look, don't worry about it. And lie still. You don't want to have to go back into hospital, do you?'

Charlotte flopped back on the cushions and stared at the ceiling. At that moment, Ginny hated herself. It was just so hard to give Charlotte anything. She always seemed to be rejecting help, rejecting advice. And here she was again, with her own plans. Jane should have checked to see what Charlotte's ideas were without urging Ginny to speak to her. But seeing how unhappy Charlotte looked Ginny tried to force out some appeasing words.

'At least I guess you won't have thought about a high chair yet. I've got Marie's old high chair, too. You can have that. Although you won't need it for a few months.'

Charlotte was silent for a moment, then she said, in a small voice, 'Thank you.'

'I don't have her pushchair or anything like that anymore. In fact, the pushchair broke.' As Charlotte remained silent, Ginny prompted, 'What are you going to do about a pushchair?'

'I wasn't going to get one.'

'How are you going to take him out?'

'I thought I'd get a sling. I'd like to feel him close to me.'

Ginny heaved a breath. Now they'd got into the conversation it was going to be hard to get out of it. She moved to another chair, where Charlotte could see her without having to twist round. Charlotte's eyes looked glazed. Whether through tiredness of boredom she couldn't really tell. But she had had a shock that morning, so she probably was feeling very tired now. And, in truth, Ginny was quite surprised by how big Charlotte had become just in a week or two. She hadn't really appreciated it before. Marie had never been that big.

'He's a big boy.' Ginny nodded at Charlotte's blanketed bump.

'Yes.' Charlotte met Ginny's gaze. Her face didn't show any particular expression. She looked numb. Perhaps she'd been given painkillers for the contractions. She certainly wasn't quite with it.

'Must be tiring, heaving that around. Marie was quite petite.'

'Yes, it is tiring.'

'You know, I do realise it's hard doing this on your own.' Ginny felt that was quite a positive step towards conciliation. An air of quietness had settled over

Charlotte, but it wasn't calmness so much as resignation. Ginny felt sympathy stirring. 'And you do know where I am, don't you? I thought you might have called me by now.'

Charlotte opened her mouth as if she would say something, then closed it again. Finally she just said, 'Sorry.'

'You don't have to be sorry. I just assumed you'd got it all sorted out as you didn't call. You normally do sort things out yourself, without any help from anyone. And I know you don't like to ask for help.' She persevered as Charlotte didn't answer. 'The thing about slings is that they can get quite hot, for the baby. It depends how long you leave him in there. It's also really hard to carry heavy shopping when you've got the baby in the sling. Pushchairs usually have some kind of basket underneath. You'd find that really helpful. And you can leave a baby to sleep in a pushchair, too, if he drops off and you don't want to disturb him.'

'I can't afford a pushchair,' Charlotte replied in a monotonous voice.

'Well, maybe not just now.'

'Not in the foreseeable future.'

'Well, come on, Charlotte, don't be daft,' Ginny tried to cajole her. 'You don't really think that Mum's going to let you struggle around, do you? Of course she'll help you with a pushchair. I can chip in, too. It's one of the advantages of you being back at home, surely?'

Charlotte looked up sharply. 'Is that what you think? That I came home so that you could all bail me out?'

221

'No.' Ginny frowned. 'It's not what I said.'

'It's what you think. That I came back here to be a leech.'

'Charlotte! That's not fair. I've never said that. I've even just said that I know you don't like to ask for help.'

'But I am asking for it, aren't I? Demanding it, in fact. By being here, being pregnant, having nowhere else to go. Emotionally blackmailing everyone into doing something about it.'

Ginny snorted impatiently. 'Before you wallow in self-pity, you could consider that I'm actually trying to help. I haven't forced my advice on you. I only came round because Mum told me too. I was quite happy to leave you to it.' It had come out more harshly than she intended. Charlotte looked very pale.

'Please don't talk to me only because Mum's told you to. I'd rather you didn't talk to me at all than do it under duress.'

'Look, I didn't mean it to sound like that.'

'It's fine, Ginny. Let's just leave it like that.'

'Like what?'

'I don't think there's much else to say.'

Ginny got up ready to leave the room in annoyance, but then hesitated on her way to the door. 'You know, Charlotte, you haven't asked me about Marie at all.'

'I did!' Charlotte sounded surprised.

'When?'

'When I came home, that evening we all spent here having dinner. I asked you about her then, and you told me she was off travelling.'

'And since then?'

222

Charlotte looked puzzled. 'She's still travelling, isn't she?'

'That's the thing about children, Charlotte. They don't just come and go. They're there, all the time, even when they're not there. Even when they're physically out of the country. It's full on, relentless, twenty-four hours a day, every day of your life from the moment they're born until – until for ever. That's what you don't realise. Marie is still my major concern, the first thing I think about when I wake up and the last thing I think about before I go to bed, and then the thing I dream about; she's the cause of every anxious moment in my life. There hasn't been a moment since you got back when I haven't been worried sick about her.'

'But. . .' Charlotte floundered. 'You seemed so relaxed.'

'No, I am not relaxed,' Ginny snapped. 'I am so far from bloody relaxed that it's unbelievable. You haven't got a clue what's going on in my life, in my head, in all the knots of nerves in my stomach. And I know you're pregnant and it's obviously a big deal for you. But you haven't once picked up the phone since you got home and asked me how I am. Not once.'

'Ginny. . .'

'Oh, get stuffed, Charlotte. Put him in a Moses basket. I don't care.'

Ginny stormed away. As she entered the kitchen she saw that Jane was on the phone. She had her back to the door and obviously hadn't seen or heard her daughter come in.

'Yes, all right, I'll meet you, Harry,' she said. 'I agree with you. It's time we sorted a few things out.'

'Mum?'

Jane rang off and sprang round with a guilty look on her face. Her cheeks were pink. 'Hello, darling,' she said over brightly.

'What's going on?'

'Oh, nothing at all. I heard voices in the other room so I left you to it. Have you and Charlotte been talking properly at last? That's good.'

'Is that *your* filofax?' Ginny indicated the battered lump of leather in her mother's hands.

'What, this?' Jane opened innocent eyes. 'Oh, no, dear, it's Charlotte's. I was just cleaning it for her.'

'Cleaning?' Ginny pulled a puzzled face, but Jane had scurried from the room, filofax in hand, and with a bolshy sister in one room and enigmatic mother disappearing upstairs, Ginny decided tiredly that she might as well go home.

Chapter Twenty-five

For the rest of the week, Charlotte and Ginny didn't speak. On Friday, after work, Ginny took the train up to Charing Cross and the tube to Wimbledon to meet Barney.

The moon was glimmering behind thin, stringy clouds, grey against the black of the sky. There would probably be a frost tonight, Ginny concluded as she hurried along a series of roads and within five minutes found herself outside a white, bay-windowed terraced house. She wiggled her fingers in her gloves, doubts creeping up on her. Should she really have come here, to his territory? What was she actually going to say in the reality of the moment? And what of his housemate or girlfriend, whichever she was – would she be there? Would it be better just to deposit the bag with the photographs in it and run?

She pressed the bell, and to her disconcertment it wasn't Barney who answered, but a slim woman with long thick curly black hair that swung down to her waist. She looked very casual in tracksuit bottoms and an oversized sweatshirt (one of Barney's?), which had the effect, as men's clothes did on some women, of looking very sexy. Her feet were bare, her toenails painted bright red – the only sign of decoration on her as she wasn't wearing make-up – and, with petite, pretty features and expressive brown eyes, didn't need to either. Flummoxed and momentarily losing confidence, Ginny opened her mouth.

'I'm sorry to disturb you, I was looking for Barney Middleton. Have I got the right house?'

'Yes, yes, of course, come in. You must be Ginny.' She stepped aside to let Ginny in, and took a bite of toast while holding out the other hand and continuing with a mouthful of crumbs. 'I'm Honey. Sorry, mouth full. I'm between shifts, grabbing a bite while I can. Go through. I think he's still in the bath; I'll go up and tell him you're here.'

'Thank you.' Ginny felt herself growing wide eyed as Honey – and what an appropriate name for such an attractive woman, Ginny decided with gritted teeth – took the stairs two at a time and disappeared along a spacious landing. Ginny edged along the hall towards an open kitchen door so as not to spy, but listened carefully. She heard a bang on the door and, yes, the door opened. So Honey wasn't averse to sticking her head round the door when Barney was in the bath, and he clearly didn't mind. She swallowed. The woman clearly was his girlfriend, and for a moment Ginny felt absurdly jealous, her skin prickling all over and her stomach churning unpleasantly. But then, as she helped herself to a seat at the kitchen table, leaning her elbows on a pile of unread Sunday supplements and edging off her gloves, she rationalised her bizarre reaction. She had come all the way to London to put a stop to any amorous undercurrents in the air between herself and Barney. What could be a more effective, more immediate, cure for an amorous undercurrent than another woman – and a sexy one to boot? Why

226

would he mess around with Ginny when he had such a woman at home warming the bed for him? Only for curiosity's sake, or old times' sake, whichever might appeal to him in a moment of recklessness. No, it was as well that she'd come here and as well that she'd met Honey. It clarified a lot. The woman herself reappeared, flicking an armful of hair over her shoulder and flashing Ginny a warm and very genuine smile.

'I'll put the kettle on. The little mermaid's on his way. He says to say sorry. He was caught in a tunnel earlier, stuck there for an hour, and he's only just got in. Some kind of meeting with the Red Cross. You know how it is with the tube.'

'Not for a long while, actually. I don't come up to London very much now.'

'That's right, Barney said.' She nodded, filling the kettle and resting it on an Aga. 'You live in Kent, don't you? Lovely to be outside London. But I have to be near the hospital at the moment. Filling in. Now I remember why I ran like hell from working in London hospitals before and went off to join M.S.F. Have no idea what I'm doing back here. Must rethink.'

'So you're a doctor too?'

'Yep. Until very recently with Médecins Sans Frontières, where I met Barney. And you? Didn't Barney meet you in med school?'

'That was—' Ginny cleared her throat. How much did Honey know? She didn't particularly want to tell her life story to a complete stranger. 'I'm not a doctor, no. I work in a lab.'

'Ah.'

'Yes.'

227

'Researcher?'

'Er. . .'

And suddenly Barney was at the kitchen door, and Ginny turned to look at him. He was in jeans and a sweater and his hair was damp. If he had been naked when Honey had put her head round the door, he had dressed in record time. Or perhaps, she consoled herself, he'd been half dressed. At least, perhaps, the bottom half. He grinned at her, then dropped the grin, seeming to realise that it was inappropriate to appear to be so happy to see her. He must have been off his guard.

'Thanks, Honey, I'll make the coffee. Shall I bring one through to you?'

'Hint taken. No thanks, I'm going to grab some shuteye while I can. I'm out of here. Nice to see you, Ginny, hope we'll talk again.'

'Oh, goodbye.'

As Honey left the room she ruffled Barney's hair affectionately. 'Be good.'

After Honey had pounded up the stairs and they both heard a door swing shut, Barney made coffee and Ginny waited for it silently, at a loss for something to say. He joined her at the table.

'Would you rather go through to the living room?'

'Let's stay in here. I'm comfortable now.' Ginny slid her coat on to the back of her chair and pushed the bag containing the photographs towards him. 'Here. All the photographs you chose of Marie. Well, all except one, I couldn't find the negatives for the fairground shot, but I hope you won't mind.'

'That's incredible of you.' Barney gazed at Ginny

228

warmly. 'I really am grateful. I hope you've put a receipt in there.'

'Well, no. It really wasn't expensive. I don't think it'd be right to charge you.'

'But I insist. It's not something you asked to do.'

'Forget it, Barney, please.'

'But I must pay.'

'Forget it!' Ginny must have raised her voice a little because he looked surprised. 'I mean, there are far more important things for us to spend our energy talking about than a couple of quid.'

'Yes.' He took a sip of his coffee and settled more comfortably. 'Yes, you're probably right. What things?'

'You know as well as I do. Emotional things.'

'Yes, yes I know.' He swallowed another mouthful of coffee. 'What kind of emotional things were you thinking of?'

Ginny blinked at him. 'Well, there's how you are going to approach Marie for a start.'

'Oh, yes, of course, that's the most important thing.'

Ginny frowned at him. Had he been thinking of something else? As Barney leafed through the photographs she had given him, his face pensive, she asked, 'So. . .your friend, Honey. You must have known her some time.'

'Hmm? Yes, a while, although we were working in different countries so we've only recently got in touch properly again. This is her house. She bought it years ago with her then-boyfriend when she was on quite a good salary and property was a lot cheaper, then she bought him out when they split up. I stayed here once before, when I was in a bit of a black hole and needed

229

a base. I was lucky to have something like this to fall back on. That was a few years ago, though. I was lucky that Honey was back in London this year. She didn't hesitate to let me move in with her. She's a gem.'

'Ah, yes, I see. Very gem-like.'

Barney shot Ginny a straight look. 'Did your boyfriend mind you coming up to see me?'

Ginny coloured, hoping he wouldn't notice. 'No. Of course not. We live in an adult world, full of imperfect situations. He's mature enough to understand that.'

'Older man?'

'No. What makes you say that?'

'I just wondered how mature he was. From what you said —'

'Barney,' Ginny said firmly, putting an end to her own discomfort, 'I don't really think it's appropriate for you to quiz me about him. I did come here to give you the photographs and to talk about Marie. That's all. And I really can't stay long.'

'You can't? I thought we might go out to eat. There's a superb Indian restaurant just around the corner.'

'Goodness me, no, I'm sorry,' Ginny said hastily. The last time they'd met had been over an evening meal. It would be a mistake to make a habit of it. Then it really would seem like dating.

'Surely you don't have to rush off? It's Friday night.'

'Well. . .that's it, you see. I do see him sometimes on Friday night so I didn't want to be away all night.'

'Oh, I see. You've got a date when you get home?'

Ginny was sure she was bright red now. Her face felt very hot. But after their last encounter in a restaurant, which had ended very steamily, at least, from her viewpoint, she couldn't risk any kind of repeat situation. 'I won't be able to stay long, that's all.'

'What a shame. I was looking forward to seeing you.' To her surprise, he was genuinely disappointed and didn't seem to be afraid to say so. His shoulders all but drooped in front of her. 'Well then, let me at least offer you a glass of wine. It's respectably late and neither of us is driving, I assume.'

Ginny hesitated. It was cold and she could actually have done with drinking something relaxing. She wasn't sure what had put her more on edge since she'd arrived at this house, Barney's apparent warmth and enthusiasm towards her, or Honey's sex appeal. Something had definitely got under her skin and rattled her again.

'Thank you. I'll have a glass of whatever you've got.'

Or perhaps, she had to ask herself with brutal honesty, it was Barney's sex appeal? As he bent to open the fridge she couldn't help eyeing a very firm rump clad in well-fitting denim. Unbidden, it brought back a memory that she'd rather have forgotten right at that moment. A thought that had flitted through her mind, nearly twenty years ago, when she had first touched his body and wondered if all the rugby playing was responsible for the beautiful firmness of his flesh. But he wouldn't play rugby now. Perhaps it was just a natural attribute. And perhaps, she concluded as she averted her eyes, she should be thinking about something else.

'So,' Barney poured them both a glass of chilled white wine, passed Ginny hers, and clinked them together, 'here's to a brief but meaningful encounter.'

'Encounter?' Ginny hesitated mid-clink.

'Tonight.' Barney explained, giving Ginny an old-fashioned look. 'Here, in this kitchen, before you run off into the cold again.'

'Yes, I knew what you meant.' Ginny sipped her wine, feeling silly. 'So, Barney, please ask me anything you'd like to about Marie. Just fire away. I'll do what I can.'

His eyes warmed with delight and Ginny felt her stomach buckle. He really did care about Marie; it was evident in every action, every shade of expression. It made her feel very strange inside.

'Well, I don't know where to start. . .'

Two hours later, Ginny found herself glancing at her watch and reacting with shock. She pulled her coat and gloves on hurriedly and stood up.

'Barney, time's just flown away from us this evening. I really do have to go now.'

'Are you sure?' He stood up slowly, rubbing his back and looking regretful.

'Absolutely. I can't believe we've had – what? Three glasses of wine? I hardly realised how quickly the time was passing. I really must fly.' Of course, self-control rather than anything else was willing her away to her empty house rather than allowing her to get too comfortable here with him. It would have been very easy to stay another hour or two, perhaps to take him up on his offer of dinner round the corner, maybe even an offer of a sofa for the night, then – what? But that was ludicrous. Honey was upstairs. He'd probably join her when Ginny had gone. She hardened her heart again.

'Then let me walk you to the station.'

'Don't be ridiculous. You're not properly dressed and I'm halfway out the door.'

But he'd already grabbed a huge padded jacket and thrown it on, and was alongside her in the hall. 'I insist.'

They parted company outside Wimbledon tube station.

'It was nice to see you, Barney,' Ginny said, feeling much more comfortable now that she was on her way home. Perhaps they had managed to set some boundaries that evening after all. It had been a trip worth making.

'You too, Ginny, though all too short. You must let me take you for a drink to make up for the photographs.'

'Oh no, that's daft.'

'I do insist on that. It's the least I can do. Let me know when you're free.'

'Well,' Ginny edged towards the ticket barrier, 'I'm not sure what Honey'll think of all these encounters. I think you'll have to consider how she feels, Barney.'

'Honey?' Barney laughed and suddenly pulled Ginny into his arms. She was too surprised to resist. He stared into her eyes, humour sparkling there. 'Honey and I are not sleeping together, Ginny. I don't have to consult her about anything.'

'Well, of course.' Ginny asserted, confused beyond measure, wanting Barney to let her go but at the same time curious to know what his cold lips, breathing white wisps of frosty air at her, would taste like at that moment. 'I only meant—'

'You are an intriguing woman,' Barney said in a low voice, and kissed her.

'Barney, no!' Ginny pulled away, perhaps not as steadily as she might have done, and put distance between them as quickly as she could. 'Goodbye.'

She fumbled as she poked her ticket into the barrier and waved overly brightly at Barney, just once, before turning away and pounding off into the night. She didn't slow down until she had reached the platform and knew that he was safely out of sight. Her heart was thumping like a bass drum.

Another kiss. And once more he had managed to turn her knees into jelly. She had come up to London to put a stop to any emotional attachments that might have been developing between them. But had she merely fanned the flames?

It was a question Ginny asked herself relentlessly in the days that followed. Her stomach churned, her mind revolved. She couldn't concentrate on work and she was distracted at home. She didn't seem to be able to keep her mind focused on anything, and kept finding her thoughts bouncing back to Barney. So much so that when she found her mother at her front door on the Tuesday evening of the week after she'd met Barney she blinked at her in confusion.

'Mum?'

'You seem surprised to see me, dear. I am expected. We fixed up that I'd come round tonight after dinner for a glass of wine and a chat, and you were going to let me send an email to Marie.'

'We did?' Ginny had been hoping for a bath and an early night.

'But if it's not convenient. . .'

Then Ginny remembered a rushed conversation that

they'd had at her mother's that she'd completely forgotten, and let Jane in. She bustled into the hall, taking off her grey overcoat and accepting Ginny's kiss and a hug.

'Of course, I'm so sorry, Mum. I'll grab you something to drink and we can go straight up to the computer. I'm just not with it at all this week. Someone's unplugged my brain.'

'Someone?' Jane quizzed lightly as Ginny poured her a glass of wine in the kitchen and led the way upstairs.

'Or something. You know.'

'But you didn't say something. You said someone.'

Ginny sighed and gave her mother a wary look as they both went into Marie's room and settled down at the computer. 'You are just too quick sometimes.'

Jane took an innocent sip of her wine. 'So you have been seeing Barney. I did wonder. You must have seen him on Friday night. I didn't really think you'd met that old friend of yours, Karen, because you never got on that well in the first place. Did you go to his house?'

'I didn't really fib to you about Karen.' Ginny felt guilty for being caught out telling a white lie. 'I have been in touch with her and we are intending to meet in London soon.'

'But you didn't want me sticking my nose into your relationship with Barney. I can understand that. Especially if things are delicate between you, as I guess they are. I'm afraid you always were in love with that boy, although I don't think he was ever worthy of your feelings until now.'

Ginny was startled. 'I'm not in love with Barney at all.'

'You aren't, dear?' Jane's voice was so kind, her eyes so understanding that Ginny felt a lump in her throat.

'No,' she almost squeaked in a pathetic attempt at denial. 'Oh, I don't know. I'm very confused about it all.' She accepted defeat. Jane seemed to have a pretty good grasp of the facts without her explaining them. It was actually quite a relief for somebody to have raised the subject. She was getting nowhere tossing it around her own head like a buckle in a tumbledryer.

'I do think he's quite besotted with you.'

'Him? God no, he's not. On his part, I'm sure it's all just novelty, Mum. I'll admit, I do feel something towards him. It's unwelcome, but there it is. But I'd be mad to get into such hot water again, and especially with Marie to consider. We'll all end up charred and burnt and much the worse for the experience, or whatever it is that happens after you've played with fire.'

'Have you talked to him about it?'

'There really isn't anything to talk about.' Ginny tried to concentrate on downloading her emails instead, staring at the computer screen intently while Jane stared at her.

'It seems to me that there's everything to talk about,' Jane insisted steadily. 'And Barney's the one to talk to. Only he can tell you how he really feels.'

Ginny tutted. 'I know how he feels. There's a bit of a frisson there, he'd probably like to explore it out of sheer devilment, then he'll be on his way again.'

'Devilment? The poor man didn't look to me like one who does anything out of devilment. He seemed most sincere. Especially where his daughter was concerned.'

'Well, there you are. If Marie is to be a factor at all,

then nothing can ever happen between Barney and me, ever. That's the end of the story. Nothing to discuss.' Ginny put her hands in the air and saw with relief that Marie had emailed again. That would be a wonderful distraction for Jane. 'Here you go.'

'Do you think you could print it out for me, Ginny? I get so cross-eyed staring at these screens.'

'Yep, of course.'

They both read Marie's email with delight, laughing at all the funny bits, Ginny feeling that familiar ache inside. Marie seemed to be having the time of her life, fascinated by all she heard and saw, just as Ginny had hoped. Just when would her daughter think about coming home? Would it really be months? The thought was dismal.

Jane typed a reply with Ginny's guidance, and Ginny wrote a page from herself. It was an hour later when they sent off their reply and watched it go into cyberspace with satisfaction.

'Quite an amazing thing, the Internet, isn't it?' Jane marvelled. 'And everyone seems to have web-pages these days. Businesses and even families have their own pages. And Joyce at the hospice shop was telling me it's so easy to do a search. I just don't know how to do these things. Maybe I should do a course.'

'You don't need to do a course to find a web page.' Ginny flicked the screen to Internet Explorer and showed her mother the search engine page. 'You'd just type a name in here and go and search for it.'

'Oh, I see. That does look easy.'

'It is. We really must get you online at home. I never realised you were so interested. Perhaps now that – well, you've got more time now that Dad's gone.'

'Not more time, dear, just more freedom to do what I want. No, I don't need a computer at home, I can always borrow yours if something interests me. So you just put a name in that box. How clever. And I expect Charlotte's school in India probably have a page, don't they?'

'Charlotte's old school? You mean the one she was teaching at in Mumbai? Well, I expect so. Why?'

'Oh, I don't know, I was just wondering. I think she's missing her friends from there. I wondered if we should – well, perhaps we should email them and tell them to write to her or something. It might cheer her up.'

Ginny was puzzled. 'Why does she need cheering up? She's perfectly well isn't she?'

'Oh, you've got no understanding of your own sister's mentality, Ginny, and it does get me down.' Jane was exasperated. 'A little insight on your part would go a very long way.'

'What?' Ginny felt further confused, but it was getting late and she was enormously tired now.

'Just go and get me a cup of coffee, will you? I feel a bit woozy after that glass of wine and I've got to drive home in a minute.'

Ginny stood up, surprised by Jane's commanding tone. 'Yes, of course I'll make you coffee. Anything else?'

'Yes. After I've gone you can ring Barney and arrange to meet him again. You won't get anywhere hiding from him and screwing yourself up into a knot.'

'Mum!' Ginny said faintly. 'Where is all this coming from?'

'Coffee, darling.' Jane gave Ginny a warm smile.

'And do find some of that brown sugar for me. And a biscuit. There's a love. I'll just fiddle about up here for a bit.'

But it was Barney who called Ginny, the following evening, to thank her again for getting reprints of the photographs for him. Even hearing his voice again sent adrenaline snaking through her veins. Wasn't Jane right? Shouldn't she talk to Barney properly about their relationship? Who else could it be more appropriate to talk to? And if she continued to have unbidden and only half-decent thoughts about him, didn't she really need firmly to put some walls up, even if only for her own sake? Weren't they mature enough by now to have an open and frank discussion about it?

'Actually, I'm glad you've called Barney.'

'You are?' He sounded pleased.

'Yes,' she hurried on. 'Because I do think we should meet again. I'd like to talk to you.'

'Well I'd love to buy you a drink to say thank you for—'

'No, I mean there are some things I want to say to you. And privately. And I think it would be better if it was soon.'

'It's not Marie?' The concern in his voice touched her, but she bulldozed on.

'No. When are you free?'

'Let's meet on Saturday night. I'll come down to you.'

'No,' she said firmly. Given the undercurrents between them, her house was far too uncomplicatedly empty and private for them to be drinking alcohol close by. 'I'll meet you close to Charing Cross. That way we both have a fairly easy journey.'

Yes, she was sure. She wouldn't change her mind. She wouldn't meet him on Saturday night – that held far too much symbolic importance for a meeting she intended to be unromantic. The date was set for the following Friday evening. The venue, All Bar One in Leicester Square.

Chapter Twenty-six

❧❧❧

On Friday, after work, Ginny once more took the train to Charing Cross and walked up to Leicester Square to meet Barney.

Apart from the recent fracas with Charlotte, which had left her feeling out of sorts, she'd had quite a good week at work and she'd tried really hard to blot out the image of her heavily pregnant sister three streets away in an attempt to carry on as normal.

It was just that she couldn't blot Charlotte out. There was something about her pallor, her stillness, that was still bothering Ginny. It was out of character. Charlotte was an effusive personality, vivacious, she could generously conclude, and had always been. If attacked, she was the first to leap to her own defence. Sometimes she leapt there before she'd even been attacked. It was, ironically enough, what had put Ginny on the defensive ever since Charlotte had returned. At times, she'd always felt, Charlotte was just damned cocky and difficult. Anybody like that was not the easiest person to shower offers of help on. But she hadn't been any of those things recently, and tiredness didn't quite seem to explain it sufficiently.

But now Ginny was walking past the Portrait Gallery, glancing idly at the posters on the railings advertising the latest exhibition, still composing the speech she was going to make to Barney. After all, she was the one who'd called the meeting. After initial overtures, Barney would be waiting for her to explain why. She swallowed, her throat dry, and headed into the tangle of tourists milling around Leicester Square.

In the end, it came out incredibly bluntly.

'You know, Barney, that there can't be anything between us.'

Ginny watched Barney sip his wine. She'd found him at a corner table with a bottle and two glasses, waiting. He hadn't poured himself a glass until she'd arrived. He seemed to savour the taste, then he took off the scuffed brown leather jacket he was wearing and hung it on the back of his chair. He gazed around the capacious bar where people were mingling and where music and voices were bouncing between the hard floor and hard ceiling. Ginny huddled into her jacket, realising that what she'd said was, of course, obvious, and that he'd be wondering why she'd dragged him out into central London on a cold November night to say something that she could have said on the phone and saved them both the embarrassment of an evening out. But when he finally did respond, his answer was not at all what she had expected.

'Why not?'

Ginny stared at him in astonishment. In a loose sweater and jeans, with a raggedy mop of unkempt hair and a little hint of stubble, he still managed to look glorious. But that was exactly what she was fighting.

'I think the answer to that's obvious,' she stated. He cocked his head, so she added, 'Use your imagination.'

'I am,' he said.

'I don't think you are.'

'Yes, I am. I think perhaps you're not using *your* imagination.'

Ginny knew she'd gone red. She'd used her imagination just a little too much where he was concerned recently. It had brought on physical sensations she'd thought were in the dim and distant past But she was feeling hot all over now because Barney was challenging her, and it took the wind out of her sails. This was not what he was supposed to be saying at all. He was meant to be agreeing with her, if anything embarrassing her by not even understanding why she was making a point about something that didn't exist. But clearly she'd been absolutely right. Chemistry did exist between them. He was being insolently honest about it.

'You don't seem surprised that this is what I wanted to talk to you about,' she told him, feeling more awkward by the second. 'You seem to have expected it.'

'Yes, I did. I guessed there were two possible reasons for you to want to see me urgently. One was Marie, and you'd already clarified that it wasn't about her. The second was that it was about us.'

Ginny squirmed and drank some wine for Dutch courage. 'Barney, I think there has been – well, something inexplicable between us the last couple of times we've met, and—'

'Not just the last couple of times. There *is* something between us. There always has been. I don't mean a history, I don't mean Marie. I mean there is a spark. I can't make it go away, I'm sorry.'

She was flummoxed again. She looked in her

handbag for a tissue she didn't need, pretended to wipe her nose, and put it away again. 'I see.' She had to think. It was very hard. Barney leant forward and studied her face carefully.

'I want to talk to you, too, Ginny. That's why I'm so glad you wanted to meet. Perhaps you'd like me to say what I've come here to say first? It might change how you feel.'

'I – well, go on.'

'I was always transfixed by you, always fascinated by you. When I first met you, you intrigued me.'

'You moved on very quickly,' Ginny couldn't help saying. 'After we'd – we'd been together. The next time I saw you, you were already moving on. But I don't want to go back to the past.'

'I came after you,' Barney said as if he was surprised that she didn't realise it 'Many times. I tried to talk to you but you didn't want to know. I pestered you to come out with me again. You blanked me.'

'I'm really not going to think back twenty years. I can't remember.'

'I can. I was obsessed with you for some time. You weren't interested in me at all.'

Ginny pursed her lips. It was such a different version of their student affair from her own memory. Could she believe it was true? He had made efforts to talk to her, teasing remarks, winks, suggestions that they go out for a drink again. She could remember all that. But she'd assumed he was teasing her, and by then she'd felt defensive. And it was so long ago, it seemed pointless to dispute it now. 'Oh, come on, Barney, this is just silly.'

'Somehow I lost you along the way, but – if this

doesn't sound too unbelievable – you've never really been out of my thoughts.'

'You can't mean that.'

He looked genuinely affronted. 'I can assure you I mean every word of it.'

'Well, okay, but the getting lost along the way bit's a bit rich under the circumstances.'

'I'm sorry, I don't know how else to put it without going back and dwelling on all the rubbish that got between us back then once you found out you were pregnant. We were both young; what happened was shocking for both of us. I behaved stupidly at the time, but I was also told a lot of lies, most of which I've only become aware of recently. I think I made it clear to you in the restaurant that there'd always been times when I wanted to get in touch, but couldn't.'

'All right, let's just leave that there for now.'

Barney took a deep breath. 'When I saw you again, in your mother's house, I was overwhelmed by you. You were incredible, just as I'd always remembered you.'

Ginny was puzzled. She'd just walked in wearing something casual, her hair all over the place, perhaps a flick of mascara and a hint of lipgloss. How could she have been incredible? She refused to be sweetened by his compliments so slapped him down instead.

'I was just me, Barney. I didn't do anything special for you. I didn't even know you were there.'

'I know. And that's what's unique about you. You're not superficial. I knew it when I first met you, and every woman I've met since then has made me realise how interesting you were. And when I saw you again, I was stunned. I knew nothing had changed.'

Ginny laughed. She couldn't help it. 'Oh, please don't look so wounded, Barney, what do you expect? Everything's changed. Nothing's the same. Not one thing. It's been twenty years, for heaven's sake.'

'The things that have changed aren't important. The thing that's still the same is.'

Ginny fingered her glass, found she was still nervous, and downed another mouthful. 'Barnaby,' she said, trying to sound severe by using his full name. 'There is nothing that is the same. Believe me.'

'I'm still intrigued by you. I have been for twenty years.'

'I – I'm very flattered,' she managed politely. This was so much harder than she'd thought. Harder even, than if he'd laughed at her and dismissed the notion that there'd been something between them. He had, instead, made it very real and very solid. Before it was a potential problem, something she could even have told herself she'd imagined. Now it was a real problem. But there was no way on earth she could admit to him that she was also fascinated by him, that if she was honest her heartbeat had risen, her breathing was tighter, her skin was dancing with life just to be in his presence. For Marie's sake, this could not be an idea that they could just play with and throw away. The implications were far too serious.

'Please don't think I've said any of this to flatter you. Apart from anything,' he gave a short laugh, 'you are the last person to be swayed by flattery. I learnt that about you when we were at university. I just feel I owe it to you to be honest. I knew I'd overstepped some boundaries the other night. I didn't mean to startle you, but I couldn't help myself.'

246

'You were flirting with me. You always were a big flirt.'

Again, Barney looked very surprised. Then his expression cleared. 'Perhaps I was, many years ago, when I was in my first couple of years at university. When you first met me. After Marie happened, all that changed. But I suppose you wouldn't have seen that. You didn't see me change, you didn't see the man I became. The consequences of our night together shocked me, and I was never the same person afterwards.'

Ditto, Ginny thought drily, but she said, 'You can tell me that, of course, but I didn't see it. All I've got is a snapshot of you then, and a snapshot of you now. I can see the same man I used to know.' It wasn't true, Ginny knew even as she said the words. He was different, he was more serious, more sensitive and far more sincere. In fact, she knew instinctively that every-thing he was telling her was true. But it frightened her to death.

'I can assure you, Ginny, I am very different from the boy you knew. I wish you would give me a chance to show you.'

Losing her nerve again, Ginny topped up her wine from the bottle. Around them glasses clinked, trays crashed, people chattered and heels clacked against the floor. They were oblivious to it.

'What do you mean?' she asked carefully. 'What do you want to show me?'

'I wish you would let me take you out. In the old-fashioned sense. I wish we could get to know each other properly, as a man and a woman.'

Now Ginny was terrified and she practically

downed her wine in one go. 'You want to go out with me?' Her voice sounded horribly high pitched.

'Yes. I'd like to ask you out. That's probably a clumsy way of putting it, but that's basically it.'

'And where on earth, Barney, do you think this would lead?'

He seemed unsure, watching her eyes, maybe trying to read her thoughts. 'What do you mean?'

Ginny considered carefully before answering. He'd been so upfront, so square with her. It had taken her by storm. But maybe, if she took a deep breath, she could do him the same courtesy. She tried. And as she began to speak, she felt a powerful conviction.

'I have to be honest with you. I have only had a few relationships since Marie was born and none of them has lasted very long. I wouldn't allow her happiness to be compromised. Not unless a man came along who was fantastic enough for me to introduce him into my daughter's life. And no man has ever been fantastic enough. Maybe if my life had been different, maybe if I'd never had a daughter, my history of relationships would be more colourful. But there it is, like it or not. I don't dabble around, I don't have affairs, I don't experiment with men. So you tell me, Barney, where do you think you taking me out would lead? I can't see it going anywhere beyond a bit of excitement and curiosity. I think the novelty of a reunion would soon wear off. I'm not prepared to mess Marie around for the sake of novelty. I'm sorry to be so unromantic, but it's the bottom line.'

'I see,' he said quietly. Ginny watched him for a while. He was thinking hard, fiddling with the cuffs of his sweater, pouring himself another glass of wine and sipping it very slowly. 'Yes, I see. Of course.'

Perhaps she could sound softer? If her nerves weren't rattling around it would be easier to be gentle. 'Barney? I think it's possible that you're a bit confused. You're having a difficult year, as you've said. You've lost your mother, and coming to meet me again and finding out about Marie is all, as you said, overwhelming. It's a lot for you to take in. I suppose. . . I can imagine that you've got Marie and me mixed up in the same package. In your mind we sort of come together. But it isn't how we are.'

'Oh God, Ginny, is that what you think? No, it's not that,' he said rather harshly, and she sat back to listen. 'I'm sorry, it's just that you're wrong. It undervalues how I feel about you to say that.'

'But. . .' Ginny scrambled for the right words, then a thought occurred to her. When he'd said he had a girlfriend, he'd never indicated it was Honey. Of course, it didn't have to be the woman he lived with. It could be anyone. 'But in case, what about your girlfriend?'

He looked straight at her, an ironic look in his eyes that made her knees melt. She'd forgotten he could do that look, sort of sarcastically sexy. She hadn't seen it since she was a teenager. It sent a bolt of adrenaline through her, especially when his lips curled slightly at the corner with dry humour. 'Come on, Ginny, we both know I don't have a girlfriend.'

'Of course I didn't know that,' she said hotly.

'Yes, you did. I lied about it. Just as you lied about having a boyfriend.'

'I didn't!' It would have been much easier just to come up here and tell Barney that her boyfriend would thump him if he ever kissed her again. She should have thought of that.

'You don't have a boyfriend, Ginny.'

She heaved a breath, defeated. 'My bloody mother,' she muttered.

He laughed aloud, lifting the mood. 'Your mother has nothing to do with it. It's purely that you are a painfully honest person, blunt to the point of rudeness sometimes, which as it happens is one of the things I've always liked about you, and you are no good at lying.'

She tried to look indignant. 'That's cheeky of you to say.'

'I'm sorry. We might as well clear the air and admit that we're both single. We've both got our histories, our reasons. I'm staying with an old friend who happens to be female, but she's got a partner, and even if she hadn't there's nothing between us and never has been. And I know we both lied about having partners to make the whole thing less tense between us. We were trying to deny the chemistry, trying to put a buffer there to prevent it. It's understandable. We're not bad people, we're just crap liars.'

'Well, even so. . .' Ginny foundered. She'd only had a couple of mouthfuls but the wine was going to her head. His tawny eyes were gorgeous, wide and enquiring. He was being incredibly honest about everything. He was laying his feelings out for her to see, or even to trample all over. Wasn't that pretty rare in a man? Was she completely mad to turn him down flatly like this?

'Look,' he said. 'I appreciate you not wanting to mess about. I'm thinking carefully about what you've said. But we're both adults. I can't tell you where it would go because I don't know. But I wondered if you would just give me a chance.'

'I – I can't, Barney. I just can't do that. It's too—'

'Strange?'

'Late.'

He sighed, a deep sigh. When he looked up at her again she could see the feelings stirring deeply inside him. 'That's what I thought you'd say.'

She sighed too. 'In another life. . .'

Barney sat up, put his elbows on the table and peered at Ginny with keen curiosity. 'In another life. . . what?'

'Oh, nothing. Not anything. I'm not thinking clearly.'

'But you feel the same way.'

'No, I didn't say that.'

'But you do.' He had shifted his chair closer to hers and was studying her eagerly. 'You do feel it.'

'I don't. . . I think. . . stop that.' He'd taken her hand and was touching her fingertips gently with his. Her stomach turned over and she tried to pull away. 'Barney!'

Too late, he had put her hand up to his lips and softly kissed the sensitive skin on her fingers. 'Tell me you don't feel the same.'

'I – look, will you stop that?'

He turned her hand over and pressed his lips to her palm. Her stomach felt as if it had dissolved completely. 'Oh God, please don't.'

Then he shifted up to her, put an arm around her shoulders and kissed her on the lips. His breath was warm, his lips soft and damp. Her head spun around and she put up a hand to restrain him.

'Barney,' she said in his ear, 'you must stop.'

He kissed her again and her lips opened. Their tongues met. The sounds of the bar faded away as Ginny lost herself in the passion of his kiss. When he pulled away again, her skin felt tender from the harshness of his bristles. She stared at him helplessly.

'You feel the same,' he confirmed, still holding her fingers and massaging them with his thumb.

'Even if I do,' she whispered to him faintly, 'I am not going to do anything about it. And neither are you.'

'But there is a reason to find out, to test our feelings, to see what's there. Don't you think we owe it to each other, to ourselves?'

'I don't think we owe each other anything. I think we both owe everything we have, every last breath, to Marie.'

Barney gripped her hand tightly. His eyes burnt at her. 'Do you know how rare this is, Ginny? Do you know how many people you meet, every day, every year, who are supposedly a good prospect for you, who you can't feel this with? Could never feel it, even if you lived with them for a lifetime?'

'Don't talk like this,' she breathed at him.

'I have to. I want you to ask yourself that question. We're not kids anymore. We're not even young adults. We've both lived long enough to know that it's unusual when sparks fly, so when they do you have to stop and take notice. It happened to us then and it's happening to us now. Don't you think that it's a good reason for us to explore what it is?'

'I think,' she said, emotion rising in her throat as her feelings swamped her, 'that you owe it to me to let me leave now.'

'I don't want you to leave.'

252

'But I'm going to.'

He sat quietly, still and unprotesting as Ginny very slowly and shakily stood up, put her coat back on and hooked her handbag over her shoulder. She looked at him before she left and their eyes seemed to be wide and hungry. 'You understand why I have to go, don't you?'

He nodded.

'This doesn't affect anything between you and Marie. You know you're welcome at our house, anytime.'

'Ginny, there's something I want you to know. Something I've always wanted to tell you, for all these years. Please let me tell you now.'

'Go on.'

'I was in love with you,' he said softly, but it was as if he shouted it. 'Back then. I was in love with you.'

She bit back the swell that rose in her throat. How could this have been? How could they both have been in love and yet not been able to communicate it?

'And I think I'm still in love with you,' he said.

She felt tears spring to her eyes. 'Goodbye, Barney,' she said in a choked voice before turning and blindly pushing her way out of the crowded bar.

Chapter Twenty-seven

Ginny still felt weak when she walked into her house nearly two hours later. She took off her coat and smoothed down her hair, examining herself in the mirror. Her eyes were still wild, her pupils black and dilated. She made herself a cup of coffee and drank it in the living room, in her favourite chair, in the dark with only the hall light casting a rectangle of yellow light on the carpet next to her. She ran Barney's words through her head, over and over again. He had been in love with her, twenty years ago, at the same time that she'd been in love with him. They'd been young, immature and gauche. They were students, only just out of adolescence, sucked into the world of display, of image, of dishonesty. They both had their own tools for dealing with rejection. He had his humour, his teasing, and had made it all look like a joke. She had her temperature control – she'd frozen him out. They had both been so convincing that their feelings had remained wrapped in secrecy. Then her pregnancy had landed on the situation like a bomb. She'd panicked and withdrawn. He'd panicked and tried to run away. Was it so strange, so unusual? Couldn't it have happened to a hundred and one other teenagers in exactly the same way? Did their ineptitude in dealing with the situation nullify the value of the feelings they'd had? That was what she couldn't answer. Events had overtaken subtleties, like a big boot print over a delicate sepia photograph.

Then as she finished her coffee and sat quietly, lost in her thoughts, confused beyond measure, she realised that the phone was ringing.

'Don't be Barney. Don't be Barney,' she chanted, going to answer it.

It was Charlotte. She sounded frantic.

'Ginny? Thank God you're there. I think my waters have broken.'

Ginny stood up straight, instantly sober and clear headed, concern for Charlotte bursting through all her other preoccupations like a sharp cold metallic spike.

'It's all right, don't worry. Where's Mum?'

'Out with Dad. I think they went for dinner somewhere, but I don't know where. I tried to call her. She took her mobile but I think she's turned it off by mistake. You know she doesn't really know how it works. I'm here all by myself and then this thing suddenly happened.'

'Okay, forget Mum. What's happened?'

'I've got all this warm water gushing out and going all over the floor.'

'What, really gushing?'

'In torrents.'

'Have you got any contractions?'

'Little ones but they seem to be getting bigger. I'm scared, Ginny. What should I do?'

'I'm coming straight round. You need to get down on your hands and knees on the floor, somewhere comfortable, so that the baby's position is stable. Did the midwives tell you?'

'Oh God, yes. Something about keeping the baby's head down.' Charlotte's voice cracked and she burst into tears. 'It's really happening, isn't it?'

'You'll be fine,' Ginny soothed. 'I'll be there in two minutes and I'll look after you.'

'But Mum was going to be my birthing partner!' Charlotte sobbed. 'I'm all on my own.'

'Of course you're not on your own. I'm here. I'll come with you.'

'Throughout the whole thing? Will you stay with me?'

'Yes, of course I will.'

'You won't just drop me off and leave?'

Ginny's heart softened and affection surged through her. 'No, Charlotte, of course I won't leave you. I promise, I'll stay for as long as it takes.'

'But you told me to get stuffed,' Charlotte sobbed.

'I didn't mean it. I'm your sister and I love you. Now get off the phone. I'll pack some stuff and come round, you just get comfortable.'

Charlotte rang off. Ginny quickly tried her mother's mobile number but it was, as Charlotte had said, on voicemail. Bloody thing, Ginny cursed inwardly. Of all the times for her mother to be unavailable. But she flung some things into a bag, thinking fast. She grabbed her car keys and left the house. It looked as if it was going to be a long night. Thank God she'd had a coffee and a baguette at Charing Cross while she'd waited for a delayed train. Now she felt completely focused.

'You've got to contact Raj!' Charlotte was crying as Ginny whisked her to the hospital in her car. They'd covered the passenger seat with towels and Charlotte was squirming.

'Sit still, darling,' Ginny tried to soothe her. 'We'll be at the maternity unit in a minute.'

'But I need him.' Charlotte dissolved into tears again, great hearty sobs that had Ginny glancing at her every five seconds with worry. 'I need him. I love him.'

'Let's just get there and you can give me all his details and I'll call him.'

'He's in India. He won't get here in time. Oh God, I've fucked this up so badly. I've really messed up, Ginny. I've made such a big mistake. I wish I hadn't left him. Oh my God.'

'Are you having another contraction?'

'Yes.' Charlotte strained, her body taut as she breathed through the pain. 'Oh God, it's horrible.'

'It's all right, we're here now. You sit still, I'm going to come round and help you out of the car.'

'Okay.'

Carefully Ginny guided Charlotte's hunched form out of the car and a couple of steps into the main entrance of the labour ward. Ginny pressed a button on the intercom and explained it was them – she'd already rung them as they'd left the house to warn that they were coming. The sister on duty was there to greet them and opened the double glass doors to let them in. She gave Charlotte a warm smile and put her arm around her, helping her towards one of the delivery rooms that led off the corridor.

'My name's Megan, I'll look after you tonight. Oh, there's no need to cry, darling, it's all natural. Let's get you settled.'

Content that Charlotte was in good hands, Ginny

stayed while she was laid carefully on a bed and wired up to a series of machines.

'There we are,' Megan assured them both in a sing-song voice that somehow eased their tension. 'A lovely strong heartbeat and here you can see your contractions on the paper. See? You're doing very well.'

'I know,' Charlotte puffed, her head flopped back on the pillow. 'I went through all this when I had a false alarm.'

'Let's just see how strong your contractions are. Have you been timing them?'

'It's about every three or four minutes now,' Ginny told her. 'They seem to have come on very strongly in the last half-hour.'

'And you have your sister's notes?'

'Here.' Ginny handed the folder over and Megan read through them.

'That's fine.' Megan smiled again.

They fell quiet, listening to the heartbeat of the baby drumming steadily, Charlotte groaning with each stronger contraction. Ginny held her hands and could feel from the pressure of her grip that she was in a lot of pain. Once Charlotte was calmer and breathing steadily, she asked the question herself. 'Is it happening now?'

'It looks as if he may be coming, darling,' Megan said. 'But these things can take a long time.'

'It feels like it's happening now.' Charlotte sat up again as another contraction gripped her. 'Am I in labour?'

'Oh no, darling.' Megan twinkled at them and Ginny smiled a knowing smile. 'Not officially, at least. That comes when your cervix is contracted by three centimetres and more; it'll be a while yet, although your little one's quite impatient, isn't he? Now, have you thought about a birthing plan?'

'I don't care,' Charlotte said tearfully. 'I just want him to be alive. He's early.'

'Well that's life, my love. They all have their own way of knowing when to come.'

'But he's early!' Charlotte insisted. 'He may not be – be properly formed.'

'Oh, he's only a tiny bit early, and I can see from your notes that your dates are a bit vague. He's a big boy, too. I'm sure he'll be all right, but we've got lots of help here if he needs it. What about pain relief? Have you got any strong feelings about it?'

'I wasn't going to have any,' Charlotte heaved a difficult breath, 'but I want some, please.'

'Can I get you some gas and air now? Yes, I can see from the monitor your contractions are quite strong now.'

'Yes, please!'

The sister bustled away. Ginny held on fast to Charlotte's hands.

'Charlotte? I want to tell you that I'm sorry.'

'I'm sorry too.'

They stared into each other's eyes, the love they felt for each other glimmering through.

'I'm sorry I didn't offer to help more. I thought you wanted to be independent.' Ginny squeezed Charlotte's fingers.

'I was scared. I didn't know what to ask you. I didn't want you to gloat over me because everything had gone wrong.'

259

'I wouldn't have gloated, but I'm sorry you thought that. It's my fault.'

'No, it's mine. I've been selfish and bloody minded. I kept thinking about Marie but I didn't say anything. How is she?'

'Oh,' Ginny laughed. 'She's fine. Of all of us, she's the most sorted I think. Having a whale of a time. She sent you her love in her last email.'

'She did?' Charlotte's face lit up. 'I can't wait to see her again. I wish I'd got to know her better. I should have made more effort.'

'It's not too late. You can see lots of her when she comes back.'

'I will.'

'And she's really excited about your baby. She wanted to know what you're going to call him.'

Charlotte sighed and instantly looked distressed again. 'I want Raj to choose his name.'

'Shall I go and try Mum again? I've left her messages all over the place and she's got all those notes at home for when she gets back. I could go outside and ring her again now if you want. I can't turn my mobile on in here.'

'Don't go!' Charlotte said in panic, her face reddening. 'Don't leave me alone here.'

'I won't, baby sister.' Ginny kissed her cheek and felt tears rising in her throat They held on to each other and hugged. 'And Raj?' Ginny enquired gently. 'Do you want me to call him?'

'Yes! Yes, call Raj then come back. Take my mobile, it's there in my bag. His number's in the address book. Just click on it and call.'

'What is it, a home number?'

'It's his mobile. Please be quick, Ginny.'

Megan reappeared with a consultant, a tall, wiry-limbed woman who Ginny couldn't possibly believe was old enough to be a doctor. It made her feel very old.

'We're going to change you into a gown, Charlotte, and just check you internally to see how you're progressing.'

'Is that okay, Charlotte?' Ginny checked as she took the mobile. 'Do you want me to wait?'

'No, ring Raj. Tell him to talk to Tom Stafford at the High Commission. He knows us, he can arrange a visa. Tell him I love him. Tell him – tell him the truth. Make him come here.'

'I will,' Ginny said and made her way to the outside of the hospital to move her car from the emergency area to the car park and make the call as quickly as possible.

Ginny couldn't get through to Raj. She tried and tried but received some strange signal that she couldn't interpret. How was she going to go back and tell Charlotte she couldn't get through? And leaving Charlotte on her own had made her feel incredibly protective. She was anxious to get back to her as quickly as possible.

She tried her mother once more. The home phone was on answerphone, as was her mobile.

'Oh, bloody Mum!' Ginny yelled into the night air, her breath creating a white, frosty puff. 'Of all the times to do a disappearing act.'

Impatiently, she tried Raj again. Still no response.

Despairing and not prepared to leave Charlotte

alone any longer, Ginny strode back across the lit car park where she'd left her car and up the path to the maternity unit. At the glass doors, she could see the back of a tall man pressing the intercom button and speaking into it.

'I am looking for Miss Charlotte Simpson, please.' Ginny's heart skipped a beat as she approached, seeing the man's dark head, listening to the exchange. 'No, I am not a relative, but I am the baby's father, if you would allow me to see her please.'

'Oh my God!' Ginny ran up to him. Now she had no doubt – a very slight lilt to his voice, a roll to the way he pronounced his 'r' confirmed to her this must be true. 'Oh God, is it you? Raj! Are you Raj?'

He swung round. As a midwife appeared at the doors and opened them, he blinked at her, He was a sturdy man, dressed in a sweater, jacket and jeans. His hair, she could see now, was thick and black, and he studied her with big brown eyes and long dark lashes. She could see instantly why Charlotte had fallen in love with him. There was a gentleness in his features, but strength, too. He was lovely. He looked cold, tired and strained, but he brightened optimistically on seeing Ginny.

'Yes, I'm Raj. You're Ginny? Charlotte's sister? I recognise you from a photo she kept by the bed.'

'She kept a photo of me by her bed?'

'You and Marie.'

Ginny couldn't help herself. It had been such a day, such an evening, such a night She burst into floods of tears and threw herself into his strong arms.

'I can't believe it I am so, so glad you're here.'

'I've had a heck of a bloody adventure getting here,'

he said, as his voice broke and she thought for a moment he was going to cry too. 'Your father had to come and sort it all out at Heathrow immigration. He's been amazing. He dropped your mother off at your home and she's just packing some bags, she said, and she'll be here in a minute.'

'What?' Ginny stood away from him, wiping her eyes. 'What do you mean?'

'It's a long story.' He smiled, looking exhausted. 'Your parents will tell you. Now I must go and see Charlotte. I have to be with her.'

Chapter Twenty-eight

Ginny hesitated as she was about to lead Raj into the room where Charlotte was. She stood back.

'You go in. I'll wait outside.'

'Thank you,' he said.

As he walked in, Ginny couldn't help herself. She had to peer through the gap and watch. Charlotte was sitting up, holding the sister's hand, groaning loudly. With her other hand she was holding a black mask of gas and air to her mouth. A contraction was just coming to an end. She pulled the mask away again and let it rest on the bed.

'There's a good girl,' Megan soothed her. 'All over now. Do you want to lie flat again for a second?'

'Hmm,' Charlotte murmured, then she looked up. She screamed in delight. 'Raj! Raj! Oh God, it's really you, you're here! I love you so much.' She began to cry and Ginny saw him leap forward and seize her hands, showering kisses on her hair, her face, her neck, her arms. 'Oh my God!' Charlotte cried, over and over.

'My lovely girl,' Raj almost shouted at her. 'You silly girl, you silly, lovely girl. Why did you leave? I love you so much. My life's nothing without you.'

'But you've come to get me!' Charlotte wailed.

'Yes, of course I've come to bloody get you. You're

going to be my wife! I won't argue about it again. Kiss me!'

'I love you!'

'I love you!'

The sister made a diplomatic exit from the room and stood outside with Ginny. She pulled the door closed, although Ginny guessed they both would have somehow liked to have been voyeurs at such a moment of extraordinary happiness. She and Ginny exchanged glances.

'I gather that's good news, then,' the sister said, raising her eyebrows.

'Oh yes. The best news. She loves him, he's the baby's father. It's perfect. I'm so happy for her.'

'Me too. I always feel a bit sad when I have to deliver a baby and there's no dad.'

Ginny almost said something but bit her tongue. In fact, she found that she just felt a little sad herself. 'Yes, I suppose.'

'It's an old-fashioned world, however modern we like to think we are,' Megan decided. 'We see it all here. The best and the worst. I like to think there's always a happy ending. I'm a romantic, really.'

'Me too,' Ginny agreed, then realised what she'd said. She'd been so stoic, so determined to do the right thing for Marie, but it was true, she was a romantic at heart. She felt nothing but delight for Charlotte, that she would find fulfilment where she hadn't.

Ginny's eyes were still damp from welcoming Raj with the explosive combination of incredulity, relief, joy. She'd had an emotional evening. And perhaps it was true that her happiness for Charlotte was tinged with envy, that Charlotte was producing the happy ending that she couldn't. That Charlotte's baby would have his two parents (because she didn't doubt it now) to love him, nurture him, give him double the love.

How might things have been different if she and Barney had been able to articulate their feelings? What if Marie hadn't happened when she did? What if she had gone out with Barney again when he'd asked her? What if they'd been like any other young couple, meeting and falling in love at university, going forward into life together, perhaps even getting married and having a family in a conventional way. Just how might her life had been different?

From inside Charlotte's labour room came the sound of loud moaning again and Raj appeared, harassed, at the door. He stared at the sister in panic.

'I think the baby's coming. Please come and help.'

'She's officially in labour now, darling,' the sister confirmed. 'Progressing well but you've still got a few hours to go. I'll come back in now if you like, we need to ask her if she'd like an epidural.'

'Yes, I want a bloody epidural!' Charlotte shouted from inside the room. 'And make it bloody quick!'

Ginny glanced at Raj, wondering how he might take this rollercoaster of manic ejections coming from Charlotte, but he glanced back, winked, and smiled tiredly. 'I see she's the same old Charlotte.'

'I'm so glad you're here,' Ginny said, her eyes stupidly brimming again. 'So glad. Now I'm going to go and find my dad.'

After they'd checked with the sister again that Charlotte's labour was progressing well but likely to be a few hours, Ginny took her father into the hospital canteen and they both collected a hot coffee and a sandwich. Jane had arrived with some bags of Charlotte's things, but wanted to sit in the visitors' room, just up the corridor from Charlotte, just so that she could be close.

'You just need to explain it all to me, Dad,' Ginny said, dazed, as she munched on an egg and cress roll. 'I don't get it. How did Raj know where to come?'

'I've been busy doing a little scheming, I'm afraid,' Harry confessed, knitting his bushy eyebrows together and pulling a face as he bit into a sad-looking salad sandwich. 'When I met Charlotte she told me the whole story about her and Raj.'

Ginny nodded but guilt lay heavily in her stomach. She'd never asked Charlotte the real story about her relationship, never encouraged her to talk about it. She'd only made judgemental noises, and now she regretted it badly. 'I only know a bit about it, really.'

'It's all right, Ginny. I know you and Charlotte haven't exactly been getting on since she came home.'

'I've been a cow to her, basically. I was so defensive. I'm really sorry about it now.'

'She was defensive too. But that's all behind you now. Blood's thicker than water. You were there for her tonight, and she'll never forget it.'

'I hope.' Ginny bit her lip. 'So what was the story with Raj?'

'She told me his family were against their relationship, that his sister had very bluntly told her to get out of his life. He was going to lose his family, his inheritance, everything because of her. So she left.'

'But didn't he protest? What about the baby?'

'She lied to him. Told him the baby wasn't his. She loved him that much.'

'God, I had no idea.' When this was all over, when Charlotte was fit again, Ginny would speak to her properly. They'd have a night out together, maybe have a few glasses of wine, and sort things out. It was time that she showed Charlotte how much she cared about her.

'So I took matters into my own hands. I'm afraid I was a bit sneaky. When I was out with Charlotte I was hoping there'd be a chance to look through her bag to find a number for Raj or something, but I didn't get the opportunity. So I spoke to your mother about it, and we decided to do something. She searched through Charlotte's things when she was asleep, but she couldn't find any kind of contact number either.'

'How did you manage it, then?'

'Your mother found the details of the school in Mumbai she used to work at on the Internet, and contacted them. Apparently he has some kind of management job there and they had a mobile number for him. So I called him, talked to him, and he sorted out a visa and a flight as soon as he could.'

'So he believed you?'

'Of course. It didn't take much to convince him she'd lied to let him go. He can see the best in her very easily. He loves her very much, you know.'

Ginny was amazed. 'You did all this without telling me?'

'Without telling either of you.'

Ginny accepted that without comment. She'd hardly shown a great deal of interest in her sister's predicament until now. 'So what happened today? I thought

Charlotte said you and Mum had gone out to dinner?'

'That was the plan. Then as I was about to leave my hotel room I got a call from Raj. He was at Heathrow and the immigration officials were giving him a hard time. They'd kept him there all afternoon and it still wasn't resolved. The poor man was desperate to get to see Charlotte as soon as possible. I was on my way to see Jane anyway, so when I picked your mother up at home we decided to drive straight to the airport to talk to them, to explain the situation.'

'Jesus. I had no idea so much was going on this evening. You've been to Heathrow and back.'

'It wasn't quite how I expected the evening to turn out myself, as it happens.' Harry grinned. 'Quite different.'

'And immigration were okay with you?'

'They were fine once they got the story from all three of us.' He paused to mutter an expletive and Ginny raised her eyebrows at him. 'Sorry. But all's well that ends well. So we got Raj home, eager to produce him for Charlotte with a big fanfare, and the house was empty. We found your notes all over the place and messages on the answerphone, so of course Raj and I leapt back in the car and drove straight up here. Your mum wanted to pack Charlotte's bags first, so she followed us in her own car.'

'Bloody hell, Dad, what a night.'

'Yes. I feel especially sorry for Raj. He's been through the mill today. But he got here in time, and that's all that counts. Thank God he's here.'

Ginny shook her head in disbelief. It was hard to believe what each of them had been going through that Friday evening. And Charlotte, having come home for

269

security, had ended up on her own in the kitchen with a plate of spaghetti Bolognese in one hand when her waters decided to break. All this and Barney declaring his undying love to Ginny in a crowded London bar. It was quite a lot to take in. And all the time she was picturing Charlotte a block away in the delivery room, understanding the pain she was in, feeling her own excitement growing about the imminent birth of Charlotte's baby. She wanted to be by Charlotte's side, gripping her hand, encouraging her. But she knew that somebody far more appropriate than her was doing that job right now.

Then suddenly something Harry had said came back to wave at her. She did a double-take. 'Hang on, Dad. You said Raj called when you were about to leave your hotel room. What hotel room? I thought you were living in a house with Denise.'

'Oh, I was,' Harry said easily. 'But I moved out.'

Ginny sat bolt upright, almost spilling her coffee. 'You did what?'

'About a week ago.'

'She threw you out?' Ginny was aghast, but delighted too. She didn't know what to think.

'No, no. She'd have been happy for me to stay. I moved out. It was my choice.'

'But – why, Dad? You spent so long telling me it was exactly what you wanted.'

'Do you know, Ginny, the strange thing is that even at my age, even when I should have built up a stack of self-knowledge over the years, I still don't know what I want. I love Jane, and in a way I loved Denise, too, but, above all, I'm just a bit lost. It's not something you'd understand, but it's the kind of lost that it

270

doesn't take anybody else to sort out. I suppose it would be a mid-life crisis if I was mid-life, but I'm not, I'm older than that. And it's not about testosterone – sorry to be blunt, I know I'm your dad. I thought it might be about physicality at one point, Denise did make me feel more alive in that department, but I know that's not it now. It's not about proving I'm attractive. I don't really, well, if you'll excuse my French, I don't really give a shit about whether young women fancy me or not. I find them very dull.'

'It's all right,' Ginny murmured while squirming quietly.

'I'm the kind of age where people get interviewed on Radio Four for suddenly going off and doing degrees in Ancient Greek, or flying round the world in a bi-plane, or writing their first novel. I'm not sure I'm brave enough to do any of those things, but that's something I need to consider.'

'So what are you going to do?' Ginny tried not to sound too startled.

'Oh, I think I might just be single for a while. Get my head together. Do some thinking.'

'But you arranged to meet Mum,' Ginny fished slyly. 'That must have been for a reason.'

'Oh, yes. We both wanted to talk.' He nodded.

'About what?'

Harry paused. 'I think that's between your mother and me.'

Ginny was surprised by the firmness of his tone, and felt admonished. She was going to protest that she was their daughter and part of the family, so she was entitled to know what was going on, but thought better of it. Were the intimate details of her parents'

271

marriage really her affair? Probably not. In fact, definitely not. She felt a little embarrassed.

'I'm sorry, Dad. I didn't mean to pry.'

'No, I know, love, don't worry. That's the thing about families. Everyone treads on each other's toes once in while. Sometimes I think there have been rather too many of us in this marriage.'

'You sound like Princess Diana.'

'Yes, perhaps I do.' He chuckled. 'Although I think Charlotte will probably marry Raj and probably live in India with him. And I'll be honest with you, Ginny, although I wouldn't put it this way to Charlotte, I think if she does your mother and I may stand a chance of ending up side by side in a graveyard after all.'

Charlotte's son was born at eight thirty in the morning. They named him Benjamin Anton Rajadurai.

Charlotte lay in a haze of drugs and happiness, her son's warm head resting on her breast, his velvety skin against hers. Raj didn't seem to be able to let go of the little hand that gripped his finger. He sat hunched in a chair, pulled up alongside Charlotte's bed, staring at the baby. He seemed unable to stop staring. His face displayed total enchantment.

'I am completely happy,' Charlotte told Ginny in a sleepy voice, although she knew she wouldn't sleep. Probably not for a week. She didn't want to close her eyes and shut out the beautiful sight of the curly black hair, the clenched fingers, the tiny toes, the little red mouth that reached for her breast with an instinct that amazed her. She was filled with wonderment. I didn't know what happiness was. I didn't understand. 'Now I do.'

'I know.' Ginny, who had been up all night with her mother and father, taking tours of the canteen, the hospital grounds, the car park, the visitors' room, and every so often, when they were asked for by Charlotte, the delivery room, was exhausted too. But seeing Charlotte with her tiny son, her love for Marie swelled again and filled her inside. She'd already phoned Marie's mobile but the reception had been awful and they'd been cut off. She would send her a long email, telling her all about Raj and her parents' dramatic Heathrow flit, and the birth of the gorgeous Benjamin. Jane and Harry had gone home, to respective home and hotel room Ginny could only assume, to get some sleep. They would be back later in the day when Charlotte was rested.

'I don't know who's cried the most.' Charlotte smiled, her mouth wide and happy. 'You, me, Mum, Dad or Raj.'

'It's a new life,' Ginny said, her voice choked again as she touched her nephew's head very gently. 'A new beginning. A chance to do everything right. It's magic.'

'Yes,' Charlotte breathed. 'Magic.' Then she turned to gaze at Ginny with hazy eyes full of love. 'I know how you felt now. About Marie. I understand what you said about thinking about her all the time. I understand the fear of something happening to her. It's so strong.'

Ginny nodded. 'Yes.'

'Isn't he the most beautiful baby you've ever seen?'

'Of course he is.'

'It's a miracle.'

'Yes. It is.'

Ginny finally went home and lay on her bed, on top

of the covers. It was early on Saturday afternoon and Mr Mistoffelees came and curled up beside her. She stroked his head and cooed at him.

'Congratulate me. I'm an auntie,' she told him wearily as she drifted into a deep sleep.

Chapter Twenty-nine

In the two days that Charlotte stayed in the post-natal ward to rest, Jane and Ginny turned Charlotte's bedroom into a nursery. Ginny had brought Marie's old cot round, they'd bought a new mattress to fit it and a selection of baby clothes, towels and toiletries, which they'd arranged beautifully in the bedroom for her to find.

'He's a lovely man, Raj,' Jane had said, glowing with happiness (as they all had been since the birth of Benjamin), while they fiddled with the blankets in the cot, and planted a huge furry teddy bear inside it as a surprise. 'I do like him. I think he's just right for Charlotte. I couldn't wish for a nicer son-in-law.'

'You think they will get married, then?' Ginny had quizzed.

'Oh yes. I think he's a traditional sort. Whatever his family might make of it, I think he'll want things done properly. He'll do it despite them. And they'll come round in the end. Especially when they see the baby. It'll take time, though. I expect his mother will be the first to crack. The rest will follow, in their own time.'

Ginny was awed by her mother's confidence, but it was convincing. 'I never thought Charlotte was the marrying kind.'

'She wasn't. Not until she fell in love. Hand me the

bunny. I think we can hang him at the top of the cot. There. Now let's get the mobile up.'

'You're quite enjoying this, aren't you?' Ginny watched her mother as she untangled the zoo mobile they'd bought.

'It takes me back. Doesn't it you?'

'Yes.' Ginny sighed. 'Yes, it does. I'm trying not to think about it, though. There's no point whatsoever in me getting broody.'

Jane, who was on her hands and knees on the bedroom carpet, sat back on her heels and stared at Ginny probingly. 'Why ever not?

'What do you mean? For obvious reasons. I'm not going to have any more children.'

'Who says?'

'Mum!' Ginny laughed. 'The God of common sense says.'

'The God of biology says you're only thirty-nine. Women have children right into their forties nowadays.'

'Yes, but however twenty-first century you want to be about it, it does still require some male participation.'

'And who's to say you won't meet the right man?'

Ginny stared at her mother incredulously, although she could feel colour rising in her cheeks as Barney flashed into her mind. 'Don't be silly, Mum.'

Jane cocked her head on one side. 'Did you see Barney again?'

Ginny pressed her lips together. She didn't want to talk about it. Thank goodness, Charlotte's baby had arrived and had superimposed itself over any other muddled thoughts she might have been having. She could just concentrate on making a fuss of the baby now and being a better sister to Charlotte. That was enough emotional output for the time being. With any luck, Barney would eventually give up any crazy notions he was fostering.

Although it hadn't happened yet. He'd sent her a dozen red roses that day and it was only a couple of days since she'd seen him. They were beautiful, she'd had to admit, and she'd put them in her bedroom so that she could ponder them as she fell asleep. She couldn't help feeling that it was a very romantic gesture. But that didn't mean she was going to weaken.

'Darling?' Jane pushed on. 'Did you see him? I was wondering.'

'Look, Mum, you're going to have one daughter happily married off. That'll be enough, won't it? Don't go turning into Mrs Bennett.'

'I am no Mrs Bennett,' Jane said, affronted. 'But I know a good man when I see one. They're rare, you know.'

'I know they're rare,' Ginny said in exasperation. 'That's why I'm still single. It's why I'm likely to remain single.'

'The only reason you're likely to remain single, my girl,' Jane said as she stood up and rattled the mobile around, 'is because you are in denial.'

'About what?' Ginny asked, round eyed, as her mother expertly screwed the plastic clamp of the mobile to the edge of the cot.

'About Barney,' Jane said, flicking a switch and sending the honky-tonk tune of *Imagine* bouncing through the air.

'There's nothing to deny.'

'Yes. There is. He's clearly in love with you, Ginny. I could see it. Why don't you give him a chance?'

'Mum!' Ginny flushed hotly. 'Really, I can't talk to you about it.'

'Why not? Seriously, Ginny,' she added kindly, 'I do think you should talk about it. I know it's complicated, but it would help you to work your feelings through.'

'And what about you, Mum?' Ginny defended. 'Who do you talk to about your feelings? I was wondering why you and Dad had gone out together on Friday.'

'Well that's for us to know and for you to guess, isn't it?' Jane raised an eyebrow.

'You know he's moved out of that dentist's house, don't you?'

'Yes,' Jane said easily.

'Doesn't that mean something? It's a step in the right direction, isn't it?'

'Oh, my dear Ginny.' Jane heaved a big breath and perched on the edge of Charlotte's bed, flicking a plastic pack of bath toys out of the way. 'There's so much you don't see.'

'Can't you tell me about it?'

Jane gazed at the wall for a few seconds as if gathering difficult thoughts together. 'When we were together, your father and I lost all our energy, all our – dynamism. Apart, we seemed to have found it again. It was as if we were staunching the flow of each other's ideas. Just by being there. Just by living in the same house. Just by living up to each other's expectations – or maybe living down to them. By maintaining the routine that we thought the other

278

person expected us to have. I know, it won't make sense.'

'I'm not sure.' Ginny thought about what her father had said to her in the hospital canteen. It was starting to make a certain kind of surreal sense. 'What if you wanted the same things, only you didn't know it?'

'Oh, my dear, not after forty or so years of marriage. You know what the other person's thinking. You can feel it, without them saying a word.'

'Yes, Mum,' Ginny thought about it, 'but what if you were wrong. What if you and Dad both wanted your relationship to be different, but you just assumed you were alone in that. What if you both wanted changes but. . . I mean, what if you wanted the same changes?'

'I think, Ginny, that if that were the case we would know it. You don't live with somebody for this many years without knowing what they're feeling.'

'In which case,' Ginny persevered with her logic, 'you must have completely expected Dad to run off and have an affair with a dentist.'

Jane sighed loudly. 'Not exactly. No, I didn't quite expect that, I have to say.'

'Well there you are.'

'But it's given me breathing space, do you see? It's given me a chance to think about my life. I'm not just a mother and grandmother, you see. I'm Jane Simpson. I was once Jane Mills. I was a person with ambitions and ideas. Other priorities take you over, change you. You know that, of all people. But it doesn't stop you dreaming. And somehow your dad and I seemed to just get each other down. But Marie spent so much time here, it was her second home, and we loved that, you know. We pulled through all those years with a common aim. Then when Marie was planning her trip away, when she was finally leaving home, oh, I don't know. It seemed to be a catalyst for both of us.'

'So, what are you saying? You were scared of being alone together?'

'Maybe, darling.' Jane nodded thoughtfully. 'Maybe we were just a little jittery about what was left. Maybe we both felt it was the last chance to seize the time we had.'

Ginny chewed her lip. 'I still think that it's possible that you want the same things, there's just something inexplicable stopping you from communicating it to each other. It would just be such a shame if you didn't talk about it, didn't really lay it all out on the table and debate it before you threw it all away.'

'There are more things in heaven and earth. . .' Jane laughed softly. 'I can never remember the rest of that quote.'

'Neither can I'

'When you get to my age, you watch Michael Palin on the television. You divide into two camps. Those who huddle up into the armchair and thank God they're at home clutching a mug of tea and cosseted by their central heating. And those who hate him for having the chance to do something we'd long to do.'

'And you're in the second camp?'

Jane nodded. 'Yes. Hate his guts. Fancy him like mad, but hate him. Lucky bastard.'

Ginny couldn't help laughing out loud, although she'd never heard Jane talk like this. She hadn't known she was harbouring such feelings. But there was something she felt she needed to point out 'Mum, I have to tell you that I watch Michael Palin, too. And I'm in the second camp, with you.'

'Well, there you are.' Jane stood up again briskly, and flicked the zoo mobile to check that it was still working. 'Perhaps we're all just a little jealous of our Charlotte when it comes down to it.'

Ginny fell silent. Her mother had a knack of being right. It wasn't worth arguing with her.

'And,' Jane went on smoothly, 'you still haven't answered my question. There's Barney, another person who's been out there exploring, living a life less ordinary, as Charlotte puts it. And it's made him an interesting man; certainly somebody worth thinking about very carefully. Now just who are you going to talk to about your feelings in that department? I can't imagine they're simple. It must be very disturbing for you to have him back in your life.'

'Well. . .'

'Especially as he's turned out so well,' Jane added, like Basil Brush trying to get the last word in.

Ginny hesitated. There was no point claiming black was white where Jane was concerned. 'I might. . . I'm seeing Rebecca for a drink in the week. Perhaps I'll talk to her about it.'

'Not your best confidante at the moment,' Jane said practically. 'No woman on the verge of divorce is going to be very optimistic about a new romance.'

'Barney's hardly a new romance,' Ginny snorted. 'He's the father of my daughter.'

'Oh, you've done things in the wrong order. There's no doubt about that. But he is very much a new romance. Perhaps if you looked at it that way you might be able to see what I can.'

'And what is that, Mum?' Ginny asked with sarcastic monotony.

'That he'd be a good husband for you.'

And leaving Ginny gaping in shock at this final announcement, Jane trotted out of the bedroom claiming she thought she could smell the dinner burning.

'We will be married as soon as you're well enough,' Raj told Charlotte gently when they were home, snuggled up together on Charlotte's bed with Benjamin sucking hungrily at her breast.

'Your family will hate that.' Charlotte still felt a stab of pain for him every time she thought about it. 'They'll disown you. Leela will make sure of it.'

Raj stroked Benjamin's warm, dark head. 'It will be their loss.'

'It must mean so much more to you than that. I know you're being brave for me and for the baby and I love you for it, but—'

'Not as brave as you were to walk away from me. I had a long flight here and I did a lot of thinking about my parents. I wrote them a letter on the plane, I've posted it, and I'll see what response I get. If there's none, too bad. If they can't see what a wonderful woman my wife is it just shows how blind they are.'

'But your family are so important, love,' Charlotte entreated, not knowing how she could advise him now.

'My family?' He kissed her cheek softly. 'My family is right here, in my arms.'

'I love you so much.'

'I know, darling. And you're tired. The baby's fallen asleep now, you should get some rest.'

'I can't rest. I just keep wanting to look at him. I'm so scared he'll disappear if I fall asleep.' She glanced at Raj cautiously. 'Where do you think we should go? Oh, my mum's being wonderful, I know we can stay here for as long as we like, until we get sorted, but after that, what do you think?'

Raj heaved a long breath. 'I've been thinking about it. I know how much you missed your home. I think you'll want to be here, near your family, in the country you know. It's natural.'

'But my home is with you now. And all the time I've been here I've missed India so much. I never realised how much I loved it until I came back to England. Everything's smaller here, greyer, more organised. I miss the colour, the noise, the smells. I miss the people, my students, and I really miss our friends. I just miss the vastness of it. I think India's in my blood.'

'So what are you saying?' Raj raised his eyebrows hopefully.

'I'm saying that I want to go back to India. For us to make our life there. We've both got good jobs and I want Benjamin to know all about his country and his culture.'

'And England? He is half English, after all.'

'We can visit any time. I think Mum and Dad would understand. I've been away for so many years, they've got used to it.'

'But now you would be taking their grandson away. I don't think they'd like that.'

Charlotte pondered, unravelling a strand of her hair from Benjamin's hand and kissing her son's tiny, damp fingers. 'I think they'll be happy if they see him regularly. I have a feeling they need some time to themselves.'

'What do you mean?' Raj looked puzzled, propping himself up on one elbow. 'Do you think your father will come back here?'

'Hmm. I'm not sure.' Carefully, every muscle in her body still aching from the birth, Charlotte shifted herself from the bed and laid Benjamin in his cot. She tucked him up and gazed at him with pure love. 'I think they need some time alone. I don't know if they can do that together or not.'

Chapter Thirty

If Ginny was looking for a cynic to ally with when she met Rebecca for a drink the following Friday evening, she might have thought that she'd found one.

Rebecca certainly looked paler and thinner as they stood at the bar and ordered their drinks. A gin and tonic for Rebecca, who asked for a double with a laugh and a conspiratorial look at Ginny, who asked for her wine to be a large one. Ginny had walked to the pub they'd chosen to meet at, as it was at her end of the town, and Rebecca had got a taxi there, she'd told Ginny as they'd arrived. Not to be a sober evening then, Ginny correctly deduced.

It wasn't a cute pub, only one they both knew to be friendly and mostly empty, and bereft of visiting bands on a Friday night. It was understood that they wanted to talk rather than to be entertained on their night out. They went to a table in the lounge bar, which was practically empty apart from two men in suits mumbling in the corner, and settled themselves. Ginny took her coat off and hung it on the back of her chair. And, of course, they first talked at length about their daughters.

'I just have a feeling things aren't going so well,' Rebecca said. 'Emma didn't sound very happy last time I spoke to her.'

'Really? I haven't managed a proper phone conversation with Marie all week, but she's sent a couple of emails. Quite short, but that's because they were travelling around, she said, trying to see some more of Thailand and get away from the beaches. I'm sure it's fine.'

'I suppose she's probably just a bit homesick, then.'

'Yes, I'm sure that's all it is. It's natural.' But Ginny wanted to turn the conversation to Rebecca. She was concerned about her nervous manner. 'You look well,' she lied. 'How's it been going?'

Rebecca took a very large mouthful of her gin, her hand trembling a little. She mopped at her lips with her finger, as if she'd clumsily spilt some. 'Do you want me to be honest?' she said finally, her eyes bright in the reddish tint of the wall light fittings. 'He and Emma are going to kill each other. I dread to think what's going to happen once the girls get back from abroad.'

'Oh God.' Ginny sat forward sympathetically and gave Rebecca her complete attention. 'What's been going on?'

'He wants a divorce!' Rebecca stated and drained her glass.

'Oh no,' Ginny sympathised.

Rebecca put her glass back on the table rather loudly. 'Yes, Gareth's going to marry his other woman. So that's that.'

Ginny couldn't find a word to say; she could only absorb the agony in Rebecca's eyes, once so wide and happy in the wedding photograph she'd seen, painted and beautiful. Now bare of make-up, raw and staring. Her pain shouted itself from her wide pupils. For a few seconds, neither of them spoke. Ginny snaked out her hand and put it on the table as near to Rebecca's as possible. Rebecca finished her drink, then put her fingers around Ginny's and squeezed them roughly, then pulled away again.

'Oh God,' Ginny said again, but in a whisper. 'I'm so sorry.'

'It's a bit of a shit, isn't it?' Rebecca laughed nervously. 'I knew it was serious, I really did. I think you just know. But I had no idea it was irrevocable. And the thing is, I have absolutely no control over this situation whatsoever. That's what makes the whole thing just so – so bloody unbearable.'

'God, yes.' Ginny nodded, leaving her hand on the table just in case Rebecca might want to return for another squeeze. As it was, she was more concerned about getting to the bar.

'Another one?' Rebecca went and fetched them the same again. When she came back, Ginny still hadn't got a clue what to say. She tried anyway.

'So – so how do you know?'

'He came round and he told me. He claims that when he first left me he hadn't made up his mind, but I don't believe him.'

'But . . .' Was there anything consoling to say? Ginny racked her brains and found something. 'You know, Rebecca, although it sounds final it may not be.'

He's going to get married!' Rebecca announced. 'At his age. With a grown-up family behind him. I think it's disgusting.'

'Yes. But, you know, he's got himself into a horrible mess but it doesn't necessarily mean he'll stay with – with this other woman.'

'Oh, he will. Gareth's always been a very old-fashioned man.' Rebecca snorted. 'I mean, now that Emma's gone, and she's the last of our brood, he's free, isn't he?'

'Is he?' Ginny sat forward, concentrating. 'Emma hasn't gone really. She'll be back, over and over.'

'Oh, perhaps at first. Yes, when they come back from their travels they'll stay at home for a bit. But they'll be aching to be off again, and then it'll be university. And then it'll be duty visits for a year or so, but soon they'll share a house and that'll be it, they'll stay away for the holidays, too, finding work, being with their friends, sleeping with boyfriends. They'll be making their own way, as adults. We'll be chasing after them far more than they'll be wanting to see us. I give it a year, two at the most before they're out of sight.'

Ginny sipped her wine, perturbed by Rebecca's vision. 'But both Marie and Emma are home birds. You know we haven't had any of the kind of nightmares some mothers have had, about discos or nightclubs or all-night raves. They've always been, thank God, happy to be at home.'

'Ginny,' Rebecca said, wrinkling her nose and staring at Ginny as if she was slightly slow, 'I can assure you, this travelling lark is only the beginning. We've lost them. Didn't you realise that?'

'Well, of course I know it's the beginning of Marie's independence. Yes, of course it is, I know that.'

'But somewhere in your heart you're waiting for her to come home, and for life to carry on as usual? It won't. She'll come back changed, she'll be itching to be out of the house all the time she's with you from now on, and then she'll make solid plans to leave. You've got to accept it. You're very much on your own from now on.'

Ginny listened, drank her wine and allowed the words to filter through slowly. But she didn't want to hear them. 'I – well, I know you're right really.'

'So that's why I'm so – so buggered up by my bloody husband's sudden announcement to me. Because I know that from now on I'm on my bloody own, and I haven't got a clue how to deal with it. But you've been on your own, for years, and you're so stable, so sorted.'

'Oh God, I'm not at all sorted,' Ginny allowed herself a tenuous laugh.

'Oh yes you are. You're very strong. And I hope, maybe, you'll give me some pointers, give me some advice, because this is all very new to me.'

'What advice can I give you?' Ginny raised her eyebrows. 'I just muddle through.'

'But you muddle through on your own. I don't know how you do it.'

'I do it by – by. . .' Ginny sank back into her cushioned chair and gazed at a dartboard on a far wall. Then she found that her real feelings formed into words. 'I do it by putting Marie first.'

Rebecca stirred her lemon around in her gin and tonic. The ice clacked against the side of the glass. There was a long silence when both of them lapsed into their own thoughts. Then Rebecca broke the silence. 'So how are you going to do it now Marie's gone?'

Ginny couldn't find an answer. She found herself gazing at Rebecca instead, mulling over her words.

'You know what's so bloody ironic?' Rebecca charged up her battery again. 'It's when the children leave that you need your husband. And I know ideally children need a father, a balanced home and all that, yes they do. But for you, as a woman, as a wife, you spend nearly twenty years suppressing every selfish instinct you have, every whim, every shred of dignity, every yearning to be desirable to your man, so that your children have a good mother. And you tell yourself that your husband loves you, admires you even, because you are such a good mother to your children. No matter that you aren't always plastered in make-up and smelling of expensive perfume when he walks in the door at night, because although you're haggard because you're so tired and you haven't had time to change into something pretty before you cooked the dinner he likes to be ready when he comes home, you know he respects you for that effort.'

'Of course,' Ginny murmured, trying to follow.

'Except that he didn't respect it.' Rebecca grimaced. 'He expected you to help the children with their homework, play with them, bath them, read them a bed-time story, be mother and father to them, because he was working late, do the dinner and then,' she slapped the table with the flat of her hand, 'then, he wanted you to be plastered in make-up and smelling of expensive perfume when he walked in.'

'I – I don't know really,' Ginny hedged, appreciating the picture Rebecca was painting for her and not liking it. On the other hand, she marvelled at the release of Rebecca's feelings that a couple of ounces of gin had produced.

'It's a funny thing,' Rebecca rumbled on, draining her glass again. 'That my husband has fallen for the woman with the perfume and the make-up. Of course, she's more alluring. But marriage becomes a routine. And what if they have children? And the bloom turns into a screaming child with a – with an exploding – exploding arse!'

Ginny giggled before she could stop herself. Rebecca's tight face suddenly creased into a smile, then she laughed, too.

'Well, I mean, after a few months of sleepless nights and exploding' – she said the word again to make them both giggle again – 'arses! Then she'd be less bloody alluring, wouldn't she?'

'She certainly would be,' Ginny agreed.

They both pursed their lips in an attempt to be serious, then erupted into giggles again.

'I hope it's a really awful wedding,' Rebecca said with emphasis. 'I hope his Auntie Muriel causes a row and his brother Steve farts all the way through the meal. I hope his father drops dead halfway through the vows and ruins everything. I hope she wears a tiny dress with a VPL and I hope it snows.'

They laughed until they both felt better. Then Ginny bought them both another round.

'So,' Rebecca let out a long breath. 'Thank you for making me see the funny side of it, Ginny. I don't want to talk about my ludicrous situation anymore. Tell me how you are instead. What's been going on with you?'

'Let's talk about you. It's far more important at the moment.'

'No, I need a distraction. Tell me about yourself. You actually do look well. I'm sure Charlotte's baby's given you all a boost, but is there something else going on?'

'Oh,' Ginny fiddled with a beer-mat uncertainly. 'Just some things.'

'What things?' Rebecca eyed her slightly manically, probably due to the gin. 'Come on, I've spilled all my beans. Let's be completely honest with each other.'

It was probably a combination of the alcohol and the moment when an acquaintance becomes a real friend that gave Ginny the release that she needed. Perhaps the alcohol was a part of making the friendship ripen on that night. That and the fact that their daughters were still inextricably bonded in companionship and by their adventure abroad. And the fact that Rebecca, her veneer of politely coping abandoned, had cried out like a wounded fox. Somehow all the barriers came down and Ginny let it all out.

Ginny told Rebecca about Barney. She found herself going back to explain the circumstances as Rebecca asked questions. It seemed that Rebecca really did want to be distracted from her own life, as she proved to be an extremely good listener and showed a great deal of attention to detail. Finally, Ginny came to the end of the story, as it had finished the previous week. She related the conversation as she remembered it in All Bar One in Leicester Square, and how Charlotte's baby had intervened.

'And nothing from him since then?' Rebecca quizzed, her eyes revolving a little but her brain showing no sign of dulling.

'Just a bunch of roses.'

'Red roses?'

'Yes.'

'Not a dozen?'

'Er – yes.'

'Goodness, how romantic. He is trying hard, isn't he?'

Ginny nodded with a cagey arch of her eyebrows. 'Too hard, don't you think?'

'Is it possible for a man to try too hard?' Rebecca pondered.

'For him, I mean,' Ginny clarified. 'He never used to be like this. It feels very strange.'

Rebecca shrugged dismissively. 'He was a boy when you knew him. All boys behave stupidly. So do girls for that matter. I wouldn't want to be judged for the rest of my life on the way I behaved when I was eighteen or nineteen. Is it more about you, really?'

'Well, yes, I'm worried about Marie.'

'No, that's not what I meant,' Rebecca said with a slight slur, her elbow slipping on the polished table. 'I know it's a bit personal, but when did you last have a boyfriend?'

'Oh,' Ginny flushed. 'It was a while ago.'

'So even if Barney wasn't Marie's father, don't you think you'd be a bit cautious about having a relationship with someone?'

'Yes, I probably would be.'

'That's it, isn't it!' Rebecca pointed a finger in the air, obviously illuminated by some insight. 'You've got to pretend he isn't Marie's father and ask yourself what you'd do then.'

'Well, I—'

'From what you've told me about him, I think the answer's obvious.'

'It is?' Ginny hoped for some clarity. 'What did I say?'

'That he's gorgeously handsome, educated, interesting, worldly, amusing, good company, sensitive and a fantastic lover.'

Ginny gaped, amazed. 'I said that?'

'Yes.'

'Oh my God, did I really?'

'Yes. *In vino veritas.*' Rebecca tilted her head knowingly. 'So you'd be very silly to turn him down.'

'God, I would be, wouldn't I?' Ginny was further and further surprised.

'So what about him being her father? How does it ruin things? I mean, couldn't it make things even better?'

'What it means,' Ginny rubbed her warm forehead, trying to think clearly against a tide of Chardonnay sweeping through her veins, 'is that he couldn't be my boyfriend, because it would force him into Marie's life, and she may not want that.'

'But Marie's in Thailand.'

'And?'

'So she's got no idea whatsoever that he's here.'

'That's right.'

'And there's no reason for her to know, presumably.'

'She doesn't know a thing about it. I'm not going to tell her anything until she comes back, and then I'm going to handle it very carefully.'

'Yes, yes, yes.' Rebecca wagged her head, waving her gin glass in the air. 'But what I'm saying, Ginny, is that what you do now, while Marie's away, is nobody's business but yours – and his of course – and there's no reason for Marie ever to know. So you could go out with him, see how it goes, and if it goes wrong you just don't tell her about it.'

'You mean,' Ginny struggled to think straight, 'you mean, see him secretly while Marie's away?'

'Yes. What have you got to lose?'

'God, I never thought of it that way.'

'Well, there you go.' Rebecca grinned. 'Sleep with him and don't tell anybody. Simple.'

Ginny began to laugh. 'It's crazy. I must be mad to even think about doing this.'

Rebecca let out such a loud sigh, her eyes suddenly tearful, that Ginny stopped laughing immediately. 'Oh Ginny,' Rebecca said, her eyes soulful. 'Give me your dilemma, any day.'

Ginny was still tipsy and full of an odd cocktail of high and low spirits when she got home very late. She felt low when she thought of Rebecca's situation and how painful it was for her. But then she felt a burst of adrenaline that felt good whenever she contemplated Rebecca's advice where Barney was concerned. Perhaps she would see him again. Perhaps with Marie halfway round the world, now was the time to try things out, to see if they did really both feel strongly? They had time – Marie would probably be away for months. And if for any reason the relationship lasted that long, when Marie came home she could hide the fact that they'd been seeing each other until she knew how Marie felt about Barney herself. And if things didn't work out with Barney, surely they were both adult enough now to walk away from it philosophically, to hide any personal feelings from Marie? And what would be lost? In essence, they'd only be back where they'd started.

Was it really so complicated? Didn't she really owe herself a favour? Wouldn't it just be fantastic to be dating a lovely man, to be sharing time with him, going out for meals, drinking wine together, sleeping with him? And especially this man, whose sexy eyes and enigmatic smile had haunted her since she was nineteen years old. She swayed around the kitchen, banging into cupboards as she clumsily made herself a cup of coffee, and realised she was humming to herself.

Then, to her shock, her doorbell rang. She stood still, staring round the kitchen, asking herself who it could be. It was eleven thirty. The bell rang again.

Cautiously she crept into the hall, then decided she could open the door as she had remembered in her drunken haze to put the chain on. She pulled it open just a crack and peered into the night.

'Who is it?'

'It's me,' came Barney's voice. 'I called you but you didn't answer. I know it's late and I'm sorry, but I've been thinking all night and I really want to see you, Ginny. Can I come in?'

Excitement and nerves shot through Ginny like a thunderbolt. How had he known? How could he possibly have known that if he turned up at her door in the middle of the night he would be welcome? That tonight, at this very moment, she was at her most receptive, possibly the most receptive that she would ever be towards him?

She opened the door and smiled at him. 'Come in.'

Chapter Thirty-one

'Ginny, I'm sorry it's so late. I had to see you. You didn't answer your phone so I just – I just drove down. If your light hadn't been on, believe me I wouldn't have rung your bell, but seeing you were still up. . .'

Ginny led him through to the living room. She flicked the standard lamp on. He seemed startled to find himself in her house. His eyes were bright, his hair dishevelled, but then she probably looked a little similar herself. He was in a denim jacket and faded jeans and he looked utterly edible. She swallowed, her body tingling already, and that was just at the sight of him.

'Shall I put some music on?' she found herself suggesting. She went to her CD player without waiting for his response and put on a soul album, one Marie loved. James Brown throbbed through the air. It was probably loud, but she didn't care. When she turned round again Barney's startled expression had been replaced by a baffled one.

'You don't mind me coming? I haven't heard from you all week and I've been building up a horrendous picture in my mind, of you hating me for coming on to you so strongly, of you changing your mind about me seeing Marie.'

'She'll make her own mind up about that, I told you. Drink?'

'Er. . .'

'I've been out this evening so I'm nicely mellow already, but I'll join you in a glass of wine if you'd like one.'

'Well, I don't know. I'm driving.'

'Not for a while yet, surely?' Ginny arched an eyebrow at him and her pulse stuttered to see the response on his face. Was she flirting with him? Yes, as she hopped into the kitchen to pour two glasses of wine, she realised she was. And she realised that she didn't care. After all, people always let down their hair when they were drunk, didn't they? She should know. He followed her into the kitchen.

'I even regretted sending you the flowers. I realised I was probably badgering you when you really wanted to be left alone. I'm sorry if I imposed on you.'

'Not at all.' Ginny sparkled at him. 'They were beautiful.'

'You liked them?'

Ginny considered how nervous she'd been to receive them at first, how confused. But she'd put them in the bedroom and felt a burst of high spirits every time she'd looked at them. And at night, gazing at them as she went to sleep, she'd felt warm inside. 'Yes,' she said simply. 'I liked them.'

'Then I'm pleased.'

'Here, drink this.' She put a glass of wine into his hand. 'And follow me. Let's go and sit down.'

She took her favourite chair, leaving him the sofa. It wasn't the right time to be sitting next to him, she felt, with stray arms and legs brushing against each other.

In the mood she was in that would be far too dangerous.

'So I needn't have panicked, then?' Barney looked at Ginny somewhat wondrously. No surprise, she guessed, since she was in a considerably different mood from the last time he'd seen her.

'No, no need to panic.'

'And,' he sipped his wine, 'I don't suppose – have you had time to think about what we talked about? Or am I rushing things. Tell me if I am.'

'I've thought about it,' she said cautiously. 'I'm still thinking about it.'

He nodded.

'And you,' she said, putting her head on one side to assess him. 'Have you thought any more about it?'

'All the time. I was back in Oxford this week, and it was very odd indeed.'

'Oh?'

'I was visiting some people at Oxfam. It was so strange being back in our old university town after seeing you. I even went and had lunch at the Kings Arms for old times' sake. It all came back to me.'

Ginny swallowed a mouthful of wine, her pulse rising. She knew exactly what he was referring to. 'What did?'

'That – that night. Sitting there, listening to the students' voices echoing around the bar, seeing the old chairs, tables, those bookshelves, the *Wisden*s piled up in the corner, knowing it hadn't changed. I could picture us so clearly on that bench in the ante-room we sat in; I could remember some of our conversation, as if somebody was whispering it in my ear. And do you know what really hit me?'

Ginny paused as a bubble of emotion rose in her throat. 'What?'

'Just how very, very young the students were.'

'Yes,' Ginny said in a low voice. 'I know.'

'It would amaze you if you went back.' Barney took off his jacket and laid it on the arm of the sofa, crossing his legs and relaxing into the sofa cushions. He was wearing a checked shirt of blues and greens that made his eyes look stunning. She wondered if he knew, but decided he probably didn't. If he'd had any vanity in him as a boy, it had vanished. 'I think if you saw these kids pretending to be adults it would make you think hard about the people we were.'

'I have an eighteen-year-old daughter,' Ginny said. 'I know exactly how young I was.'

Barney gave Ginny a very long look and she felt her cheeks warming under his relentless scrutiny. Then he finally said, very softly, '*We* have an eighteen-year-old daughter.'

'Yes,' Ginny whispered, then couldn't speak. She looked away.

'Oh, Ginny,' he said. 'What did we do?'

'I – I,' but the combination of alcohol and emotion suddenly produced a response in Ginny that was unwelcome. She felt the tears rise, then swell in her eyes, then dribble silently down her face.

'Oh God, come here.' Barney stood up and strode towards her chair. He took her hands, pulled her to her feet and gathered her into his arms. 'Let me hold you. It's all been so hard. I messed up so badly. I'm so, so sorry.'

Ginny let herself cry. She no longer cared what he might think. It felt so good, so extraordinarily good to

300

be held tight, to feel his hand stroking her hair, to smell him. Then to feel his lips softly kissing her ear and neck.

'What are you doing?' she managed, but her head was hazy and her body was warm against his. She didn't want him to pull away.

'I don't know.' He kissed her cheek and her eyelashes. 'Do you like it?'

'Yes, I do. I want you to hold me.'

'I will. I'll just hold you.'

She clung to him as his powerful arms supported her. How had she forgotten over the years just how incredible it was to be held by a strong man, to be held by the man she had been so painfully, agonisingly in love with. How could she have ever have imagined that he might one day walk back into her life and hold her again? Finally he spoke again, breaking the spell.

'Are you all right now?'

'I think so.'

She thought he was going to retreat back to the sofa again, but he coaxed her with him and they sat on the cushions together. He draped an arm round her shoulders and pulled her to his chest. She swayed towards him without protest and he ran his hands through her hair. She could feel his breath on her skin. Aretha Franklin pulsed sensuously through the air.

'Just tell me when you want me to go.' Barney dropped a kiss on the top of her head.

Ginny snaked a lazy arm round his waist and settled on his chest. It felt so damned good. She could hear his heartbeat, loud and fast, under his shirt, and feel the heat of his body.

'I don't want you to go.'

'You don't?' he queried almost in a whisper.

'Not yet.'

She turned her head so that she could look up at him. It was so easy to get lost in his eyes, in the intensity of his expression.

'You are so beautiful,' he said.

'Kiss me, then.'

He hesitated, but she could feel his body hardening under her. 'Ginny, are you sure?'

'Yes, I'm sure.'

He lowered his mouth to hers and kissed her softly. It was unbearably exciting. She spread her fingers on his chest and stroked him. Eventually he pulled away and his eyes were bleary and dark with passion.

'Be careful, Ginny.' He half-smiled, that killingly sexy smile that melted her knees completely. 'It's been a long time.'

'For me too.'

They kissed again, and Ginny unwound her body. They fell easily together on the sofa and she felt the full weight of him over her as his kisses became more passionate. Then, as she was losing herself completely in the magic of the moment, he raised his head and looked down at her, stroking her cheek with his finger.

'I think I should go now.'

'No, don't go.'

'But I want you to think about this. I don't want you to rush into anything.'

'I'm not rushing anywhere. I'm far too drunk.'

'I thought so.' He looked very concerned. 'And the last thing I want is to take advantage of your mood. It would be so crass, especially in our case. Especially since. . .' he tailed off.

'Especially since you took advantage of me nineteen years ago?'

'Yes,' he said seriously.

'Rest easy, Barney. You didn't take advantage of me. I wanted it to happen.'

'You did?'

'I knew exactly what I was doing then. I probably shouldn't have done it, but I knew. And I know what I'm doing now.'

'Just,' he pushed a hand through his hair and it flopped back into loose, untamed curls, 'just be sure, Ginny. Please don't let's get this wrong.'

She gave him a direct look. 'Are you going to take me to bed, or not?'

He was silent, gazing at her incredulously, a glimmer of light in his eyes. When he spoke again, his voice was throaty. 'Ask me again.'

'Are you going to—?'

'Yes,' he said, and lifting her up, carried her up the stairs to her bedroom.

Chapter Thirty-two

Ginny pulled the cords of her bathrobe tightly round her body, opened the front door a fraction and squinted out into the daylight.

'Yes?'

'Well, that's a fine welcome to receive.' Marie rolled her eyes and put a hand on her hip. 'I left my door keys here, don't you remember? Sorry if I woke you up.'

Ginny allowed the door to swing open and stared at her daughter in disbelief. '*Marie?*'

She was wearing the same baggy combat trousers that she'd left in, and a T-shirt with *Bangkok* emblazoned on the front. Her hair was longer and messier, she looked tired and somehow grubby, and her face was deeply tanned. But most all she looked relieved to be home.

'Let's just say, Mother, that travelling isn't all it's made out to be.'

Ginny stared. Upstairs, Barney was in her bed, naked.

'Marie?' she repeated, bolts of adrenaline shooting through her as if fired from above.

Marie blinked several times. 'Can I come in, then?'

'Oh, darling, come in. Of course. Just let's get you inside.' They got as far as the doormat. Ginny hedged, blocking Marie's entrance. Was Barney about to prance down the stairs and see what was going on? 'Oh my God, I'm just so surprised to see you.'

'And happy, you forgot to mention,' Marie reminded her.

'Oh and happy. Of course, oh God, how happy to see you home and safe.' Ginny swept Marie into her arms and hugged her tightly, subconsciously feeling for loss of weight. She was a bit thinner, but she seemed healthy, and Marie pulled away first.

'Can I smell booze?'

'Not at all. Oh, maybe. I had some friends here last night, perhaps that's what you can smell.'

'Hmm. Well, we flew into Heathrow and I rang, but then I thought it was better just to get on a train and come home and get on with it. No point in faffing about. And I just wanted to get home as quickly as possible, so don't nag me about asking for lifts or anything, it wasn't necessary. I got a taxi from the station, though, my rucksack weighs a ton. I don't know how it's heavier than when I left, but I just couldn't drag it all the way home.'

'So you had English money for the taxi?'

'Hmm? No, he's outside. I thought you might pay him. Is that okay?'

'Oh, of course.'

Ginny tiptoed outside with her purse and stuffed a ten-pound note into the driver's hand as it was all the change she had. He seemed surprised given the fare was only half of that, but she nodded at him and gestured him away before springing back inside the house again, eager to see that nothing had happened in the split second she'd been in the road. Her hangover

305

fired at her like a piston as she somehow bundled Marie and her baggage inside the house and deposited everything in big, untidy heap. Overcome in equal measure by guilt and panic, she felt suffocated, and let Marie take the lead.

'Emma's gone home too. We fell out. Can you believe it? Never go on holiday with your best friend, that's my advice to you. I'm dying for a cup of tea. Shall I make it?'

Ginny watched in a daze as Marie took control, gliding into the galley kitchen, flicking the switch on the kettle and rummaging through the cupboards, her cupboards, as if she'd never been away.

'So what...?' Ginny faltered. 'So why didn't you call me? I thought you'd call me.'

'I did call. I left a message on the answerphone, and your mobile was switched off, or it's run out of credit. You should check it regularly. Where's my herbal tea? You haven't thrown it away, have you? Ah, here it is. So you're not picking up your messages?' Marie frowned in mock reproof. 'Why? Have you been busy? Come to think of it, you look a right state. Have you been out on the piss? Typical, while the cat's away the mice will play.'

'Oh no, darling, that's not the case, Ginny gabbled. I just didn't hear the phone and I can't imagine why I didn't get your mobile message.'

'I can.' Marie gave Ginny a sly look. 'You're hung-over, aren't you?'

'No!'

'You are. That's all right, I'm glad you've been enjoying yourself while I've been away. Who did you have round?'

'Oh, but that's not important Are you all right? Is Emma all right?'

'We're both fine, Mum, don't fuss.'

'But you were going to be away for another couple of months. Something must have gone wrong.'

Marie gave a long sigh, and looked at Ginny as if she had a very limited understanding of human nature. 'You have no idea what it's like to be in a strange place with somebody you think you know. You find out you don't really know them at all. Oh, we loved it at first, but we wanted to do different things. And I loved the places we went – we've seen the most amazing things, Mum, really incredible things – but in the end I got tired and we were running out of money, and as soon as money becomes an issue everybody starts getting tense, and so we started rowing all the time, and in the end we both agreed that we wanted to come home. That's about it really, we just decided we'd had enough. Oh, Emma's all right really, but she's so – well, she's just so anal about things. I couldn't bear it. It was like having my mum with me. No offence, but you know what I mean. And I couldn't really take off and leave her on her own, that wouldn't have been fair. But she wouldn't do anything I wanted to do, it was always, "but what if this happens, what if that happens?" She's a big whinger at the end of the day. I'd never thought that of her.' Marie prodded her tea bag, screwing up her face. 'I'm glad to be home.'

Momentarily, Ginny wondered what kind of changed circumstances poor old Emma, branded the big whinger, was about to walk into in her own home.

'And you're sure Emma's got home all right too?'

'Mum! We only parted company at the station, when

307

we got in separate taxis. Hers took her home, and mine brought me here. Unless she's been mugged somewhere between the station and Orchard Avenue, I think we can assume that she's arrived home safely.'

'You are quite sure about that?'

'Yes!'

Ginny took Marie in her arms again and held her tightly while she panicked and wondered wildly what she was going to do. 'I'm glad you're home, love. Of course I'm delighted. I'm just so – so surprised! And especially now! Of all times, *now*!'

'Why? Oh, because you're hungover. God, don't worry, we had a few hangovers in Bangkok, don't fuss, so where's Mr Mistoffelees?' She began searching for the cat and ended up in the hall, peering up the stairs. 'Is he in your bedroom? I'll go and get him. I can't believe I missed the stupid cat. How prosaic is that?' She began to mount the stairs.

'No!' Ginny leapt in front of Marie and blocked her way. 'Oh, darling, don't go up there just yet, it's not tidy or Hoovered and I really did want things to be lovely at home for you so that you had a proper homecoming. I just wish you'd called.'

'I did call,' Marie repeated very slowly as if she was talking to somebody very thick. 'Look, if you don't believe me I'll prove it to you.'

She bounded into the living room and pressed the play button on the answering machine. 'Here you are. You've got two messages you haven't even heard yet. So much for you hanging on the telephone waiting for my every call, Mother.' Marie rolled her eyes comically, and before Ginny could stop her had pressed the button.

308

Barney's husky voice was the first message.

I'm coming round. I have to see you tonight.

Ginny swallowed, gazing around the room as if it must have been an aberration, ignoring Marie's immediate stare in her direction. The second message was Marie's. She couldn't believe that they had been so preoccupied early that morning that she hadn't even heard the phone ring. Or, on second thoughts, she could believe it, but the timing was absolutely terrible.

Mum, it's me, I'm at Heathrow, we're home but I'll tell you more later. Are you there? Hello? Earth to Mother? Okay, heading home now, I'll see you when I get there. Don't worry I'll get a taxi from the station. Bye.

'Oh, yes, you did leave a message,' Ginny said over brightly. 'Darling, I'm sorry, I'll confess I did sleep in this morning and I must have missed it. I am sorry, do you forgive me?'

'Who was that?' Marie said, her eyes alight with curiosity.

'Hmm?'

"The bloke's voice. Anyone I know?'

Anyone she knew? That would be an understatement. 'Oh, no. Oh, that was just a wrong number, that's why I didn't even pick it up. I heard it last night when I was watching television but it wasn't for me, so I didn't even move. You know how cosy I get when I'm in my chair watching a good film.'

'You said you had friends round.'

'Oh, I did.' Ginny nodded stupidly. 'And then they left and then I watched a film and then the message. . . came.'

Marie watched her mother squirm, and Ginny watched Marie. It was like seeing a calculator working through a complicated sum, knowing with a sinking heart that any moment it was going to hit on the right answer. 'Is he your boyfriend?'

'I don't have a boyfriend. Don't be silly. So come on, let's talk about you.' Ginny patted the sofa. 'Come and sit here.'

A thump came on the floor from upstairs. Marie cast her eyes up to the ceiling. Then, just as Ginny thought she was going to declare with absolute correctness, 'He's up there, isn't he?' Marie in fact said, 'Mr Mistoffelees! He's heard my voice and jumped off your bed. And he's not getting any thinner, is he? I'll go and get him.'

'No!' Ginny yelled, leaping into the hall first then smiling broadly to cover her panic. 'No, darling, you sit down and relax, I'll let him out of the bedroom. He's going to be so pleased to see you. To be honest I'm horribly hungover. I did drink too much last night and as you're the expert on hangovers perhaps you could make me a cup of tea and find me an aspirin from the drawer. Please?'

'All right.' Marie tutted. 'You are hopeless when it comes to drink, aren't you? Always have been a lightweight.'

'Yes, that's me,' Ginny called as she flew up the stairs. 'Lightweight.'

She flung herself into her bedroom and slammed the door after her, leaning on it with all her weight for good measure just to be sure that Marie couldn't follow her up the stairs and burst in.

Barney was standing up, next to the bed, stark naked. At the sight of the alarm on Ginny's face he grabbed the first thing he could and held it in front of his genitals. It turned out to be George, the motheaten toy dog.

Ginny gasped, trying to get her breath back.

'What is it?' he asked, absorbing her nerves. 'Who's here?'

'It's Marie!' Ginny gulped. 'She's come home.'

Barney froze. He seemed completely unable to move or speak.

'You have to hide,' Ginny instructed, trying to think clearly. 'You'll have to get under the bed.'

Barney tried, but under the bed were several suit-cases and full bin-bags containing winter clothes, spare bedding and a sleeping bag just in case of visitors. There was no room. He stood up again, still speechless, still clutching George.

'The wardrobe.' Ginny pulled open the door. Barney tried to get into the wardrobe. 'Jesus Christ, they don't make wardrobes like they used to,' Ginny wheezed, shoving him inside and wishing she'd had more money so that she could have invested in something taller and deeper. Her B&Q flatpack was just not going to be big or strong enough to contain Barney's body. This was confirmed when they tried to close the flimsy wardrobe door and heard a resounding creak followed by the loud bang of the wooden bottom giving way under Barney's weight.

'Are you all right?' she hissed through the door at him.

He emerged, shaken and seemingly in a worse state of shock. 'I'll have to climb out of the window,' he said.

'I don't have a balcony. I don't even have a window-box,' she reasoned in a hoarse whisper. 'You can't do that.'

311

'*Mum!*' Marie's voice broke through the fog of their panic. She was right outside the bedroom door. 'What is going on in there? Have you broken something? There was this loud bang.'

The bedroom door began to open from the outside but Ginny grabbed the handle and forced it shut again.

'Darling, just wait a moment I'm just – just trying to find Mr Mistoffelees. *The cat!*' she mouthed at Barney. 'Where's the sodding cat?'

He shook his head, but then Ginny spotted the cat's ginger form in the corner, snuggled among the clothes she'd shed the night before. She pointed at him while she leant back against the door.

'Get him.'

'Mum?'

'Just coming, darling.'

Barney picked the cat up and carried him carefully towards the door.

'Just fling him outside when I open the door,' Ginny breathed. Barney nodded. Ginny then stood aside, opened the door a crack, and Barney, standing back so as not to be seen, pushed Mr Mistoffelees' fat ginger body through a small gap in the door. He gave a meow of complaint. Ginny then pushed her weight against the door quickly and it snapped shut again.

'There he is, darling,' she called over loudly and over brightly. 'I'll just – let me just clear up a bit in here and I'll be out in a minute.'

There was a long silence, long enough to have both Ginny and Barney shivering with discomfort. Time passed. Ginny wondered if Marie had gone downstairs again. She stood, cringeing, wondering what to do next.

Ginny was off her guard. Marie opened the bedroom door so firmly and quickly that Ginny couldn't stop her coming in.

Across the room, behind the bed, Barney stood naked with nothing but George to cover his modesty.

'Oh my goodness,' Ginny declared, horrified. 'Marie, it's not what it looks like—'

'You only needed to tell me you had a man in your bedroom, Mum,' Marie said, giving them both withering glances. 'I'd have understood. I'll see you downstairs when you've both got dressed.'

Chapter Thirty-three

❧

'What the hell are we going to do?' Ginny hissed into the air, throwing clothes around the room in a blind panic. Barney managed to make it into his shirt before sinking on to the edge of the duvet and putting his head into his hands. He made a low moaning noise. 'Barney? Are you all right?'

'Jesus, this is awful. Oh God, it's unbelievable. After all the careful plans I had. I was going to be so sensitive.'

'Well, so was I,' Ginny flapped, buttoning her shirt with trembling fingers then giving up, ripping it over her head and pulling on a sweater instead. 'But that's all blown out of the water now. We have to think. Think, think, think.' She pulled her jeans on roughly.

'I should never, ever have spent the night here,' Barney uttered. Ginny stopped in her panicking to stare at him. He wasn't regretting it, was he? It had been wonderful. Barney glanced at her. 'Not here, where she lives. We should have gone somewhere else.'

She felt relief wash over her. She could have kissed him again, but there wasn't time. 'It's not your fault. You didn't know she was about to turn up on the doorstep. I didn't know. It's just Sod's bloody Law.'

'And now she's seen me, for the first time, with nothing on.'

'It's not ideal, I agree.'

'And I'm shaking. I'm actually shaking.' He struggled into his jeans. 'I can't believe I've finally seen my daughter. She's so beautiful, except she's got my nose.'

'Your nose?' Ginny paused as she put on an odd pair of socks.

'Didn't you ever notice it? It's just like mine. She's going to realise who I am as soon as she looks at me properly.'

'No, she's not.' Ginny tried to be practical. 'She's eighteen. She's too obsessed by herself, luckily for you.'

'But how do we handle it now?' Barney finished buttoning his shirt and raked his hands through his hair. 'What do you want me to do?'

'I'm thinking.' Ginny brushed her hair roughly. 'I don't know what to do. Yes I do. There's only one thing to do. It's obvious. We have to tell her who you are.'

'What?' Barney went white.

'We don't have any choice. It's the only decent, honest thing to do.'

'But she's just seen me in the nude,' Barney croaked.

'I know. It's going to be a bit of a shock.'

'A bit? It doesn't give me a snowball's chance in hell of winning her round. Isn't there another way?'

'No. Not if we're going to be fair to Marie.'

'But I wanted to build a relationship with her,' Barney choked, near to tears. 'I wanted to introduce myself slowly and carefully, so that she might like me.

315

If we meet for the first time like this, she's going to hate me. All these years of waiting will be blown away in a single morning. We just can't tell her today, not now, not like this. Think about it, Ginny. She'll be trapped. She'll have no time to think about her reaction. It'll be awful for her.'

Ginny was racked with painful indecision. Barney looked agonised, his eyes pleading. 'You might be right,' she agreed.

'Please think of another way.'

'Right.' Ginny thought fast. 'Change of plan. We'll have to do it completely differently. You cannot, under any circumstances, tell Marie who you are.'

'No, I agree.' He looked immensely relieved.

'You're right. It's just what I didn't want, for her to be cornered. So we'll have to lie.'

'Okay, what's the lie?'

'We'll – we'll have to just tell her you're my boyfriend.'

'Why is that a lie? I was hoping I *was* your boyfriend.'

'You what?' Ginny was flustered, trying to find a lipstick and putting coverstick on her mouth by mistake.

'After last night. And this morning. Ginny, it's been so fantastic. Please, don't shut me out. I know we're both in shock, but you will see me again, won't you?'

Ginny paused, foundation all over her fingers, her breathing painful and shallow. She looked at his mad hair, his sensitive mouth, the fear in his eyes. Those beautiful eyes that were still her undoing. 'Yes, Barney,' she said. 'I'll see you again, but I'll have to keep you away from Marie.'

'Away from her?' He looked panic-stricken again. Ginny realised, even in her nervous state, that however bad this was for her, it was absolutely terrible for him. And what shock, what overwhelming emotion must he be feeling to have finally met his own daughter? It was hard for her to imagine. She softened quickly.

'No, Barney, I don't really mean that. We'll just have to play it very carefully. We'll have to tell her the truth as soon as we can.'

'Yes, of course, I agree.'

'So,' Ginny said as they were both finally clothed, decent and brushed. They stood and looked at each other. 'What do we do now?'

'Can I sneak out the back door?'

'There's not much point in that. She knows you're here.'

'But I don't know what to say to her. What if she talks to me? I'm so nervous I'll probably mess it up completely.'

Ginny thought fast. 'I don't think it's very elegant for you to skulk out of the door just because she's here. It makes it all look – well, a bit cheap and tacky. I don't want her to think I'm having a one-night stand.'

'So what shall we say?'

'Let's say you're my boyfriend but that you've got to rush away because you've got an important meeting. You can say a polite hello to each other then you can leave.'

'It's Saturday.'

'An important – doctor's appointment. You've got to see the doctor.'

317

They stared at each other aghast. 'That makes it sound like I've got VD.'

'Well then – what about the dentist?'

They both froze as there was hammering on the door. Marie's yell broke through their mutterings.

'Breakfast's ready! I've put aspirins out for both of you. And a valium for George. He looks as if he needs one.'

They waited with bated breath and Marie clumped down the stairs again.

'George?' Barney asked jumpily. 'Who's George?'

'The pyjama case.' Ginny sighed. 'Welcome to your daughter's sense of humour.'

'So, who are you?' Marie arrowed bluntly at Barney as he and Ginny edged sheepishly into the kitchen. Marie had filled two frying pans with bacon, eggs, sausages and fried bread. It smelt delicious. Ginny realised that it was up to her to make the situation as elegant as possible. She knew bluntness was all part of Marie's style, but Barney may not realise it. To a stranger, she could sound confrontational. You'd have to see the twinkle in her eye half the time to realise she was having fun. But Barney had looked so pale as they'd headed out of the bedroom, at that moment Ginny was almost more concerned for him than she was for her resilient daughter.

'Marie,' Ginny explained in the most coaxing tone she could produce, 'I'm sorry you've walked into a situation you weren't expecting. I think we both want to apologise to you for that.'

Marie nodded and Ginny saw the dreaded twinkle. 'So, who *are* you?' she shot at Barney again, who was standing staring at her in fascination. 'Am I going to have to chase you off the grounds with a shotgun, or are you going to do the honourable thing?'

'Marie. . .' Ginny warned, but Barney's warm voice interrupted her.

'And who are *you*? I didn't realise the staff worked at weekends.'

Ginny watched in amazement as Marie chuckled. 'I expect you've worked up a bit of an appetite. Is that your denim jacket in there?' She flicked her head towards the living room.

'Yes. Like it?'

'It looks as if it's seen a bit of wear.'

'It has.'

'Oh, stop looking so worried, Mum.' Marie poked the sausages and turned them over. 'It could have been worse. You could have left your clothes strewn all the way up the stairs.'

'Marie, that's enough now,' Ginny said gently.

Marie pursed her lips, then she said, 'So were you going to introduce us? I'll do it then. I'm the daughter.' She eyed Barney again quizzically. 'And I assume you're the boyfriend, even though my mum denied she'd got one. My name's Marie.'

Ginny leapt in. 'This is Bar – Bar –' She stopped dead.

'Christ, Mum, you sound like a sheep.' Marie stared at her. 'Have you developed a stutter while I've been away?'

But Ginny had realised that she couldn't use Barney's real name, because Marie knew it and it was unusual enough for her to raise an eyebrow, if not to put the pieces together instantly.

'I'm Bartholomew,' Barney said.

'God, really?' Marie pulled a face. 'Poor you. Poor ewe. Get it? Oh, don't worry. I'm sorry, I'm a bit high. It was a long flight and I didn't sleep a wink and I've been fantasising about an English breakfast for weeks. I've eaten some fantastic things, don't get me wrong, but one can have enough rice packets.'

'I know,' Barney agreed.

'Do you?' Marie glanced at him again, and Ginny knew her well enough to know that this time she was feeling a little shy. 'Where have you been, then? Did you take that denim jacket with you?'

'I've been to a few places. I had the best rice packet ever from a stall by the side of the road just outside Dhaka. I don't think I'll ever forget it.'

'You were in Bangladesh?'

'Yes, for while.'

'Cool. I think I need to get out and about more. I might go to Bangladesh next.'

'I've never been to Thailand, though, and I've always wanted to go.'

'Oh, don't. It's been spoilt.' Marie put out her hands expressively. 'I mean, do go if you want. But it's so full of poseurs and you've got to stay away from the beaches, they're a nightmare now. Everybody's pretending they're something out of an Alex Garland novel and it makes you nauseous. And what makes it worse is that everybody disses Alex Garland when really they hope they're going to be handed some kind of blood-stained map by a junkie. That makes it even more nauseating. How many sausages do you want?'

'Oh Bar – Bar – Bartholomew can't stay.' Ginny stepped in.

'Mum.' Marie gave her a pitying look. 'Are we going to have to get that stutter seen to? Or should we put you through the sheep dip? Perhaps the shock will sort you out.'

'I have to go I'm afraid,' Barney piped up, pressing his hands together. 'It's been lovely to meet you, Marie. Ginny. . .' He dried up and Ginny exchanged a glance with him.

'It's been lovely to meet you, too?' Marie suggested, finding plates from the cupboard and putting them on the unit. 'At least stay for breakfast, Bar-Bar-Bartholomew. I'm starving but I can't eat all this.'

'Oh, Bar – he can't stay.' Ginny shook her head. 'He's got an urgent appointment with a dentist.'

Marie looked up with a deadpan expression. 'It's not Denise, is it? Because if so, I have to tell you, Mum, you'd better go with him if you want to keep him.'

Ginny bit her lip in an attempt not to laugh. Marie had, of course, known enough about Jane and Harry's issues before she'd left the country.

'No, it's not Denise.'

'So are we going to have to plough through this lot on our own?'

'Well, yes, why not?' Ginny pretended to busy herself finding knives and forks for the two of them. 'And you can tell me all about your trip.'

'Yes, but I've told you most of it on email. Hot, damp, noisy, gawdy, fantastic, but too many tourists. And a whining best friend who got on my nerves. And after I've eaten all this I'm going to have to go to bed with Mr Mistoffelees and sleep for a week. I've been fantasising about that, too. Isn't it amazing how in England you can just drink water out of the tap?' She turned to Barney. 'Don't you think there's a lot we take for granted here?'

Barney suddenly looked serious and his eyes became pensive. 'Yes,' he said. 'As it happens, I do think that.'

Marie nodded her approval and flipped a can of baked beans into a saucepan. 'Okay then.'

As Marie seemed to have finished sporting with Barney, Ginny gesticulated to him and they both went out into the hall, Barney collecting his jacket on the way. They parted at the front door. They looked into each other's eyes, and Ginny wasn't surprised to see that his pupils were as dilated with anxiety and pure adrenaline as hers probably were.

'Was that all right?' he whispered to her croakily.

'I'm stunned,' Ginny said, because it was true. 'I can't believe how well you handled it.'

'She's a really interesting girl. It was easy,' he said, and she could see from the warmth in his eyes that he really meant it. 'The last twenty-four hours have been so incredible that I think I'm going to have to pinch myself all the way home. I still can't believe any of this.'

'But you're happy?'

'More than you could ever know, Ginny. I'll have to go before Marie gets interested in us again. Goodbye then, have a great weekend with Marie. And I guess, well, I guess we'll talk again soon. I'll leave it up to you to contact me. Just – just don't leave it too long, Okay?'

'Yes.'

'You promise you'll be in touch?'

'Yes, of course.'

He stepped out of the door, then came back again,

grabbed Ginny's shoulders and planted a huge kiss on her lips. She kissed him back.

'You're fantastic,' he said.

'Go on, be off with you before our daughter gets her shotgun out,' Ginny, said in a hushed, urgent tone. But when she closed the door on him, she leant back against it and closed her eyes, a flood of warmth and happiness flowing through her body. What if. . .? Could she really allow herself to believe, after all these years of famine, that she'd earnt her feast? That Barney was for real? That Marie would like him? It was too much, far too much to ask. It wouldn't happen to her. Such things didn't happen to her.

'Mum!' Marie bellowed. 'Where's the blimmin' Lea and Perrins? You have no idea how much I yearn for Lea and Perrins.'

'In the top cupboard, above the kettle.' Ginny went back into the kitchen, her cheeks warm, her lips throbbing. She gave Marie a big hug. 'I'm so, so glad you're home. I missed you so much, you've got no idea how much.'

'I missed you, too.' Marie returned the hug and turned herself to the business of dishing out the breakfast. 'It's a bugger that Bar-Bar didn't stay. I've cooked far too much.'

'Marie,' Ginny said as they both settled at the breakfast bar to eat. 'I just want to say again, especially now Bar – he's gone, that I'm so sorry that you walked in on us. It must have been really embarrassing for you.'

'Not really. I think it was embarrassing for you, though.' Marie plunged her teeth into a sausage, groaned with delight, spread Lea and Perrins over the rest of her food then looked at Ginny properly. 'How do you know him, then?'

'Oh, I don't really know him very well yet. I'm only just getting to know him.'

'How did you meet him? Was it very romantic?'

'I. . .' Ginny thought. 'I met him in a library.'

Marie pulled an elaborate face. 'Intellectual type, is he? Or was he mooning over the Barbara Cartlands?'

Ginny laughed and put her hand out to stroke Marie's hair. 'Probably a bit of both.'

'And is he going to stick around? Or were you just having a mad fling while I was away?'

'Well, I don't know,' Ginny said very carefully as she played with her breakfast with a fork. 'What do you think?'

'Don't ask me.' Marie widened her eyes. 'I'm rubbish with men. No insights whatsoever in that department.'

'I mean, did you like him? I know you didn't see much of him, but—'

'Mum.' Marie grimaced. 'I saw practically all of him. If it wasn't for George. . .'

Ginny decided to reject that image, although she thought later she'd probably find it funny. She tried to move on quickly. 'Would you like it if I saw him again?'

Marie heaved a slice of fried bread into her mouth and chewed on it. 'I don't mind. It's up to you, isn't it?'

'Well, yes, but. . .'

'The thing is, Mum, I'm not really going to be here so much from now on, am I?' Marie's voice softened, and Ginny had a definite sense of being prepared for something. 'I mean, with university coming up soon and I

324

know this trip's gone a bit pear-shaped but I'm not sure what I want to do with my gap year now. Something interesting, anyway. I mean, don't get me wrong, I love home, but I don't think I'm going to be here as much as I was. I'm not at school anymore.'

Ginny felt an infusion of sadness and gladness. Rebecca had been right. Their little girls were getting ready to fly the nest.

'I know, darling,' Ginny said, trying not to sound emotional. 'And that's all fine by me.'

'Good.' Marie looked relieved. 'So what you do next's fine by me too. I actually think it'd be really cool if you had a boyfriend. Really, I just want you to be happy and I'd hate to think of you here all by yourself. It would be a bit of a guilt-trip, wouldn't it?'

'Yes, I guess it would.'

'So Bar-Bar can come back again,' Marie finished with her habitual twinkle. 'And I think you'd like that, wouldn't you? I can tell.'

'How?' Ginny flushed, pretending to be fascinated by a piece of bacon that wouldn't stay on her fork.

'Well, he must be one hell of a kisser. Your lips are all swollen and red. You look like Mick Jagger.'

Chapter Thirty-four

⚜

'Oh my God, he's amazing!' Marie sat awkwardly on the sofa at Jane's with Benjamin in her arms, absorbing every tiny detail of him. Charlotte cuddled up close to her and put her arm around her niece's shoulder, kissing her hair.

'I'm just so glad you're here, with him. It seems right.'

'Well, he's my cousin, although it's a bit weird having a cousin young enough to be my nephew, but I guess that's what happens when you've got an abnormal family like ours. I'll have to look after him as he gets older. Or maybe you'd like me to be the one who does all the corrupting. What do you think?'

'I think looking after will be fine. You can always throw a bit of corrupting in for good measure when he's older.'

'God, yes. He'll need some reality checks. Hello, little one!' She stroked his button nose. 'Wow, Auntie Charlotte, you really know how to steal the show, don't you?'

Charlotte laughed. She lowered her voice, as Raj was in the kitchen with Jane, making some plans or other about an evening meal. 'And what do you think of my man, then? Approve?'

'Wow, yeah!' Marie's eyes widened into saucers.

'Too old for me but I bet he was tasty when he was younger. I'm not into English men either. I approve of your choice of husband, Auntie Charlotte, so go forth and be happy.'

'Why don't you just call me Charlotte?' Charlotte smiled affectionately at Marie. Talking together like this, she felt more like they were old buddies than aunt and niece. It was such a shame that she hadn't realised how fast Marie was growing up before now. But no time for regrets. She had a new baby. It was all about the future, not the past. Now she could build a proper relationship with Marie. Now was the right time. Everything happens when it does for a reason, Raj had said. He was probably right. 'I feel too young to be an auntie.' Charlotte shook her head. 'It's doubly strange being a mother. I think that takes time to sink in.'

'I think he's going to sleep now.' Marie gazed at Benjamin in wonder.

'Thank God. He seems to be awake most of the day. I always thought babies slept all day, but that's some kind of bizarre myth I must have got from old films or something. In fact, I spend all day trying to make him go to sleep, then I spend all night poking him and waking him up just to make sure he's still alive.'

'Do you?' Marie wrinkled her nose without comprehension.

Charlotte chuckled. It was something she had said to Ginny recently, and Ginny had understood immediately. It was such a bond between them now, motherhood. It was warm, feminine and powerful. She had never realised just how powerful it was, and she was thankful beyond words that her family ties had grown and become stronger in every possible sense due to this little, squirming miracle of a baby.

'You must be knackered, then,' Marie concluded. 'And Raj spends all day staring at him. When do either of you get any sleep?'

'Here and there. I've become like a cat, napping when I can.'

'Like Mr Mistoffelees. He's a fat bastard now, I can tell you. Not like the scrawny kitten we took from you all those years ago. But he's company for Mum, and that's a good thing. Thank God she's got someone at home. And now this Bar-Bar bloke, some kind of boyfriend. He seems quite cool. It's important that she has someone apart from me, you know, because, well, I don't like to be rude about Mum, but there's something I wanted to say to you.'

'What's that?' Charlotte sidestepped the brief mention of Barney. Both Ginny and Jane had given her rough outlines of what had happened when Marie was away, and how Marie had come back to find Ginny and Barney in bed together. Privately Charlotte had thought it was hilarious, but she understood that from Marie's angle it was very delicate territory indeed, and Charlotte didn't want to stray there. But fortunately Marie didn't want to talk about her mother's new boyfriend – well, at least not directly.

'Well, Charlotte, the thing is, I think I take after you and I don't think I'm going to be at home much in the future. I must get it from someone, this desire to travel. And I know everyone does it at my age, or at least us lucky ones do, but it's more than that.' She screwed up her face thoughtfully. 'It's something very real to me. I want to do something with it. Like a career that takes me abroad a lot on trips, or even something where I live abroad. And I really mean it. I'm not just fantasising like kids do. I can feel it, like a strong pull, inside me.'

'Yes, I can see you do.'

'So I don't get it from Mum,' Marie stated factually. 'She's boring in that way, which is no offence to her but she wasn't even really into holidays abroad when I was growing up.'

'They're expensive when you're on your own, I know that much.'

'Well, yes, as I said, I'm not being rude, but she's a bit clueless. She was great about Thailand but it's not as if she could really give me any guidance. And yes, I know Gran would tell me off and say that's because she had me instead of gallivanting around, but it's so good that you're here now and that I've got someone to talk about gallivanting with.'

'When you're working abroad it doesn't seem so much like gallivanting, but it certainly is the life I've felt was shaped for me and I never questioned it. Perhaps you're similar, you'll have to experiment and see. It's a shame you never came to see me in the places I lived,' Charlotte said, then stopped herself. She moved on. 'What I mean to say is, I hope that from now on you'll take advantage of me and stay with me whenever you like.'

'Do you really mean that?' Marie's eyes lit up.

'Of course.'

'And you're going back again? Abroad I mean?'

Charlotte gave Marie a thoughtful look. 'I haven't really discussed this with Mum yet, but my guess is we'll be in Asia more than we'll be here. Not a word to

Bessie, I have to be diplomatic about how I break that kind of news.'

'I won't say a word,' Marie promised. 'But I hope, for my sake, that you do go away again. No offence, but it'd be much more fun. Now that we're proper friends I could really make the most of it. Can you speak any Indian languages?'

'Some Hindi, that's very handy as a common language in India. And it's on TV a lot.' Charlotte nodded. 'And some Tamil words that I've learnt from Raj. Mostly rude ones. But it's much more important to me now that I do learn Tamil properly, because we want Benji to be a native speaker both at home in India and in England. And he'll probably need Hindi too.'

'Crumbs,' Marie gasped. 'He'll be trilingual then.'

'Languages are fun. You enjoy them too, don't you?'

'Yes, love them. And I'm good at them.' Marie warmed to her subject. 'I thought I'd probably learn Russian next, but maybe I'll start with Hindi.'

'I've always found the best way to learn them is by immersion. I never spoke decent Spanish until I went to South America and got a job.'

'So I could come and stay with you and learn Hindi? And while I'm there I can change a few nappies for you too, if you like.'

Charlotte nodded eagerly as Benjamin stirred and gave a croaky cry. 'Want to start your nappy training now?'

'Okay,' Marie said with a nervous laugh. And as Charlotte took her son into her arms and Marie watched in awe, she said to Charlotte shyly, 'I'm so glad you came home, Charlotte. Thank God somebody understands me.'

330

*

'I know I said I wouldn't ring but I had to.' Barney's voice was urgent and Ginny glanced around the lab before disappearing into a deserted corridor to take the call more privately.

'I'm at work, Barney. It's not easy to talk.'

'I know, I'm sorry, I just had to know what was going on. How has it been?'

Of course, she didn't need to ask what he was referring to. She let out a long breath and rubbed a corner of her eye tiredly. 'I'm muddling through. Marie's on top form, loves her new nephew, she's spending most of her time round at my mother's with my sister, Charlotte. Or she's out with friends.'

'So you haven't – I mean – have you. . .' He tailed away, but she could hear the anxiety in his voice.

'I've been waiting for the right moment but she's dashing around and it's hard to know when to catch her.' Ginny sighed. 'I feel absolutely awful that she doesn't know. Especially as she's mentioned you a couple of times.'

'She has?' Barney brightened instantly, then sounded anxious again. 'Oh God, it was about me being naked – wasn't it?'

Ginny allowed herself a small smile. 'No, in fact it was about your travelling experiences. That was what she noticed most about you, thankfully for all of us. She's really got a travel bug, so your casual mention of Dhaka seems to have made quite an impact.'

'I wish I could talk to her about it,' he said wistfully. 'I hope I can share it with her. It's what I've dreamt of.'

'We just need to do things in the right order,' Ginny

insisted, guilt surging through her again. If only it hadn't happened like this. If only Marie had waited until Barney was out of the house before she'd turned up on the doorstep. Indecision and panic rose whenever Ginny had a moment to stop and think. And she still wasn't sure whether they'd done the right thing in not telling Marie straight away that Barney was her father. But, then again, she would have been put in an impossible situation, just back from halfway across the world, presented with that bombshell, and Barney seemed so desperate to find another way to tell her. . . The wheels of indecision turned again. 'Just let me handle it when I can.'

'But – I've been thinking about that, too – don't you think it's better if I handle it myself? I mean, after all, I was going to make contact with her and tell her in my own way.'

'Barney, I can't really think straight now.' Ginny rubbed her forehead, feeling confused again. 'Can we talk about it later?'

'Of course. But I just wanted you to consider this. If I mess it up, you know, the way I tell her now that she's already met me without knowing it, then I've got to live with the consequences. But if you tell her, I'll always be wondering. Maybe if I'd done it, maybe if I'd been the one to look her squarely in the eye and say sorry, instead of lurking in the background like a shadow.' He paused for breath. 'Do you see what I mean? It's not that I don't trust you, it's more that it's so important to me that I'm desperate to do it myself. That way if she wants to punch anyone it'll be me. And that'll be quite right. Do you see?'

'Sort of. Look, Barney, I'm sorry I've really got to go,

I'm in the middle of some timed cultures. I'll talk to you later.'

'You promise you'll call me?'

'I promise.' She softened her voice. 'And, Barney? Don't panic. I'm sure we'll find a way to do this properly.'

But as Ginny slipped her mobile phone back into the pocket of her lab coat and pushed the heavy swing door back into the lab, she wondered with a sinking heart whether they were indeed going to find a way to do things properly, or whether the time for that had already passed.

Chapter Thirty-five

❧

Finally a week had passed and Ginny decided that she had to do something.

'Marie, can we sit and talk for a moment?'

'I really wanted a long bath. Is it urgent?'

'Well, yes in a way,' Ginny said, leading Marie into the living room so that they could sit comfortably and settling down on the sofa with her.

'All right then,' Marie said, all big mocking eyes. 'What's the problem? Is it about Bar-Bar?'

Ginny forced a laugh. 'Don't be silly.'

'I just wondered why he hadn't been back. Do you think I put him off?'

'No, not at all. No, he's just busy that's all. He lives in London and he's got things to do up there.'

'So aren't you going out with him then? I thought you were.'

'Well, only sort of.'

Marie looked sceptical. 'You're avoiding him because of me, aren't you?'

'Well, no not really.' In fact that was exactly why Ginny was avoiding Barney, but of course Marie didn't know the half of it.

'I liked him,' Marie announced factually. 'Why doesn't he come here again? What are you doing tonight? Are you seeing him? It is Saturday night.'

'And?'

'Well, Saturday night's going-out night, isn't it?'

'For some people, yes, but I thought I'd spend it with you instead.'

'I'm going out,' Marie stated.

'Are you?' Ginny was surprised. 'Your first proper weekend home? I thought – well, it doesn't matter what I thought. Where are you going?'

'Don't know yet. It depends who's around.'

'Oh.' Ginny couldn't help feeling a little dejected. Marie had obviously made her mind up to go out with whoever might be free.

Marie looked worried. 'You did believe me when I said I'd probably spend less time here from now on, didn't you? I really don't want you to mope around when I'm out. Can't you call him and go for a drink or something?'

'I can't just ring him up and ask him out.'

'Why not?'

'It doesn't matter why not. I'm not really in the mood to see him anyway. I just want a quiet night. If you're going out I'll probably go round and see Mum and Charlotte.'

'Well, don't blow it, will you?' Marie said earnestly. 'Don't go all super-cool like you did with those other men. You'll only scare him away. And you need a boyfriend now, a proper one. I think Bar-Bar, aside from having a ridiculous name, could be a good thing.'

'You do?'

'Just got a feeling about him. I think he really is into you in a big way. It was the way he looked at you. And the other thing was that I got the feeling he liked me.

You can just tell with people, if they're just trying to be polite or if they're genuine.'

Ginny nodded, heartened. But, on the other hand, her nerves increased. It was a delicate juggling act. She didn't want to say too much about Barney, because the reason she'd brought Marie into the living room was to give her Barney's letter. She would hate her to think that she'd already been introduced to this man, albeit by a twist of fate that nobody expected or would have wanted.

'While you were away, something came through the post for you. I—' Ginny tried to find the right words, couldn't, and so just handed over the envelope. Marie took it and turned it over. She squinted at the writing on the envelope.

'Who's this from?'

'It's—'

The metallic tune of Happy Birthday tinkled out from the envelope. Marie laughed. 'Brilliant. Who's it from, then? Somebody who doesn't know when my birthday is, obviously. It was weeks ago.'

'Actually he does know. He knows exactly when your birthday is, and especially when your eighteenth birthday was. That's why he's written to you now.'

Marie stared at the envelope again. Ginny could all but see the cogs of her brain whirring into action. She looked up at Ginny. She seemed paler. 'It's not – you know. It's not him is it?'

'Who do you mean, love?' Ginny queried softly.

'Is it from my dad?'

Ginny paused. 'Yes, Marie, it's from your dad.'

Marie was very thoughtful. 'How do you know it's from him? Have you read it?'

'No, of course not. It's addressed to you and it's private. But he sent me a covering letter with it.'

'Oh.'

'It's up to you what to do with it. You're eighteen and it's entirely your business. You don't even have to open it if you don't want to.' As Marie stared at the envelope Ginny decided to make a diplomatic exit. 'I've got some things to do in the kitchen now, but I'm there if you want me.'

'Why are you leaving the room? Are you being tactful?'

'Yes.'

'Actually, I might just go up to my bedroom for a bit.'

'All right, love. I'll be making dinner.'

''Kay.'

Marie went off, slowly trudging up the stairs, the envelope swinging between her fingers. Ginny held her breath until she'd heard her bedroom door click shut. Then she let her breath out and leant against the units, rubbing her face. Had she done the right thing? Well, she was never intending to hide Barney's letter from Marie, so nothing had changed there. But what now?

She made a casserole for dinner and read the paper for an hour. It was all still quiet upstairs. Then eventually she heard Marie running a bath. Later, she appeared downstairs, dressed up and ready to go out.

'I won't be late. I'm meeting Emma.'

'Oh?'

'Yeah, apparently there's been some huge drama in her house since we've been away. Her dad's left home. Did you know anything about it?'

337

'Just a little, from Rebecca.'

Marie pulled a face. 'Bit ironic really. Her dad's disappeared, mine's appeared.'

Ginny nodded watching her daughter's face carefully. 'Everything all right, then?' she asked as neutrally as possible.

'Christ, no.'

'No?'

'Apparently her mum's falling to bits and her brother's threatening to come home and duff him up. Emma's the only sane one left. I feel sorry for her, so I'm going to give her some moral support. That's what friends are for, after all.'

'Oh, yes, poor Emma. Yes, give her my love, won't you? You know she's welcome here any time.' She chewed her lip, vowing to call Rebecca again in the next couple of days. But at that moment she was more worried about her daughter's reaction to her father's card and letter. 'And with you? Is everything all right with you?'

'Yep, fine.'

'And, so, casserole when you get home?'

'Yes, can't really face it now. Lost my appetite. See you later.'

In fact, Barney called Ginny on her mobile as she was walking round to see Jane. He asked if he could drive down and see her that evening. Ginny pretended to be busy.

'Tomorrow, then?'

'It's not really a good time.'

'Ginny,' Barney said after a short silence, 'are you shutting me out?'

338

'Not at all.' She laughed it off. 'No, I just—'

'You just want to keep me and Marie apart for now.' Barney finished for her, and sighed. 'I can understand why but I miss you like crazy. Isn't there any other way we can do things?'

'I don't really see how.'

'Can't I pick you up from the house, take you out, and drop you back off again? Marie needn't see me at all.'

'But she'll know I've been out with you.'

'Does it matter? She doesn't know who I am. We can still avoid any personal contact.'

Ginny pondered, her mind turned over and over, the fog of confusion descending again. She wanted to see Barney so much. She wanted them to consolidate what had happened the previous weekend, needed to see his face, hear his voice, believe that it was all true, that it wasn't going to disappear.

'All right then. I'll have Sunday lunch with Marie as usual. You could pick me up after lunch, we could go for a walk or something. That would be nice.'

'Great I'll see you then. And, Ginny? I really meant it when I said I missed you. I've thought about you all week.'

Ginny smiled, warmth spreading through her body. 'I missed you too.'

Charlotte, Raj, Jane and Harry were all sitting in her parents' living room, cooing over baby Benjamin. Well, in reality, Charlotte had huge bags under her eyes and was falling asleep on Raj's shoulder, but the others were cooing. Ginny was quite taken aback to see her parents sitting in the same room, at home. It had been months since there'd been such a sight, and even before Harry had left it had been a very long time since they'd spent their evenings in the same room. One of them had usually been out, or Harry had been in the garage or the shed or in one of the spare bedrooms, or Jane was reading a book upstairs or doing something in the kitchen with the radio on while Harry sat and watched television. . . The more Ginny observed the rare sight of her parents chatting together, their focus combined on account of their grandson, united by events, the more she realised that they had both been right when they'd tried to tell her that they'd been living separate lives.

Much later when Charlotte was awake again, Ginny found herself alone with her in the kitchen. Without hesitation, she put her arms around her sister and they held each other tightly.

'I'm so happy for you, Charlotte.' Ginny kissed her. 'It's all worked out for you.'

'I'm so lucky.' Charlotte glowed. I wish everybody could be as lucky as me.'

'And what about Mum and Dad?' Ginny raised her eyebrows. 'Don't you think that's promising?'

Charlotte nodded. 'It might be. But there's one thing that needs to happen before they'll be able to think anything through clearly.'

'What's that?'

'Raj, Benji and I need to leave.'

'I'm sure there's no mad rush,' Ginny soothed her.

'No, it's time,' Charlotte said with a loud, happy sigh. 'It's time for us to go home.'

Chapter Thirty-six

In fact, Marie went out for Sunday lunch. She came through the kitchen at half past eleven with her coat on, and told Ginny she was meeting some friends for a pub lunch in town. Ginny paused, wounded, as she basted a chicken. She hadn't gone the whole hog with roast potatoes and stuffing, but she still felt that their traditional dinner routine was being abandoned.

'You're going to say what about the lunch you've cooked, aren't you?' Marie pulled a pained expression. 'I'm sorry, Mum, you didn't ask me if I was going to be around. I didn't realise you'd done a chicken. I didn't smell it until I was coming down the stairs.'

'Well, now,' Ginny stood up and wiped her hands on a tea towel, 'it really doesn't matter. We can have it cold later.'

'Oh, don't make me feel guilty.' Marie was suddenly stroppy.

'What?'

'I always feel guilty when I go out, and it's not fair. I am eighteen now.'

'I don't make you feel guilty,' Ginny defended.

'You don't *make* me feel guilty, I know. I'm sorry, Mum, I know you don't mean to do it, but it's always as if I'm abandoning you. I'm not, you know. You really should go out more. You've got to ring this

341

Bartholomew bloke and see more of him. He's really nice, and he's good looking, too. Why don't you go out with him?'

'Hang on,' Ginny shifted uncomfortably. 'You want me to date Bar – him – so that you can go out without feeling guilty?'

'Partly.' Marie went red. 'But I just want to know that you're happy. If you're having a good time I can have a good time. And I don't see what's wrong with him. He's sophisticated, he's obviously been around a bit, and he really likes you. He's a cut above any of the usual blokes around here. He's got a bit of va-va-voom. Why don't you think you deserve that? You do deserve to be happy. I wish you'd see that instead of being – being, you know.'

'Being what?'

'Being martyrish about it.'

'Marie, I am not being a martyr. It's just not as simple as you think. But, in any case, I am seeing him, later this afternoon in fact.'

'You are?' Marie brightened slightly. 'Good.'

Ginny was troubled as she washed up the greasy utensils and set them to drain. It sobered her to think that Marie was feeling guilty about leading her own life. Is that really what her own years of solitude had resulted in? That instead of protecting Marie from outside influences, she was inhibiting her from being free? It was far from what she wanted. But there was something else on Marie's mind. She could tell. Marie still looked awkward as she hovered around the kitchen, poking at some bills and rearranging some mugs. 'I'm going to really piss you off now.'

'What is it?' Ginny tried to smile but was warned by the serious expression on Marie's face.

'It's about my dad.'

Ginny nodded, feeling her mouth go dry. Had Marie guessed? She waited tensely. 'Yes?'

'I – I've written back to him. I'm sorry.'

Ginny was stunned on two counts. Firstly that Marie had decided to reply to Barney, but, more importantly, that she was apologising for it. She frowned at her daughter as she nervously played with things lying around on the unit tops, unable to meet Ginny's eye. Where was this coming from? Ginny hadn't thought this far ahead at all, and she hadn't been prepared for the psychology of the moment. Eventually, flummoxed, she had to ask. 'Why are you sorry?'

'Oh, you know.'

'No, I don't know. Tell me.'

'Oh, it's you. You've, you know. You've done it all for me. It's been really hard for you. That kind of thing.'

'I don't really understand.'

'Yes you do,' Marie said impatiently. 'You've sacrificed everything, haven't had boyfriends, lived your life for me, always put me first. You didn't become a doctor, didn't get married, didn't have proper holidays, all that stuff. And now my father comes along and writes me a letter, and you must be really put out.'

'No,' Ginny asserted. 'I'm not put out. I'm pleased if you're pleased.'

'Really?'

'Yes, really.'

'You're not angry with him?'

'No, not at all. I never have been, you know that. Why are you asking me now? Do I look angry?'

'No.'

'Well then.'

'It's just – that guilt thing again.'

'Now you listen to me, young lady.' Ginny took a step towards Marie. 'I don't want to hear any more rubbish about being guilty. I am very happy with the way my life's turned out. As it happens I like my own company, but aside from that I've got family, friends and perhaps even a boyfriend. I like my job. So my life is full. You can go out as much as you like and you can certainly write to your father if you want to. It's completely up to you.'

'You won't be annoyed?'

'Of course not.'

Marie played with a pepper grinder, not looking up. 'Did you like him?'

'Who?'

'My father. When you knew him. Did you like him?'

'Oh, darling.' Ginny regarded her daughter affectionately, her stomach somersaulting just at the thought of Barney, then and now. 'Yes, I liked him.'

'So you must have been really hurt when he didn't want to live with us.'

Ginny swallowed. This was very delicate ground. 'He had his reasons.'

'Did he?' Marie glanced up, her eyes foil of questions. 'Like what?'

'I think that's something you need to talk to him about yourself. He has his own story, just as we all do.'

Marie absorbed this quietly. 'Does he look like me?' she shot at Ginny.

'Oh. . .' Ginny hedged, becoming nervous again. 'Well, a bit. It's more in your manner really, some of the things you do. A look in your eyes at times. And,' she found herself adding, 'I think you've got his nose.'

'This is his nose?'

'Well, yes. It is.'

'Bastard!' Marie exclaimed, and Ginny was filled with relief to see the twinkle back in her eyes.

'So go on, bugger off,' Ginny said bravely. 'My boyfriend's coming in an hour or so and I'd like to have a bath and get changed first.'

Ginny wondered whether she should tell Barney that Marie had written to him. He'd find out for himself in due course and she had realised as she'd lain in the bath and thought it through that it would be wrong for her to be an intermediary. If she reported Marie's reactions back to Barney it would feel as if she was spying. They would have to work out their relationship on their own.

Marie had already gone out by the time Barney arrived. He drove them out to a footpath through a wood. They left the car and scrunched through the dry brown and amber leaves, passing dog-walkers and occasional couples and families.

'You look gorgeous,' Barney said, taking her hand and squeezing it. 'Did I tell you?'

'That's about the third time,' Ginny said. 'I don't know how I can look so good. It's only an old coat.'

'I didn't notice the coat.' He lowered his voice as a tweedy woman stalked past them calling after a bulldog named Jasper. 'I was thinking about what was under it.'

'Barney!' Ginny felt her face grow hot.

'How cold is it, do you reckon?' Barney pushed a hand inside her coat and wound his arm around her waist. She shivered with pleasure.

'Pretty cold. Why?'

'Hmm. I was just wondering whether we could. . . at least the ground's dry.'

Ginny glanced up at him, expecting him to be joking, but his eyes were smouldering at her. 'You don't mean what I think you mean?'

'What do you think I mean? I've got a big jacket. There's a quiet little path over there leading into the thick of the woods. Nobody around over there. What do you say?'

Ginny didn't say much for the next hour. When they emerged from the trees again, pulling twigs from their hair, she felt as if every person they passed must have been able to read her mind. It was difficult to stop smiling. Although her body was cold now, her face was warm, her lips stinging. She'd never felt so alive.

They walked to a lane where they stopped and had a drink in a country pub. It was so easy to talk. Not only were they interested in many of the same things, the conversation somehow kept reverting back to Marie. 'You know, Ginny,' Barney said, playing with a scarcely touched pint of bitter. They'd been so busy talking, there hadn't been much thought of drinking. 'I've been thinking really hard about how to handle this with Marie.'

'You and me both. I've thought about nothing else.'

'I want to suggest something to you. I know your immediate reaction will be to say no, but if you think about it you might change your mind.'

'What is it?' Ginny widened her eyes.

346

'Well . . . the fact is, Marie has already met me. We've already had a conversation and she already thinks that I'm your boyfriend.'

'Yes,' Ginny said warily, wondering what was coming.

'And since she has, and since we got along quite well when we met, I was wondering if. . .' He seemed pained, then he shook his head. 'No, it's no good. You'll just say no.'

'Come on, out with it, Barney.'

He sighed then met her gaze squarely. 'I wondered if I could continue to get to know Marie, to gain her trust, to let her discover who I am as a person, not as her father. It's a process we've already started without planning to. I just think – don't you think it would be much better for her to know something about me before my identity's stuck in front of her nose? Don't you think it would be much easier all round if she's spent some time with me first?'

'Oh God, you mean without telling her who you really are?'

'Yes. Then once I've built up her trust in me as a person, once she knows I'm genuinely interested in her, then I could tell her.'

Ginny blanched. 'No.'

'I knew you'd say that.'

'It's impossible, Barney.'

'But I'd like you to think about it.'

Ginny sipped her wine and tried to consider dispassionately. But her emotions screamed back at her that this was deception on an unforgivable scale. 'I can't trick Marie. She'd never forgive me. She'd never forgive you.'

347

'That may be true, but I don't think so. I've thought this through over and over again. Look, Ginny, the damage is already done. We didn't tell her when she first saw me, so we've already kept the truth back from her. It's not about an ideal situation now, it's about how to salvage the best of a bad job.'

'I know.' Ginny hedged. What would Marie feel? She tried desperately to put herself inside her daughter's head. Yes, she liked Barney, she'd said so a number of times. But to put them together without her consent? Would it be better or worse for her? Might it be better for her to find out that her father was a man she was already fond of?

'What do you think, Ginny? What's the right thing to do?'

'If only I knew, Barney.' Ginny shook her head, confused again. 'You'll have to give me some time to think.'

'All right.' He nodded. 'Let's mull it over for a day or two, then let me know your thoughts. I'd just really like you to consider this angle – if you let me do it my way, you won't be able to blame yourself. Please think about it.'

'Agreed.'

'And in the meantime, I'm dying to know more about her trip to Thailand. What has she been telling you?'

It struck Ginny, wondrously, that if she'd been with any other man she'd probably have been apologising for her constant references to her daughter. But, as it was, it was a shared obsession. Barney leapt on any mention of Marie like a hungry dog.

How could this be, Ginny thought when they finally

made it back to the car in the early twilight. That things could all suddenly fit together like this? How could I be so happy? Was Marie right? Had she really persuaded herself over the years that she didn't deserve any personal happiness because at university she'd done a stupid thing? Because she'd compromised other people by her mistake?

Barney walked her to the front door of her house, and as they were saying goodbye it was thrown open by Marie, making them both jump as the light from the hall lit up the gloom of the doorstep.

'Ah, there you are! I was going to send a search party out,' Marie quipped into the cold air, and Ginny was happy to see that her earlier difficult mood seemed to have lifted.

'I'm just dropping your mother off,' Barney said comfortably. 'Thank you for lending her to me.'

'Oh, you can have her. I'm sure we can come to an amicable arrangement,' Marie answered a little too readily for Ginny's sensitivities. 'You coming in, then? Mum cooked this huge chicken earlier but I heartlessly went up the pub so we've got to eat it now. And I feel guilty because I had a massive pizza and I'm not going to be able to eat enough before bedtime to make my mum happy. D'you want some?'

'Oh, darling, Bar-Bar, he has to go really.'

Marie gave Ginny an irritated look, then glanced right over her head at Barney, ignoring what Ginny had said. 'Do you play chess?'

'Yes.' Barney raised his eyebrows curiously. 'I do, as it happens. Do you?'

'Yes. I'm pretty good. D'you fancy a game?'

'I'd love to play with you some time.'

'Now, I mean.'

Barney looked at Ginny keenly. She was hopping from foot to foot, seeing as Marie was still firmly planted on the doormat, blocking her mother's entrance to the house and forcing them into a dialogue.

But Ginny was now thinking of a conversation she had with Barney in the pub. Here was the ideal opportunity for them to get to know each other. But was it right? And what of the letter Marie had written to her father? Here, without her knowledge, was the man she had written to. How would she feel if she found out? Or was it just a question of when? Would she feel cheated? Tricked? But, on the other hand, if she liked Barney, which she genuinely seemed to, and as she'd decided to reply to her father's letter, would it matter in the long run? Ginny was utterly frustrated with her own indecision, not knowing what to do for the best. 'Look, Marie, I don't think now is a good time really, it's late.'

'No it's not. Bartholomew? Why don't you come in. You look freezing.'

'It is getting a bit chilly out here, I have to say.'

'Well, come in then.' Ginny gave way finally, stepping into the hall as Marie stood back to allow them in, a triumphant grin on her face.

'If I may just use your loo?' Barney asked politely.

'Up there.' Marie pointed, then tutted. 'Of course, you know where it is.'

While Barney was in the bathroom, Ginny took off her coat and tried to smooth down her hair, finding tiny pieces of dry leaves everywhere. 'Marie,' she said to her in a stage whisper, 'you don't really know what you're doing. It would be better to let him go home now.'

'Why?'

'You – you can't force relationships.'

'You can force people away though.'

'What do you mean?'

'Mother,' Marie hissed, 'I may be a complete amateur when it comes to men but even I can see that you're doing it all wrong here. You'll lose him unless you make more effort, it's as simple as that. I like him, I think you should go out with him, so I'm giving you a helping hand. If I leave you to get on with it he'll just wander off with a broken heart and you'll have ruined it. Christ, what did you do to your hair? Did you fall over?' Marie stared, then the penny dropped. 'Oh my God. You didn't? You did?' She opened her mouth wide and pulled a shocked face. 'You're incorrigible, but I understand. You're making up for lost time. Right, I'll go and set the chessboard up in the front room. You can put the veg on.'

'Oh, he won't—' Ginny panicked, feeling the situation was being wrenched out of her control. 'Bar – he won't stay to eat.'

'Yes he will,' Marie replied factually, dancing away.

Chapter Thirty-seven

Ginny prepared vegetables as she had been instructed and set them to one side as Barney and Marie settled into a game of chess. She heard their conversation clearly through the open door. She wandered around the kitchen in agitation, on hand ready to burst in just in case things took an awkward turn.

'Let's toss for white. Have you got a coin? Go on, you toss then. Aha, I'm white. Great. Mum! Can you bring us some drinks?'

Ginny appeared, trying not to look as if she'd been eavesdropping. 'What would you like?'

'I think you've got wine in the fridge, haven't you? Can I have a glass of that?'

'Wine?' Ginny frowned.

'I am eighteen, Mum,' Marie said in a bored voice. 'And I'm sure Bartholomew would like something too.'

'Oh, I'm fine, Ginny,' he said, looking apologetic.

'No he's not. He'd love a glass of wine too.'

Ginny gave Marie an admonishing look for her tone, but she collected wine for them both anyway, then, as they seemed to be focused on the chessboard, wandered back into the kitchen, at a loose end.

'So you've been to Bangladesh?' Marie said as the game progressed and Ginny heard occasional comments punctuating concentrated silences. 'You'd be better not to put your knight there, but I'm not going to tell you how to play. What were you doing there?'

'I was working.'

'Oh? Doing what? You're not one of these engineers who earns thousands of pounds a week are you? I met some of those in Thailand. There were these guys, about sixty years old with teenage girlfriends. I didn't think much of them.'

There was a slight pause. 'Actually, I'm a doctor.'

'Really? I thought of doing medicine once. But I'm better at languages really, so I'm going to do languages at university. I hope I'm going to travel with them, though. I don't want to be one of those people who ends up translating things in London and never travels, or even worse just doing something completely different. I'm quite good.'

'It's a valuable skill overseas and here. It makes a big difference if you don't expect everyone to speak English to you.'

'My Auntie Charlotte did languages and she's lived most of her life abroad. Do you know Charlotte?'

'No, I never did meet her.'

'Never did – what, when?'

'I mean,' Barney corrected quickly, 'I haven't met her yet.'

'She's great, just not around very much. So how did you become a doctor in Bangladesh? Did you work anywhere else?'

'Yes, I worked in Africa mostly.'

'What, for a charity or something?'

'Yes, Save the Children.'

'Oh.' Out of sight, sipping her own glass of wine, Ginny held her breath as the game went on. 'My mum could have been a doctor.'

'Really?'

'Yes. But she's probably told you this already. It's my fault she's not. I turned up and messed everything up. But she was good. She went to Oxford, you know. Did she tell you that?'

'Well, I think she must have done. I knew about it, definitely.'

'Where did you study?'

Only a beat, a slight pause that Ginny appreciated and Marie wouldn't even have noticed. 'In fact, I was at Oxford too, but we were in different years. Coincidence.'

'Yeah, isn't it? You can't do that, you'll be in check. So did you like Oxford?'

Again, Ginny felt rather than heard Barney take a breath. She gripped her glass. 'Yes. Mostly.'

'I didn't apply for Oxbridge. I don't know why really, but I probably wouldn't have got in anyway. I just wanted to do my own thing. I'm going to Bristol. I want to do modern languages and start learning Russian, too. Have you been to Eastern Europe much?'

'Not so much. It's changing all the time, though. I'd like to go.'

'My queen there and bingo, you're in check again. I think you're dead in the water now. So why did you work for Save the Children? Haven't you got any children?'

Ginny panicked. She grabbed a baking tray from the draining board and threw it on the floor, then made elaborate noises of pain. There was silence from the living room so she put her head round the door. 'Sorry about that. Are you ready to eat? I'll put the veg on, shall I?'

'Not yet,' Marie said. 'Have you done any gravy? Oh, please do your fantastic chicken gravy. My mum does the best chicken gravy you've ever tasted. She's a brilliant cook but she's so modest she never goes on about it. Which is a bit of a waste, really, because I'll eat anything.'

'I'll do gravy, then.' Ginny retreated to the kitchen, grateful for having created a distraction.

Marie won the first game. They chatted on through a second, which Barney won, and started a third decider.

'I love games,' Marie said. 'Mum taught me chess. She's brilliant at it. Have you played her yet?'

Ginny put her hand to her chest. Of course they had played, years ago. It had been quite an occasion. Did Barney remember it as clearly as she did?

'Actually, we've only played once. Barney's voice hid a half-laugh. 'She beat me, of course.'

'We used to play all the time when I was a child. And cards, too, but there's a limit to the card games you can play when there's only two of you. I'm a beast at Gin Rummy. What else do you play?'

'Well, my favourite game is actually one I learnt in Africa,' Barney said, and Ginny could tell that he had Marie's rapt attention. 'It's called Wari.'

'I've heard of that. How do you play it?'

'It's quite hard to explain but you have to count your blots back into your home board and you can steal your opponent's pieces if you're clever enough.'

355

'Have you got a set at home then? Can you show me?'

'You don't really need a special board. You just need a grid of some kind, and the kids and old men play it with stones. They often just draw the grid in the sand. It's easy to play anywhere.'

'Could we play it here?'

'In theory.'

'It would be so great to turn up to university knowing how to play Wari. Will you teach me?'

'Next time,' Ginny said, walking in decisively. 'When you've finished that game I'd really like to eat. I'm hungry.'

'I think I'm winning again,' Marie told Barney. 'Unless you've got a secret plan to get out of the mess you're in.'

'No plan.' Barney sighed.

'Then I'll finish you off.' Marie moved her bishop into place and grinned. I'll give it six moves.'

'Marie's demolishing me.' Barney smiled at Ginny as she sat on the sofa and watched them for a moment, either side of her small table, Barney on the edge of her favourite armchair, Marie on a stool. They turned back to their game, focused. And it was just as well that Marie couldn't see them both from this angle, in profile, noses down – she just might have started to suspect something. They looked completely at ease together. It made Ginny want to take a mental photograph and keep it for ever. Who knew where things would go from here. For just one moment, one fleeting evening, everything had fallen into place.

*

It was time for Charlotte to speak to Jane. She tapped on her mother's bedroom door and let herself in, stopping in amazement to stare. Jane looked gorgeous. She was wearing a trouser suit with loose crêpe trousers and jewellery. She smelt of Chanel No. 5, her favourite perfume, which Charlotte hadn't caught a whiff of for years. She was fluffing up her hair with a comb. Charlotte felt a buzz of happiness. Harry was due round that evening in an hour or so. This was definite evidence of the upturn in their relationship. When had her mother last made such an effort with her appearance?

'Oh, hello, darling, come in.'

'I just wondered if you've got a minute to talk. Wow, you look nice.' Charlotte went and sat on the edge of the bed. 'Dad will be so pleased.'

'Hmm?'

'When he gets here. He'll be bowled over.'

'Yes, I expect I'll just have a chance to say hello to him before I leave. If he's on time. Do make the most of him though, won't you, Charlotte. I know he can't feed Benjamin but he can clear up a bit and talk to Raj while you get some sleep. Give him some washing up to do or some other practical jobs and he'll excel himself.'

'Why, where are you going?' Charlotte was disconcerted.

'Oh, I'm just going out for a couple of hours. I don't expect I'll be late.'

'Out? Where? You're all dolled up.'

'Is it too much, do you think?' Jane twirled in front of her full-length mirror.

'Well, it depends where you're going.'

'I'm going to try out that restaurant that Ginny went to recently with Barney. It sounded so nice, very atmospheric.'

Charlotte was confused. 'On your own?'

Jane gave Charlotte an old-fashioned look. 'No, of course not on my own. With a friend.'

'Oh. Who?'

Jane paused, poked at her hair again and blinked at her reflection. 'Actually, I'm having dinner with Malcolm.'

Charlotte sat bolt upright, wishing she hadn't as her stomach contracted painfully. She put a hand over it and rubbed. 'Not the handyman? I thought he'd vanished out of sight.'

'No, no. He's still around. He asked me out to dinner and I thought I'd go.'

'But, Mum, now Dad's on his own again and you two are getting on so well. . .'

'Yes, we are getting on well. That's true.'

'So why would you want to ruin it by seeing someone else?'

'Really, Charlotte,' Jane said, a small smile hovering on her lips. 'What on earth makes you think that me seeing someone else will ruin it?'

Charlotte stared, uncomprehending. 'What do you mean?'

'I'm just going out, that's all.' Jane picked up her handbag and checked inside. 'It's not such a big deal, is it? I'm sure nobody minds, and I'm quite sure that your father has no cause whatsoever to complain about it.'

'But – do you like Malcolm, really? I thought he was boring and long-winded. Not your type at all.'

'Well, perhaps he isn't my type. I'm not sure that it matters. I'm going out because I've been asked and because it will be a change.'

'And what about Dad? At least you could just say you're seeing one of your other friends instead.'

'Why?' Jane gazed innocently at her daughter.

'Because it'll wind him up if he thinks you've tarted yourself up like this to have dinner with another man.'

'Oh, will it?' Jane breathed ironically. 'Jolly good.'

Charlotte continued to stare as Jane gathered a smart coat from her wardrobe. Was she being dense? Was her mother trying to make her father jealous? Was she trying to hurt him, or to get her own back, or was it more complicated than that?

'Anyway,' Jane went on breezily, 'what did you want to say?'

'Oh, just that, Raj and I have been thinking.'

'Yes,' Jane sat on the bed next to Charlotte and kissed her lightly, brushing a smear of newly applied lipstick from her cheek, 'I thought you might have been.'

'We both want to thank you so much for everything you've done for us. Letting us stay here, being so patient, not minding when Benjamin screams all night. You've been amazing. But we think it's time for us to move on.'

Jane nodded slowly. Her eyes were sad, but she pursed her lips philosophically. 'I know, love.'

'We thought we'd wait until Benjamin's six weeks old. Then I'll be fitter, we'll both have our health check and hopefully we'll both be right as rain. Then we thought we'd go home.'

'Yes, you do need to be at home with your new family. I understand. Where will you go?'

359

'Back to Mumbai. We'll look for something a bit bigger, maybe a little house, and we'll – we're going to settle there. I hope you understand.'

Jane took her daughter in her arms and gave her a strong hug. They kissed again.

'It's absolutely what I expected.'

'You don't mind?'

'Not at all. You must live the life that's mapped out for you. I'll come and see you, though. It's about time I took part in your life instead of expecting you to come back here and take part in mine. I'll want to see little Benji growing up.'

'And I'll bring him back here, all the time. I promise you'll see as much of him as you want.'

'I know, darling.'

'So, we've actually booked our flights.' Charlotte watched Jane for her reaction. She gave a warm smile.

'Good. That'll make you both feel much more settled.'

They were peaceful together as Jane stood up again and slipped her coat on.

'Have a lovely evening tonight,' Charlotte said. 'You really deserve to do something for yourself. You've spent so much time doing things for other people.'

'Thank you, Charlotte.' Jane nodded her head in acknowledgement 'And do make sure you tell your father all about it, won't you?'

'Of course, we'll tell him we've booked our flights. I think he'll understand, too.'

'No,' Jane said, putting another layer of lipstick on, 'I mean about my dinner with Malcolm.'

Chapter Thirty-eight

'She's written back to me!' Barney told Ginny. Excitement reverberated through his voice.

Ginny cradled the phone to her cheek and listened, eyes closed. It was a moment she had been equally looking forward to and dreading. It moved things on, either way. That had to be a good thing, didn't it? It was a dull, wet night and Marie was visiting Charlotte again. Apart from Mr Mistoffelees snoring on the sofa, she had the house to herself.

Barney bounded on. 'I assume you knew she'd replied to me? Or maybe you didn't?'

'Yes, I knew.' Ginny chewed her cheek. 'I didn't want to say anything. I thought you'd rather it was private. I didn't want to play piggy in the middle.'

'Of course, yes, I understand,' Barney said warmly. 'Do you want to know what she's said?'

'Well. . .' Ginny wavered. 'Not word for word – but I'll admit I'm curious.'

'She didn't tell you?'

'I didn't ask. I felt it was between the two of you.'

'Thank you, Ginny,' Barney said. 'I really respect the way you're handling this.'

'So she – is she positive? I don't want to pry but it would be helpful to know roughly which way she's heading.'

'Yes,' Barney said triumphantly. 'Positive but with a thread of black humour, which now I've met her makes perfect sense.'

'Good.' Ginny was relieved. A positive response was good. It was a start, at least. Now they just had a small mountain to climb, and the question was, how to go about it.

'So I was thinking,' Barney went on enthusiastically, 'that this is an ideal time to see her again. Before I've responded to her and before it all becomes set in stone.'

'What do you mean?'

'You know, things went so well on Sunday night. Better than I'd ever dreamt. I'd like to build on that. It probably sounds sentimental to you, but I really felt we were a family.'

Tears stung Ginny's eyes. Sentimental? No. Warm, sensitive, wonderful? Yes. She'd really felt they were a family too. It had been fantastic, a moment to treasure. 'I do know what you mean, Barney. I felt it too,' she replied softly.

'I'd just like to make something of my relationship with her, just one more chance to meet her naturally before it's all out in the open.'

'You're not going to reply to her?'

'Yes, yes. As soon as possible. But could I see her once more first? This week? I could come down and take you both out, for a pizza or something. We could just relax together, as we did on Sunday night.'

'Oh, I don't know, Barney.' Ginny took the phone to the sofa and curled up in a ball next to Mr Mistoffelees. He rolled over on to his back and carried on snoring. 'Sunday was more by accident than design.'

'I disagree. It all happened on Marie's insistence. It

362

wasn't an accident. Fate, perhaps?'

Ginny sighed, the wheels all spinning in different directions. 'Fate, perhaps. But we didn't plan it that way. It would seem very deceitful.'

'But I think it's working, that's my point. Can you imagine how I feel to know that my daughter, my real, live, wonderful daughter is actually enjoying spending time with me, actually likes me? Just to run her comments through my head, her questions, her observations. To savour that feeling of joking with her, having fun with her. I've fantasised about this for years. I can hardly believe it's real. I – I can't explain it, Ginny.'

'You don't have to. I understand. I saw it.'

'I just—' He sounded close to tears again and Ginny felt hard faced and obdurate for trying to stand between him and his dream. 'I just don't want it all to crumble into dust. Not just yet.'

And maybe, Ginny thought, that's exactly what Barney expected to happen once he told Marie who he was. Perhaps he thought he was stealing time, seizing moments with Marie that didn't really belong to him. If he had to do it as an impostor, perhaps he felt that was better than nothing.

The pendulum swung back again.

'All right, Barney. Let's go out for a pizza, if she's up for it. But that has to be the last time. After that you must promise to contact her and deal with this properly.'

'I promise.' He expelled a long breath and she could hear the joy and relief in his voice. 'Thank you, Ginny. You are so wonderful.'

*

'So guess what?' Marie told Charlotte as, on their knees side by side on the bathmat, they bathed Benji. Charlotte was holding him tightly and Marie gently swilled warm water over his stomach. 'My dad wrote to me.'

'Well, well,' Charlotte said non-commitally. She knew, of course, through the Ginny-Jane grapevine that Marie had replied to Barney. She didn't know any of the details, though. It was better for Marie to tell her if she wanted to. 'How do you feel about that?'

Marie shrugged, peering down at Benji's brown stub of a belly button. 'Is that really supposed to look like that?'

Charlotte laughed. 'Yes. That's a healthy one. It rots, and then falls off.'

'Disgusting.'

'I suppose so. Quite a lot about babies is disgusting, really. But when it's your baby you don't notice.'

'Oh, I'm not sure about that.' Marie raised her eyebrows. 'I watched Raj gagging like mad while he was doing a nappy the other day.'

'Well that's a man thing,' Charlotte said knowledgeably. 'The trick is not to breathe through your nose, but he hasn't mastered that yet.'

'I suppose men will never really take over from women on the baby front, will they?' Marie mused. 'I mean, if it'd been the other way round. If it'd been my mum who'd run off into the sunset and my dad who'd been left with me wailing in his arms, I just wonder what would have happened. He'd probably have given me to someone else after five minutes. His mum, probably.'

'I'm not sure,' Charlotte said neutrally. From what

364

she'd always heard about Barney's mother, that scenario sounded pretty unlikely. And from what she'd heard about Barney, he seemed the sensitive type. Not so sensitive that he hadn't run away, though, so in a way Marie was probably right. They hoisted Benji from the bathtub and wrapped him in soft towels. They padded out to the bedroom together, Charlotte keeping up a running monologue on their actions for the sake of her bleary-eyed baby.

'Do you talk to him all the time?' Marie quizzed.

'Yes. I have to. That's how he's going to learn about things.'

'Bit early though, isn't it? He's not listening to you.'

'Oh, I don't know.'

'I suppose women are good at talking to babies because they're used to talking to men.'

'And?'

'Well, men don't listen to you either.'

Charlotte smiled. 'And what about your dad? Where do you go from here?'

Marie let out a long breath and handed Charlotte a clean babygrow from the drawer. 'I suppose I'll meet him.'

'Is that what you want?'

'I don't really know what I want. I suppose I've got some questions I'd like him to answer, but it's not as if I care about him or anything. It's not as if I even like him. I've got no feelings towards him at all.'

'Hmm,' Charlotte mused. And yet she knew that Marie had met Barney in another guise and had confessed to liking him quite a lot. What to say? 'Maybe you'll grow to like him.'

'I don't know.' Marie pulled a face. 'And it's not as if

Mum cares. She's all wrapped up with this new boyfriend, and good luck to her. He's pretty cool, and he really cares. You know, you can just tell with some men that they'd never be the type to just run off and dump you. Well, this Bar-Bar bloke she's met, he's like that. Far more worthy than my blimmin' absent father.'

Charlotte wriggled uncomfortably as she fed Benji's resistant arms into his babygrow. It was probably best to say nothing.

'Do you know what I'd like to see?' Marie ejected, her eyes sparkling. 'My dad turning up at the door and Mum's boyfriend answering. That'd be a poke in the eye for him, wouldn't it?'

'I think,' Charlotte said very carefully, 'that it really would be a sight to behold.'

'You've got to do something about this,' Charlotte told Ginny kindly but firmly. She'd found her older sister in Jane's bedroom. She'd left Marie singing to Benji to try to settle him in his cot, and hearing voices along the landing had walked in on Jane and Ginny, side by side on the bed, deep in conversation.

'About what, dear?' Jane interjected.

'Barney.' Charlotte plonked herself down on the bed alongside the others. 'Marie's fantasising about Barney turning up and Barney answering the door and showing him who's boss.'

'What?' Ginny pulled an expression of incomprehension.

'Yes.' Charlotte nodded gravely. 'Exactly. So just when are you going to spill the beans?'

'Actually, I've just been talking to Mum about it.'

366

Ginny sighed, and Charlotte could instantly see how white faced and tense her big sister was. She took her hand and stroked it.

'Hell, I'm sorry. Barging in here as if there's a simple answer to it all. I just thought Marie was getting confused and it might be best to put a stop to it before it gets any more convoluted.'

'Well I agree,' Ginny said, although her eyes betrayed her uncertainty. 'I was just telling Mum that Barney's coming down tonight to take me and Marie out to Pizza Express but I'm thinking of cancelling it.'

'And I think Ginny and Marie should go out with him,' Jane piped up. 'Barney wants just one more meeting with Marie as himself before the – what is it they say? The shit hits the fan.'

'Mum!' Both daughters ejected as one, then laughed.

'Blimey,' Charlotte said as she considered the facts. 'It does seem a bit risky. There again, it does give him a chance to build up her interest first.'

'That's exactly what he says,' Ginny said weakly.

'And he's going to contact her immediately afterwards and then there'll be no more illusions, only facts,' Jane said. 'So I've told Ginny not to be silly. She should go out tonight and enjoy herself. There's plenty of time for questions and answers later. My goodness, life is so full of quizzes and justifications, recriminations and defences. It really is a waste of time when it comes down to it.'

Ginny looked at Charlotte for help and received a shrug. 'Maybe Mum's right. I don't know. I think you should tell Marie before you go out. At least then she'll know who's buying her pizza.'

'But Barney wants to tell her himself, in his own

way,' Ginny protested. 'I've promised him now I won't spill the beans. Especially as now he's written to her and she's written back. It's really not for me to interfere.'

'Hmm.' Charlotte was unhappy about it.

'No more dilemmas,' Jane said decisively, standing up and leaving her two daughters lolling against each other on the soft mattress. 'You'd made up your mind to go out tonight, Ginny, so why don't you stick to it? Besides, it's too late to cancel it now. He'll be on his way already.'

'Christ, yes.' Ginny looked at her watch and leapt up.

'Benji's asleep. Who's on his way?' Marie walked in and stuck a hand on her hip. 'What are you lot talking about?'

'Bar-bar. . .' Jane began, frowning at herself.

'*Him*,' Ginny said knowingly. 'I told you. Let's go home and get ready.'

'And I suppose you'll hog the bath for the next hour.' Marie rolled her eyes as they left the room together and went down the stairs.

Charlotte let out a breath once Marie and Ginny were out of earshot. 'That was close,' she said in a hushed voice to her mother.

'One more night, then we'll all know,' Jane said wistfully.

'We'll know?'

'Whether Barney really is the answer to Ginny's prayers that I think he is, or not.'

In the event, Ginny hardly got a word in edgeways.

Marie seemed a little shy when Barney appeared at

the door again, but she insisted on answering it and letting him in, and offering him a whisky, which he refused – which was just as well as Ginny knew for sure that they didn't have any. He was looking stunning in a faded black denim shirt over a polo shirt and casual jeans. He smelled lovely too, but Ginny hoped that Marie wouldn't notice and blurt out some tactless remark about perfume. Together they climbed into his car and headed up the road into the town, and instantly Marie took over, leaning forward from the back seat.

'Is this your car, then?'

'No, it's actually my housemate's car. I'm just borrowing it because she doesn't use it much.'

'She?'

Ginny groaned silently. Not a conversation about Honey, please. Her nerves were shredded enough without provoking her slumbering insecurities about Barney's gorgeous housemate.

'We're old friends. Nothing more.'

'Okay. Don't protest too much. My mum'll get jealous.'

'Marie!' Ginny snapped.

'See? Still, jealousy's a good sign, isn't it? I was talking to Emma about it. Emma's the one I went round Thailand with. Emma says if you don't feel jealous when your other half so much as looks at another person then there's probably something wrong. You have to care about losing something, don't you? Otherwise you probably don't value it much. You can park here, go left into this side street. Don't go into the municipal, you'll lose your wing mirrors and maybe your wheels, too. I know, idyllic little market town this is. You should hear the language on the

369

school bus, it'd turn you grey overnight. But I suppose you've been to far rougher places, haven't you?'

The conversation continued at the table in Pizza Express, after they had ordered their drinks. Ginny had decided to stick to lime and soda, just to be alert in case the conversation started to drift in a dangerous direction. Barney had ordered a Coke, probably for the same reason, she guessed, as much as for the fact that he was driving. Marie, giving them both astonished looks, had ordered a large glass of red wine.

'And don't make me keep stating my age to you, Mum. I'm starting to feel like one of those old ladies who accosts you in supermarket queues and shouts "I'm ninety-seven".'

'I know how old you are, love. You can drink wine if you want.'

'Thank you. I suppose you both drank *occasionally* when you were my age. You must have enjoyed the odd little tipple when you were at university.'

Barney didn't miss the heavy irony in her voice. 'Oh, I used to enjoy a small one now and then, as I recall,' he rejoindered.

'Vodka was your poison, wasn't it?' Ginny twinkled at Barney, then went red. Then she went white and clammed up, swallowing painfully. She picked up a menu and flapped it. 'I had something with chicken and peppers in here once. It was delicious.'

But Marie, sharp as a Sabatier, was staring at Ginny relentlessly. 'I thought you two didn't know each other when you were university?'

'We didn't,' Barney said smoothly. 'But we've talked about it a lot. As you can imagine, both having been to the same place. We've got a lot in common.'

Marie nodded, glancing from Barney's innocent smile to Ginny's flushed face, her eyes determinedly fixed on the menu. She scratched her chin. 'I suppose you must have known some of the same people?'

'A few,' Barney went on, discreetly slipping a hand on to Ginny's knee and squeezing it. 'None of them very interesting. I'd much rather hear about you and your university plans. Is Emma going to Bristol too?'

'Top marks.' Marie held out her glass in salute to Barney and took a swig of her wine. 'You remembered where I was going to university and my friend's name. You'd have made a good journalist. Did you ever think of doing that?'

'No.' Barney laughed. 'There's only ever been one vocation for me.'

'Hmm. And what if someone had given you a baby when you'd been in university and told you to look after it? What would you have done about your vocation?'

Ginny blanched, almost knocking over her glass as she summoned the waiter. Marie's sudden changes in direction were usually amusing, but where Barney was concerned they were positively seizure-inducing.

'I really don't know.' Barney answered Marie seriously, his voice softening. 'And it's a very good question.'

'Do you think so? I was talking to my Auntie Charlotte about it. I suppose she's done everything in the right order so it's easy for her to be theoretical about it, but it's been on my mind recently.'

'And why's that?' Barney asked gently.

'Oh, no, no,' Ginny intervened drastically, waving the menu. 'We've got to order now. Marie, I'm sure

371

Bar-tholomew doesn't want to hear all about our business over dinner like this.'

'Okay.' Marie shrugged and picked up her menu. And as Ginny was about to relax, added, 'After dinner then.'

In fact, the conversation turned in so many directions that Ginny became dizzy. Barney kept up admirably and many times father and daughter had each other laughing with a dry remark or an unexpected retort. As Marie downed the last of her chocolate ice-cream she sat back and eyed Ginny and Barney through narrowed eyes.

'I suppose it's a bit sad really, me going out for a pizza with my mum and my mum's boyfriend.'

'Tragic,' Barney said. 'Especially as you're paying.'

'Ha, ha, on my budget. But actually you're both quite fun and nobody saw me so no harm done.'

Ginny held her breath, waiting for her to bring up the subject of university and babies again, but as she watched Marie drain her glass of wine, her eyes hazy, Ginny realised with some relief that she'd forgotten about it and moved on. Marie looked at her watch.

'Shit. Sorry, I don't want to be rude or anything, but can I leave you two to it now? I said I'd meet Emma in the Stag for a quick one before I went home.'

'You what? Darling, you didn't say anything. How are you going to get home?'

'Where's the Stag?' Barney asked Ginny pleasantly.

'Oh, just up the road, but there are no buses after nine thirty and I'm not sure—'

'We'll be here for another hour and a half,' Barney told Marie. 'I'm going to have another coffee and maybe a small brandy. We might even go mad and

372

order the cheeseboard. See you back here at ten thirty for a lift home?'

'Fine,' Marie said, standing up and putting her jacket on. 'I don't want a late night anyway. One can only hear so much about someone else's parents' marital difficulties before the eyes glaze over and start revolving. But her dad's such an arse, and she needs someone to get drunk with occasionally. Sorry, Mum, but get over it. We're going to form a Dads Are Arses club, or something like that. We've got to work on the name. Bye then, see you later, and thanks so much for the dinner. It was scrummy, Bartholomew, as I assume you're paying. See ya!'

They watched Marie leave the restaurant in a flurry of activity. The room seemed duller the moment she had walked out.

Barney picked up his spoon and poked a piece of pineapple around his plate. 'Dads Are Arses.'

'I'm sorry, Barney, you just never know what she's going to say. And it's not as if she knows—'

'That's exactly it,' he said seriously. 'It's time that she did know.'

Chapter Thirty-nine

When she thought about it afterwards, Ginny realised that she should have known what was going to happen next.

The time that Barney had spent with them had been wonderful. She'd been nervous throughout, but Marie and Barney had sparked off each other so well that she kept reassuring herself that there was no harm being done. Taking a long view, could that possibly be a bad thing? After their meal in Pizza Express, Barney had come in for a quick coffee before driving back to London, and eventually Marie had wandered off to her room, she guessed so that she and Barney would have some time together alone downstairs.

Worrying again, Ginny had gone upstairs and put her head round Marie's door. She was immersed in a book. She glanced up at her mother.

'Go and play with Bartholomew.'

'Darling, I just want to say. . .' What did she want to say? That she was being dishonest? That somehow, through the turn of events, they were tricking her into meeting her own father without her knowledge?

Marie turned over and lay on her front. She widened her eyes. 'Mum, I like him. A lot. You have my blessing. Go and see to him or he'll get bored and go home.'

374

'I – Marie, you know sometimes things happen that you don't plan.'

'I know.'

'Sometimes events go a bit fast for you, get a bit out of control.'

'Yes?'

'That's – that's what I want to say.' Ginny hesitated, her anxiety knotting in her stomach. Should she say something else? Was now the time? But with Barney sitting downstairs sipping coffee there wasn't really anything else she could say. Now she probably had to restrain herself. Any interference, any clumsy revelations at this stage could wreck everything.

'Well, goodnight then, love.'

'Goodnight, Oh Cryptic One.' Marie's attention was already caught by her book again.

But as Ginny had dreaded, things were going to change.

Ginny had just got in from work on Friday evening. It was a foul night, the wind whipping the rain against the windows, and she was glad to be inside. She took off her coat, dumped her umbrella, notched up the thermostat on the central heating and went into the kitchen. Marie was sitting at the breakfast bar with a letter folded in her hands.

'Hello, darling,' Ginny said, putting the kettle on. 'Good day?'

'He's written back to me,' Marie said blankly. 'I was out all day. I've just come in and picked it up. I didn't think he'd answer so fast.'

Ginny stopped what she was doing and stood and stared at Marie instead, her heart beating hard. 'Yes?'

'Well, that's it really. It's moving on.'

'It is?' Ginny stood stock still, swamped with nerves. 'How?'

'I'm going to meet him.'

Ginny just stood in silence for minutes before Marie looked up at her. 'Are you all right? You've gone white.'

'Yes, of course, I'm fine. I just need a hot coffee to warm up. Such a horrible night, isn't it? We're really into winter now. And the shops plastered from wall to wall with Christmas things, they don't let you catch your breath, do they? It was so cold in the lunch hour, I wished I'd taken a warmer jumper. Did you get cold today?'

'Mum, are you panicking?'

Ginny dropped her teaspoon, jitters overcoming her. 'No, why?'

'Because I've just told you I'm going to meet my father and you're talking about the weather. Why don't you sit down and calm down.' Ginny sat at a stool, taking her black coffee with her. She eyed Marie cautiously. Marie went on. 'I don't know why you're so nervous. I'm the one who should be nervous.'

'And are you nervous?'

'I wasn't at all before we talked about meeting up. But I am now.'

'And who – who suggested meeting?'

'I did, when I wrote to him. So he's said he'd like to. And we're going to meet on Sunday.'

Ginny wanted to shout *Oh my God* at this point, but she managed to bite it back. 'Oh my goodness. That's – that's soon.'

'Yes, it is. I'm a bit shocked now that it's really happening.'

'Do you know where?'

'I'm going to ring him. He's given me his mobile number.'

Ginny gulped. Would she recognise his voice on the phone? Would the cat be out of the bag immediately? How terrifying would the recriminations be, for Barney and for Ginny herself? She quaked at the thought. 'Are – are you sure it's what you want to do?'

'Yes.'

Marie was so definite, so unequivocal that Ginny was daunted. It occurred to her in the midst of her panic that Marie may have wanted to meet her father for many years, however casual she'd seemed about it. This was obviously an enormous emotional event for her. Ginny tried to pull herself together. 'Darling, I'm happy for you.'

'Are you?' Marie sounded unimpressed. 'You don't sound happy.'

'I'm sorry. It's just quite sudden.'

'For you? How does it affect you? It's not as if he's going to come here or anything.'

'Er – no, but where will you meet him then?'

'I'll fix something up when I talk to him. He offered to come and pick me up and take me out somewhere, but I think that's too childish. I'd rather get a train and meet him somewhere else. Maybe I'll go to London, that's where his address is, in South-West London somewhere. Maybe we'll meet in a café or something. I don't know how you're supposed to do this. But we're not exactly going to ask you to join us, are we?'

'No,' Ginny said faintly.

'So what difference does it make to you?' Marie stared at Ginny as if she was failing to understand her at all. 'Oh, all right I suppose it's a blast from the past for you too. Sorry, I'm being a bit insensitive. Look, if it makes you feel any better I won't talk to you about it again. I was just a bit on edge because I'd only just opened the letter and then you walked in. I should have taken it up to my bedroom.'

'Oh, no, darling, don't feel like that. You don't have to hide any of this from me.'

'I'm not exactly going to be able to talk to you about him though, am I?'

'Why not?' Ginny swallowed.

'Well, if you react like this all the time. . .it's a bit offputting.'

Ginny's head was spiralling as Marie was speaking. What should she do? How could she react to the sudden news that Marie and Barney were going to meet? That Marie was going to realise that they'd already met, but under a veil of ignorance? Should she just tell Marie now and put it all out on the table for her to see? Or was that really up to Barney now, when it was his relationship with her that stood to be damaged?

The worst thing was that, above everything else, in that emotional moment, Ginny had a screaming desire to tell her daughter the entire truth before she headed out to keep her appointment with her father. The meeting was going to shake Marie up anyway, how could Ginny add to that by *not* warning her who she was about to meet? Wasn't withholding evidence a serious crime? Didn't it go against all her instincts to protect her child, to let her go into this new and daunting situation without this knowledge?

It had been a terrible idea, Ginny suddenly concluded, to promise Barney that he could have the sole rights to divulging the information. The most natural thing, of course, would have been for Ginny and Barney to sit down together and for him to introduce himself. No, that would have been strange. For Ginny to have introduced him while they were sitting side by side. No, that would have been even stranger. For Barney to have introduced himself while Ginny was in the other room just in case she was needed. . . stranger and stranger. Any of those options would have cornered Marie.

No, the best thing would have been for him to have written to her first, and then if she'd decided that she wanted to meet him Ginny could have introduced him to her. Or he could have introduced himself. But she'd come full circle. Wasn't that what they were doing anyway? Oh God Almighty, she just did not know what would have been best.

But what if there'd been no spark between Ginny and Barney? What if he'd been a passive figure, drifting into their lives because of his link to Marie but with no other emotional or practical resonance for Ginny in the short or long term? Ginny's thoughts spiralled. What would have happened then?

Probably, she reasoned, he would have written first, then if he'd received an encouraging response, made an appointment to meet Marie that did not involve Ginny. And that was what they *were* doing. Barney was going to explain it all to Marie in the privacy of a one-to-one meeting.

If Barney was going to explain it all to Marie,

wouldn't he want to tell her face to face, rather than through the cold medium of the telephone? In which case, wouldn't that bring them back to meeting each other, which was what they were planning to do anyway? After all, Ginny hadn't heard from Barney about the meeting, which showed that he must have made his own mind up about it without feeling the need to consult Ginny for her advice.

Muddled and scared, Ginny couldn't think of a thing to say as Marie studied her.

'Christ, Mum, I didn't realise it all meant so much to you. You look like you've seen a ghost' Marie frowned at her. 'Oh, hang on. Is this about Bartholomew? Are you worried he's going to get wind of it and think that the old devil's back to make trouble for you again?'

Ginny made a small noise, not really a recognisable sound.

'Okay,' Marie scraped her stool back and picked up her letter. 'You've turned into a guinea pig so I'm going up to my room now. Don't worry about it, and don't give it another thought. I'll deal with it.'

'No, Marie, before you go,' Ginny tried to clear her head. 'When you meet Bar – Bar—'

'Barney,' Marie finished, tutting. 'God, Mum, what is it with you and men with funny names?'

'When you meet him,' Ginny snapped, her nerves frazzled, 'you might find that he's not what you expected. I – I just want you to be prepared.'

'Why? Is he a two-foot midget with a mohican?'

Failing to appreciate her daughter's humour Ginny ploughed on. 'I just want you to remember, when you meet him, that I'll be thinking of you. That

– if it's confusing, I'll be here to talk to when you get back.'

'Okay,' Marie said.

'Barney Middleton's phone?'

Ginny paused, thrown, as she was about to launch into a nervous rattle of a sentence. It was Honey's voice. It was a fairly intimate thing to do, answer someone else's phone – and their mobile phone at that. For a second she went completely and utterly blank, visions of long dark curly hair and red toenails prancing unhappily across her mind.

Then she pulled herself together. This didn't concern Honey and she had to contact Barney.

'Hi, it's Ginny,' she breezed. 'Is he there?'

'Yep. I'll get him.'

Ginny waited, her chest heaving, to hear Barney's voice. For some utterly inexplicable reason having to encounter Honey at a moment like this made her want to slap him. But it didn't make sense. And remembering Marie's soliloquy on jealousy, at another time she would have smiled, but not now.

'So you're going to meet her,' Ginny said brittly as an announcement as Barney picked up his mobile phone.

'Yes.' He stopped short of elaborating, but she could tell by his terse breathing that he was either nervous or excited about it, or probably both. Either that or he'd just run down a flight of stairs.

'You have to let me warn her before she comes to you. Let me say something. I feel absolutely awful.'

There was a long pause where she could tell that he was deliberating, maybe passing the phone from one

381

hand to the other, certainly pacing, by the way the phone was sliding in and out of distortion.

'I just feel—'

'Can you just stand still!' Ginny issued. 'You keep going out of focus.'

'Is that better?'

'Yes. Just stop pacing and stay there. Bite your nails instead.'

He gave a soft laugh and her heart melted too. They weren't at loggerheads over this. When it came to the moment of truth they were on the same team.

'What did you want to say?' he asked her gently.

'I just – I was thinking that it would be much nicer if we told Marie together. Or if you let me talk to her before she comes to meet you.' Ginny faltered as his thoughtful, non-committal silence went on and on. 'I mean, I just feel I must have some input into this.'

'Yes,' he said gruffly. 'I can understand that.'

But again his words were followed by silence and she knew, of course, that it was the complete opposite of what he really wanted, which was to handle the situation with Marie privately and on his own.

'I'm sorry, Barney. I know it's not what you want.'

'No, it isn't. I can see your point of view, but I can see mine too. I've had so many years to think about this, to savour it, to have nightmares about it going wrong, have dreams about it going right. I – I just feel. . .' He dried up.

'You feel that it has to be your call.'

'Yes.'

Ginny found herself nodding. In a strange way she was thankful for his obstinacy. It showed just how much he cared about Marie. Compared to men she might have met over the years, what kind of problem was this? If anything, Barney cared too much. Or – maybe not too much – maybe he just cared as much as she did, which was why they had been head to head on this issue since the morning when Marie had arrived home.

'Ginny?' he said quietly. 'We'll do whatever you decide. It's hard for me, but you're Marie's mother and you brought her up. You have to make the final decision. I know how much it means to you. You just give the orders and I'll go along with them.'

It was amazing, she thought later, how capitulation was often the key to success. Because of course her eyes filled with tears at his sensitivity, and she gave way to him completely.

'I won't breathe a word,' she promised, her heart full of love for them both. 'But please be careful with her, won't you?'

'She's as precious to me as you are,' Barney said. 'Trust me.'

Marie didn't speak to Ginny about the meeting again that weekend, and, for all her misgivings, Ginny didn't broach the subject. Marie seemed to make every effort to be out, probably to avoid talking about it. When Sunday came Ginny was up and out of bed early, channelling her nervous energy into cleaning the kitchen. Marie came down mid-morning, dressed casually, but with more make-up on than usual and her hair plaited. Although Ginny knew Marie was being fashionable, it made her look painfully young and she felt a pang in the pit of her stomach.

'That's it then,' Marie said, hitching a bag over her shoulder. 'I'm off. See you later.'

'Darling.' Ginny followed her to the door as she strode out purposefully. 'I'm here for you. You can ring me or anything you like, any time you like.'

'Okay, thanks. I'm sure it won't be that bad.'

'No, I didn't mean. . . Do you know where you're going?'

'Some restaurant in Piccadilly. We thought we'd make it central.'

'So you spoke to him?' Ginny's mouth was as dry as a desert.

'Last night. I phoned him from the pub when I was out with Emma.'

'Oh, you did?'

'Yeah, with a bit of Dutch courage. Didn't want to make a big thing of it. See you later. No idea what time.'

And she was gone, leaving Ginny flapping her hands at the door, tongue-tied and helpless. Now she was just going to have to let fate take its course.

Ginny couldn't go to bed, even as the time slipped past nine, towards ten, past ten. Marie had been out all day and she hadn't heard from her once.

Ginny had sent Marie a neutral text at about nine o'clock and received no reply. She didn't want to badger her daughter, especially on a day that was so important. She'd promised herself that she'd keep a low profile and let Marie set the pace. But finally, when the clock showed eleven, a deadline Ginny had mentally set, she buckled and called Marie's mobile number. It was on voicemail. She left a message and began to worry, this time about Marie's safety. At that point the phone rang. It was Charlotte.

'Oh, hi, Charlotte, look I'm sorry to do this to you but Marie's out and I need to keep the line clear in case she calls me. Can we talk tomorrow?'

'Marie's here at Mum's with us,' Charlotte said. 'She's asked me to tell you she's going to stay the night here.'

'Oh God, what happened?'

Charlotte lowered her voice. 'I'm in the kitchen, she's in the other room with Mum and Raj so she can't hear me, but basically she's had a long day and she's quite wound up. I'm going to give her some of Mum's whisky then try to persuade her to go home, but at the moment she's vowing she's going to sleep on the sofa here. It might be better if she does.'

'Oh God.' Ginny sank into her chair, her hands over her eyes. 'Won't she talk to me?'

'I'm sorry, Ginny. Not at the moment. She's too stirred up by it all.'

'So when did she come to you?'

'She's been here about two hours.'

'And she'd rather talk to you than me about it? Oh Jesus, what have I done?'

'Don't take it personally,' Charlotte said gently. 'I've seen quite a lot of her recently and she obviously feels I'm an ally of a sort. I'll do what I can to smooth things over.'

After they'd rung off, Ginny fetched herself a glass of wine, intending to call Barney and talk to him, but she was reluctant to contact him without speaking to Marie. It would seem even more like a conspiracy. And however muddled the circumstances of his meeting

385

Marie properly for the first time, it was a private matter, between him and his daughter. And now the fallout between herself and Marie was a private matter, between herself and her daughter.

As she reminded herself, Barneys come and Barneys go, but Maries stay. Any further conversation about this had to be with Marie.

She sat with an untouched glass of wine, the phone on her lap, into the night.

Chapter Forty

'I'm going to India with Charlotte,' Marie announced when she came home the following morning. Ginny had rung in sick, something she rarely did, so that she could be there for Marie. She'd jumped off her kitchen stool as soon as she'd heard the door and was standing waiting in the kitchen, all but wringing her hands.

'Marie, we need to talk.'

'Not now. I'm tired and a bit hungover.'

'Now, Marie,' Ginny asserted. 'Sit down. I'll make you a cup of coffee.'

'Mum, I really—'

'Sit down!' Ginny instructed. She hadn't been sure how she would react on seeing Marie again but now she knew that she had to take some control of the situation. She put the kettle on, grabbed two mugs from the cupboard and made coffee. She handed Marie her mug and sat down again, looking her daughter squarely in the eye. Marie stared back. It wasn't a friendly stare, but it wasn't full of hate either and Ginny took some comfort from that.

'I take it that you met Barney yesterday?'

'Haven't you spoken to him already?'

'No. I wanted to talk to you first.'

'Yes, I met Bar-Bar-Bar.' Marie imitated Ginny. 'No wonder you got confused.'

'Right' That confirmed that the truth of the situation was out. Ginny took a deep breath. 'I don't know what Barney said to you. That's between you and him. But I want to say some things to you. The first is that I'm dreadfully, agonisingly sorry about the way things have turned out. It started when you came back from Thailand unexpectedly and it's all gone wrong from there. But it's my fault, nobody else's.'

Marie chewed her lip. 'Yes, that was my conclusion.'

'I wouldn't have dreamt of bringing Barney into your life without your knowledge, or your consent, if it hadn't been for that morning when you walked in. After that, it was already done and I didn't know how to put it right. That morning I – he – we thought it was better if you just thought he was a boyfriend. I couldn't tell you the truth.'

Marie didn't answer. She watched Ginny carefully with an inscrutable expression.

'So,' Ginny went on, 'I tried to stop you from getting to know him. I tried to send him home last Sunday, I tried to prevent you from spending time with him without knowing who he was. But I failed in that, and as a result you relaxed around him and started to get to know him without any idea at all that he was really your father. Then it seemed to work so well, he asked for one more meeting with you before the truth was out. That was Pizza Express. I want you to know that I can't forgive myself for that. I keep thinking there's something else I should have done. It just got out of control. And I'm very, very sorry. It isn't at all how I wanted things to be. It was my worst nightmare. I don't know how to make it up to you.'

'You can't really.' Marie was factual. 'It's done now.'

Ginny sighed and gave Marie a long, soulful look. 'I expect you want to punish me for it. I don't blame you.'

Marie didn't answer. She sipped her coffee noisily.

'I realise too that you will have found a lot of things out yesterday, things you didn't know, and all that information's probably quite overwhelming.'

'You kept a lot of secrets from me,' Marie said finally. 'About all kinds of things.'

'Go on.'

'You never told me you'd sent my father photos of me all my life.'

'He – he didn't get them,' Ginny said carefully. 'I expect he told you that.'

'Yes, he did tell me.'

'I'm sorry if that upset you. I couldn't ask your permission when you were a little girl. I thought it was the right thing to do.'

'Gran knew too. She didn't tell me either.' Marie pulled off her coat and let it fall on to the floor. She hunched her shoulders over her coffee and took another slurp. She seemed dazed, and no wonder.

'Can I make you some breakfast?' Ginny suggested.

Marie didn't seem to hear. 'Gran went out on a date last night, can you believe it? When I got there Granddad was in tears and Charlotte was trying to cheer him up. Then Gran came back and they went off and had a row in the kitchen and I talked to Charlotte and Raj. Then Granddad left and Gran came rushing up to me and told me it was all her fault because she'd told you that Barney would make a good husband. So I told her that if that's what she'd said it *was* her fault. Emma thinks she's got problems. My whole family's gone completely mad. Apart from Charlotte. She's sane. Except that Raj's whole family have disowned him. And Charlotte said that's all *her* fault, and it's hard to disagree with that. So I thought I'd go to India with Charlotte and help her look after the baby. It is my gap year, after all. She thought she could get me a job at the language school she teaches at, doing something. It won't be anything special. Probably admin or she said I could be some kind of teaching assistant, but it will mean I can earn a bit and pay my way as I go along. I don't expect you'll mind, will you?'

Ginny held her breath. 'I – whatever you want to do is fine by me.'

'I didn't realise you'd had such a nightmare time with his parents back then. You never told me.'

Ginny accepted that Marie was jumping around on stepping stones. Her head must have been very jumbled. 'It was all right. We survived it.'

'Bar – my father – Barney, he said his mother was quite cruel to you. But he said it was all *his* fault.'

'What – back then?'

'Oh, then, now and everything in between. He said he's got broad shoulders and I should put the blame on him. So I did that too.'

'All right.'

'Then in the middle of the night Granddad came back with a bunch of flowers he'd bought at that twenty-four-hour service station up the bypass and gave them to Gran, and he said it was all *his* fault. So she took them and shut the door in his face. But I'd had a whisky or two by then so it's all a bit vague.'

Ginny watched Marie carefully. Perhaps she was still a bit drunk from the night before? She wondered how much whisky Charlotte had fed her before putting her to bed.

'And I asked Barney what his intentions were towards you, because I said it would be quite nice to know whether my own father was going to be hanging around or not, and he said he was serious about seeing me but he didn't mind whether he carried on seeing you or not. I suppose he thought that might make things better. He said he was really into seeing you for a while, but he'd sort of gone off the idea. That's the essence of it, although he put it much better than that.'

Ginny cleared her throat nervously and drank some coffee quickly.

'I suppose you knew that, did you?' Marie glanced up suddenly with dark, tired eyes. 'That the novelty had worn off for him? Or have I shocked you?'

Mother and daughter stared at each other. Ginny had seen this mood in Marie once or twice before, but it was rare. She had a way of punishing a person, a way of hurting. She used bluntness and tactlessness.

'I know you want to get a reaction, Marie. I understand. You've been through a lot in the last twenty-four hours.'

'And it's all *your* fault, I know. So you did know then? That's a relief. Wouldn't want to blow the gaff.'

'I don't think my relationship with Barney's important anymore. You are more important.'

'I'm glad that you're both taking that attitude,' Marie said. 'Especially as he's still in love with Honey. I know I'm not supposed to tell you, but he's living with this woman who he's been seeing for years, on and off, and he told me its been a confusing time for him, but he's still in love with her. I don't think he really meant to tell me as much about it as he did, but we sat in the restaurant for a long time and he had quite a few glasses of wine.'

Ginny swallowed, her eyes smarting. Marie may have been trying to hurt Ginny by blurting it out, but to Ginny's sensitive mind in an emotional state the facts would fit. She had no doubt that Marie was deliberately hurting her with her tone, but in some way she believed her.

'It's all right, Marie. You aren't shocking me.'

'Good. I suppose it must have been exciting for you both to play with the idea of getting back together for a while, but at the end of the day it's a lot of water under the bridge, isn't it?'

Ginny bit her lip. Marie carried on talking and she listened. She talked about her future plans and about how she was going to book a flight to travel with Charlotte and Raj. She speculated about how India would be different from Thailand, and occasionally she referred back to Barney again.

'I suppose I'll meet him again soon. It'd be interesting to talk to him about Bangladesh.' Marie stood up, stretched and yawned. 'But I'll keep him away from you if you like. I don't want to upset you. I'm going to have a kip now.' She turned as she reached the bottom of the stairs. 'Mum? I'm sorry if Barney wasn't what you thought he was. You'll get over it. Plenty of fish in the sea and all that.'

After Marie had gone back to bed, Ginny sat alone in the kitchen listening to the buzz of the clock on the electric cooker.

At first when Barney had told Ginny he was staying with an 'old' friend who happened to be female, of course her curiosity had been aroused. And when that friend turned out to be the appealing package that constituted Honey – well, in honesty she had been appallingly jealous. But Barney had eased that jealousy away. How? Not through constant protestations, but simply because she believed his simple statement that they weren't sleeping together. Was there any reason for Ginny to change her mind just because her hurt, confused daughter was lashing out?

No, she reasoned. There was no reason to believe Barney had been lying to her. Could events have moved on between himself and Honey? Could there be a grain of truth in Marie's statement that Barney had always been in love with her? Perhaps. The biggest question was, did it matter?

What mattered was that Marie was clearly tortured with confusing thoughts, with the knowledge that she'd been lied to, with the fact that her own mother had betrayed her trust. Ginny felt worse about it now than at any time since Barney had first shown up in her life again. Her throat was constricted, her stomach tight, her head aching. She was full of deep regret and self-recrimination. Was there anything, anything at all that she could do now to help to put things right?

She couldn't undo the decisions she'd made, however flawed. But she could prevent any further mistakes being made. She could make sure that she didn't compound Marie's unhappiness by seeing Barney again. Whatever else was true about the situation, it was clear from the verbal assault that

393

Ginny had received from her daughter that evening that Marie did not approve of her relationship.

It had to end.

Later, when Marie was fast asleep, Ginny took herself out. Exhausted and sad, she put on her coat and walked round to see her mother. There was obviously a lot of news to catch up on there, and she wanted to hear their version of events. On her way she phoned Barney from her mobile, knowing what she had to do. The last thing on her mind was to ask for any kind of explanation or to recriminate, but she had to remove herself from the situation now, as quickly and in as dignified a way as possible. He sounded relieved to hear her voice, but his first question was about Marie, not her, and Ginny's resolve was unshaken.

'Marie's fine,' Ginny said firmly. 'Don't tell me about yesterday, it's private between you and Marie and I'd like it to stay that way. I don't want to know what either of you said. It's far better now to keep our relationships with her separate.'

'Do you think so?'

'Yes. And I won't mess around, I have to tell you, Barney, that I'm afraid it's over between us now.' She felt tears rise in her throat and she battled with them. 'Let's not put ourselves through any torture over it. We knew it was an experiment and I think we can be philosophical about it.'

'An experiment?'

'Please let's not talk about it. I'm on my mobile and running short of credit, but I have to ask you please not to come and visit anymore, especially now that Marie's at home. I'd rather we didn't speak.'

'Ginny?'

'Goodbye, Barney. I'm sorry we couldn't create the happy ending, but at least we can say that we tried.'

She pressed the 'off' button on her phone and marched on to her mother's house, tears streaming down her cheeks.

Chapter Forty-one

꧁ꙮ꧂

'We could have done this at home,' Jane advised Ginny as they squeezed past each other in the kitchen holding serving dishes full of vegetables.

'This is home,' Ginny reminded her with a tired smile.

'Of course, dear, I only meant it's a bit cramped, isn't it? What with us all barging in on you like this. I could have saved you some work.'

'But I wanted to host. God knows when I'll see either my sister or my daughter again. And you've always done Christmas for us.'

From the living room, where Ginny had opened out her rarely used foldaway table, appended an old picnic table from the shed and draped a discreet tablecloth over the lot, there was a lively buzz of conversation punctuated by Benji's croaky cries. Piled inside her tiny house were Charlotte, Raj and the baby, Jane and Harry, and, of course, Marie. The dinner was in honour of Charlotte's return to India and – since Marie was indeed going with her – of Marie's second departure that year for distant shores.

'Well it's good of you.' Jane popped a kiss on Ginny's cheek as they both attempted to keep their balance. 'I'll just put these on the table and come back for more.'

'You sit down and have a glass of wine with Dad. Send Marie out to help,' Ginny said with a frown. 'I did send that message via Charlotte just now. What's she doing?'

'She's ignoring you, dear.' Jane pulled a face. 'I'm afraid it's quite obvious.'

Ginny sighed and her unhappiness must have been plain to see because Jane deposited the carrots on the breakfast bar and gave her a hug.

'It'll pass. Trust me.'

'Not for a very, very long time, if ever,' Ginny said bleakly. 'It's been like this ever since she found out, and as they're all flying off tomorrow it doesn't leave much time for a reconciliation, does it?'

'And no news from. . .from him? Any effort to get in touch and resolve things?' Jane raised her eyebrows.

Ginny tutted impatiently. Her decision was made and there really was very little point talking about it. It only twisted the knife in her stomach even harder. 'There's nothing I can do anything about, so please let's not go over that again. I seem to have fallen on very stony ground. And serve me right.'

'You know, Marie will get over this. I only wish I could convince you.'

'The only person who can convince me of that is Marie herself. And seeing as I'm public enemy number one where she's concerned, we're a long way from that. The last couple of weeks have been absolutely awful. She's treating me like dirt. I know she's angry, but it's pretty hard to take.'

'I know, dear. I just think you shouldn't give up hope,' Jane finished in a hushed whisper as Marie herself appeared in the kitchen doorway. Her face was flushed – she'd probably had a glass of wine already, Ginny correctly surmised, but it hadn't mellowed her hostile expression. She addressed her remarks to Jane, not Ginny.

'Where are the other bottles? We need another one.'

'Oh, darling, you need to ask your mum that,' Jane said, inching away. 'I'll just take these carrots through and leave you two alone.'

Jane disappeared. Ginny wiped her hot forehead, oven gloves on, leaving a smear of meat juices over her eyebrows.

Marie pouted. 'Bottles? There's a drought in there.'

'Why don't you ask Granddad where he put that nice Bordeaux he brought with him? He could open that now ready for the dinner.'

'He's already done that,' Marie said as if it was obvious. 'We just need some more white while you're hiding in here. It's getting boring waiting.'

Ginny gave Marie a severe look, her patience over-stretched by an early morning preparing food and Marie's uncooperative attitude. 'A little help from you, Marie, would have made my life a lot easier.'

'Okay, we'll drink the Bordeaux then. I just thought there was some white in the fridge but I'm not going to fight you for it.'

'Oh, take the bloody white!' Ginny raised her voice, yanking open the fridge door. 'Help yourself. But save some for me, please. I might need a glass or two if I'm going to survive another twenty-four hours of you punishing me before you leave!'

'Jesus, Mother, get over it will you?'

The living room fell silent. Ginny instantly regretted

her outburst and softened her voice. 'Here, Marie, take the wine and open it. I've nearly finished dishing up then we can eat.'

'Thank *you*,' Marie said with sarcastic emphasis before leaving the room again with the wine.

Charlotte sent Raj in to help Ginny bring in the rest of the food and eventually the whole family were seated, rather haphazardly, around the makeshift dining table, elbows clashing, voices gaining volume with each glass of wine that was refilled. Charlotte laid Benji in his buggy in the hall, tucked him up and crept back into the room with her fingers crossed.

'I think we've got an hour before he wakes up again. I hope we have.'

'And you're sure you won't have wine?' Harry asked Charlotte jovially.

'No, Dad. Breastfeeding. Don't want to give the poor boy hiccups.'

'We'll only be up all night if his milk disagrees with him.' Raj smiled. 'And I'll stay off alcohol in sympathy with Charlotte, so she won't feel left out.'

'I'll have a top-up, Gramps.' Marie held out her glass.

'Marie?' Ginny entered automatically. 'How many have you had?'

'Oh, shut up, Mother,' Marie muttered.

'Marie!'

'It's all right.' Charlotte touched Marie's arm and winked at her. 'I'll make sure this one doesn't fall off the plane tomorrow.'

'I just –' Ginny took a sip of her drink to try to dispel the ball of tension in her stomach. 'I just wanted to be sure Marie didn't get into such a relaxed state that she forgot to pack anything, that's all. I'm not being prudish.'

'It's all right, darling, we understand. We're all family here,' Jane joined in, holding out roast potatoes to Ginny as if they were a balm that might somehow ease the pain. It was amazing how often the offer of food or a drink could be employed in the attempt to dissolve a difficult atmosphere. 'Have some more of your lovely crispy potatoes. I tell you, Marie, you'll go a long way in this world to find a better cook than Ginny.'

'She's always been wonderful,' Harry chimed. 'Just like her mother. Do you know the first meal Jane ever cooked for me?'

'Goulash,' Ginny and Charlotte said together.

'Yes, but that was very exotic in those days,' Harry insisted. 'I know you eat everything these days, but back then it was quite a thing to have paprika. I thought, "Aye-aye, here's a hot and spicy young minx, trying to get me hot blooded." Wondered what she wanted from me!'

'Dad!' Charlotte pulled a good-humoured face at him. 'You're putting me off my chicken.'

'But it's true,' Jane tittered, touching Harry's arm with feathery fingertips. Ginny realised with a shock that she was flirting with him. 'We did experiment quite a bit in those days.'

'Jane!' Harry raised his eyebrows and they both giggled.

'Mum!' Ginny frowned, starting to feel like the resident party-pooper. 'I'm not sure poor old Raj wants to know all the gory details.'

'Not prudish at all, obviously,' Marie uttered under

her breath.

'Well I suppose you're used to spicy food, Raj,' Harry went on haplessly. 'You probably think we're all ridiculous for making such a fuss about it.'

'God, Gramps, you shouldn't assume Raj eats chilli all the time just because he's from India,' Marie complained.

'I'm not. I didn't,' Harry defended. 'I'm just curious, that's all. I've never been there. Did you learn to cook at home, Raj?'

'I think it's best not to talk about Raj's family,' Marie stumbled on. 'They're not exactly flavour of the month with Charlotte and Raj at the moment.'

There was an awkward silence.

'Really, it's fine to talk about it.' Raj gave everyone a bright smile, although he seemed a tad paler. 'Most of my mother's recipes are a sworn secret. In answer to your question, I don't really like hot food much myself. My favourite food was always pizza when I was a kid. Although my mum is quite traditional.'

'Anyway, I'm not going to India to learn how to cook a curry.' Marie rolled her eyes as if she was surrounded by idiots. 'That's the sort of thing Mum would assume.'

'Thank you,' Ginny said archly, trying to cover the fact that she was actually very wounded by Marie's implication. She had tried to widen her daughter's horizons, not narrow them. As far as she knew she'd been broadminded and encouraged Marie not to think stereotypically. It felt like a slap in the face. One of many she'd received in recent days. 'In fact you're quite wrong. I've got more imagination than that.'

'Oh thank you,' Harry said, affronted at last. 'I didn't

mean to display my lack of imagination.'

'It's all right, Harry,' Jane said swiftly, touching his hand, an alliance Ginny was surprised to see displayed so publicly.

'Well, really,' Harry huffed. 'I was just trying to make conversation to distract from the bickering.'

There was another silence and everyone heaved a deep breath before taking another mouthful of chicken.

'So!' Jane said brightly, then couldn't think of anything to say.

'So! India!' Marie mocked.

'So! Teenagers!' Charlotte ribbed Marie, with another wink and a playful look at Ginny.

'Well, *bon voyage*, everyone,' Ginny said, raising her glass and finding that her eyes filled with tears and her voice became choked.

'Thanks, sis.' Charlotte leant over and hugged Ginny, who couldn't stop a tear from dribbling down her cheek.

'I'll miss you.' Ginny sniffed into Charlotte's shoulder.

'And you'll come and see us soon?' Raj said hopefully.

'Yes, I'll do my very best. Perhaps once. . . Maybe once Marie's home again. I wouldn't want to crowd you.'

'That's if Marie comes home,' Marie said, glancing up at the ceiling insouciantly.

'I'll – I'll just go and get the pudding,' Ginny managed to utter before fleeing to the safety of the kitchen to wipe her eyes again.

*

'So what is all this about, young lady?' Charlotte quizzed Marie in the privacy of Marie's bedroom, where they had taken Benji for a nappy change. 'You're being pretty hard on Ginny. Are you quite sure it's all deserved?'

'I don't care, Charlotte. She was such a cow over the whole thing with my father, I'd really rather be halfway across the world so that I don't have to think about it.'

Charlotte calmly poked Benji's dirty nappy into a nappy bag and whipped out the wet wipes, thinking hard as she did so. She was very concerned that Marie was on the verge of leaving the country before settling matters amicably with Ginny. They needed to have some kind of reconciliation. Otherwise Ginny would be left torturing herself long after Marie's departure.

'I know,' she sympathised. 'It's been rough on you the last few weeks.'

'Nothing I can't handle,' Marie sniffed, although she looked tearful suddenly.

'It must have been a heck of a shock to realise that you'd met your own dad without knowing it.'

Marie nodded. 'It was.'

'Yes, I can imagine. But you know the thing that really bugs me about it?' Charlotte said, puzzled. 'It's that I know the last thing in the whole world your mum would do is deliberately hurt your feelings. When you think about it, it just doesn't make sense, does it?'

'Oh?'

'You know, the whole life-sacrifice kind of thing. The way she's dedicated everything to you, to your happiness. I keep thinking to myself, why would she

403

suddenly blow it at the last minute? She doesn't love you any less. If anything, she loves you more than ever. So what on earth could have happened to make her act like this about your dad?'

Marie shrugged. 'Beats me.'

'But it's a puzzle, isn't it? Can you hand me the nappy? Thanks. I can't work it out. What do you think?'

Marie sank on to the edge of her bed and picked up George, the battered old toy pyjama case. She pulled at his ears, agitated. 'I suppose he turned up out of the blue and she realised she still fancied him.'

Charlotte considered it, pulling elaborately thoughtful faces for Marie's benefit. She just hoped to God that this tactic was going to work. 'You think so?'

'Well, it was probably a bit more than that.'

'True. They've got you in common for a start. They both care about you, that much is obvious.'

'Yeah, and they slept together in this house while I was away, so that's not going behind my back at all? Bloody sneaky pair.' Marie suddenly tossed George across the room with distaste, as if a memory had just come back to her. 'They didn't care about what I felt. They just got on with it.'

'Hmm. And yet, Ginny was so shocked when you suddenly came back from abroad. She told me about it. She went into a terrible panic. I mean, can you imagine! I suppose she just didn't know what to do. What would you have done?'

'I wouldn't have been shagging him here in the first place.'

Charlotte took a deep breath. 'No, but Ginny thought you'd be away for a long time. And she's had so little romance in her life. Everybody needs a little bit of romance, Marie, take it from me. I suppose Barney must have quite bowled her over, reappearing and being so charming. Not at all as she remembered him.'

Marie listened.

'After all, when you've had a very hard life, with very little affection in it, the smallest kindness means a great deal to you. I can only imagine how overpowering it would be to have a handsome, thoughtful man turn up on your doorstep, a man who you used to be very much in love with—'

'Was she?'

'Oh yes.' Charlotte nodded as she snapped the poppers on Benji's babygrow and snuggled him to her chest again. 'Yes, she was in love with Barney. But he was young and thoughtless. And selfish. I think we're all selfish when we're young but we don't even realise it.'

Marie sighed, flopping back on to her bed and punching a pillow. 'You mean me, don't you?'

'No, not at all. I'm talking about your dad. But can you imagine it, that young man suddenly coming back into Ginny's life with all the bad bits removed and replaced by good bits. . .and, to add to that, it turns out that he cares passionately about Marie! The one thing that Ginny cares more about than anything else in the world. I'm quite awed, actually. If I'd have been Ginny, I'd have been as confused as hell. Especially once you were back from Thailand and – God! You'd even started to like this guy! I don't know what Ginny must have thought then.'

'She probably thought it was too good to be true.' Marie stared up at the ceiling.

'You think so?' Charlotte appeared to weigh it all up as she rocked Benji. 'Yes, I think you're probably right. But she should have sent him packing straight away. She shouldn't have let you get close to him.'

'Yeah, but I was the one who insisted that he came into the house.' Marie picked up her *Rough Guide* from the bedside table and played with it.

'So, she should have said no and put her foot down, surely? That was a bit bad of her.'

'No, it was me. It was a Sunday afternoon and they'd been out for a walk or something, so I made him come in and have dinner with us and play chess. Then Mum told me another time he wanted us to go out for a pizza but she said she didn't think it was a good idea, but I said we should go.'

'Oh?' Charlotte feigned astonishment. 'So she did ask your opinion? Well I didn't know that. It does change things a little.'

'I pushed her into his arms, if you really want to know.' Marie rolled over on to her stomach and stared down at her pillow. 'But it wasn't my fault. I didn't know he was my father, did I?'

'No, of course you didn't,' Charlotte soothed. 'I wonder what was going through your mum's head then? And what about Barney? From what I've heard from Ginny, he was pretty desperate to do everything right by you. I mean, how on earth can they have let him spend time with you without telling you who he was? I'm baffled. What were they thinking?'

There was a pause before Marie answered in a small voice. 'They thought it would be better if I got to know him and like him as a person before I knew who he was. They thought it would be better, since I'd met him anyway.'

'Ah.' Charlotte rocked Benji increasingly faster, gaining hope. 'Well, I suppose in a way that would make sense.'

'Did they ask you, Auntie Charlotte?' Marie glanced up. 'Did you ever give your opinion?'

Charlotte nodded, deciding honesty was best. 'Only about the pizza. I told Ginny she should tell you the truth and she promised it would happen after that night. I could see that she was in a very difficult position. It made my situation with Raj look simple.'

'Really? You're not just saying that?'

'No. I really do think Ginny's been in a horrible dilemma, and I could only hope that if I were in her shoes I'd handle it half as well as she has.'

There was a long silence as Benji suckled from Charlotte's breast and Marie lolled on the bed, thinking, and every so often flicking unseeingly through her travel guide.

'Charlotte?'

'Yes.'

'Do you think I've been unfair to Mum?'

'Honestly?' Charlotte smiled kindly. 'Not initially, no. But now? Yes, I do. I think it's time to try and see it through her eyes.'

'Do you really think Mum's in love with Barney?'

Charlotte paused. 'Yes, I do.'

'And do you really think she'd give him up, just for me?'

'Yes, love. She already has.'

Marie put her hand over her face, and when she

finally removed it Charlotte could see that she was
crying.

'Shit,' she said. 'What have I done?'

Chapter Forty-two

❧❧❧

It was a farewell gathering at Heathrow airport the following day as Charlotte, Raj and Benjamin departed for Mumbai. With them was Marie, a holdall and rucksack packed for her trip. Seeing them off were Ginny, Jane and Harry. They checked in their baggage and trooped up towards the departure gate.

'It only seems five minutes ago that we were here seeing you and Emma off for Thailand,' Ginny said to Marie as they all grabbed a coffee at Starbucks while Charlotte took Benjamin off to change him. 'And yet it seems like ages ago. A lot's happened.'

'Tell me about it.' Marie pulled a face.

'But we got through it somehow, love, didn't we?' Ginny said uncertainly.

At least they had spent a peaceful night after everybody had left. Marie had come into the living room and found Ginny pretending to read a book. They'd hugged each other and both said sorry before Marie had scampered upstairs again, avoiding conversation. Now Ginny ruffled Marie's hair but Marie pulled away awkwardly.

'Don't get emotional, Mum.'

'I won't.'

'And you won't be sad about me going, will you? At least you know I'm with Charlotte and I'll be looking after the baby. It's more like a family holiday really.'

'I'm very happy that you and Charlotte get on so well. She's a good role model for you. And you've always been interested in languages and travelling. I think she'll inspire you.' Ginny realised that she meant it. She was proud of all the things Charlotte had done: she was well qualified in her field, knew her job and loved it, she'd helped people along the way and she'd battled with her own demons too. In their own ways, both of their lives had taken unexpected turns and they'd made the best of them.

'So what will you do while I'm away?' Marie looked uncomfortable as she prodded the froth of her hot chocolate with her finger.

'Oh, I've got lots to do. I've been looking at some courses, maybe I'll even think about retraining. Charlotte's given me a lot to think about too. Perhaps my life has been too much of a straight line. I've enjoyed it, but I've got bit more freedom now. I think I'll try to make the most of it.'

'Okay.' Marie seemed troubled and Ginny could see that she regretted the friction they'd experienced in the last weeks. Maybe it was possible that she wished she hadn't made so many jibes – about everything but especially about Barney. Perhaps she'd noticed the letters he'd sent being whisked off the mat by Ginny and put in the bin. Maybe she'd realised that Ginny had ignored his phone calls, leaving the phone on answerphone. By now Ginny hoped Marie could be reassured that whatever had happened was all over.

Marie let out a long sigh. 'Yes, it is strange that I was here with Emma. Going off on my gap – month.'

'But you did sort things out with her, and I'm

pleased about that. Friendships are important and you've got so much in common.'

'I don't want her to come out and visit me in India though.' Marie blinked expressively. 'Try and put her off if you see her or send subtle messages through her mum. Tell her I've got constant dysentery and I've been mugged twice a day. That should do it.'

Ginny had been putting off seeing Rebecca as she'd felt she had enough to deal with after all the disturbances. She would contact her soon though, probably even ring her that evening and arrange to go out again. Perhaps they could form a deserted mothers club? Play badminton and go on walking holidays together? Isn't that what single middle-aged women did? Perhaps it wasn't such a bad idea. Although even thinking about it Ginny felt the familiar lurch of her stomach that missing Barney produced. She fought it. She'd felt it before, and the pain had eased in time. It would happen again.

'I suppose we can't all be as lucky as Charlotte and Raj,' Ginny mused, watching Charlotte return with her wriggling baby, and watching Raj jump up and help her back into her seat, his hand brushing hers as they settled together again to talk to her parents. He kissed her cheek and took the baby in his arms, Charlotte watching him with pure love in her eyes.

'I think I'm going to be a bit of a gooseberry,' Marie whispered to Ginny.

As their flight details were called, the group stood up and moved off. Harry, Ginny noticed, kept creeping towards Jane and touching her elbow possessively. Perhaps that was also a situation destined for a happy ending, or perhaps it wasn't. Although Jane had been flirting outrageously with Harry the previous evening, Ginny had a feeling today that her mother was more keen on keeping him at arm's length. Maybe she was unsure of herself, or maybe she didn't want him to be too sure of himself? Either way, Ginny couldn't tell whether the state of affairs was likely to endure or not.

At the departures gate, they all hugged and kissed. Charlotte burst into tears, and Ginny held her tightly. It was such a relief to see this display of emotion. Every other time that Charlotte had left the country she'd only ever seen her eager to get away.

'I'm going to miss you all so much,' she cried into her mother's jacket. 'I'll phone you and write to you all the time.'

'You'll put your own family first.' Jane hugged her back. 'And we'll be here for you, whenever you need us.'

'And, Ginny.' Charlotte sniffed as they embraced. 'You've been such a wonderful sister. You will come out to India, won't you?'

'Not while I'm there,' Marie reminded everybody again.

'I'd love to.' Ginny tried to ignore the rebuff and take it humorously. 'You just tell me when and I'll do it.'

Ginny stood with her parents, the three of them misty eyed, as they watched Raj, Charlotte and Marie inch their way along the queue towards the immigration desk. As Marie got closer to the gate, she turned and looked back at Ginny with huge, soulful eyes.

Ginny waved cheerfully, swallowing back her regret. 'Bye, darling,' she called. 'Look after yourself.'

'She looks very sad,' Jane observed to Ginny,

squeezing her arm. 'Perhaps she's going to really miss you?'

'I think it's more likely that she can't wait to get away,' Ginny remarked, still waving.

Then Marie muttered something to Charlotte and made her way back along the queue. She pushed her way past the disgruntled human traffic and back to the rope barrier where Ginny was waiting. She reached her, breathless. Her face was red and wet from tears. She hadn't changed her mind about going, had she?

'What is it?' Ginny was alarmed.

'I can't go without telling you something.'

'What is it?'

'You lied to me, Mum,' Marie blurted out, 'so I lied to you too. I'm sorry.'

'What do you mean? What did you lie to me about?'

'About my father. About Barney. What I told you wasn't true. I just wanted to upset you.'

'What wasn't true?' Ginny gripped Marie's hand. 'Tell me.'

'That he'd got bored with you and that he was in love with that woman, Honey. It's not true. That isn't what he said.'

'Oh, Marie.' Ginny's heart leapt up and down, then fluttered uncertainly. Of course, she'd guessed it might not be true but the uncertainty had been damaging. What was more important, though, was that it was Marie who was telling her this. 'What did he really say?'

'He said he loved you. He said he'd always loved you. He asked me—'

'What?'

'He asked me if he could marry you,' Marie sobbed.

'And I was angry with you both so I lied about it. I didn't think you'd believe me when I went on about that other woman, I only wanted to shock you like I was shocked. I just wanted to see the expression on your face. But then you believed me and you ended it with him and it was too late. And you did all that for me and I'm so sorry because I know you love him too.'

'What – how do you know?'

'Because I heard you crying in your room at night and because he told me. I'm sorry, Mum. I was fed up with being the odd one out; I thought, here we go again. Everyone's parents are getting divorced and mine are going to get married.'

'Oh, Marie.' Ginny grabbed her daughter across the rope barrier and held her in a bear hug. 'It's all right. Everything's all right. I understand.'

'But you've got to explain it to him because I lied to him, too. I wrote to him and I told him you wanted to finish it because you'd got fed up with him. I'm so sorry, I've been such a cow.'

'It's all right.' Ginny's emotions surged wildly, sadness and happiness blustering around like clouds in a storm. 'What will be will be.'

'And I had to tell you all of that now,' Marie said, sounding panicked and pulling away.

'I know, love, it's best to get things all clear before you go away. I understand.'

'No, it's because he's right behind you, and I'm in really big trouble now.' Marie clamped her mouth shut.

Ginny spun round. There, striding towards the gate, looking rugged and as loveable as he'd ever been, was Barney. He looked anxious as he reached them, his

414

curly hair flying in all directions as he pushed a hand through it.

'Thank God I've made it in time. When you told me when you were flying, Marie, I vowed I'd be here to see you off but I got caught in a traffic jam and – well, I'm here.'

'I'm sorry, Dad,' she said, and Ginny caught her breath to hear the word 'Dad' coming from her so naturally. 'I'm sorry I lied to you. Mum didn't want it to end. She loves you too. I lied to both of you but I hope you can sort it out now.'

'Marie!' Charlotte called from the gate. 'We've got to go now!'

''Bye. Take care of each other.'

'One moment,' Barney said; and he leant over the barrier and gave his daughter a hug. Then, to Ginny's delight, Marie put her arms around his neck and kissed him. She kissed Ginny again too, a big, wet, tearful kiss.

''Bye Mum. Bye, Dad. See you soon.'

And with that whirlwind of activity over, Marie threaded her way back to the front of the queue (to much complaint from her fellow passengers) to where Charlotte had held her place. They waved as their passports were handed back to them, and together they moved off through security and out of sight.

'Our grandson,' Harry said, mopping his eyes.

'Yes,' Jane said and cleared her throat noisily. She turned to Ginny. 'Harry and I are going now. We'll see you back at home. . .whenever.'

Ginny nodded, tensely happy. Jane winked at Barney. Then her parents wandered away, stopping to look at the window display in one of the shops. They looked like any other happily married set of grand-parents out passing the time together.

Barney turned Ginny around by her shoulders so that she was facing him.

'You didn't return my calls.'

'No.'

'You didn't answer my letters.'

'No.'

'Why?'

'I couldn't.'

'I've been going crazy being apart from you,' he said, and she could see the truth of it in the glint in his eyes, that he was overjoyed to see her again. 'Marie told me you'd changed your mind, that any feelings you had for me had gone. That you'd moved on. It seemed so harsh, so sudden. I didn't want to believe it, but the fears I had were whispering to me that it could be true. Maybe you had decided to shut me out, however amazing we were together. And then when you wouldn't reply to me. . . I didn't know what to believe.'

'I'm sorry, Barney. I had to be alone with Marie while she worked this through. I thought I might have to be alone for ever. She's been so angry. And it's not her fault, it's our fault. I don't blame her for it.'

'And neither do I. In my head I knew she was punishing me, punishing us both, but in my heart. . .' he took Ginny's hand in his and laid it over his chest. 'Do you feel it? Crashing just to be near you again.'

'I feel it,' Ginny was almost whispering back to him, and they devoured each other with their eyes, so close that the bustle of Heathrow around them melted away. And stupidly Ginny found herself insecure in the presence of this man, daunted by the strength of her feelings for him. She had to say, 'And Marie teased me, would you believe, about Honey.'

'Oh God!' Barney laughed aloud. 'Marie! She's a minx, that girl. She knows just where to bite. You never believed her, did you?'

'Not really,' Ginny said, although she allowed herself a rueful smile that to a discerning eye may have revealed the truth, a woman's secret truth, that however rational she normally was, her heart could be wrenched out of shape through jealousy over the man she really loved. But looking into Barney's eyes, at the shining happiness there as he held her close, she felt at ease. 'No, I didn't believe it. I don't believe it.'

'So. . .' Barney said, heaving a long, relieved sigh. 'Thank God we're together again now. And we're forgiven. I really think Marie is happy for us now.'

'Happy for us to. . .?' Ginny peered up at Barney tentatively. Where did it go from here? They were in love with each other, that much was clear and in the open now. They always had been. But could it really work out, even with Marie's blessing? Shaped by years of hardship and disappointment, Ginny could only watch Barney's face, mesmerised, wondering what he might say next. She was awed by the power this man held over her heart but gratified to realise that she, too, held his heart in her grasp. Was it really her fate to have a happy ending?

'I feel that it's only right that I should do the decent thing,' Barney said, his lips twisting in that ironically humorous way that she found so sensuous.

'Don't you think it's a little late for that?' she sparked back at him.

'Not at all. I think a good, clean shave should put things right with your mother and we'll be sorted.'

'You're still convinced that you can impress my mother with your shaving habits. You are brilliantly old fashioned.'

'Hmm. Maybe you're right to be sceptical. Perhaps I should throw in a packet of custard creams as well.'

'Oh, Barney!' She glowed with pleasure, squirming with delight over his teasing. 'You managed to win my mother over just by being you. I think she got used to the idea of you being back in my life even before I did.'

'You're right, of course. You're not a woman to be rushed into anything. Perhaps we should now have an eighteen-year engagement just to be sure about how we feel.'

'Eighteen years? Engagement?' Ginny blinked at him.

'Maybe eighteen days then?' He stroked her cheek, suddenly serious. 'You look a bit surprised. Will that be enough time to get a really great dress?'

'Barney, what are you saying?'

'Only that I want to marry the woman I love. The woman I've always loved. Isn't that what doing the decent thing is? Making a man and a woman who have always been in love as happy as they can be?'

A shiver of excitement spread over her skin, the romantic girl inside her blossoming with hope and lighting up the eyes of the woman she had become.

'Barney, I don't know what to say.'

'Yes, you do, Ginny,' he said softly, feathering a kiss on her lips. 'You know exactly what to say.'

A lump rose in her throat, a swell of pure happiness.

'I can't believe it,' she managed in a husky voice. 'I thought it was all over.'

'It's far from over,' Barney said, holding her close and lowering his mouth to hers. 'It's only just begun.'

Reading Between the Lines

Linda Taylor

When she chucked in her safe job to read English at Oxford, Julia Cole didn't give a thought to the future. But now she's thirty, newly graduated and it's pay-back time – at least as far as the bank is concerned. With a cat providing her only male company, *Blind Date* her only Saturday night engagement and her last relationship further in the past than a pay cheque, she can't help wondering if she's missing the point.

Until tall, handsome Rob strides into the class she teaches. And then his alarming brother Leo, a barrister with a penchant for cross-examining, strides into her friend Maggie's party and puts Julia on the stand. Suddenly, Julia's life is hotting up.

But is she taking both brothers at face value? And is she over-looking the obvious? Perhaps Julia should try reading between the lines . . .

arrow books

Going Against the Grain

Linda Taylor

Louise isn't sure where her life took the wrong turning, but it's not shaping up as well as she might have hoped. She's just turned thirty-two, her job for a party planner – the latest in a long line of occupations – might kindly be described as not her natural forte, and she watches helplessly as her dynamic elder sister charges up the career path. The only road Louise seems to be on is the one paved with good intentions.

Scatty, disorganised, bad at co-ordinating her wardrobe, Louise resolves that it's time to get it together – even her boyfriend is party-time. But then she discovers she's succeeded at one thing: getting pregnant . . .

arrow books

Beating About the Bush

Linda Taylor

Ella Norton has opted for the simple life. Gone are the power suits, the high earnings and the high stress of city life – and instead she's got her own cottage, a course in horticulture, and a crush on her dynamic tutor Matt.

But life isn't all rustic paradise . . . Ella has two lodgers – gorgeous, worldly Miranda and unglamorous, naïve Faith – who can't stand each other. And then there's the matter of Matt's wife and the fact that something dodgy and possibly illegal seems to be going on next door.

When the police arrive and set up a stakeout in Ella's bedroom, things begin to spiral seriously out of control . . .

arrow books

Rising to the Occasion

Linda Taylor

Cathy Gordon has made a discovery. Adopted at birth, she finds out at the age of twenty-eight that she has a grandfather. But when she arrives at a cricket match to meet Frank, there is no trace of him – only an alarmingly sexy man called Nick.

Heading off to Frank's home in leafy Oxford, she encounters a grumpy old man who only takes pleasure in two things: cricket and arguing, especially with his lifelong friend, Barbara.

Determined to bond with her only living relative, Cathy takes up the challenge – a challenge which means her path crossing with Nick's once again. But as the summer heatwave continues, Cathy realises that there is more at stake than family ties. Will any of them – including Frank's beloved England team – rise to the occasion?

arrow books

Shooting at the Stars

Linda Taylor

Caroline Blake longs for a night under a cloud-free sky with the telescope of her dreams. Busy, happily single, and passionate about her hobby, her life is as ordered as the science classes she teaches.

Lizzy Carter is living the life she'd longed for. With a lively young family, and adoring husband, good friends, and almost enough money, she appears to have it all.

Antonia Clarke is a divorcée with a teenage daughter, an ailing car, an obstinate mother and a lodger she needs to placate. She yearns for twenty-four uneventful hours – but the gods have other plans.

When the engaging Tom Grainger moves into each of the women's lives, things start to change. Three women whose paths have already crossed find their fates are about to collide.

arrow books